WOMAN
of COURAGE

WANDA & BRUNSTETTER

WOMAN
of COURAGE

COLLECTOR'S EDITION

SHILOH RUN PRESS

An Imprint of Barbour Publishing, Inc.

Woman of Courage © 2014 by Wanda E. Brunstetter
Woman of Hope © 2018 by Wanda E. Brunstetter

Print ISBN 978-1-68322-787-8

eBook Editions:
Adobe Digital Edition (.epub) 978-1-68322-968-1
Kindle and MobiPocket Edition (.prc) 978-1-68322-969-8

All scripture quotations are taken from the King James Version of the Bible.

This book is a work of fiction. Names, characters, places, and incidents are either products of the author's imagination or used fictitiously. Any similarity to actual people, organizations, and/or events is purely coincidental.

For more information about Wanda E. Brunstetter, please access the author's website at the following internet address: www.wandabrunstetter.com

Cover Design: Faceout Studio, www.faceoutstudio.com
Cover Photography: Steve Gardner, Pixelworks Studios

Published by Shiloh Run Press, an imprint of Barbour Publishing, Inc., 1810 Barbour Drive, Uhrichsville, Ohio 44683, www.shilohrunpress.com

Our mission is to inspire the world with the life-changing message of the Bible.

ecpa Member of the
Evangelical Christian
Publishers Association

Printed in Canada.

DEDICATION

To my friend Jean Otto, a woman of courage.

Finally, my brethren, be strong in the Lord,
and in the power of his might.

EPHESIANS 6:10

PROLOGUE

Dansville, New York
1837

A shiver of excitement ran through Amanda Pearson as she gazed at her mother's wedding dress lying across the end of her bed. Once more this dress would be worn to honor a new beginning. Tomorrow, Amanda would become Mrs. Nathan Lane, and she could hardly wait.

Nathan was all she had ever wanted in a husband. He was attractive, with thick blond hair and pale blue eyes. Nathan owned his own carriage-making business and was doing quite well financially. But it wasn't Nathan's good looks or lucrative occupation that attracted her to him. What Amanda found most appealing about her future husband was his confident attitude and good standing in their Quaker church. Everyone said they made the perfect couple. Even Amanda's father, a widower and preacher, approved of Nathan and seemed quite eager to see Amanda happily married.

A knock sounded on Amanda's bedroom door, halting her musings. "Come in," she called.

The door opened, and Papa stepped into the room. "Nathan is downstairs, Daughter. He wishes to speak with thee."

Amanda glanced at the clock on her bureau, noting that it was half past eight. "Nathan is here now? I didn't expect to see him until tomorrow evening, when we become man and wife."

Deep wrinkles formed across Papa's forehead as he scrubbed his hand down the side of his face. "Nathan said it's urgent." Papa shifted uneasily, his pale blue eyes blinking rapidly. "I asked if something had happened in his family, but he wouldn't say. All I could get out of him was that he wanted to talk to thee and it couldn't wait until tomorrow."

A tremor of fear shot through Amanda.

"I shall retire to my room for now so that thou mayest speak to Nathan privately," Papa said.

Amanda paused in front of her mirror, pinched her cheeks to give them a bit of color, and followed her father out of the room.

Downstairs, she found Nathan in the parlor, pacing from the window to the settee.

"Good evening, Nathan," Amanda said, stepping up to him. "I understand thou wishest to speak with me."

Nathan stopped pacing and averted his gaze, looking over her shoulder toward the door.

"What is it? Has something happened at home—to one of thy parents, perhaps?"

"Mother and Father are fine." Nathan began pacing again. He stopped beside Amanda and reached for her hand. His fingers were moist. "I—I should have told thee sooner, but I cannot marry thee tomorrow."

Amanda's spine stiffened as she tried to digest what he had said. "Wh–why not?" she asked in a whispered voice.

He took a deep breath, then cleared his throat. "I am in love with someone else."

Amanda quickly withdrew her hand as shock coursed through her veins. She grabbed the back of the settee for support. "Who has stolen thy love from me, Nathan?"

"Penelope Goodwin. We have been seeing each other secretly for many weeks." Nathan placed both hands against his temples, making little circles with his fingertips. "I thought it was just a passing fancy, but as time went on, it became much more."

Penelope Goodwin. The words echoed in Amanda's head. *Oh Penelope, how couldst thou have done this to me? I thought we were friends.*

"I'm sorry," Nathan said, "It was wrong to let our relationship go on this long, and I know it's a lot to ask, but I hope thou wilt understand. It wouldn't be right for us to marry when I am in love with someone else."

"No—no, of course not." Amanda blinked back tears and swallowed the bitter taste of bile in her mouth.

He took a step toward her, but she turned away. "There is nothing more for us to say," she murmured.

Amanda cringed when she heard his heavy footsteps retreat. The door clicked shut behind him. She breathed deeply, trying to calm her racing heart. Her dream of becoming Mrs. Nathan Lane lay destroyed. The months during which Amanda had thought their relationship blossomed into something that meant so much had just been ripped away as if they had never happened. Had she been blinded by the truth? Was she a fool for trusting Nathan so deeply? Whatever the answers to those questions, Amanda was certain about one thing: she was destined to be an old maid. As clearly as the full moon beamed through the parlor window, she knew she would never fall in love again.

CHAPTER I

Three months later in early spring
Wyoming Territory

Amanda tried to hide it, but she was tired and out of sorts. She wasn't used to sitting sidesaddle on a horse for hours on end, but that's what she had been doing since they'd left Fort Laramie early that morning. Harvey Hanson, the guide Papa had hired for their journey west, said they needed to make as many miles as possible during the daylight hours. He also warned them to be on the lookout for hostile Indians who might already be aware of their departure.

When Amanda and her father had first arrived at the post and met up with Harvey, the burly looking man had explained that Fort Laramie wasn't a military fort, but a trading post established by fur traders in 1834. Its true name was "Fort William on the Laramie," but most folks referred to it as simply "Fort Laramie." Just last year the post had become the headquarters for the American Fur Company.

Amanda had felt a bit nervous, seeing all the Indians camped in areas outside the post, but Fort Laramie was the central location for trading with the Sioux and Cheyenne. Trading buffalo robes, the fort's primary commodity, was fast replacing the once-prevalent beaver fur trade. The Indians exchanged the robes and furs they'd brought for tobacco, blankets, powder, lead, beads, and unfortunately alcohol.

While those facts interested Amanda, she shuddered, remembering Harvey's stories about some of the aggressive Indian tribes. He'd mentioned torture such as thrusting sharpened sticks into prisoners, heaping red-hot coals on their bodies, or cutting off their fingers and toes. While Amanda trusted the Lord to protect them every step of the way, she would keep a wary eye out for enemies. She could never endure such agonizing pain, and knowing what was possible made her feel as if their every move was being watched by some Indian's keen eyes.

Harvey was strictly business. He seemed to be better at barking out orders than engaging in idle chitchat. He spit a lot, and each time, Amanda cringed. But Papa had been told that Harvey was good at what he did, so Amanda was grateful that he was their guide. She could ignore his annoying habits in exchange for a safe, uneventful journey.

When Harvey removed his worn-looking beaver-skin cap earlier that morning, she'd noticed a scar on the back of his head. No hair grew in the small area, and Amanda wondered what had happened. Maybe he'd been attacked by a hostile Indian and managed to escape with his life. Or perhaps he had tangled with some wild animal. It was probably best not to know.

She glanced over at Papa, slouched in his saddle, seeming half-asleep. As if sensing she was watching him, he sat up straighter, stretched his back, yawned, and slumped once more. This trip seemed to be taking its toll on him. Soon after they'd left the fort, Papa said he felt light-headed and short of breath. Concerned for his welfare, Amanda had suggested they go back to the fort to rest a few more days, but Papa assured her that he would be fine and was determined they continue. Amanda wasn't surprised. Although blessed with many endearing qualities, her father could be a bit stubborn.

Of course, the same could be said about me, she reasoned. *But Papa's really a dear man.* She reflected on how he had insisted on coming with her on this trip. After Amanda's engagement was broken, she'd announced that she wanted to go west and join the Rev. and Mrs. Spalding in their mission to bring the Good News to the Nez Percé Indians. "I will not send my daughter into the wilderness to face unknown dangers alone," he said.

While Papa received no pay for his service as a Quaker minister back home, he'd worked as a cabinet maker for a good many years and had saved up some money. Since they didn't know if or when they would return to New York, he'd sold their home, his business, and all their belongings except for the few things they would need for this trip. Using some of the money, Papa had secured passage for him and Amanda on a steamboat, which took them to Cincinnati. From there, they'd boarded another steamboat to St. Louis, and then a third boat to Liberty, Missouri. Continuing on their journey, they rode in wagons with some fur traders, following the Platte River to Fort Laramie, where they met the man who would guide them to the mission. Harvey had said the rest of the journey would be best made on horseback without taking any wagons over the mountains.

Papa's remaining money would be used for supplies along the way and anything they might need once they got to Lapwai Creek in Oregon Territory, where the Spaldings had set up their mission. Amanda figured their expenses would be minimal once their journey ended and they got settled in. Unlike Henry and Eliza Spalding, who'd gone west under the direction of their mission board, Amanda and her father would receive no monetary support from their church and were pretty much on their own.

Amanda shifted in her saddle, trying to find a comfortable position, glancing at her father again. "Art thou alright?" she asked when he met her gaze. "Should we ask our guide to stop awhile so you can rest?"

"I'm a little tired, but I'll be fine," he said, offering her a weak smile as he pushed his dark, broad-brimmed hat farther back on his graying head. "Please do not worry. There is no need for thee to ask our guide to stop."

Amanda smiled in return, but it was hard not to worry when she saw such a look of fatigue on his pale face. Papa had never been a strong man, but for the last several months he'd taken more naps than usual and slept longer at night. She'd also noticed times when he had trouble catching his breath. At Amanda's insistence, Papa had seen the doctor for a checkup before embarking on this trip.

He'd returned home later that day, saying everything was fine and that Dr. Stevenson had given him permission to travel. To Amanda's knowledge, Papa had never lied to her about anything, so she had no reason not to believe him. She figured he'd just been doing too much lately and that the tonic the doctor had given Papa would put the spring back in his step. Truthfully, Amanda was glad he'd decided to go west with her, because she would have missed him terribly if she'd come alone—not to mention having to deal with their uncouth, unfriendly guide. Still, Papa's pallor and growing weakness concerned her.

As they rode, she focused on taking in the scenery. If she thought of other things, it helped her not to worry about Papa or the possibility of a hostile Indian encounter. Tucking in a piece of loose hair under her dark Quaker bonnet, she shuddered as a chill went through her body. Her slender arms ached, and her fingers could hardly bend from holding the reins so tightly. She'd ridden horses before, but not for this many hours at a time. Hopefully, as each day passed, she would become better adjusted to long hours in the saddle.

Looking around, it wasn't hard to realize that they were far from home. Gone were the fertile farmlands and lush rolling hillsides, thick with trees. Here, it was practically treeless and flat, with grasslands and sagebrush. Steep bluffs rose out of the flats where the Great Plains merged with the Rockies. Amanda had never been this far west, and she could only imagine what Oregon Territory might look like.

She turned in her saddle and looked ahead at the two pack mules carrying all of their supplies. Harvey had said their names were Jake and Jasper. With the exception of her Bible and toilet articles, which she carried in the reticule tied to her saddle, everything Amanda owned and all their provisions were in the care of those mules.

After what seemed like an eternity, Harvey finally announced that it was time to stop for the night. They made camp in a small clearing by a wide stream. After stretching her tired, aching limbs, Amanda went down to the stream to wash up, while her father tended to his needs, and Harvey built a fire and put up a canvas shelter for them. Amanda didn't look forward to sleeping on the ground, but at least they had several blankets to rest upon. And it would give her a break from the monotonous motion of the horse, not to mention the uncomfortable saddle.

Harvey, a rugged-looking, brown-haired man in his early forties, said he preferred to sleep on a buffalo hide in front of the fire. He'd told Papa that he liked gazing up at the stars, but Amanda had a hunch the real reason Harvey chose to sleep outside was to guard their camp. If a wild animal or enemy Indians should come upon them, he'd be ready and waiting with his loaded rifle. Harvey also said he slept with one eye open so he could watch for bears. While Amanda would never consider using a gun herself, she felt a measure of comfort in knowing they had the protection of their guide.

Pulling her thoughts aside, Amanda dried her wet hands on her apron and began fixing their supper over the campfire. When they'd hired Harvey at Fort Laramie, he'd made it clear that he wasn't much of a cook, so Amanda had readily agreed to fulfill that duty in order to see that they were properly fed. Tonight, she planned to make some corn bread and serve it with a hearty venison stew.

Her stomach growled noisily as she cut the dried meat and vegetables and placed them in the pot of water Harvey had set over the hot coals. When that was done, she glanced across the clearing to check on her father. He was seated on a large rock, Bible in his lap and head bowed as though he was praying. Amanda figured as tired as Papa was, he had probably nodded off.

He's not getting any younger, Amanda reminded herself. Papa would be fifty-one next month. They'd have to celebrate his birthday on the trail. She smiled, reflecting on how last year she had invited several friends over for supper to celebrate Papa's fiftieth birthday. Nathan had been among those who had come.

Amanda gripped the sides of her dress. *There I go, thinking about Nathan again.* She grimaced. *I am making this trip to forget about him, and I need to keep my thoughts on other more important things.*

Taking a seat on a log, Amanda thought about a middle-aged Indian woman she'd seen at the fort. She wished she'd had the chance to talk with her a bit and perhaps even give the woman a Bible. But Amanda was told that the Indians there were part of a Cheyenne tribe and spoke no English. If she could have communicated with the woman, Amanda would have explained that there were some white people, like her, who wanted to help the Indians. Then too, if they could have talked to each other, perhaps the woman might have given Amanda some insights about the Indians and their customs. Going to the mission without being able to communicate with those she was planning to teach presented challenges; however, Amanda felt sure that by the time she and Papa reached Oregon Territory, the Spaldings would have begun educating the Nez Percé, and that at least some of them would understand a little English. At the very least, she would be able to help Mrs. Spalding with cooking and cleaning, which she'd been doing since she was a child. Although she'd written a letter to the Spaldings, letting them know she and Papa were coming to help out, they'd left New York before an answer had come. Even so, she felt sure the reverend and his wife would welcome their help.

Amanda's thoughts turned to her mother and how she had died giving birth to Amanda. Papa had never remarried or shown any interest in another woman. He'd been devoted to Amanda since her birth, twenty-two years ago, and had made sure, under the tutorage of her aunt Dorothy, that she learned to cook, clean, and sew. Papa had told Amanda on more than one occasion that he wanted her to learn all these things, not just to provide for their needs, but so she could be a good wife someday.

Amanda wished she'd had the opportunity to meet her mother and get to know her, the way Papa had for the first four years they were married. But that was not to be. Papa had said Amanda got her beautiful flaxen-colored hair from Mama, but her blue eyes came from him. The only things Amanda knew about her mother were what Papa had told her. So in a sense, she did know her mother a little bit, although it wasn't the same as if she'd been alive during Amanda's childhood.

She cringed. Thinking about Papa's marriage had drawn her thoughts back to Nathan. Had he and Penelope gotten married yet? If Nathan truly loved Penelope, then he surely would have made Penelope his wife by now. Nathan Lane! Would she ever quit thinking of him?

"Oh!"

At the sound of her father's cry, Amanda leaped to her feet and rushed to his side. "Papa, what is it?"

Papa's thin lips contorted as he pointed to his chest. "It—it hurts, right here."

"I shall get Harvey." Amanda, fearing the worst, started to turn, but his desperate plea stopped her from going after their guide.

"No! I must tell thee something," Papa said, looking up at Amanda through glassy eyes.

Amanda went down on her knees beside him. "What is it, Papa?"

He blinked several times, as though trying to focus his thoughts. "Give me thy word."

"My word on what, Papa?"

"Promise thou wilt go and teach the Indians about God."

She placed her hand gently on his arm. "Of course, Papa. We shall both go and preach the Good News."

Papa clutched his chest. "I should have told thee before but knew if I did, thou wouldst not have made this worthy trip."

A sense of fear coursed through Amanda. She could barely breathe. "What hast thou not told me?"

"My heart is failing. The doctor confirmed what I already suspected when I went to see him before we left home." He reached out a trembling hand and with shaky fingers stroked her cheek. "I need thy word that if I don't make it, thou wilt go on alone."

Tears sprang to Amanda's eyes as she gripped her father's cold hand. "No, Papa! No, I cannot!"

"Thou must," he implored. "The Lord told me in a dream that this is His will for thee. There is nothing for thee in New York. Thy future lies in the west—among the Nez Percé people, and. . ." Papa's

16

words were halted as he drew in a shuddering breath. "My work is done here on earth, Amanda. It—it is time for me to be reunited with thy mother."

"No, Papa, not yet!" Amanda clutched his arm, willing him to hang on. "I need thee. I cannot go on without thee."

"Thou must. Promise me this, Amanda. I beg thee to give me thy word."

Amanda nodded slowly as tears coursed down her cheeks. "Yes, Papa, I will go."

Her words seemed to offer the comfort he needed, for he smiled slightly, and then his head fell forward onto his well-worn Bible.

"Papa! Papa!" Amanda screamed.

No response.

She placed her hand under his nose, but there was no breath. She felt no heartbeat in his chest. "No, Papa! No!" Despite her denial, Amanda knew her father was gone. What she didn't know was how she would go on without him.

Chapter 2

Amanda sobbed as she watched while Harvey dug a shallow grave in an area outside their camp and then placed her father's body within it. As the sound of the digging echoed in her ears, she still couldn't comprehend that Papa was gone. *He just can't be dead,* Amanda told herself over and over again. It had to be a horrible nightmare that she would wake up from in the morning, and they would continue their journey west. But with each shovel of dirt that covered the grave, Amanda began to face reality. Papa's heart had given out on him. The trip had been too much, and it was her fault. If only she hadn't decided to embark on this journey, Papa would still be alive. *Or would he? Is it possible that Papa would have died even if we'd stayed in New York? If his heart was weak, Papa might not have survived no matter where we lived.*

"Would ya like to say a few words over your pa before we bed down for the night?" Harvey asked, jolting Amanda's thoughts.

"What? Umm. . .Yes, I. . .I need to do that," she said, swallowing hard in an attempt to regain her composure. She glanced at the log where Papa's Bible lay and knew she ought to read some scripture. But before she could make a move, Harvey, as though reading her thoughts, went to get it.

When he returned, he handed her the well-worn Bible and said, "I ain't no religious fella, but even I know that a man like your pap deserves a Christian burial."

Amanda managed a quick nod, and with trembling fingers, she opened her father's Bible and read from the twenty-third Psalm: " 'The Lord is my shepherd; I shall not want. He maketh me to lie down in green pastures: he leadeth me beside the still waters. . . . Yea, though I walk through the valley of the shadow of death, I will fear no evil: for thou art with me.' " Amanda paused and drew in a shaky breath. She was sure that Papa hadn't been afraid of death, for he had died so peacefully. The Lord had been with Papa, offering comfort as he passed from this earth.

Now, as she stood looking at the fresh mound of dirt, she consoled herself with the knowledge that her father was no longer in pain and that he and Mama, after all these years, were finally together again.

" 'Thou preparest a table before me,' " she continued to read, as emotion clogged her throat, " 'in the presence of mine enemies: thou anointest my head with oil; my cup runneth over. Surely goodness and mercy shall follow me all the days of my life: and I will dwell in the house of the Lord for ever.' "

Amanda closed the Bible, bowed her head, and prayed a simple prayer: "Heavenly Father, we commend my father's spirit into Thy hands. I thank Thee for the short time I had with Papa. Now, I ask Thee to give me strength to go on without him. Amen."

Amanda thought about her mother's engraved headstone, nestled between two maple trees in the graveyard behind their meeting place back home. *Papa should have been buried there by her side. He too ought to have a nice headstone. But then,* she reminded herself, *Papa's spirit is not here—only his body, which will soon become one with the earth.* Knowing her father as well as she did, Amanda didn't think he would mind that his place of burial had no marker.

Tears coursed down Amanda's cheeks as she moved away from the grave and headed back to their camp. It hadn't really been a proper service; at least not proper enough for a man like Papa. But under the circumstances, it was the best she could do. As difficult as it would be, Amanda knew she must keep her promise to Papa. She would go to Oregon Territory and share the Word of God with the Nez Percé Indians.

When Amanda awoke the following morning, she felt groggy and disoriented. She'd had a horrible dream and hadn't slept well. Glancing across the lean-to, to see if her father was awake, she frowned. He wasn't there, and neither was his sleeping mat. Maybe he'd rolled up his bedding and gone down to the stream to wash up. Yes, she was sure that must be the case.

Amanda yawned and rubbed her eyes. She needed to get up and fix breakfast so they could be on their way. After she'd stepped out from under the lean-to, she spotted Harvey, poking at the smoldering embers of the fire.

"Were ya able to get any sleep last night, missy?" he asked when she approached him a few minutes later.

"I did sleep some, but it was a restless kind of sleep. I had a horrible nightmare," she replied, pulling her arms back to get the kinks out of her limbs.

"That's understandable, under the circumstances and all," he said, rubbing one finger down the side of his slightly crooked nose.

"Where is my father?" Amanda asked. "Is he down at the stream washing up?"

Harvey squinted his beady brown eyes. "What was that?"

"I said. . . . Oh, never mind. I need to go there myself, so I'll talk to him then." Amanda hurried off toward the stream. She heard Harvey call her name but kept going. She felt a desperate need to talk to Papa. Yesterday he'd looked awfully tired, and she'd been worried about him.

When Amanda arrived at the stream, Papa wasn't there. *Where in the world could he be?*

She turned and studied the surrounding area, searching desperately for any sign of her father. Then, as she moved back toward their camp, her gaze fell on a mound of dirt. Two sticks tied together to form a small cross had been stuck in the ground at the head of the mound. A cold chill swept over Amanda as reality set it. Beneath this ugly mound of dirt lay Papa's body. It hadn't been a dream after all. Her beloved father had died last night, and she had read scripture over his newly dug grave.

Amanda dropped to her knees and wailed, "Dear Lord, why didst Thou take my father?"

"Missy, ya ain't doin' no good fer yourself like this," Harvey said, placing his hand on her trembling shoulder.

She looked up at him through a veil of tears, surprised not only by the gentleness in his tone, but also that he had followed her here to the gravesite. Harvey hadn't been this nice or spoken so kindly to her since they'd left Fort Laramie.

"Come on over and get yourself warmed up," Harvey said, motioning to the fire he'd started. "You'll feel better once you've had some hot coffee."

Amanda shook her head. "I do not drink coffee, sir."

"Well, it's all I got, and it'll warm ya from the inside, while the fire takes the early mornin' chill outta your bones." Harvey extended his hand. "Come now, missy. It ain't doin' a thing for ya to stay here like this."

Dazed, Amanda took his calloused hand and rose to her feet. She followed him silently back to the camp.

"Why don't ya take a seat over there?" Harvey motioned to a log near the fire. "Once we've had ourselves somethin' to eat, we'll clear up the camp, load up Jake and Jasper, and start back for the fort."

"You mean, Fort Laramie?" she asked, tipping her head as she looked up at him.

He gave a quick nod. "We're only a full day out, so I can easily take ya back."

"Oh no." Amanda shook her head determinedly. "I have already come a long way, and my father hired thee to take us to the Spalding Mission, so that is where I plan to go."

"Well, if ya do, you'll be goin' without me," Harvey said, narrowing his gaze. "I ain't takin' no lady that far by myself."

"Why not?"

" 'Cause it wouldn't be right. Besides, I never did think it was a good idea for a sickly looking old man and a little slip of a lady, who looks like she might break, to be goin' on no trek through the wilderness with some dumb idea about preachin' to the red-skin people."

Amanda squared her shoulders and stared up at Harvey with a renewed sense of determination. "For thy information, Mr. Hanson, I am not as fragile as I may appear. I'm a hard worker with a determined spirit, and I won't go back on the promise I made to my father."

"What promise was that?"

"Before Papa died, he asked me to continue the journey west to minister to the Nez Percé Indians." She clasped her hands tightly, as though in prayer. "With or without thee, I intend to keep that promise."

Harvey tipped his head back and laughed. "You're sure a feisty one, I'll give ya that much."

She made no comment, feeling anything but feisty.

Harvey shook his head and muttered, "Women! They're impossible creatures to figure out."

"What is that supposed to mean?"

"You're either very brave or just plain dumb to all the trials that could come upon us along the way," Harvey said sarcastically.

Amanda folded her arms in an unyielding pose. "I am neither of those, sir. I am a woman of faith who is trusting in the Lord to give her courage."

Harvey spat on the ground. "Is that so?"

"Indeed. Now wilt thou continue to act as my guide?"

Harvey broke a branch off a nearby tree, snapped it in half, and tossed it on the fire. "I may be loco for agreein' to this, but yeah, I'll see that you get to where ya wanna go."

Amanda smiled. "I thank thee for that."

Amanda reached up a slender hand to shield her eyes against the glare of the harsh afternoon sun, while clucking to her horse. "Slow down, Betsy. Thou art going much too fast."

"She's jest followin' my lead," Harvey called over his shoulder. "Hang on tight to the saddle."

"That is what I am trying to do," Amanda said breathlessly. "It's hard to stay on the horse when I'm sitting sideways like this." She bit her lip out of frustration, while opening and closing her stiff fingers. She would never admit it to Harvey, but she really wasn't cut out for this. *What made me believe I could make a journey of this sort when I know so little about survival in the wilderness?* Amanda wondered.

The words of Ephesians 6:10 ran through her mind: *Finally, my*

22

brethren, be strong in the Lord, and in the power of his might. A renewed sense of purpose welled in Amanda's chest. *I can do this. With God's help I can do whatever He asks me to do.*

"We can remedy your situation real quick," Harvey announced. He halted his horse, and the pack mules stopped behind him.

Amanda pulled her horse up too. "Why are we stopping, Mr. Hanson?"

"I want ya to put on a pair of your pa's trousers, and then you're gonna ride that horse like a man," he said, dismounting.

Amanda gasped. "Dost thou expect me to wear men's clothes?"

"That's right, and I wish you'd stop *thee*in' and *thou*in' all over the place. Can't ya jest talk like a normal person?"

"I am a 'normal' person," Amanda replied tersely as she slid off her horse. "And I would appreciate it if thou wouldst not speak to me in that manner."

Harvey lifted his hand. "Hold your britches, little lady; I meant no offense. It's just hard to understand when ya talk thataway."

"It is how we Quakers who attend the Friends' church speak," she said, trying not to sound so defensive this time.

"That's all well and good, but there ain't no Friends' church around here, and I'd be much obliged if you'd say *you* instead of *thee* when you're speakin' to me."

Amanda wasn't sure she could abide by that request, as it simply wouldn't sound right to her. But rather than start a disagreement, she nodded and said, "I shall try."

Harvey grinned; then he pointed to her father's valise. "When ya find some trousers you can go behind one of them trees and change. In the meantime, I'll put your pa's saddle on your horse, and we'll leave the sidesaddle here on the trail 'cause ya won't be needin' it again."

Amanda groaned inwardly. This man surely liked to give orders. Well, as much as she hated to admit it, perhaps wearing Papa's trousers would be a good idea. It would mean she could sit a little easier on the horse, and it might keep her legs from getting so chafed. She wouldn't, however, remove her skirt. She would simply put Papa's trousers on underneath.

CHAPTER 3

As Amanda and Harvey mounted their horses the following day, the sunlight filtered through the tree branches overhead, casting rays of misty splendor. Amanda winced, despite the beautiful morning. A few more days in the saddle and she was certain she'd be permanently crippled. She thought by now that she'd be used to it, but even wearing Papa's trousers and sitting in a regular saddle hadn't helped that much. She was beginning to feel a sense of bitterness about this trip and the inconvenience of sleeping on the ground every night. Riding on the back of a horse that wouldn't listen to her for hours on end didn't help either. There were times when Amanda wanted to throttle the mare, and more often than not, she would end up hollering, "Slow down, Betsy!" or "Get going, Betsy!" The sturdy quarter horse, with a medium brown coat and a white patch between her eyes, definitely had a mind of her own. It was enough to test Amanda's patience.

How can I minister to the Indians if I continue to feel this way? Amanda asked herself. *Perhaps I should have turned back when Papa died.* She clenched her teeth and squared her shoulders. *If I'd gone back, it would have been admitting defeat, and I am not a quitter.*

"You'd better stay alert, and keep that horse of yours right beside me," Harvey warned. "We're travelin' through Blackfoot territory now, and I aim to be extra careful."

"Didn't thou sayest the Blackfoot people can be quite hostile?" Amanda asked with a tremor in her voice.

"Ya got that right, missy," Harvey replied. "Some of 'em go to the tradin' posts and Rendezvous to barter and trade their goods, but there ain't a one of 'em that I'd trust as far as I could throw 'em. They're not like some of the other tribes that are a mite friendlier."

Amanda swallowed hard and gripped Betsy's reins. "Why are they called 'Blackfoot'?"

"I've heard that it's 'cause of the dark moccasins they wear on their feet," he replied.

"Dost thou think we will see any Blackfoot, Mr. Hanson?"

He shrugged his broad shoulders. "You sure do ask a lot of questions, and I don't rightly know if we'll see any Injuns, but I'll be ready for 'em if we do."

"Ready? What dost thou mean?" she asked with a feeling of trepidation.

"Well, I ain't gonna start shootin', if that's what yer thinkin'. I weren't born yesterday, so I ain't stupid enough to take on a whole tribe of Injuns. Some of them redskins will kill just for the sport of it." Harvey gave his gun a tap. "Now, if it's just two or three hostile red men, then I'll give 'em my best shots."

Amanda's face warmed. "Oh dear. I hope we will not have any bloodshed on this trip."

"There won't be none if I can help it." Harvey turned and looked over his shoulder at the two pack mules following, along with Papa's horse, which was now carrying some of their supplies. "We've got plenty of goods and a few trinkets we can trade to the Injuns, so I'm countin' on that to save our hides, should the situation arise."

Amanda drew in a quick breath to help steady her nerves. She hoped the Indians she'd be ministering to at the Spalding Mission weren't hostile.

"What dost thou know about the Nez Percé Indians?" Amanda asked, feeling the need for a change of subject.

He frowned. "I told ya before to stop usin' *thee* and *thou*. I'd rather you'd just say the word *you* when you're speakin' to me."

"I can't make that promise, but I shall try."

"I appreciate that. Now about the Nimiipuu. . ."

Amanda blinked. "Who are the Nimiipuu? Is that how you say it?"

He nodded.

"But I thought we were talking about the Nez Percé Indians."

"We are. Nimiipuu is the name they call themselves. It means 'real people.'"

"Then why do white men call them 'Nez Percé'?" Amanda asked.

"Well, the way I understand it, when some French explorers arrived in 1805, they saw some Injuns with shells in their noses, so they gave 'em the name 'Nez Percé,' which means 'pierced noses.'"

"Do all Nez Percé people pierce their noses?" Amanda could hardly believe anyone would do such a thing.

"Nope. It ain't even a common practice from what I understand."

None of this made much sense to Amanda. "What else do you know about them?" she questioned, pleased that she had remembered not to say *thee*.

"I've learned that most of 'em are friendly and peaceable—unless ya get their dander up. There'd be a heap of trouble if someone tried to take their land, or if another tribe, like the Blackfoot, made war on 'em."

"Art thou—I mean you—saying that the Nez Percé aren't hostile or violent by nature?"

Harvey shrugged. "I guess not, but they'll fight to protect what's theirs, and I sure can't blame 'em for that."

Amanda reflected on that, then asked if there was anything else Harvey could tell her about the Nez Percé.

"At one time, they ate mainly fish—especially salmon. They could dry and store it for winter use. Sometimes ice caves were used for storage too."

"You said 'at one time.' Does that mean they no longer eat fish?" she asked curiously.

"I suppose they do when they're at their winter home, but durin' the warmer weather, they travel to the high country to dig roots and bulbs, like *kouse*."

"I don't believe I've ever heard of a kouse root. What do they do with it?"

"After it's cleaned, they boil the root whole or grind it into mush. Sometimes it's shaped into small cakes and dried for later use." Harvey rubbed the back of his neck. "By July the Indians move farther onto the prairie to gather sweet camas bulbs. Then after the harvest of bulbs, most of the Nimiipuu return to the rivers to fish for salmon, while some of the men hunt for elk, deer, moose, and bear. Durin' the winter months, the Injuns live on whatever small game they can capture as well as the food they've dried or buried under the ground."

Amanda let go of Betsy's reins for a moment to wipe the perspiration from her forehead. "You seem to know a lot about the Nimiipuu Indians, while I know so very little in comparison."

"Just what do ya know, missy?" Harvey asked.

"I know from what I've read that they need to be educated—to learn the white man's ways, and of course, to know God in a personal way."

Harvey grunted. "I doubt they'd wanna learn the white man's ways, but I guess they do wanna learn about God, or they wouldn't have sent a party of men to St. Louis a few years back to ask for Bible thumpers."

Amanda tipped her head. "Bible thumpers?"

"Yeah. Folks like you and your preacher pa. Ya carry a Bible and preach from it, don't ya?"

She nodded.

"I'm guessin' you ain't never been called a 'thumper' before?"

"Not until now."

Harvey gave a low grunt.

Amanda was surprised at how he could be so chatty one minute, and then go silent the next. Well, a time of silence was alright, she decided. It gave her time to think and pray.

They rode along quietly until midday, when Harvey announced that it was time to stop and water the horses and mules. Amanda was thankful for that, as she really did need a break.

After Harvey helped Amanda down from her horse, he led the animals to a small pond surrounded by a cluster of trees. Their presence spooked a mule deer that had been drinking there, and it quickly scampered away. It was a beautiful animal, a buck, Amanda noted, and much bigger in body than the white-tailed deer back home. Ever since they'd begun this trip, her nerves had been rattled, but seeing the deer with the beginnings of his new rack had given her a sense of peace.

Amanda took her valise and stepped behind a clump of bushes, wondering if she'd ever get used to using the bare ground as her toilet. Maybe she wasn't cut out for life in the wilderness. Perhaps Harvey was right, and she should have returned home. *No, I am not a quitter*, she reminded herself. *God will give me the strength to complete my journey, and perhaps I will be stronger for whatever trials I must endure.*

Amanda was about to step out from the bushes, when a blood-curdling scream pierced the air. It was unlike anything she'd ever heard, and it left her trembling and unable to catch her breath. Maybe some wild animal had ventured to the pond to get a drink. Harvey had told her there were wildcats in this territory. Could it be a bobcat cry she'd heard?

Too frightened to look out, but afraid not to, Amanda clutched her valise and cautiously poked her head between the two bushes. Her legs started to cramp in the crouched position, but she didn't move. What Amanda saw made her flesh crawl, and she felt sure that her heart had nearly stopped beating. Amanda would have much rather seen a wild animal, but instead, in the middle of the clearing were a dozen half-naked Indians on horseback.

One of the red men had already seen her. Her legs were nearly numb, but Amanda's fear got her up. Moving quickly, she started to run. She could hardly feel her feet as they whisked over uneven ground. The Indian caught up with her, reached down, jerked off her bonnet, and grabbed a handful of her hair so roughly that the combs came loose from her bun. Amanda gasped as her hair tumbled down her back in a tangle of curls.

"Ouch! Thou art hurting me!" she cried, tears stinging her eyes as she held on tightly to her valise. It felt like her hair was being pulled out by the roots, and Amanda's only defense was to slap the man's horse with her valise. To her surprise, the horse didn't budge, and the Indian merely gripped her hair tighter.

"Don't fight him, or it'll only get worse," Harvey hollered from across the clearing, where he stood with his arms pinned behind his back. One of the Indians stood behind Harvey, with his knife held dangerously close to Harvey's throat.

"Oh!" Amanda squealed. "What art thou going to do about this, Harvey?"

"There ain't nothin' I can do. At least, not yet," he said through tight lips.

The Indian holding Amanda by the hair let loose, stepped down from his horse, and yanked her roughly to his side. His face was painted with yellow-and-white stripes, and his long, coal-black hair hung loosely down his bronzed back. He was tall and muscular, with foreboding, deeply set, dark eyes. His strong jaw was accentuated by a long, jagged scar.

Despite her fear, Amanda couldn't help thinking, *Here it is early spring, and these Indians have bare skin showing. How can they not be cold?*

Her mouth went suddenly dry, and she shuddered as she closed her eyes, clasping the leather valise to her chest. *This is it*, she thought fearfully. *Unless God performs a miracle, I am about to join Papa in the Promised Land.* While Amanda felt certain she would go to heaven, she wasn't quite ready to die. Unbidden tears slipped onto her hot cheeks and she began to silently pray. *Oh Lord, if Thou art still with us, please show Thyself in some way. Protect Harvey and me from these savages, and I pray it will be soon.*

The Indian turned Amanda's body toward his, so that her full weight pressed against his rock-hard chest. Looking at one of the other Indians, he mumbled something in a deep guttural sound—something she could not understand.

The Indian holding Harvey captive grunted and said something in response, but it was completely foreign to Amanda.

"Aapi ahki," Amanda's captor said, releasing his grip on her with one hand and running a finger down the side of her face.

Amanda squeezed her eyes shut. *"Finally, my brethren, be strong in the Lord, and in the power of his might,"* she quoted to herself. *If this is my time to die, Lord, then help me not to be afraid, and give me a sense of peace.*

"I can't speak the Blackfoot language," Harvey shouted, "but I think he wants you for his woman."

Amanda gulped. She had not come all this way to be taken captive; she would rather die first. If only there was something she could do to dissuade the hostile Indian.

Opening her eyes, she looked up at the man and said, "Please, let me go."

"That ain't gonna do ya no good, 'cause he can't understand a word you're sayin'," Harvey hollered. "If my hands weren't bein' held behind my back, I could try signin' or make pictures in the dirt to let 'em know we have goods to trade. For that matter, I'd gladly give the stuff to the redskins if it meant savin' our hides," he quickly added.

The man holding Amanda said something else, releasing her hair but holding tightly to both of her arms.

Amanda, feeling light-headed and unsteady, feared she might be about to faint. If all Indians were like this, then she had to be out of her mind to embark on this terrifying trip to the West. "Harvey, please, canst thou do something?" she pleaded. "Offer them my horse. Maybe they would want her instead of me." Amanda figured giving up Betsy wouldn't be so bad. She would ride Papa's horse instead.

"I wish I could, missy," he growled, "but as you can see, I ain't in no position to do much of anything right now."

"Well, we can't just stand here and let them murder us," she retorted.

"If you've got any bright ideas, I'm all ears."

The Indian tipped his head, apparently interested in what Amanda and Harvey were saying. He released his grip on her arms for just an instant, and she seized the opportunity to run. That was a mistake. One of the other Indians dismounted from his horse, stuck his foot out, and tripped her. Amanda's valise flew out of her hand as she fell to the ground. There hadn't been enough time for her to close it properly when she'd been accosted, so the handles easily flew apart, dumping the contents out.

Along with her personal items, Papa's Bible had been inside the valise, and she reached out quickly to grab it. Clutching the Bible tightly to her chest, Amanda prayed out loud, "Dear God in heaven, please help us now!"

CHAPTER 4

Time seemed to stand still as Amanda rose to her feet and continued to pray, her breath coming in shallow gasps. "Oh Lord, if they are going to kill us, then let it be done swiftly."

The Indian who had held Amanda captive only moments ago backed slowly away, never taking his dark eyes from the Bible she held. When he reached his horse, he quickly mounted and shouted something to the other men. His face wore a look of fear, which made no sense at all since he had a weapon, while she had none.

The Indian holding Harvey shoved him to the ground, leaving him sprawled facedown, and skillfully jumped on the back of his painted steed. Amanda watched in stunned silence as the Blackfoot Indians rode quickly out of the clearing.

Harvey stood and brushed the dirt from his buckskin shirt and pants. "Well now, if that don't beat all," he said, slowly shaking his head.

Amanda's shoulders tensed, and her voice trembled. "Are we safe now, Harvey?"

"Sure looks that way." Harvey grinned widely, revealing stained, crooked teeth. "If I hadn't seen it with my own eyes, I wouldn't have believed it."

"I thank Thee, Lord," Amanda murmured, looking upward in appreciation. "It was truly a miracle."

"I'd call it luck," Harvey said.

"I'm not sure what happened, but I think it may have had something to do with this." Amanda held up her father's Bible. "I could not understand what that Indian said to the others, but I believe he was afraid of the Bible."

Harvey nodded. "Yes, ma'am, I'm thinkin' that too. Most Injuns don't have a clue about Bibles or any other kind of books for that matter, but I think this one did."

"God answered my prayers," Amanda said reverently, although she could hardly believe it herself. "He heard, and He answered."

Harvey shrugged. "Don't know 'bout that, but I do know we need to hightail it outta here, in case them redskins change their minds and decide to come back."

"I am sure they won't," Amanda said with conviction. "God drove them out, and they will not return."

Harvey scratched his shaggy beard and frowned. "Just the same, it's time we hit the trail. We're wastin' good daylight standin' here, chewin' the fat."

Amanda pursed her lips. "What art thou talking about? I am not chewing any fat."

"Gabbin'," he snapped. "We're wastin' time flappin' our gums!"

A slow smile pulled at the corners of her mouth. "Oh, I think I understand now. Dost thou mean we are talking?"

"That's what I mean, alright. Now gather your stuff that's scattered all over the ground and mount up." Harvey turned toward his horse but suddenly whirled around. "And one more thing—you're still theein' and thouin', and I wish you'd stop. It makes ya sound too uppity when ya talk like that!"

Amanda grimaced. After what they had been through, the man was worried about the way she talked? "I am sorry if the way I speak offends you," she said. "I will try to do better from now on."

"Thanks, I appreciate that."

———

"Tomorrow is the Sabbath," Amanda mentioned to Harvey as they were setting up camp that night.

"What about it?" he asked, not bothering to look up from the fire he was tending.

"The Bible says that God rested on the seventh day of creation. It was His example to us."

"Uh-huh," Harvey muttered with disinterest.

"If God rested, then so should we."

"You can rest tonight on your sleepin' mat," Harvey shot back.

"I am referring to a full day's rest—on the Sabbath," she said, stepping up to him.

"How you gonna rest, knowin' we've got all that ground to cover?" he asked gruffly. It was obvious that his irritation was mounting.

"I think it would be best if we only traveled six days of the week and rested on the seventh," she insisted, standing her ground.

Harvey muttered an obscenity and spit on the burning logs. "Have ya gone loco, woman? We don't have time to be sittin' around on our backsides all day, restin'. I thought you was chompin' at the bit to get to Oregon Territory and the Spalding Mission."

"I am," she answered sweetly, hoping to soften the man's temper. "But since the Lord rescued us from those terrible Indians earlier today, I think it is only right that we should honor His commandment to keep the Sabbath day holy."

"I'll tell ya what, missy," Harvey said, squinting his beady eyes, "you can ride on that horse of yours, prayin' and even readin' your Bible if ya want to, but we ain't stoppin' our travels for no day of rest, and that's final!"

"But. . .but I thought. . . ."

"Well, ya thought wrong!" He tossed another log onto the fire. "Now, if ya don't mind, I'd like to have some supper, 'cause I'm hungry enough to eat a bear and a couple of jackrabbits besides."

Amanda placed her hands on her hips and thrust out her chin in defiance. "May I remind thee, sir, that I am the one paying thee to act as my guide? Therefore, I feel I have the right to decide when we will travel and when we shall rest."

He stepped close to her, so they were almost nose to nose. "Is that a fact?"

"Yes, it certainly is."

Harvey's deeply set eyes narrowed into tiny slits. "And may I remind you, Missy Pearson, that it's me who's gonna get ya safely across the Rocky Mountains, not God!"

"What about the things that happened today?" she retorted. "Was it not obvious that God intervened on our behalf?"

"Maybe He did, and maybe it was the fact that the Injun knew you were a Bible-thumper. Or it could have been just plain luck. Most Injuns are superstitious, and it don't take much to spook 'em. Either way, I'm in charge here, so what I say goes!" Harvey slapped his calloused hands together.

"Well, I do not like it one bit!" Amanda snapped back.

"Whether you like it or not, we're in Injun territory, and I say that come tomorrow mornin', we're gonna get up early, saddle our horses, and travel till the sun goes down." He raised his bushy eyebrows and scowled at her. "Unless, of course, you're fixin' to let God take ya to Oregon Territory without any help from me."

Amanda pushed her lower lip out in a pout. "Does that mean thou wouldst leave me here in the wilderness, alone and unprotected?"

He nodded, and spit again, just missing the toe of his boot. "You wouldn't be alone. You'd have God with ya, remember?"

Knowing she had lost the battle, Amanda whirled around and marched off to get the needed supplies for making their evening meal. "What's the use in arguing? Men can be so pigheaded," she muttered under her breath. Amanda paused and looked upward. *Forgive me, Lord. I know I should not be so ungrateful or stubborn, but thanks to my equally stubborn guide, I will be forced to travel on the Sabbath. I hope Thou wilt understand and will not hold it against me.*

———

Amanda spent most of the following days quietly following Harvey's instructions as they continued their journey. She barely managed to squeeze in time for her morning scripture reading and prayer, when Harvey ordered her to mount up. He meant what he said about traveling on the Sabbath, and as the weeks passed, Amanda realized she would never have a day of rest until they reached the Spaldings' mission.

That man is deplorable, she fumed. *He's uncouth, ill-mannered, and doesn't seem to care about God. It's no wonder he isn't married. No woman in her right mind would be desperate enough to marry a man like him.* Amanda wondered why Papa had hired Harvey as their guide. *But then,* she reasoned, *wilderness guides aren't easy to come by, and Harvey does seem to know his way around. He should, I guess, since according to him, he's been doing it a long time. And he surely understands the Indians a lot better than I do. I suppose I should be more grateful.*

"Looks like we might be in for a storm," Harvey said, breaking into Amanda's thoughts. "The wind's pickin' up, and a few raindrops just splattered on my nose."

Maybe that is because thy nose is so big, Amanda mused. Feeling guilty, she reminded herself that a good Christian woman, on her way to preach the Good News to the Nez Percé Indians, should not be entertaining negative thoughts about another human being—especially one who was trying to get her safely across the mountains.

Amanda had been so busy reflecting on her companion's negative qualities that she hadn't even noticed the change in the weather. Harvey was right, it was beginning to rain. The once crystal-blue sky had darkened with gray clouds, and the wind lashed angrily at the tree branches on all sides of the trail. She shuddered as the trees groaned, swaying from the force of the wind. The spooky, creaking sound teased her nerves.

"Are we going to stop and take shelter?" Amanda called to Harvey.

"Not yet," he replied. "There's too many trees here. Don't wanna chance one of 'em blowin' over on us. We'll keep ridin' till we find a clearing that looks safe."

Amanda figured Harvey was probably right, although being in the seclusion of trees made her feel safer than when they were out in the open where they could be watched more easily. He always seemed to be right, though, and that irritated her more than she cared to admit. She reached behind and pulled a small tarp from one of her packs, while holding firmly to her saddle with the other hand. With difficulty, she managed to drape the covering over her head and shoulders, hoping it would shield her from some of the drenching rain.

"Is it always like this here in the Rockies?" she yelled over to Harvey. The rain pelted so noisily on the tarp that Amanda had to strain to hear his answer.

"Mostly in the springtime," he hollered back. "It rains a lot in the mountains, ya know."

No, she didn't know. Until now, Amanda had never been in the mountains. She'd never been away from New York until this trip. She'd never seen anything like the vast greatness and majesty of these mountains.

Amanda shivered and wiped some raindrops from her cheeks. When she and Papa had first left home, she'd foolishly thought this trip would be a fun adventure. So far, there had been nothing fun or pleasant about her journey. The routine of riding all day was exhausting. Camping outdoors and cooking over an open fire were inconvenient. Her mission was worthy, and she shouldn't complain, but there were times like today when she felt irritable and out of sorts. The damp weather had done nothing to cheer her melancholy mood either. To make matters worse, she missed Papa something awful, and she didn't think she'd ever stop blaming herself for suggesting this trip.

As they traveled on, the weather grew steadily worse. The wind howled eerily, and rumbles of thunder shook the earth with such force that Amanda wondered how the horses and mules stayed on their feet. Lightning zigzagged across the sky, and rain pummeled the ground with the fury of angry warriors, changing the trail to a sludgy mud. She held herself so tightly in the saddle and felt so tense with worry that she wondered how much longer her muscles could endure the stress.

Back East whenever there was a storm like this, Amanda would watch it through a window from the safety of their home. Those thunderstorms had never frightened Amanda like this violent weather. She figured it might be because they were outside with no protection. It felt so cold.

Just when Amanda thought she could take no more, the sky lit up with a jolt of lightning that streaked toward the ground and slit a tall pine tree right down the middle. It struck so close that the hair under her bonnet felt charged. Harvey's horse whinnied and veered to the left, but it was too late. The tree fell with a mighty force, landing on top of both horse and rider!

Amanda screamed. "Harvey, no!"

CHAPTER 5

Amanda screamed again, but it was drowned out by the fury of the wind and rain. Both Harvey and his horse lay motionless on the ground, pinned beneath a heavy tree.

She reined in her skittish mare and quickly dismounted. Stepping around the fallen tree, she dropped to her knees next to her guide. "Harvey, canst thou hear me?"

No response.

Amanda called his name again and again, but he lay there, unmoving, dark blood oozing from a gaping wound in his head. She placed her hand against his nose to feel his breathing, but the air was still. Harvey's arm lay free from the tree, and Amanda felt for his pulse. Nothing.

Amanda watched helplessly as the last breath of life shuddered from the horse's nostrils. As much as she hated to admit it, both Harvey and his horse were dead. As she reached out to close Harvey's eyelids, sobs of anguish, coming from the depths of her soul, poured out. She'd not only lost her father, but now her guide was gone. Amanda was all alone, with nothing but two horses and two pack mules. She had no idea how to get to the Spaldings' mission, and even if she did, what chance would she have of providing food, shelter, and protection for herself along the way?

"Oh Lord, what am I going to do?" Amanda wailed. Despite Harvey's rough exterior and disinterest in spiritual things, the poor man was one of God's creations, and he deserved a proper burial. She was fairly confident that she could manage to dig a grave, but how on earth was she going to move that tree off Harvey's body?

Amanda's horse whinnied, and she suddenly realized how the task might be accomplished. She would tie a rope to her horse's saddle, and secure the other end to one of the larger limbs on the section of tree that had fallen on Harvey. If the horse could pull the tree aside, Amanda would be able to free Harvey's body before digging his grave.

A strangled sob caught in her throat. "Dear Lord, please help me. I have never dug a grave before!"

Amanda's legs trembled as she rose to her feet. The raging storm was slowly diminishing, with the thunder and lightning ebbing away, but the heavy rain continued. Maybe the rain would make the ground soft for digging. But if the ground became too muddy, it would be harder to dig. She took a rope from one of the supply bags and set to work. After nearly an hour, she managed to get the tree off Harvey and his horse. By then, the rain had stopped and the storm had moved on, although she could still hear thunder in the distance. Now she faced the chore of digging a shallow grave for the unfortunate man.

She found a shovel in one of Harvey's packs and began digging into the wet earth. Once the hole was deep enough, Amanda gritted her teeth, and using what strength she had, she rolled Harvey's body in. Then she covered him with a tarp and began the job of filling in the grave with rain-soaked dirt. When that was done, she piled several rocks on top, tied two sticks together to form a cross, and placed it at the head of the grave. There was nothing she could do about Harvey's horse. He was too big and heavy for her to consider trying to bury. The animal would have to lie on the trail, to be eaten by the buzzards or whatever creatures might come along to claim it for a meal.

Amanda's muscles ached so badly that it was all she could do to stay on her feet. Since they hadn't stopped for their afternoon meal, she hadn't eaten anything since breakfast. But despite her fatigue, she felt no hunger. Her stomach had begun to churn, and she feared she might get sick. Turning away from the grave, Amanda went to the river, filled her canteen, and washed up. What she wouldn't give to soak in a tub full of warm water. After taking care of Harvey's body, Amanda had been splattered with mud, but the river's water, cold from melting snow, was better than nothing.

I need to say something over Harvey's grave, she told herself, rising slowly to her feet. *He deserves that much.* Amanda winced. Unless Harvey had gotten right with the Lord before his death, which seemed unlikely, he had not made it to heaven. "It's my fault," she whispered. "I feel like a failure. I should have told Harvey more about God and the Inner Light. I've proclaimed myself to be a missionary, yet I haven't led one person to the Lord. If I had known Harvey was going to die, I would have said more."

Removing her Bible from her valise, Amanda stood beside Harvey's grave and read the Twenty-third Psalm: " 'The Lord is my shepherd; I shall not want. He maketh me to lie down in green pastures: he leadeth me beside the still waters. . . .' "

When she came to the fourth verse, she nearly choked on the words. " 'Yea, though I walk through the valley of the shadow of death, I will fear no evil: for thou art with me; thy rod and thy staff they comfort me.' "

Amanda stopped reading. Without Harvey as her protector and guide, she was in the shadow of death herself. Was her faith strong enough to believe that God would provide for her in this seemingly hopeless situation? Did she have the nerve to go on?

She swallowed hard and offered up a simple prayer: "Heavenly Father, please show me what to do and then give me the strength and courage to do it." She thought of a verse from the Gospel of Luke: *"Ask, and it shall be given you, seek, and ye shall find: knock and it shall be opened unto you."* If she could muster up enough faith, then surely God would answer her prayers. After all, the Lord had saved her from the Blackfoot warriors, so He could certainly show her the way through the mountains ahead.

It was already growing dark, and Amanda knew she could not spend the night next to a dead horse and its master's grave. Besides, the trail they'd been on was narrow, with no adequate place for setting up camp. She secured the pack mules to her father's horse, mounted her own mare, and rode on.

Sometime later, Amanda came upon a small clearing where she set up camp and built a fire. At least she knew how to do that much.

After her recent ordeal, Amanda really had no appetite for food, but if she was going to keep up her strength, she needed to eat. She would change out of her wet clothes and cook supper. Maybe then she could think more clearly and decide what to do.

Once the fire had died down some, Amanda set a kettle of water on the burning coals to cook some dried rabbit she'd found in Harvey's pack. It wasn't much of a supper, but it would have to do. She'd already watered the horses and mules and tied them out to graze on some tall grass, as she'd seen Harvey do whenever they stopped for the night. But what about all the things she didn't know how to do? She'd never handled a gun or dressed wild game.

Amanda wasn't sure how long her supply of dried meat, beans, and grain would hold out. They'd finished their fresh vegetables a couple of weeks back. And even though she was feeding only one person now, eventually she'd need to find a food supply or she'd run out of things to eat.

Amanda's thoughts turned from food to travel. She could either stay put, hoping someone would come along and escort her to the Spaldings' mission, or she could make an attempt to get there herself. *Maybe by morning I'll know what to do,* she decided. *Perhaps God will speak to me during the night and give some direction.*

Bedding down on her mat was pure torture. The night sounds and pitch-black sky created an eerie, nerve-racking scene, and Amanda felt the cold chill of fear sweep through her. She'd never spent a night by herself, much less in the wilderness, where all kinds of dangers posed any number of threats.

Earlier, the clouds had parted, and now, gazing up from her bedroll, Amanda felt small in comparison to the vastness of the star-filled sky. In her exhaustion, she didn't bother to put up the tarp cover, hoping there would be no more rain. When she'd first slept on the Plains, she'd felt so confident about her decision to go West. Now, staring at the stars, she questioned her intentions. Instead of making a snap decision to leave New York, she should have prayed about it more, seeking God's will. Well, it was too late for that. She was here by herself, and Papa and Harvey were gone. Nothing could change that, no matter how much she wished for it.

Amanda sighed and tried to relax as she huddled under her blanket. She'd put a few extra logs on the fire before lying down on her sleeping mat, remembering that Harvey had said once that a good fire would keep wolves and other animals away from the campsite. But what if some not-so-friendly Indians happened upon her? Other than Harvey's gun, Amanda had no protection.

As Amanda lay awake, listening to the night sounds, she had the strange feeling that someone was watching her. Whether it was her imagination or the truth, Amanda prayed that whoever was watching would remain simply curious and leave her alone, unharmed.

The fire felt good as its warmth spread toward her. She clutched her blanket closer, watching as sparks floated higher into the darkness. The wood snapped and popped as it burned steadily, and Amanda's eyes grew heavy. Just before falling asleep, she reached inside her valise and pulled out the Bible, which she knew offered words of wisdom and comfort. "Thy Word will protect me, Lord," Amanda whispered, clutching the Bible tightly to her chest. "I must have the faith to believe that. Oh Lord, help Thou my unbelief."

CHAPTER 6

Amanda sat up with a start, unsure of what had awakened her. Had she heard a noise? Had she been dreaming? Could it have been God's voice?

She propped herself up on one elbow and glanced cautiously around. As far as she could tell, she was alone, just as she had been the night before, and the night before that. It had been two full days since Amanda had buried her guide along the trail, and from the time she had begun traveling by herself, she'd prayed for a miracle. Amanda had come to the conclusion that she had no other choice but to keep moving because so far no one had come along to help. It was either travel on, or sit and wait to die. She just hoped and prayed she was heading in the right direction.

Amanda knew that the sun set in the west, so when the sun rose each morning, she traveled in the opposite direction. Of course, she had no idea how far it was to the Oregon Territory, or how she would know she was there, if and when she reached her destination. God willing, she would find a band of Nez Percé Indians along the trail. If she could communicate with them, they might show her the way.

Why am I thinking such foolish thoughts? Amanda berated herself. *I wouldn't know a Nez Percé Indian from a Blackfoot, even if I rode into one of their camps. I cannot believe how unprepared I am for this trip.*

She released her breath in a moan and forced her aching body to stand, stretching to get the kinks out. Her stomach rumbled, but she was in no mood for another breakfast of dried meat and biscuits. What she wouldn't give for a decent meal, a nice hot bath, some clean clothes, and a soft bed. Nothing Amanda had imagined about making this trip had come close to what she'd experienced. The wilderness had taken Papa and Harvey, and short of a miracle, it could very well take her—if not due to some freak accident or Indian attack, then from lack of proper nourishment.

Amanda's thoughts went to the band of Blackfoot Indians who had confronted her and Harvey a few days ago. She had never been so frightened. Somehow she'd managed to conceal her fear, even though her heart had felt as if it were beating louder than thunder.

How proud and stoic those Indians had stood. They had showed no real emotion, other than to glare at her and Harvey as if they were intruders, traveling through land the Indians thought was theirs. In a way, Amanda felt sympathetic toward the red men. After all, they were here first, but white people were encroaching on the land the Indians had previously shared with only God's creatures.

When they had first left Fort Laramie, Harvey had tried to explain that Indians were one with the land. They blended in with the nature surrounding them and respected Mother Earth. They were not constricted by material things many white people felt they couldn't live without. Nowhere in this Indian territory had Amanda seen trash strewn about or the land and animals abused by anyone other than the white men who had already ventured through here. No forest had been cleared by the red men. The land seemed to be untouched, as if God had just created it.

Amanda hadn't missed the way the Blackfoot people had eyed her. If they could have communicated, Amanda wondered what they would have said to her. She especially wished she'd known what they'd thought once her Bible had been revealed. At that moment, she'd known for certain that God was with her, for she could only imagine what might have happened if His Word hadn't tumbled out of her valise.

Amanda closed her eyes, lifted her gaze toward the rising sun, and whispered a prayer. *Dear God, please give me the strength and courage I need for this day. Be with me and calm my anxious heart as I continue this journey.*

From the time she'd awakened, to the time she prepared for bed that night, Amanda had carried an uneasy feeling. Was it just her nerves, or was it the fact that she was all alone in a dense forest at the bottom of a steep trail?

No, it is more than that, she decided. There had been no evidence to cause her to believe so, but for some reason, she still felt as though she were being watched. *Perhaps it is God, watching over me. Oh, how I hope that is the case.*

Tucking a blanket beneath her chin, Amanda held Papa's Bible firmly to her chest. It gave her a sense of peace to have it with her—especially when she slept. It was difficult to close her eyes at night, knowing anything could happen during those long, dark hours. So she tried something different and erected the tarp as a makeshift tent. Maybe with this little shelter overhead, she would feel safer.

A good night's rest is what I need, she thought, yawning and barely able to keep her eyes open. Amanda lay listening to the hoot of an owl and the soft nicker of one of the horses and allowed the sounds to relax her. "Things will look better in the morning," she mumbled softly as her eyes finally drifted shut.

Amanda came off her sleeping mat as though she'd been stung by a hornet. A terrible racket outside her small shelter could have wakened the dead. She threw her covers aside, crawled out of the small enclosure, and clambered to her feet. If someone planned to kill her, it wouldn't be while she slept. No, she would meet the intruder face-to-face, no matter what the outcome.

Fully prepared to see a band of hostile Indians, Amanda was surprised to discover two bear cubs running through the campsite, making a shambles out of everything. They had ripped open all but one of the packs, and everything—from Amanda's clothing to her food staples—was strewn about in the dirt.

"Oh no!" Amanda gasped. She snatched up a piece of wood and began chasing the mischievous cubs. "Get out of here! Leave my things alone!"

The cubs continued to frolic, which caused the horses to whinny and the mules to bray. At wits' end, Amanda picked up some small rocks and heaved them at the bears, shouting, "Get out of here, right now!"

As though they knew she meant business, the twin cubs ran bawling into the woods.

With hands planted firmly on her hips, Amanda surveyed the damage. Her food supplies were nothing more than scavenger pickings. Her plain, dark dresses and Quaker bonnet were dirty. The only pack the roguish little bears had not gotten into was full of Papa's things. Amanda knew that unless she wanted to die in the filthy black dress she presently wore, she'd have to put on one of Papa's shirts to go with the trousers she wore hidden beneath her dress.

Unsure of which trail to take, and with few food provisions left, Amanda was certain that unless God intervened, she wouldn't last many more days.

Amanda hadn't moved from her campsite all day. She was too weary to travel, and since she was unsure of which way to go, she'd decided it was best to spend the day resting, praying, and reading her Bible. She desperately needed God's wisdom and guidance if she was going to find the strength and courage to go on.

Amanda had hoped that other travelers going in the same direction might find her and invite her to journey with them. But all day long, her only friends were the sky, the mountains, and the birds serenading her with melodies.

With a lightweight blanket draped over her shoulders, Amanda placed a log on the fire. As she sat, holding her Bible, while watching the sun go down, she tried not to think about the ache in her stomach. She'd had a refreshing drink of water from a nearby stream, but thanks to those cavorting bears, she was forced to ration her remaining food.

Dark clouds drifted across a stunning sunset, vivid with color. Even the clouds feathered the sky with oranges, reds, and purples, as the sunlight touched them. In these dangerous lands, God's beauty could be seen in every direction. Despite her fear of the unknown, Amanda couldn't help but take in all this grandeur.

Back home, the maples would be coming to life. The red buds

sprouting on every branch always gave an illusion of autumn instead of spring. Up here in the Rockies, she saw no leafy trees—only pines that stood massively reaching toward the heavens.

The landscape was beautiful, and some of the animals Amanda had seen along the way were different from those she was familiar with back East. She'd had her first glimpse of antelope and had even heard wolves howling during the night—thankfully at a distance.

Everything is so different here, Amanda thought as a shudder coursed through her tired body. Tears streamed down her face, and she looked toward heaven. "Dear Lord, hast Thou brought me this far, only to abandon me now? Wilt Thou allow me to die out here in the wilderness alone?"

A sob erupted from Amanda's throat. She couldn't remember ever feeling such despair. She closed her eyes and tried to sleep, but sleep would not come. She wondered if the bear cubs would return. What if, this time, the mother bear was with them? In New York, where black bears were numerous in the mountains, people were always warned never to confront or get between a mother bear and her cubs. That was when they were the most vicious and had no fear of showing rage to protect their young. Amanda knew the cubs that had raided her campsite were black bears. While a black bear was something to be on guard for, her worse fear was that she might encounter a giant grizzly along the way.

As if there couldn't be one more thing to make the situation even more difficult, the sound of thunder rumbled in the distance, and raindrops followed. *Another spring storm?* Amanda shivered. *I wonder what kind of wrath this one will bring.*

Chapter 7

For five days, Amanda sat in the same place, waiting for the rain to stop and pleading with God to send her some help, but to no avail. The small lean-to she'd managed to erect had blown over in the wind and had done little to protect her from the relentless rain. The weight of the water had completely saturated her father's hat. She'd been hot and sweaty one minute, and chilled to the bone the next. If the rain didn't stop soon, she'd be completely water-logged. Amanda no longer wore her dress, just Papa's shirt and trousers. She'd put all her soiled dresses inside her valise. She was sure that she looked more like a drowned kitten than a prim and proper Quaker woman. No matter how hard she tried, she seemed unable to get dried off or warmed up. Her lips were numb, her teeth chattered hopelessly, and her arms and legs were stiff and achy from holding them so tightly against her body for whatever warmth she could muster.

The horses and mules seemed to be managing, as they drank from the nearby stream and ate grass and leaves from the rain-soaked bushes. Amanda got water from the same stream, but her food supply continued to dwindle. What made it worse was that she couldn't build a fire to get warm or cook the dried meat. Although she knew how to use the piece of flint in Harvey's pack, the logs and branches were too wet to ignite. Over the past couple of days, she had developed a horrible cough that caused her sides to ache. Her throat felt raw and swollen. Never before had she suffered such a bone-wrenching weariness.

Feeling light-headed and exhausted beyond belief, Amanda sat with a blanket over her head under the branches of a tree, praying for a miracle, and fearful that none would come. For the last couple of hours, she hadn't been able to stop the strange images she'd begun seeing—no doubt brought on by her increasing weakness. Once, she'd become almost jubilant when she thought she'd seen a covered wagon approaching. As she'd reached out her hand to a smiling woman and her family, they suddenly vanished, making Amanda realize they were never there.

Another time, she'd seen an Indian approach, alone and riding bareback on his painted pony. In Amanda's desperation, even an Indian would be unexpectedly inviting. But that illusion turned out to be just like the last, disappearing as fast as it had come.

Amanda's last hallucination was the worst of all, when she'd thought a pack of wolves had surrounded her, ready to pounce. She sat frozen with fear.

Amanda knew she was sick and needed medical attention, but that wasn't going to happen—not here in the wilderness. She needed to find the nearest fort, but had no idea where it would be, for as much as she hated to admit it, she truly was lost. *Perhaps I should get the livestock ready and ride, trusting God to show me the way.*

Despite her wooziness, Amanda made her way over to the place where she had staked out the horses and mules. She freed Jasper first, and then Jake, tying their rope to the saddle of her horse, Betsy. She'd just untied Papa's horse, when something spooked him. The horse's nostrils flared as he whinnied and reared up, flipping his head from side to side as he pawed the air.

Amanda screamed as the horse's hoof came straight for her.

———

Buck McFadden rode his buckskin, Dusty, slowly through the pines, stopping to check each of his trap lines. Some were near streams where beaver were still plentiful, and other traps he'd set deeper in the forest. Trapping had been in Buck's blood since he'd met his friend Jim Breck, and he knew from experience that the traps should be approached cautiously until he'd identified what animal was caught. He'd learned some time ago to be keenly alert to his surroundings, for in the wilderness, it took only seconds to change one's life forever. If not careful, a bobcat, a lynx, or even a wolverine might give a nasty bite when approached in a trap—a bite that could cause infection or eventually death. Despite all of those dangers, Buck loved these mountains. Their jagged peaks were a part of his soul. He was an adventurer, roaming the trails, rivers, and valleys that he respected so deeply.

The Rockies had been Buck's home since he was twelve years old, and it wasn't until two years later that he'd crossed paths with Jim, his only real friend. Buck had no family—not since he and his mother had been separated. He had dreams of finding her one day, but from what he'd been told, she was dead.

All these years, whether hunting, fishing, trapping, or relaxing on the front porch of Jim's cabin, Buck had found joy living in this wilderness. Jim had taught him everything he knew about trapping and hunting. Now Buck's skills rewarded him with abundant furs for trading whenever the two of them went to Rendezvous or visited one of the mountain forts to replenish the supplies they needed.

As Buck rode silently on, a hawk followed overhead, never leaving Buck out of his sight. "Enjoy the air, my winged brother," Buck whispered, watching as the hawk circled high above. He knew the awesome bird, flying close to the clouds, must feel the same freedom Buck did swaying in the saddle to his horse's rhythm on these familiar mountain paths.

The hawk, a beautiful creature, was just a ball of fluff when Buck had first found him a few years back. He and Jim had been checking traps when they'd come upon the half-dead hatchling. After unsuccessfully checking the surrounding trees for a nest it may have fallen from, Buck decided to care for the hawk, hoping to save its life. After that, the winged creature grew stronger, depending on Buck for food. As time went on and the hawk grew, Buck taught it to fend for itself. Now, this noble bird of prey was as skillful as other hawks, even though it had been raised by a man.

The uniformly colored tail of the hawk—reddish above, light pink beneath—and the dark bell band made the bird unique. Red-tailed hawks preyed on rabbits and rodents, so it brought Buck joy to watch his winged brother swoop down and catch a small rabbit with ease.

When fully grown, Buck's hawk had adapted to its natural instincts and could leave anytime it liked. Buck had no constraints on the bird, but it had decided to stay nearby. All Buck had to do was whistle, and the hawk, calling to him with a high trill, would swoop down and land gently on his outstretched arm, just as it had done during its younger years.

Bringing his mind back to the present, Buck dismounted and checked the last of his traps. As he was preparing to head back to his cabin, he spotted a horse with no rider running toward him. It wasn't an Indian pony, he was certain of that, as there was a bridle, a saddle, and a supply pack half-secured on the horse's back. The horse slowed when Buck started waving his hands, and finally the animal came to a stop, pawing at the ground, snorting. The horse's flanks weren't lathered, so Buck figured it hadn't run very far.

Buck grabbed the reins, tied the runaway to his saddle, and tightened the cinch that held the saddle and pack; then he mounted his steed and rode in the direction the horse had come. Looking ahead, he saw the shadow of his winged brother fly directly overhead, screeching, as though urging Buck on.

A short time later, Buck entered a small clearing, where another horse and two pack mules milled about. As he drew in closer for a better look, he was shocked to see a man's body lying on the ground near one of the horses. Was the poor fellow dead? Had he been attacked by hostile Indians?

Buck climbed down from his horse and secured him to a tree; then he sprinted across the clearing and dropped to the ground beside the man. The fellow looked young, probably in his early twenties, and his face was smudged with mud. The man's shirt and pants hung loosely over his mud-caked arms and legs. The poor lad was skinny as a twig. *How long has he been out here?* Buck wondered.

Buck put his hand over the man's nose and was relieved to find a breath, although it seemed shallow. When he spotted blood on the ground near the man's head, Buck realized the man had been injured.

Buck removed the man's black hat to get a closer look, and his hand froze in midair when a mass of flaxen hair came tumbling out from underneath. This wasn't a man at all; it was a young woman with hair the color of straw. But what was she doing in men's clothing, and where was her man? Surely she wouldn't be out here alone without someone to protect her.

Buck gulped. A gaping wound marred the woman's forehead. If he didn't get help soon, she could die.

CHAPTER 8

Mary Breck had just put some wood in the stove when a knock sounded on the cabin door. Instantly alert, she grabbed the rifle her husband, Jim, had left for her when he'd gone to check on his traps. With the exception of Jim's friend Buck McFadden, they rarely had company, so she was nervous about who might be at the door.

"Who there?" she called.

"It's me, Mary—Buck."

Mary breathed a sigh of relief, set the gun aside, and quickly opened the door. She was surprised to see Buck standing on the stoop, sopping wet, and holding a young woman in his arms. A bloody cloth was tied around her forehead, and she was dressed in a man's clothes. Her skin was pale, and long yellow hair, matted with blood, hung down her back. What Mary didn't understand was what such a fragile-looking woman was doing here in the mountains, or why Buck was holding her like a sack of grain.

Before Mary could voice her questions, Buck announced: "This woman is hurt, and she needs your help."

"Come inside." Mary opened the door wider. "Put her on bed."

Buck followed her to a small room at the back of the cabin. The bed, which still seemed foreign to Mary, had been made by Jim. She knew that because the first day he'd brought her to this cabin, he'd told her so, and said the bed was off-limits to her.

"She your woman?" Mary asked as Buck leaned down and placed the white woman on the bed.

He shook his head. "Found her when I was out checkin' my traps earlier today, but there was no sign of anyone else around. Didn't think it'd be right to take her back to my place, so I decided to bring her here." Buck swiped at the sweat rolling down his forehead. "Sure hope ya don't mind, but since you know a lot about healin' and such, I figured you'd know what to do."

Mary drew in her lower lip, wondering what her husband would say when he returned to the cabin and learned about this. Would he have objections? Jim Breck could be a harsh man at times, but surely he wouldn't throw the injured woman out.

"I do what I can for her," Mary said. "You come back in a few days, alright?"

Buck nodded. "I sure will, but I'd like to stick around for a while. I wanna find out who she is and what happened to the rest of her party, 'cause I don't think she would've been traveling alone." He glanced around the cabin. "Where's Jim? I didn't see his horse in the lean-to."

"He out checkin' traps. Left early mornin'. You stay if you want. I need tend to woman."

"I'll sit at the kitchen table while you do that, and then I'll go as soon as I know whether she's gonna live or not."

Mary gave a nod, and as soon as Buck left the room, she turned back to the bed. She hoped the pale-faced woman didn't die because it would be kind of nice to have someone other than Jim and his faithful dog, Thunder, to talk to for a change.

Feeling a chill in the room, Buck picked up two pieces of wood lying on the floor and tossed them into the stove. Even though it was nearly summertime, it could still get cold here in the mountains, and since the injured woman in the next room had felt cold when he'd picked her up, he figured some heat might help take the chill out of her bones.

"Sure hope she lives," Buck murmured, closing the door on the stove and going back to the table. If anyone could help the white woman get well, it would be Mary. He thought about how she had come to be Jim's wife. Jim and Buck had both been at the Green River Rendezvous last year. While they were there, several Blackfoot showed up, wanting to trade a young Nez Percé woman for blankets and guns. Buck didn't know why, but for some reason they'd singled

Jim out, and he'd ended up with a wife. There was some preacher man at the Rendezvous who said he and his party were heading to Oregon Territory to begin a mission work. After witnessing the trade between the Blackfoot and Jim, the preacher insisted that Jim marry the Indian woman, and said he'd be glad to perform the ceremony. Said it wouldn't be right for him to take her if he didn't make it legal. Jim had said no at first, but then for some reason, he'd changed his mind. It had never made much sense to Buck, because Jim had told him some time ago that he'd been married once and would never tie the knot again. Buck thought about that day and Mary's frightened expression as she was turned over to Jim and forced to become his wife. He remembered seeing the same fearful look on his mother's face the last time he'd seen her.

Since Buck spoke the Nez Percé language, he'd tried talking to Mary, but she would barely look at him and refused to say a word. Since that day, Buck had gotten to know her a little better, and small talk had become more comfortable to her. He had learned that Mary's real name was Yellow Bird, and that a group of Blackfoot Indians had stolen her from her people one night two years ago. For the last year she'd been living as Jim's wife in the mountains. Mary still spoke very little to Buck, and during his frequent visits, he'd noticed that her eyes remained sad. Early on, he'd suggested that Jim look for her people, but the answer had been a firm no. Now that Mary was heavy with child, Buck figured it was best for her to remain with Jim. After all, Jim was the baby's father.

Mary reminds me of my mother, Buck thought. *She has the same dark eyes and gentle spirit and is always willing to help someone in need. For all the good my mother's sweet spirit did her,* he fumed. *She should have fought back.*

As Buck sat at the table, he felt the heat from the fire burning steadily in the woodstove. Even though his buckskin pants and shirt kept him warm enough, he was chilled after the exertion of bringing the injured woman inside, so the fire's warmth was inviting.

Sometimes Buck felt like a lifetime had passed, instead of just his twenty-four years. Other than his shoulder-length red hair, Buck looked as Indian as Mary. His dark-skinned muscular body was tall and lean, without an ounce of fat, and dark brown eyes constantly assessed his surroundings.

Buck's mother had been married to a white trapper, Jeremiah McFadden, until he'd been killed at the hand of a Blackfoot warrior. Buck's mother had been pregnant with him at the time, and some Blackfoot Indians had taken her captive. When Buck was born, she'd named him Red Hawk and explained early on how they'd come to live in the Blackfoot camp. Until he was five years old, Red Hawk and his mother had lived with the Blackfoot tribe. Then they were traded to a white man named Silas Lothard. Silas was cruel, often beating Red Hawk and his mother into submission. He taught them to speak white-man-talk, and had changed Red Hawk's name to Buck. Silas claimed to be a Christian, and he constantly reminded Buck's mother, whom he'd called Sarah, that she was nothing but a heathen who made a good slave. He forced Buck and his mother to listen while he read from a black book he called "God's Word," which Buck quickly came to resent.

Buck's jaw clenched as he remembered how one day his mother had tried to take him and run away. They'd been caught, and as punishment for her disobedience, Silas had traded her to another man. But he'd kept Buck, who was then ten years old, continuing to mistreat and belittle him, often threatening that if Buck didn't do as he said, he would die, and his soul would go straight to hell. Silas also told Buck that his mother had been killed and that the only family he had left was him.

One day when Silas began beating him with a strap, twelve-year-old Buck decided to fight back. In the process of the struggle, Silas fell on his own knife. Once Buck realized the man was dead, he lit out on his own. At the age of fourteen, he met Jim Breck, who trained him to hunt, fish, and trap. Buck vowed to always treat people with kindness, the way his mother had done.

Buck's thoughts were interrupted when Mary stepped into the

room. "The woman very sick," she announced. "Need rest, food, and drink."

"Is she awake? Can I talk to her?" Buck asked, jumping to his feet.

Mary shook her head. "She not wake up yet. I cleaned wound and stitched skin in place. Now she need rest."

Buck craned his neck, trying to glance around Mary for a look at the woman lying on the bed. "Maybe I should stay until she comes to. I'd like to talk to her—find out who she is."

Suddenly, the cabin door opened, and Jim stepped inside, a wide smile on his bearded face. "I thought ya must be here," he said, striding across the room and clasping Buck's shoulder. "Saw your horse, and two others, plus a couple of mules. Where'd ya get 'em? Is someone here with ya?"

Buck nodded and motioned to the bedroom.

Jim headed quickly for the back room. He returned a few seconds later, red-faced and squinting his brown eyes at Buck. "I don't know who that woman is lyin' on my bed, but she'd better be gone by the time I get my horse fed!" With that, he jerked the cabin door open, stepped out, and let it slam shut with a *bang*.

CHAPTER 9

Jim's hands shook as he poured oats into a bucket and set it in the small corral he'd built for his horse. He was overreacting, but that woman lying on his bed reminded him of Lois. *What is she doing here, and why did Buck bring her to my cabin? Of course,* Jim reasoned, *Buck don't know what Lois looked like, since I've never described her to him.* Truth was, Jim had said very little to Buck about the life he'd led before coming to the mountains.

Watching his horse eagerly eat, Jim leaned on the fence and reflected on his past. He and his childhood sweetheart, Lois, had grown up on farms near St. Louis, Missouri. It was expected that Jim would follow in his father's footsteps and take up farming too, but Jim had other ideas. He loved being in the great outdoors and wanted to do something that could earn him money without having to rely on the right kind of weather to produce good crops. He wanted to live in the mountains, where the air was clean and a man could survive off the land. Jim had dreams of adventure, and his enthusiasm for it had led him in that direction.

Jim ended up going west, where he'd taken up trapping and trading. During those early years, he'd done quite well, and when he wasn't setting or checking his traps, he'd built a small but cozy cabin, nestled deep in the woods. A river flowed nearby, making it an excellent place to trap beaver, fox, otter, and rabbit. A multitude of deer, elk, and bear roamed the area as well, and barring anything unforeseen, Jim figured he'd have a good many years to enjoy trapping, trading, and selling his furs.

Once the cabin was finished and Jim had enough money saved up from two years of trapping and trading, he left the mountains and returned to Missouri, where he married Lois. Three days later, they headed west. Jim was filled with excitement and eager to show his new bride the rustic home he'd built for her. Lois's folks had been against the move, saying they were worried about their daughter living in the rugged wilderness. But like Jim, Lois was adventurous and daring, so she'd eagerly agreed. Being the good Christian woman that she was, she'd quoted some scripture to her folks about cleaving only unto him and said in no uncertain terms that her place was now with her husband. Then she'd looked at Jim and, quoting something more from the Bible, said, " 'Wither thou goest, I will go: And where thou lodgest, I will lodge.' "

Jim drew in a deep breath and released it slowly. His beautiful blond-haired, blue-eyed Lois had taken sick before they reached the cabin, halting their journey. Jim did his best to bring her fever down, but it raged on for several days. Jim begged God to save his wife, and it felt like a spike had pierced his soul as he stood by helplessly, watching her slowly slip away. His young heart nearly broke when she died and he had to bury her beside the trail. He returned to his cabin in the Rockies alone, crushed of spirit, and for weeks that was where he stayed, until he had to get back to the task of living. Jim had vowed never to love another woman. He blamed God for taking Lois and determined in his heart that no matter what situation he faced in the future, he would never call on God, for He obviously did not answer prayers—at least not his, anyway.

If God is truly loving, as Lois often said, then how could He take her from me? Of all people, Lois, who fully trusted in God, should not have died, Jim fumed. It had been ten years since Lois's death, but there were times like now when it felt like only yesterday. He'd thought he had pushed the memories aside—until he discovered that woman on the bed he'd made for Lois. Even Mary didn't sleep in that bed; she slept on a mat in the loft overhead. However, it was getting harder for her to climb the ladder now that she was heavy with child, so it wouldn't be long and she would need to bring the mat down and sleep on the floor near the fireplace, which was where Jim spent most of his nights when he needed to be alone.

Jim and Mary had been married a year, and he had to admit, she was a good wife, always eager to please and obedient to his wishes. He felt no love for her, though; just a healthy respect. But then, he was sure the feeling was mutual.

Jim still couldn't figure out why he'd let that preacher man at the Rendezvous talk him into marrying the Indian woman. For that matter, he'd never really understood how he could have made the deal with the Blackfoot Indian to trade two blankets and a gun in exchange for Mary.

"I had to be outta my mind," Jim mumbled. "Either that, or it could've been that I just wasn't thinkin' straight 'cause of all the whiskey I'd drunk that night."

The only good that had come from the trade was that he now had a wife to cook, clean, and do other chores, which gave him more free hours to hunt, trap, and enjoy the great outdoors.

When Jim had brought his Indian bride home, he'd given her the name Mary and taught her to speak English. She'd caught on fairly fast, although her sentences were broken, but at least they could communicate. Even though Jim didn't love Mary, he enjoyed her womanly company.

Jim's horse whinnied and nuzzled his arm, bringing his thoughts back to the present. "I know ol' boy. I wish we could hightail it outta here again, but we just got home." As much as he didn't want to admit it, a white woman was lying on his bed, and he needed to go back inside and find out who she was.

"You want more coffee?" Mary asked, holding the coffeepot out to Buck.

He shook his head. "Thanks anyway, but I've had enough." He glanced toward the cabin door. "I wonder what's takin' Jim so long. He's been out there a long time, feedin' his horse."

"He upset." Mary set the pot back on the stove. "He be back when he ready."

Buck gave a nod. If there was one thing he'd learned about Jim Breck, it was that whenever he got mad, it was best not to bother him until he'd cooled off.

"Any idea why Jim's upset about the white woman being here?" Buck asked when Mary took a seat at the table.

She lifted her shoulders in a brief shrug. "He not like intruders. He very private man."

"Yeah, I know what ya mean." Buck raked his fingers through the ends of his hair. "He wasn't too keen about me hangin' around when we first met neither."

Mary leaned back in her chair and stroked the yellow feather tied to the end of one of her long dark braids. Buck had never seen Mary without that feather, and he knew the reason she wore it was because many moons ago, when she was a young girl, she'd gone into the hills to pray and fast until she found *Weyekin*, her guardian spirit, just as all young Nez Percé children were expected to do. Mary had shared with him once that a yellow bird had come to her one morning during her time alone, and it had sung her a special song. Mary had been sure that *Hanyawat*, the Great Spirit and creator of all things, had sent her guardian spirit in the form of a bird. This Weyekin would be with her to offer assistance throughout her life. From that moment on, Mary wore a yellow feather, and had taken on the name of "Yellow Bird." Of course, Jim never called her by that Indian name. Said she was Mary, and that was all there was to it.

Buck was about to ask Mary if she thought they should check on the woman in the next room, when the cabin door opened, and Jim stepped in. He lumbered across the room, grabbed a tin cup and the pot of coffee, and poured himself some of the muddy-looking brew. Then he pulled out the chair next to Buck and sat down with a grunt. "So, who is this woman?" he asked, motioning to the bedroom, "and why'd ya bring her here?"

"He not know. He find her along trail," Mary spoke up before Buck could respond.

Jim slammed his hand on the table, jostling his cup of coffee and spilling most of it out. "I asked Buck, not you!" he hollered, squinting his eyes at Mary.

Mary winced as though she'd been slapped; then she leaped out of her chair and began wiping up the mess with a rag.

Buck felt sorry for her. He didn't understand why Jim spoke to his wife in that tone of voice. She'd done nothing wrong and didn't deserve to be talked to that way. Jim had been good to him and taught him life skills, but it took all of Buck's willpower to keep his mouth shut when he heard Mary spoken to like that. She had been taken from her people, just like his own mother, and it wasn't her fault she was here. Having no choice in the matter, she'd stoically taken on the life that was dealt her. Yet Buck had noticed that there were other times when Jim silently looked at his Indian wife with respect and admiration. Maybe he talked to Mary that way only when Buck was around, trying to prove something. What, he didn't know. Maybe he should ask, but knowing Jim, he'd probably get mad, and it could ruin their friendship. No, he figured this was one of those things that was better left unsaid.

Jim turned to Buck and leveled him with a look that could have stopped a pack of wild horses dead in their tracks. "Well? Why's there a white woman lyin' on my bed?"

Buck quickly explained how he'd found her and said he'd seen no sign of anyone else.

"Humph!" Jim grunted, folding his muscular arms across his chest. "She had to be with someone. No white woman in her right mind would be up here in the mountains all by herself."

"I'm sure she was with someone, at some time," Buck countered. "But there was no sign of anyone else, and since she was hurt and needed help right away, I wasn't gonna stick around to see if somebody showed up. The way she was bleedin', I couldn't take the chance. So I gathered up her livestock and things and brought her and everything else over here."

Mary filled Jim's cup again, and after blowing on it, he took a drink. "Couldn't ya have taken the woman back to your place?" he complained. "Did ya have to bring her here?"

Buck lifted his hands. "Didn't think it'd be right to take her to my dinky cabin. Besides, Mary knows about healin' herbs and such. The woman probably woulda died in my care," he added. "What would you have done? Left her there to die?"

Jim stood and began pacing. "Well, she can stay till she wakes up and is feelin' better, but then she'll have to go!"

"Go where?" Buck questioned. "I just told ya, I ain't takin' her to my place; it wouldn't be right."

Jim stopped pacing and tapped his foot, while raking his long fingers through the ends of his full beard. "Guess we'll take one day at a time for now. When she's well enough to travel, one of us will have to take her to the nearest fort, and they can decide what to do with her." Jim lumbered across the room and got the big iron tub. "Mary, would ya heat up some water for me? I need to wash up."

Mary nodded and went to the stove.

Buck, grinning inside, was glad that Jim had relented and would let the woman stay so Mary could nurse her back to health. He had an inkling, though, that it would be him taking the woman to the fort, not Jim. Since Mary was with child, Jim would no doubt use that as his excuse to stay put, but Buck couldn't blame him for that.

"Well, I have one more trap line to check before I head back to my cabin," Buck said, rising from his seat at the table. "Thanks for the coffee, Mary."

It was the first time today that a hint of a smile passed across Mary's lips, yet she said nothing.

Buck gave Jim's back a quick thump. "I'll be back in a few days to check on the white woman."

Walking toward his horse, while whistling for his winged brother, Buck wondered if Jim was softening a bit because he was on the verge of becoming a father.

Chapter 10

As Mary opened the cabin door to breathe in the cool mountain air, she placed her hand gently against her stomach and smiled. The babe had been active today, kicking in her womb almost every time she moved. Jim was outside chopping wood, and she'd been busy cooking and cleaning, so some time outdoors felt good.

After several minutes, Mary meandered back inside and headed into the small room, partitioned off from the kitchen by several deer hides that had been sewn together and draped over a thick rope. Noting that the cabin had grown chilly, she headed for the lofty stone fireplace at one end of the room. Nearby sat two split-log chairs, and a black bearskin rug covered a good portion of the floor. The rug gave the room a feeling of warmth, even when it was cold outside.

Mary stoked the embers in the fireplace, then went to check on the woman fitfully sleeping in the next room. Sometimes, when the fever spiked, the woman would moan or cry out for someone or something she called *Pa-pa*. Mary wasn't sure what that word meant.

Thinking about her husband, Mary wondered once again why Jim had reacted so strangely when he'd first seen the white woman. She had asked him about it, but he'd pushed her aside and said, "It's nothin' for you to worry about. Just do your doctoring and stop askin' questions."

It had been seven days since Buck brought the woman to Jim's cabin, and she'd been running a fever most of that time. She had opened her eyes a couple of times, but not long enough to ask who she was. On more than one occasion, Mary had thought the woman might die, but she seemed to have a fighting spirit and had hung on. That was good. It took a fighting spirit to survive in this wilderness.

Courage too. Mary knew that better than anyone. Still, seven days with a fever was not something to be taken lightly. The blond-haired woman looked so small and frail lying in that big bed.

Mary thought about the day Jim had brought her to his cabin. Mary could hardly take it all in, for she'd never been inside a white man's home before.

Although larger than what she had been used to, the cabin felt confining. She remembered hearing for the first time the door shut behind her. She had to take in deep breaths, almost suffocating without fresh, outside air. As each day passed, Mary had gotten used to her new routine and became more accustomed to her surroundings.

At first, Mary had been puzzled about many of the things she'd seen in the cabin—especially the big fire-box in the kitchen. She had watched curiously as Jim opened the fire-box door, piled kindling inside, and set it on fire. Mary's people's source of heat, and for cooking, was an open fire, and Mary didn't have the vaguest notion what to do with such a strange-looking thing. As Jim had continued to feed the fire, Mary wandered through the cabin, clutching her parfletch to her chest. When she'd peered into Jim's bedroom, her eyes had become pools of confusion, seeing the huge bed. She'd never seen anything like it, and had no idea what its purpose could be.

Jim had stepped into the room then, and shouted something at Mary, wagging one finger in front of her face. Then he'd pointed to the ladder leading up to the loft and nudged her in that direction. It didn't take Mary long to realize that was where he expected her to sleep. Fortunately, sleeping in the loft was easy to adapt to. Like a bird high in the trees, finding shelter in a nest, Mary felt comfortable there. Even now, while heavy with child, she was content to sleep on the floor of the loft, although it was getting harder to climb the ladder.

The other thing that had surprised Mary was the big gray-and-white dog sleeping near the fire. The camp dogs among the Blackfoot, where she'd been living since being taken from her own home, had been downright vicious, often snarling and snapping at anything that moved. Mary wasn't sure if she could trust having the animal in the cabin. It hadn't taken her long, however, to realize that the dog Jim called "Thunder" and who was part wolf wasn't vicious at all. He'd quickly become her constant companion. She felt safe with him around, especially whenever Jim left for several days to check on his traps. Many times while Mary sat by the fire, the dog would come over and lay his head in her lap, looking up at her with his big brown eyes. Thunder and Mary seemed to bond with each other in a silent understanding.

In all the moons she had lived here, there were many things Mary had adapted to. But always in her heart was the life she'd been ripped away from so long ago.

Mary had just bent down to put another log on the fire, when she heard the white woman holler, "Pa-pa! Pa-pa!"

Unsure of what to do, Mary waited and listened. Sometimes, as in the past, the woman would mumble for a while, then fall back into a fitful sleep. Other times, she would continue to holler until Mary came and soothed her feverish brow with a wet cloth. Today seemed to be one of those times, for the woman continued to shout, "Pa-pa! Pa-pa!"

Mary set the wood aside, rose to her feet, and hurried into the other room.

———

Amanda opened her eyes and blinked several times. Where was she, and why did her head feel so fuzzy? She was in a bed; she knew that much, but where? This wasn't her bed. Or was it?

She tried to sit up, but her limbs felt too weak. When a small, dark-skinned woman, who was obviously with child, approached Amanda's bed, a ripple of fear shot through her veins. Had she become the captive of an Indian? But if that was the case, she wouldn't be in a bed, would she?

"It good that you awake," the Indian woman said with kindness. "You been sick long time."

"Wh–where am I?" Amanda asked, rubbing her throbbing forehead.

"Home of Jim Breck." The woman touched her chest. "Me, Mary—Jim's wife."

Jim Breck? Amanda thought hard. She didn't know anyone by that name.

Amanda placed her hands against the sides of her head as she tried to remember what had brought her to this place. She had no recollection of coming here. What was the last thing she did remember?

Drawing in a deep breath, she closed her eyes and thought hard. She was a Quaker woman, who lived in Dansville, New York, with her father. She was engaged to marry Nathan Lane. No. No, that wasn't right. Nathan had broken their engagement to be with her best friend, Penelope Goodwin. Soon after that, Amanda and her father had left New York and headed west so they could help the Spaldings minister to the Nez Percé Indians.

Amanda's eyes snapped open. "Papa!" she cried. "Oh Papa, why didst thou have to die and leave me alone?"

The Indian woman touched Amanda's arm. "Who Papa?" she asked, tipping her head.

Tears coursed down Amanda's cheeks. "He's my father, and he. . . he's dead." She nearly choked on the words. Not only had Papa died, but their guide, Harvey, had died as well. Amanda shivered, remembering the fear she'd felt when she'd been left alone and had tried to find her way out of the mountains. She'd been trying to get on her horse when it kicked her in the head. Then the world started spinning, and everything went black.

"How did I get here?" she asked, opening her eyes.

"Buck bring you," Mary replied.

Amanda rubbed her temples, trying to make sense of things. "Who is Buck?"

"Buck McFadden. He Jim's good friend."

Amanda tried to take in all that this woman who spoke broken English had told her. She was thankful she hadn't been abducted by hostile Indians or torn apart by some savage animal.

How many days have passed? she wondered.

Hearing a grunt, Amanda rolled her head in the opposite direction and saw a large gray-and-white dog watching her from the corner of the room. She cringed and gripped the edge of the blanket.

The woman, Mary, must have noticed Amanda's fear, for she quickly explained, "He no bite. Thunder friendly mutt."

Just then, a big, burly man with shoulder-length brown hair and a matching beard strode into the room. He was a mountain of a man, and wore buckskin pants and a fringed shirt. He looked more menacing than the big dog. Was he an Indian too?

Amanda shook her head, trying to clear her mind. He couldn't be Indian. He had brown hair and also a beard, which she knew Indians never had. Amanda was sure that underneath that scraggly beard, the man's face would most likely be white.

He stopped at the foot of the bed, squinting his pale blue eyes. She didn't know why, but she was sure this man with the slightly crooked nose did not like her. The question was, why? Did she dare ask?

Chapter 11

This husband," Mary said, motioning to Jim. Seeing the young woman's wide-eyed expression, she sensed her fear. Mary could relate to that, since she'd felt the same way when she'd first met Jim Breck. He was a bear of a man, with piercing blue eyes and a grim expression that made him look like a hungry animal about to devour its prey. Mary hoped the young woman could draw on her inner strength, for she remembered, if not for her own courage, she never would have made it through all the changes and pain that had been forced upon her.

"Who are you, and where are ya from?" Jim asked, moving closer to the bed.

"My name is Amanda Pearson, and my home is in Dansville, New York." The woman's voice was raspy, and a circle of red erupted on her cheeks. "I am a Quaker, and I'm on my way to Oregon Territory to help at the Spalding Mission and teach the Indians about God."

Jim frowned. "So you're one of those Bible thumpers, huh?" Before Amanda could respond, he quickly added, "Where's your man? No white woman would be out here in the wilderness by herself."

Amanda slowly shook her head, tears pooling in her eyes. "When I left New York, my father was with me." She paused and drew in a shaky breath. "He died soon after we left Fort Laramie, and then a few weeks later, our guide, Harvey Hanson, was killed when a tree fell on him during a terrible storm."

Mary's heart went out to the white woman. She had obviously been through a lot. She hoped Jim would say something to offer her comfort. Instead, he shrugged and said, "The wilderness ain't no place for a woman like you. Ya oughta go back where ya came from."

Amanda shook her head once more. "I promised my father I

would continue this journey, and somehow, I will go on. The Nez Percé Indians need to hear about God and how—" Overtaken by a coughing fit, she stopped talking. When it subsided, she lay with her eyes closed, drenched in sweat.

Mary stepped forward and turned to face Jim. "Woman need rest. She not well yet."

Jim grunted. "I s'pose you're right, but she can't stay here forever. As soon as she's well enough to travel, I'll see if Buck will take her to the nearest fort." He turned and started for the door. "Right now, I'm goin' outside to feed my horse. Get some coffee made while I'm gone!" He glanced down at his dog. "Come on, Thunder, let's go!"

Mary flinched as he slammed the cabin door. He was still upset about the young woman being here, and she wished she knew why. Her husband, even when sober, had a gruff way about him, but this was somehow different. She wished she felt free to ask why he was so angry. Eventually she might figure it out herself.

Sure hope Mary can get that Quaker woman back on her feet soon, Jim stewed as he stepped into the yard. *I'll never get Lois off my mind if I have to keep looking at that gal's pretty face.*

Jim knew he should let go of the past, but seeing Amanda Pearson made him miss Lois all the more. *A man comes on love like Lois and I had only once in a lifetime,* he thought. Despite not being in love with Mary, she was carrying his child, and he looked forward to becoming a dad. He knew that Mary with her gentle ways would be a good mother too.

Just then, Thunder bounded up to Jim with a stick in his mouth.

Jim chuckled. "Ya wanna play fetch, don'tcha, boy?

Thunder dropped the stick at Jim's feet. *Woof! Woof!*

Jim bent down, grabbed the stick, and gave it a toss. The dog raced off and returned a few seconds later with the stick, ready to do it again. Jim quickly complied, and this went on for the next several minutes, until Thunder disappeared into the woods. Thinking the dog had given up on the game, Jim headed for the corral where he kept his spotted horse, Wind Dancer.

When he'd been able to trade for Wind Dancer at one of the Rendezvous, Jim had been surprised that anyone would want to give it up. It was a beauty. Its front half was black, like the mane and tail, but the horse's back half was white with black spots throughout. Jim had seen many Indians at Rendezvous with the same type of horse, but none were any prettier than his. Some horses were covered with spots, others had just a few, but Wind Dancer was unique.

He'd just given the horse some oats when Thunder bounded out of the woods, yipping and running in circles.

"What's the matter, boy?" Jim called. "Did ya tangle with some critter out there?"

As the dog approached, a noxious odor wafted up to Jim's nose, and he knew exactly what had happened. "Phew! You've been sprayed by a skunk, haven't ya, boy?" Jim pointed at the dog, whose fur still glistened from the spray. "Stop right there! Don't come any closer! You won't be comin' into the house till that disgusting smell wears off."

Thunder whined, dropped to the ground, and rolled over on his back. With his feet in the air, he twisted this way and that, as though trying to rub the horrible stench off his back. Jim knew all too well that skunk odor could linger for some time. "Well," he said, "guess the least I can do is give ya a bath, but I sure don't relish the idea of gettin' that close to you, Thunder, ol' boy. By the time I'm done, I'll probably smell like skunk too."

As if Jim had just pronounced a fate worse than death, the dog rolled back over, leaped to his feet, and darted into the woods. Jim figured the mutt probably wouldn't return for a few days. Maybe by then the smell would be less intense so he could stand giving the dog a bath—if he could coax him into the river, that is. Thunder might be brave when it came to taking on some other animal, but he didn't like water at all.

———

Buck urged his horse, Dusty, forward. He was anxious to get to Jim's and see how the white woman was doing. He'd stopped there a few days ago, but she'd been sleeping. Mary said the woman was still running a fever, which wasn't a good sign. Buck wondered if the woman might die, despite Mary's best efforts.

Buck's thoughts went once more to his mother. It wasn't fair that she'd been taken from him. Had she really been killed, or was Silas lying when he'd told Buck that? He wondered if Silas had only said that to make him more miserable. Or maybe it was so the tyrant could have more power over Buck.

Bitterness welled in Buck's soul. He still hated Silas, even though the man was dead. *How could anyone claim to be a man of God and treat people the way he did?* Buck fumed.

Buck didn't believe in the white man's God. He'd been taught by his mother to worship Hanyawat, the Great Spirit and maker of all things, but Buck refused to do even that. *Well, I no longer have to worry about Silas,* Buck thought. *He's exactly where he should be!*

Pulling his thoughts aside, Buck guided his horse up the trail leading to Jim's cabin. As he entered the clearing, the Brecks' property came into view. Jim was in the corral, brushing his horse.

"It's good to see ya," Jim called with a wave. "Can ya stay awhile this time?"

Buck nodded. "I can stay long enough to have some of Mary's good coffee, if she's got any made, that is."

"I'm sure she does," Jim replied. "I told her to make some before I came out here to feed Wind Dancer." He motioned for Buck to bring his horse into the corral.

"Ya got a skunk around here?" Buck asked, sniffing the air. "Smells like one's close. I can almost taste the critter."

"Before you got here, Thunder tangled with one somewhere in the woods. He went runnin' off when I said I was gonna give him a bath." Jim chuckled. "Ya know he don't like water."

"Guess the dog will be sleepin' outside for a while, huh?" Buck said, thumping Jim's back.

"Yep. I reckon the mutt won't be none too happy about that," Jim agreed as he finished brushing his horse. "Can't have the dog smellin' up the cabin though."

"I came to see how the white woman is doin'," Buck said, taking their conversation in a different direction.

Jim punched Buck's shoulder playfully. "Is that so? And here I thought ya came to chew the fat with me."

Buck snickered. "That too." He lowered his voice. "Seriously, how is she today?"

"She's awake. Least she was before I came out here."

"Well, that's a good sign," Buck said. "Did she say who she is or what she's doin' here in the Rockies?"

"Her name's Amanda Pearson, and she's on her way to the Spalding Mission in Oregon Territory. Have ya heard of it?"

Buck nodded. "Heard it's near Lapwai Creek."

Jim shrugged his broad shoulders. "Don't think she's goin' there now though. Not unless she finds herself a guide."

"Who was she traveling with?" Buck asked.

"Said she left New York with her pa, but he died on the trail." Jim grimaced. "Then a bad storm hit and their guide was killed by a falling tree."

Buck whistled. "I'd say she's had her share of bad luck."

Jim nodded. "If ya ask me, she needs to go back to where she came from."

"Guess I'll go inside and have a talk with her." Buck moved toward the cabin.

"Before you go in, I need to ask you something," Jim said, walking beside Buck.

"What's that?"

"When the woman's up to traveling, would ya be willing to take her to the nearest fort?" Jim paused as they reached the cabin door. "I'd do it, but Mary could have her babe most any day, and I won't leave her alone."

"I understand that," Buck said. "I'll have to think about it though." Truth was, he wasn't sure he wanted to be alone with the white woman.

When Buck and Jim went inside, Mary greeted them at the door. "Good see you," she said, smiling at Buck.

"It's good seeing you too, Mary."

"You want coffee? It ready on stove."

"Maybe after a while, if that's okay," he said, even though the thought of a hot cup of coffee was inviting. "I'd like to speak with the white woman first. Jim said she's awake."

Mary nodded. "Come see."

Buck followed Mary into the other room, while Jim remained in the kitchen. He found the woman lying on the bed, her eyes open. Even in the dim lantern light, he could see that she looked pale and weak.

"This Buck," Mary said. "He find you; then bring here." She looked at Buck and motioned to the woman. "This A-man-da."

Amanda smiled slightly. "I want to thank thee for finding me and bringing me here. I am not well yet, but I'm doing better. Mary has taken good care of me."

Buck gave a nod. "Jim said your pap and your guide are both dead."

Amanda nodded slowly. "Papa and I were on our way to the Spalding Mission to help teach the Nez Percé Indians about God." She paused and drew in a shallow breath. "If thou knowest of the area, wouldst thou be willing to take me there?"

Buck shook his head vigorously. "I'll take ya to the nearest fort when you're well enough, but I ain't goin' into the Nez Percé winter homeland!"

CHAPTER 12

When Buck left Jim's cabin later that day, his mind whirled with unanswered questions. Had he said no to Amanda's request to take her to the mission because he didn't want to be reminded of his mother's people and where he'd come from, or did it have more to do with the fact that Amanda was a Bible thumper? It didn't matter. Either way, he wasn't going to act as her guide. He might consider taking her to the fort, but that was all. Maybe she could find someone there who'd be willing to take her where she wanted to go—someone who had no ties to the Nez Percé people.

Buck had never admitted this to anyone, but he blamed his mother's people for letting her marry Jeremiah McFadden. If she had married one of her own and stayed with her tribe, there would have been less chance of her being taken captive by the Blackfoot tribe.

Of course, Buck reasoned, *Mary Yellow Bird was stolen from her tribe—right out from under her parents. Well, the past is in the past, and nothin' can be changed.* Buck had no desire to visit the Spalding Mission. He'd heard about the missionaries who were trying to teach the Nez Percé how to live like the whites and worship their God. None of that seemed right to him.

Buck often wondered how things would have been for him, as well as his mother, if his white father hadn't been killed. Would Jeremiah have taught Buck all of the things he'd learned from Jim? Probably so, since Buck's mother had mentioned that Buck's father was a trapper too. His father had died before Buck was born. But he knew from the things his mother had told him that she'd loved her husband.

Engulfed in the solitude around him, Buck gave his horse the freedom to run. As they raced through the woods toward his cabin,

Buck enjoyed the feel of the wind in his face, and the power of the steed he sat upon. Both horse and rider were meshed together, in tune with the other's movements. It was at times like this that Buck could forget about the bitterness in his soul, become one with nature, and hold close to his heart that which had been untouched by mankind.

In the sky above, which no man could destroy, Buck's red-tailed hawk soared high in broad circles. His raspy, *kree-eee-ar*, was mingled with another's, when a second raptor circled just below him.

"Ah, my winged brother, I see you have a friend—possibly a mate." Slowing his horse, Buck smiled, watching in awe as the two hawks ascended. He wondered if someday he'd have a wife and perhaps a child of his own—maybe a son to teach all the good things about living here in the Rockies. Part of Buck wanted to get married and raise a family, but another part said he was better off being free. Free like the birds, who could go anywhere, whenever they wanted.

"Something smells good in here," Amanda said when she made her way to the kitchen and found Mary stirring something in a big black pot on the woodstove. Her legs were still wobbly, but the pleasant aroma drew her to the table.

Mary turned, offering Amanda a smile. "You hungry?"

Amanda nodded, her stomach growling noisily as she leaned on a wooden chair for support.

"That good sign. You eat. Gain strength back." Mary added some salt to the pot. "When stew is done, we eat." She motioned to the chair that supported Amanda. "I cook. You sit and rest."

Amanda did as Mary said. She would have offered to help, but knew she wasn't up to doing anything more than sitting. Her hands shook as she tried to smooth the wrinkles from her dress, which Mary had found in Amanda's valise and apparently washed for her. The effort to walk from the bed to the table had stolen all of Amanda's strength, but the need to get out of bed and talk with another person was more powerful than her own weakness. Besides, she was tired of being sick and useless.

"Is there anything I might do to help thee?" Amanda questioned, feeling the need to ask at least.

"You rest. Just nice to talk with another woman," Mary said.

"How long have you lived here with Jim?" Amanda asked, anxious to know more about Mary.

"Many moons. He say one year," Mary replied, continuing to stir the pot of stew.

"What Indian tribe do you come from?"

"Ni-mii-pu."

"Oh, you're part of the Nez Percé?"

Mary nodded.

"I'm curious," Amanda said. "How did you come to marry a white man?"

Mary didn't say anything at first, but then she took a seat at the table across from Amanda. "Me stolen from my people by Blackfoot."

Amanda gasped, thinking of the Blackfoot Indians who'd come into her and Harvey's campsite. She had heard tales about captives who had escaped and the hardships they'd endured while being held. Other captives, both men and women, had ended up being part of the tribes who stole them. Years after, when they'd had chances to escape or be rescued, the captives chose to stay, enjoying life as an Indian instead of returning to the white community they'd been born into. Amanda could have easily been taken captive, but God had spared her.

"Did Jim rescue you from the Blackfoot?" she asked.

Mary shook her head, her dark eyes looking ever so serious. "Smoking Buffalo trade me to Jim."

"He. . .he traded you?" Amanda could hardly fathom such a thing.

"Traded for blankets and gun," Mary said in a matter-of-fact tone, as though it was perfectly normal for a man to do so.

Amanda wondered if it was a common occurrence for Indians to trade people for things. If so, they really did need to know about God and learn of His ways.

"So did you and Jim get married?" Amanda dared to ask.

Mary nodded. "He marry me at fort in white-man ceremony.

White preacher say the words over us."

"I see." Amanda couldn't help wondering if Mary was happy being Jim's wife. Maybe the reason she'd seen no warmth or tenderness between them was because Mary had been forced to leave her people and hadn't chosen him to be her husband. Jim seemed angry when he spoke to Mary, as if he felt no love for her at all. But if he felt that way, then why had he married her?

Amanda thought about how difficult it must have been for Mary to be taken from her people and end up getting traded to a white man. Amanda was not the only one who had suffered a great loss. Mary had obviously been through much grief, yet she seemed to have accepted her lot in life and was making the best of things.

Amanda looked at Mary with even more respect, for this woman who'd been taken from her family and her heritage had great courage to have made it this far. Amanda hoped she could be just as brave in her venture to the Spalding Mission.

"Can I ask you something else?" Amanda said.

Mary gave a quick nod.

"I've been wondering about the young man Buck. Do you know why he's not willing to take me to the mission?"

The cabin door opened and Jim entered the room. "I'm hungry as a grizzly bear and need somethin' to eat!"

Mary stood and ambled back to the stove. "Where Thunder?" she asked.

Jim wrinkled his nose. "He tangled with a skunk awhile ago, so he'll be stayin' outside till the stink wears off." He turned to face Amanda, barely making eye contact. "I see you're up. Does that mean you're feelin' better?"

"Yes, some," she replied, "but I am still very weak."

"Need more rest," Mary said, glancing over her shoulder as she stirred the pot of stew. "Need eat and gain back strength."

Amanda's stomach rumbled just thinking about food. She had to admit she was quite hungry.

Mary took a tin plate from the wooden cupboard, filled it with steaming stew, and set it on the table in front of Amanda. "You eat. Good stew."

"What about me?" Jim growled. "Don't I get anything to eat?"

Mary bobbed her head. "Yes, Husband. There plenty of stew for you." She filled another plate and gave it to Jim, then fixed one for herself and took a seat.

As they sat around the table, Amanda asked if they would mind if she said a prayer.

Jim shook his head vigorously. "You can pray in your head if you've a mind to, but nobody prays out loud at my table!"

Amanda cringed. Did everything she said make this man angry? Why would he object to her saying a prayer?

"What is pray-er?" Mary asked.

"It's talking to God. . .saying thanks for the food and all that He's done," Amanda explained.

"Who is God?" Mary asked.

"He created the world and all of mankind," Amanda replied.

Mary's brow furrowed as deep wrinkles formed across her forehead. "Hanyawat, the Great Spirit. He made everything."

Amanda looked at Jim, hoping he would say something, but he grunted and began eating his stew.

Amanda wondered about the Great Spirit. Could the Indians be worshiping the same God as she and not even realize it? Perhaps He was the same God called by a different name. There were so many things she didn't know about these red-skinned people. Perhaps the fact that she'd ended up here in this cabin with a Nez Percé Indian had been God's plan so that she could learn more about the Nez Percé and their ways. This would help her when she got to the Spalding Mission. Of course, she had to find a way to get there first. In the meanwhile, for whatever time she remained in Jim's cabin, she would learn all she could from Mary. Perhaps in the process, she could teach the young Indian woman about the one true God.

CHAPTER 13

Amanda yawned and stretched as she crawled out of bed. She hadn't slept well last night, having had several bad dreams. But at least she felt a bit stronger now, with no sign of a fever. Mary's good cooking had given her body new strength, and each new day she was able to do a little more.

Amanda had spent the last week resting, eating, and sitting outside in the fresh air as she got better acquainted with Mary. She'd learned that before the young woman's capture by the Blackfoot tribe, she'd planned to marry a Nez Percé Indian brave named Gray Eagle. Tears had welled in Mary's eyes as she'd told how Gray Eagle had tried to rescue her and been shot and killed with an arrow before the Blackfoot left their camp and moved on to another. Mary's story had been interrupted when Jim came home with two rabbits he'd asked Mary to clean. However, Amanda hoped that sometime later today she would have the chance to visit with Mary some more. Though sad, the young woman's story was quite interesting, making Amanda yearn to learn even more.

Buck had come by twice to see how Amanda was doing, but he never mentioned taking her anywhere, not even to the fort. She said nothing about it but hoped by the time she was well enough to travel he would reconsider and act as her guide. He seemed like a nice man, though whenever he looked at her, she detected wariness in his eyes.

Amanda had asked Mary about Buck's dark skin, as it didn't go with his shoulder-length red hair, which he wore pulled back and tied with a thin piece of leather. Mary had explained what she knew of Buck's story and his friendship with Jim.

Dismissing her thoughts, Amanda got dressed and splashed water on her face from the bowl on the rustic wooden dresser in the small room where she slept. She wondered if Jim had built the simple piece of furniture. Feeling a sudden chill, she opened one of the drawers to look for her woolen shawl, since Mary had said she'd put all her things in there. Sure enough, there were her other dresses and underclothes, although wrinkled, along with her and Papa's Bibles. Seeing no sign of the shawl, Amanda opened the second drawer, where she found her shawl, as well as another Bible. Wondering whom it belonged to, she lifted it out of the drawer and carried it over to the bed. Taking a seat, she opened it to the first page, where she saw an inscription. "To our daughter, Lois, and her husband, James, on their wedding day," she read aloud.

Amanda's lips compressed. *So Jim must have been married before. I wonder what happened to his wife. It seems strange that they had a Bible yet he wouldn't let me pray out loud at the table.*

Clutching the Bible, Amanda rose to her feet. She hoped Jim hadn't left yet, because she wanted to speak with him about this.

Jim had just taken a seat at the table to have one last cup of coffee before heading out to check on his traps, when Amanda emerged from the bedroom, holding a Bible. He didn't recognize it at first, not until she placed it on the table in front of him and opened it to the first page where his and Lois's names had been written.

"Where'd ya get that?" he shouted, his face heating.

"I-I found it one of the dresser drawers," Amanda stammered.

"Well, ya shouldn't be snoopin' around where ya don't belong!"

"Me put her clothes in there," Mary quickly interjected.

Jim glared at her. "Nobody asked you!"

"It's true," Amanda said, coming to Mary's defense. "My clothes were in the drawer, and when I was looking for a shawl to wear I stumbled upon the Bible."

Struggling with his emotions, Jim snatched up the Bible. It was all he had left to remind him of Lois, yet he could barely stand looking at it. Lois had been religious, but where had that gotten her? Nowhere but an early grave!

Because of Lois and her strong religious beliefs, Jim had gotten to know God better, and had wholeheartedly thanked the good Lord every day for bringing Lois into his life. Now God was a stranger to him. All those prayers of thanks had fallen on deaf ears, when this so-called God allowed Lois's life to slowly drain away to nothing. Lois had told Jim once that when a person died and went to heaven, their soul lived on. Jim hoped that was the case for his precious wife, but he felt as if his own soul no longer existed.

Jim pushed back his chair so quickly that it toppled over. Then he stormed across the room, opened the stove, and tossed the Bible in. Barely hearing the women gasp, he stood watching as the flames consumed the book, but it did nothing to soften the anger he felt toward God. Slamming the stove door shut, he turned to Mary and said, "I'm goin' out to set some traps, and I won't be back till dark. Make sure you have my supper ready." He grabbed up his things and went out the door, letting it bang shut behind him.

Amanda couldn't believe how upset Jim had become when he'd seen his first wife's Bible. And throwing it into the fire—well, that was incomprehensible! What in the world had the man been thinking? Didn't he know or even care that God's Word was holy?

Amanda glanced at Mary, who sat at the table with a pinched expression. The way Jim talked to his wife was terrible, yet Mary never objected. Why, it wasn't a marriage at all. Mary was nothing more than a slave to that man!

"Jim angry," Mary said. "He blame himself for death of first wife."

Amanda's mouth dropped open. "Did he tell you that?"

Mary shook her head. "Just know. I see on his face." She winced and placed one hand on her stomach.

"What is it, Mary?" Amanda asked with concern. "Is your baby kicking?"

"No kick," Mary said. "Baby coming soon."

"Yes, in a few more weeks, right?"

"No." Mary rose from her chair. "Pains have started. Baby come today."

Amanda's eyes widened. "You can't have the baby today. It's too soon, and Jim's not here."

Mary began pacing, while rubbing her lower back.

A sense of apprehension crept up Amanda's spine. She'd never helped bring a child into the world or even witnessed the birth of a baby, and she wasn't prepared to do it now. Maybe Mary was wrong. She might not be in labor at all. Amanda hoped that was the case, because there was no way she could help Mary deliver her baby!

CHAPTER 14

No worry, Amanda," Mary Yellow Bird said, seeing Amanda's fearful expression. "Baby will come when ready."

"But I don't know what to do." Amanda's voice quivered.

"Do nothing now." Mary touched her chest. "Me birth baby." Having grown up with nature's ways and the knowledge of herbs, she was fully prepared to deliver her own child. She wished, however, that she was at home with her people, where their medicine woman would be on hand in case there was any trouble. But so far, her labor seemed to be progressing normally, so this helped her feel more confident.

"Are you sure you won't need my help?" Amanda asked, her forehead etched with wrinkles.

"I let you know when." Mary continued to pace, and every once in a while she stopped to take a drink of the birthing tea she had concocted earlier that morning when the pains first began.

Amanda sat at the table, with hands folded and head bowed, like she did when she prayed silently before a meal. Mary didn't think she needed the white woman's prayer, but she guessed it couldn't hurt. In the meantime, Mary sent up her own prayers to Hanyawat, asking that her guardian spirit would protect her and the child and offer a speedy delivery, without complications.

When the pains came closer, Mary reminded herself not to fight them. She remembered her mother telling other expectant women in their tribe to flow with the pain, just as a leaf falls slowly from a tree.

Another pain, sharper than the last, came and went. Beads of perspiration gathered on Mary's forehead, and she hurriedly greased her loins with bear grease she kept in a can. Then, moving over to be closer to the warmth of the fire, she squatted down.

"Wh-what are you doing?" Amanda called, jumping to her feet.

"It best if I sit on haunches. Need clean rags, water, and herb tea on stove," Mary said between ragged breaths.

"I will get them."

As she had been taught, Mary concentrated fully on bringing this new life into the world. Despite the sharp pains, she remained calm and composed.

Amanda dipped a piece of cloth into the bucket of water she'd brought over and wiped Mary's damp forehead. When the next contraction subsided, Amanda offered her a drink of tea. She sipped it appreciatively, knowing the birthing tea would get things moving quicker.

"Tell me what else to do," Amanda said in a panicked tone.

"Sit on floor behind me," Mary instructed. "I lean on you."

Amanda did as Mary requested, and as Mary took deep breaths, she was able to relax against Amanda's chest between contractions.

When she knew the time was right, Mary began to push. "Head coming now," she said, excitedly. As Mary gave one final push, the baby slipped from her womb and into her outstretched hands. "It's a boy!" she cried, tears coursing down her cheeks.

A few seconds later, a loud cry filled the room. Mary breathed a sigh of relief, knowing her son was alive. "Thank you, Hanyawat," she whispered in awe. Lowering herself the rest of the way to the floor, she said to Amanda. "Bring knife."

Amanda's face paled. "A knife? Why would you need a knife?"

"Cut cord," Mary replied.

"Oh, I see."

Once the cord was cut, Mary washed her son gently with a wet, clean rag. Then she wrapped the infant in a small blanket she'd made and handed him to Amanda.

Amanda looked at her quizzically.

"Hold baby while I clean up."

Amanda took the child and sat in the hickory rocker near the fire while Mary tended to her own needs.

"You need to rest now," Amanda said. "I think you should go to the bed and lie down."

Mary shook her head. "Jim no like me sleep there. He be angry when he come home."

Amanda frowned. "I don't care what Jim says. You and the baby need to rest comfortably. When Jim gets here, I'll tell him that I have decided to sleep upstairs in the loft, and that you need the bed."

Mary, too tired to argue, followed Amanda into the next room. When she crawled onto the bed, it felt strange, but there was lots of room, and she knew it wouldn't be long before she fell asleep. First, though, she must try to feed her baby.

Amanda placed the baby in Mary's arms, covered them with a blanket, and quietly left the room.

After cleaning the cabin, she prepared something for Mary to eat and drink. *I wonder what Jim will think when he gets home and discovers that he has a son. I hope this baby will soften his heart and cause him to be kinder to Mary. She has such a sweet spirit and deserves only the best.*

After Mary finished eating a bowl of rabbit stew and fell back to sleep, Amanda took out her Bible and sat at the table, reading Isaiah 26:3–4: "Thou wilt keep him in perfect peace, whose mind is stayed on thee: because he trusteth in thee. Trust ye in the Lord for ever: for in the Lord Jehovah is everlasting strength."

Those are such comforting words, she thought.

Thunder barked outside. Fear clutched Amanda's heart. Could Jim be back already? It wasn't even dark. Or was someone else outside?

A few minutes later, Jim entered the cabin, dripping wet.

"What happened? Why art thou so wet?" she asked as Jim removed his jacket and coonskin cap.

"Slipped on a rock and fell into the river," Jim grumbled. He looked around. "Where's Mary? Did she get my supper made?"

Amanda motioned to the bedroom. "Mary's in there, with. . ."

"She knows that room's off-limits to her!" Jim slapped his hands together so hard that it caused Amanda to jump. She'd never met anyone with such a fiery temper. Before Amanda could offer an explanation, he stormed into the bedroom, dripping water from his wet clothes all over the wooden plank floor.

Amanda left her seat at the table and followed, fully prepared to defend Mary if necessary. She entered the room in time to see Jim screech to a halt at the foot of the bed. He stood with his mouth gaping open as he gazed upon Mary and the baby.

Mary's eyelids fluttered, and a soft smile played on her lips. "Come. Meet son."

"It's a boy? You had the baby while I was gone?"

Mary nodded. "He a fine boy too. Come see."

"Well, I'll be. . . ." Jim moved to the side of the bed and grinned as he bent down to look at the baby. It was the first time Amanda had seen such a pleasant expression on the burly man's face.

"You want hold son?" Mary asked.

Jim nodded, then quickly shook his head. "I'm all wet, Mary. My foot slipped, and I fell in the river when I was settin' one of my traps."

She smiled. "You change clothes. Then hold baby."

Jim nodded. "I'll do that in a minute. Right now I need to know something."

"What?" Mary asked.

"How are ya feelin'? Are ya doin' okay?"

"Me fine. Baby fine too," she assured him. "Amanda take care of us. She good woman."

Jim turned to Amanda. "I'm glad you were here when the baby came. Thanks for helpin' out."

"Thou art welcome, but I really didn't do that much," Amanda replied. "Mary delivered the baby herself, and I did whatever she told me."

"It's a comfort to know you were here. If somethin' had gone wrong, it wouldn't have been good for her to be alone." Jim cast another look at his sleeping son. "I'm gonna get outta these wet clothes now, but when I come back to the room, you and me have a job to do, Mary."

"What job?" she asked, looking up at him with a curious expression.

"We need to name our son."

"Yes," Mary agreed. "He need good name."

As Jim left the room, Amanda's throat constricted. Behind Jim's harsh exterior lay a kind, gentle man, and all it took was seeing his precious son to bring that out of him. Now if she could just get Jim and Mary to see their need for salvation, Amanda's mission here at this place would be complete, for she felt certain that was the real reason God had brought her to this cabin. "God works in mysterious ways, His wonders to perform," she whispered.

CHAPTER 15

As Jim stood looking down at his wife and baby, an emotion welled in his chest he'd never known before. He had a son—someone to care for and carry on his name. For the first time since Lois died, Jim felt like he had a reason to live—a real purpose for his life. The love he felt for the tiny infant lying in his mother's arms was undeniable. It was an emotion he thought had died with his first wife. All these years he'd protected himself from getting too close to anyone, even Buck. But now Jim's heart lay wide open, eager to experience this newfound joy he felt seeing his newborn son. Was it possible that he felt something for the child's mother too? He knew he could never love Mary the way he had Lois, but if he were truly honest with himself, he'd have to admit that he did feel something for the Indian woman who'd borne him a son. What did he feel, anyway? Was it friendship? No, they'd never really been friends. In fact, Jim treated Mary poorly much of the time. In spite of his hostilities, though, she'd remained loyal and obedient, much like his dog.

As he continued to study Mary as she suckled their son, Jim realized that what he felt for her was respect. This young Indian woman had endured many hardships, before and after he'd brought her to his cabin. She had cooked his meals, cleaned his house, done many of his chores, and even made friends with his dog. Yes, Mary was deserving of Jim's respect, if not his love. And now she'd given him the greatest gift of all—a beautiful, healthy son.

He pulled thoughtfully on his beard and smiled down at her. "So, what shall we call this little fella?"

Mary turned her gaze to the now sleeping babe, then looked back at Jim. "What name you choose?"

With no hesitation, Jim said, "I was thinkin' Joseph would be a fitting name. That was my pa's name, and he was a good man. I think he'd be right pleased to know he had a grandson to carry on his name."

Mary lay silently for a while, then she said, "Joseph a good name, but he need Indian name too."

At first, Jim was tempted to argue that point, but he changed his mind. After all, little Joe was Mary's son too, and she had every right to choose a name. "Guess that'll be alright," he said. "What name did ya have in mind for him?"

"Little Wolf. I like he be called Joseph Little Wolf."

"The boy's name is chosen then," Jim agreed. "There's one thing though."

Mary looked at him with questioning eyes.

"He can be told of his Injun name when he's older, but I wanna call him Little Joe for now."

"It be as you wish, Husband. You want hold Little Joe now?" she asked.

"Oh yeah." Jim took a seat on the edge of the bed and Mary placed the baby in his arms. As Jim gazed at his son's tiny face, his vision blurred, and he swallowed hard, unable to express the way he felt. He couldn't get over the baby's dark hair, as coal-black as his mother's. He'd done nothing to deserve it, but Jim felt as though he'd been given a second chance at happiness. He could hardly feel the weight of the little person he held in his arms, yet his heart felt as if it had grown ten times larger. He looked forward to the days ahead, raising Little Joe, and teaching him to hunt, fish, and trap. But that would come later, when the boy was grown. As Jim tucked his little finger into the baby's fist, he sighed when his son grasped it strongly and held on. What more could a man ask for in this life? he wondered.

———

Buck prided himself on his expert hunting skills. He'd bagged more deer and elk than he could count, along with many buffalo, moose, antelope, and even some black bear. Today, he hoped to get his catch quickly and go home with plenty of fresh meat for the table, as well as some to dry and store for the days ahead. If he did well, he would share some of the meat with Jim.

Buck left his horse grazing in a grassy meadow and entered the forest of pine and fir trees on foot. It wasn't long before he spotted a cow elk stepping out of the trees into a clearing. Taking a deep breath, he loaded his gun, steadied it, and was about to fire, when he noticed a young calf standing next to his prey. "That critter wasn't there a minute ago," he grumbled. "Must've been lyin' in the grass." Annoyed, Buck lowered the gun. He couldn't bring himself to kill the mother or her baby, even if they were only dumb animals. Maybe he was getting soft. He shook his head in dismay and turned in another direction. He'd try his luck elsewhere.

Crossing the clearing, Buck headed for the woods on the other side. He had barely reached the stand of trees when he heard a loud rumbling noise. Swiveling, he glanced in the direction of the sound, and stopped short when he saw an enormous, brown grizzly bear emerging from the forest. Of all the animals in the wilderness, grizzlies were the most feared by Indians and white men alike. Sometimes towering over eight feet in height, the vicious animals were equipped with terrible needlelike claws. Buck knew that a single swipe could decapitate a man.

His mouth went dry as the giant grizzly lumbered toward him slowly, then stopped to sniff the ground. Grizzlies were noted for their poor eyesight, but they did have a keen sense of smell, and it soon became obvious that the bear had picked up Buck's scent.

Taking off on a run, Buck dodged the pine and fir trees, until the forest became a blur. If he could just get to his horse quickly enough. Buck was running so fast now that he could hear his heart beating, like drums inside his ears. To his left, as he ran forward, he caught a glimpse of more brown and realized it was a grizzly cub. No wonder this bear was coming after him. Somehow, Buck had gotten between the cub and its mother—the worst thing anyone could do.

The bear was gaining on him. He could hear her low growl and the branches snapping under her heavy weight. The ground shook like it did during an earthquake. Feeling a sense of panic, Buck glanced back over his shoulder and saw that the bear had drawn closer. He could almost smell the grizzly's rancid breath as it let out another roar.

Buck pivoted on one foot, planning to fire his black-powder rifle at the rushing animal. Too late. The grizzly let out an ear-piercing roar and blindly charged, knocking him off his feet. Buck rolled quickly to one side, narrowly escaping the bear's cruel teeth. A huge paw came down on Buck's chest, and he was quickly aware that his buckskin shirt had been torn clear through. His flesh was cut deeply, and warm blood pressed against his skin.

Buck turned this way and that, but the bear, with its relentless strength, kept him pinned to the ground. It continued to tear into Buck's flesh at every opportunity.

Buck was drenched with perspiration and blood. Saliva from the raging animal mixed with his own fluids, saturating him. He could taste his own blood and smell his own fear, but Buck fought with all the energy he could muster. His gun had been knocked from his hand when the bear attacked, and it lay several feet away. Buck knew his only chance was to reach it and shoot the bear in the head. Each time the grizzly made another pass at him, Buck rolled inches closer to his rifle. Finally, with nearly all his strength used up, his fingers touched the tip of the gun barrel. Buck was thankful he'd loaded the gun before he decided not to shoot the elk and that it hadn't gone off when he dropped it. Frantically, he pulled the gun to his side, raised it slightly, and shot the grizzly between the eyes.

As the bear's blood splattered and blended with his own, the animal staggered, swayed, and sagged heavily onto its forepaws. A thick flow of dark blood poured from its skull as it went down and lay motionless, inches from where Buck sat sprawled on the ground.

Gasping for breath, pain stabbing at his chest, arms, and neck, Buck realized that his body was full of gashes where the bear's claws had made deadly contact. He tried to stand but was too weak, so he did the only thing he could. He crawled on his belly toward his horse, knowing if he didn't get help soon, he would surely bleed to death.

Clutching the gun tightly in one hand, Buck used the other arm to pull himself along. He'd only gone as far as the stream, when his strength gave out. He lay there in the tall grass, within reach of the water's edge, unable to move. His mouth had gone dry, and his thirst was fierce. Short of a miracle, Buck knew he was a goner. As everything started to fade, the last thing Buck heard over the ringing in his ears was the bubbling of water as it spilled over a rock like a miniature waterfall. If only he could quench his thirst before he relinquished his soul to death.

CHAPTER 16

When Jim woke early the following morning, a sense of exhilaration coursed through his veins. He was a father now and would do his best to see that his wife and son's needs were always met. Everything he did—hunting, fishing, trapping—had more purpose. Jim was glad he'd set some new traps yesterday and wouldn't have to venture far from the cabin today. He wanted to be nearby to see that Mary got the rest she needed and to spend time holding their son.

Jim smiled as he glanced at the loft overhead where Amanda had made her bed last night. As much as he'd fought having her here, he had to admit her presence now that she was feeling better would be a benefit. He could go out to do his chores, hunt, fish, and trap without having to worry about Mary. If she were alone in the cabin with the baby, she'd probably try to do too much.

Thinking about the bed in the other room, Jim realized how foolish he'd been to forbid Mary from sleeping in it. For that matter, he ought to be sharing that bed, instead of sleeping on the floor by the fire. *Guess my stubborn pride got in the way of common sense,* he told himself as he slipped into a deerskin parka.

Jim had noticed when he'd first gotten up that he could see his breath. Despite the month of June bringing warmer weather to the mountains during the day, nighttime and early morning hours were still a bit chilly. While spring was usually wet, on occasion they got snow, even as late as July.

First things first, Jim told himself. He needed to go down to the stream and fill a couple of buckets with water. If he did that before the women awoke, they would have fresh water for washing as well as for their breakfast preparations.

Whistling for Thunder to join him, Jim picked up the two buckets sitting outside the cabin door and headed for the stream. Only a hint of skunk smell lingered on the dog's coat, so it wouldn't be much longer before Thunder could come inside. Jim was glad because once he began traveling farther to check trap lines, he'd feel better knowing Thunder would be back in the cabin, guarding the women and keeping them company.

As Jim headed to the stream, he caught sight of some colorful wildflowers blooming nearby. *Them flowers are sure purty.* Jim reminded himself to pick a few for Mary before he went back to the cabin. He might pick a bunch for Amanda too because she deserved some kind of thanks for helping around the cabin.

Jim and Thunder were halfway to the stream, when he spotted Buck's horse grazing in the meadow across the way.

Thinking Buck must be somewhere nearby, Jim moved on. As he drew closer to the water, he heard a low moan. Jim halted and cocked his head, listening intently.

Another unmistakable moan came from several yards away. Thunder growled, then whined, hair down the center of his back bristling and teeth gleaming against the light of the early morning sun. Cautiously, Jim inched his way along the grassy banks, wishing he'd had the presence of mind to bring his rifle along. He almost never left the cabin without it. *What was I thinking?* he bemoaned.

Looking over the area, Jim was shocked to discover Buck lying in a crumpled heap near the stream, shirt soaked with blood and eyes shut.

Jim rushed over and knelt beside his friend. It was hard to tell how badly Buck had been hurt, but several bloody gashes tore across the back of his neck and into his hairline, indicating that Buck may have tangled with a bear or mountain lion.

Jim placed one hand over Buck's nose, to check for breath. Thankfully, his friend was still alive, although his breathing was shallow. Jim bent close to his friend's ear and spoke softly. "Buck, it's me, Jim. I need to get ya back to my cabin to clean your wounds and see how bad you're hurt."

A low moan escaped from Buck's swollen lips, but he made no intelligible sound.

Knowing he didn't have a moment to lose, Jim dropped his water buckets and hefted Buck over his shoulder. "God, if You're up there, help me now," he pleaded.

While Buck wasn't a big man, he was no lightweight either. Each step Jim took was done with great effort, and it took all his strength to keep his balance as he carried Buck carefully toward home. When he finally made it to the cabin, he wondered how he was going to get the door open without having to put Buck down. The door suddenly opened, and Amanda greeted them.

"Oh my!" she gasped. "Is that your friend Buck?"

Jim nodded and pushed past Amanda.

"What happened to him?" she asked as Jim laid Buck on the floor in front of the fireplace.

"He's been hurt. Found him down by the stream, and from the looks of things, I'm guessin' he's been there awhile."

"Was it an Indian attack? Has he been shot with an arrow?" Amanda questioned, her eyes widening like a frightened child's.

"Can't ya see the claw marks on his neck, arms, and chest?" Jim's temper flared. This prissy woman sure didn't know much. "I reckon Buck's had a run in with a bear. And I'll bet it was a big one, too."

Thunder, who'd slipped in the door with them, began licking Buck's face.

"Get away, dog!" Jim hollered.

Tail between his legs, Thunder moved aside obediently but remained nearby, whining as though in sympathy for the injured man.

Jim pulled out his knife and cut the tattered shirt away from Buck's battered body. Amanda let out a painful gasp. "Oh my. . .the gashes on his chest are so deep. It—it looks like the muscle is showing!"

"You're right, and his wounds are gonna need to be sewn together." Jim went to one of his parfletches hanging on a wall peg across the room, retrieved the necessary animal tendons, and threaded a large porcupine needle. Then he took out several pieces of cloth and, using what was left from the bucket of water still in the cabin, he washed Buck's wounds. Next, Jim began the grueling task of stitching him up, while Amanda looked on with obvious concern. Jim was surprised she hadn't fainted dead away at the sight of so much blood. Maybe Miss Pearson had more gumption than he'd given her credit for.

Except for an occasional moan, Buck lay silent and unmoving. It was an agonizing process, and with a steady hand, Jim finished stitching the last deep gash. The whole process left him exhausted and drenched in sweat. The fact that he'd had nothing to eat or drink yet this morning didn't help.

Jim covered Buck's injuries with a poultice of comfrey, then wrapped them with clean cloths. The wounds on Buck's neck and arms were not as deep as those on his chest, but Jim cleaned them thoroughly and applied healing herbs to them as well.

"What's that you're putting on his wounds?" Amanda questioned.

"It's an herb called comfrey," Jim replied. "It's used freely among the Indians and has been known to mend wounds of all sorts."

"How do you know so much about the use of herbs?" she asked.

Jim looked up at her and shook his head. "In case you've forgot, I'm married to an Indian woman. Mary's taught me a lot about healin' with herbs."

Amanda's face reddened. "Oh, I see."

Next, Jim mixed some alfalfa and dandelion with water and tried to get Buck to drink it. When he didn't respond, Jim pried his mouth open, hoping to get some of the liquid in, but it only dribbled down Buck's chin.

"I've gotta get him to drink this," Jim mumbled. "It'll help with his loss of blood."

"Let me see if I can help." Amanda knelt on the floor and lifted Buck's head so it rested on her knees. Then she pinched his nose. Almost immediately, Buck's mouth opened. "Go ahead and pour a little in," she said. "Just a small amount at a time though. We don't want him to choke on it."

"Well, I'll be. . . . Don't know why I didn't think of that." Jim did as she said, and as the liquid trickled into Buck's mouth, Amanda gently rubbed his throat, helping it to go down.

Through it all, Buck never opened his eyes, and Jim was relieved that his friend hadn't choked to death.

"He needs to rest now," Amanda said. She placed one hand against Buck's forehead. "His skin is moist and hot, so I am sure he has a fever."

When Buck began to shiver, Jim told Amanda to step out of the room.

"How come?" she asked.

"So I can get his wet clothes off. Go in the bedroom and get some blankets. Oh, and while you're there, check on Mary and Little Joe."

Amanda lowered Buck's head to the floor and hurried into the bedroom. When she returned, she came in backward, calling over her shoulder, "Here are the blankets. Where shall I put them?"

"Just drop 'em on the floor. I'll get 'em as soon as I get Buck's clothes the rest of the way off. How's my wife and baby doin'?" Jim questioned.

"They are both sleeping."

"Good." Jim was glad. Had Mary known about Buck's injuries, nothing would have stopped her from getting out of bed to help. Jim knew he could do no more for his friend at this time. His doctoring was finished, and now the waiting began.

Amanda started back to the bedroom, but halted when Jim called, "You'd better start prayin' to that God of yours, 'cause short of a miracle, Buck's likely to die."

CHAPTER 17

Two days later, between taking care of Buck and doing the cooking and cleaning, Amanda was exhausted, although she wouldn't admit it. Mary had said that she was capable of resuming her duties, but Amanda insisted her friend rest for the first few days following her baby's delivery. Little Joe had been fussy and demanding, so Amanda assured Mary that she could manage and would let her know if she needed anything or had questions about caring for Buck's wounds.

Yesterday, when Jim flopped down a turkey he'd shot, Amanda wasn't sure what to do with the bird. Jim had looked at her strangely when she admitted that to him, and she'd been relieved when he'd merely shrugged his shoulders and taken it back outside. Awhile later, he returned, with the turkey feathers removed. Amanda had thanked him for doing that. Later, she felt good when the nicely browned roasted turkey sat in the middle of their supper table. Everyone ate their fill of the succulent meat. Jim had even said how good it was, a nice surprise considering how irritable the man had been when she'd first come to his cabin. Since Buck wasn't up to eating anything yet, she'd made him some turkey broth.

Amanda yawned and reached around to rub the small of her back, in readiness to begin a new day. She didn't think she would ever get used to sleeping on the floor in the small loft overhead. Even with the thick buffalo hide beneath her, the floor was unyielding. The loft was hot and stuffy, making it hard to sleep.

Amanda opened the cabin door and stepped outside for a breath of fresh air before starting breakfast. She observed the sights and sounds of nature, and a flicker of homesickness washed over her. The mountains were so beautiful, but they reminded her just how far from home she truly was. Even with those reminders, the grandeur of the Rockies could not go unnoticed, for they were surely glorious. The majestic mountains, with their high jagged peaks and snow-covered tops, were the backdrop to pines and fir trees mixed with oaks, providing shades of green among all the other colors. A meadow to one side bloomed in a rainbow of wildflowers that any artist would enjoy painting.

This area was far different from the rolling mountains she'd been accustomed to back East. Amanda's father had said many times how he loved those rolling hills, and Amanda had come to appreciate them too. Oh, how she missed Papa and the love they had shared. She missed the familiarity of their home in Dansville too. But that was all behind her now, and she had to go on from here, experiencing the beauty of everything God had created and making the best of each new day, no matter what the challenges were.

As Amanda reentered the cabin, she glanced at Buck sleeping on the floor in front of the fireplace. When she'd gotten up this morning, she had checked on him and discovered that he'd thrown the covers aside and was trembling. She'd immediately begun to bathe his face with cool water and given him small sips of the willow bark tea Mary had prepared. Amanda was grateful he'd cooperated, even though he hadn't appeared to be aware of her presence. She was even more thankful when Buck finally drifted into a deep sleep. His injuries looked somewhat better than when Jim had first brought him back to the cabin, but as Jim had said last night, "He ain't outta the woods yet." Amanda had been praying for Buck, asking God to bring down the man's fever, keep his wounds from becoming infected, and give her the strength to keep up with things. It hadn't been so long ago that she'd been the one with the fever, so her strength was still lacking. She was trusting God to give her the endurance to do whatever was needed each day. So far her prayers had been answered, as she felt stronger each day.

Amanda had just begun cooking a pan of cornmeal mush, when Buck started moaning. Since Mary and the baby weren't up yet and

Jim was outside doing chores, Amanda removed the pan from the stove and went to see about Buck.

Buck opened his eyes and tried to speak. "The bear. . .my gun. . ." A spasm of pain ripped through his body like a jolt of lightning, and when he coughed, his sides ached like he'd been kicked by a mule. Buck's face felt like it was on fire, and his body dripped with sweat. "Wh–where am I?" he rasped as a woman's face blurred before his eyes.

"Thou art in Jim Breck's cabin. Please, drink this," she said, lifting his head and putting a tin cup up to his dry lips.

"What is it?"

"It's willow bark tea. Mary said it will bring down thy fever and help with the pain."

Buck winced as he gulped down the bitter liquid. "Thanks," he whispered gratefully. His eyes felt like red-hot pokers, and when he reached up to rub them, the woman's face became clearer. Oh yes. Now he remembered. . . . It was that Quaker lady he'd saved a few weeks ago—Amanda Pearson. Buck thought she looked even more beautiful than he'd remembered. Amanda was like a vision he'd seen long ago. Or maybe it was just his imagination. Buck's head felt fuzzy, making it hard to reason things out.

"Do you remember what happened to you?" she asked.

Buck's head pounded as he squeezed his eyes shut and thought. He'd been out hunting, and then. . . He moaned. "A grizzly. She came at me fast. I tried to fight, but her claws kept connecting to my body." Buck paused and moistened his lips. "I. . .I managed to grab my gun, and then I shot that old bear right in the head."

"You're right. It was a bear," Jim said as he strode into the room. "Didn't see any sign of her when I found you by the stream, but after I got ya to the cabin and tended your wounds, I grabbed my rifle and walked out in the woods." He stared down at Buck with a grim expression. "Found the dead grizzly bear that got ya some distance upstream. Seen two cubs not far from her too. You're lucky to be alive, ya know that, friend? Nothin' worse than a mama bear protecting her young."

Buck nodded weakly and groaned when he tried to sit up.

"Whoa now!" Jim put his arm on Buck's shoulder and held him down. "It's too soon for ya to be tryin' to get up."

"Jim is right," Amanda put in. Her piercing blue eyes looking ever so serious seemed to bore right into Buck's soul. Was she really concerned about him or just the compassionate type?

"Move around too quickly and thou art likely to tear the stitches Jim worked so hard to put in," she said. "Thou hast lost a lot of blood and art still running a fever, so thou really dost need to rest."

Buck knew Jim and Amanda were right, but he had traps to check and traps to set. There was no time to be lying around on his backside. Not if he planned to haul some of his furs and hides to the next Rendezvous.

"I know what you're thinkin'," Jim said. "You're worried about your traps."

Buck gave another short nod, biting his lips against the pain that coursed through his body when he tried to move.

"Well don't trouble yourself 'bout that, 'cause I'll take care of things while you're letting your body mend." Jim motioned to Amanda. "This here little lady's been takin' good care of you, so just do what she says and try to relax."

Buck wasn't sure he liked the idea of anyone taking care of him, because he'd been taking care of himself for a long time. But right now, he guessed he didn't have much choice. He just hoped it wouldn't be too long before he was back on his feet. The idea of the Quaker woman taking care of his needs made him nervous. What if she tried to push her religious ideas on him? Well, if she did, he'd have to set her straight, because he had absolutely no interest in God!

CHAPTER 18

It had been four days since Mary had given birth to Little Joe, and she decided to go outside and bring in some more wood for the cooking stove. "I go out to get wood," she told Amanda, who sat at the table reading her Bible. "You watch Little Joe?"

Amanda smiled. "Of course I will, but wouldn't thee rather that I get the wood so thee can stay inside and care for thy son?"

Mary shook her head. "Me need exercise and fresh air. Get tired of being in cabin so much."

"Are thee certain thou art feeling up to it? Thee just had a baby. . . ."

"Indian women have babies all the time. No lie around unless very sick."

"I understand, but please be careful and don't overdo it trying to carry too much wood," Amanda cautioned. "If thou dost too much, thou mayest start bleeding heavily."

"I be fine," Mary asserted. She motioned toward the bedroom. "Little Joe asleep on bed. You want hold him while I gone?"

Amanda nodded eagerly. "That would be nice. I have been so busy taking care of Buck that I haven't had much time to hold the baby."

"You hold whenever you want," Mary said. "I care for Buck if he need me."

Amanda smiled. "As long as thou art able, I guess it would be alright if we take turns."

Mary tipped her head. "Take turns? What is that?"

"It means that I will take care of Buck whilst thou art busy with the baby, and then thou canst care for Buck while I watch the baby."

Mary gave a nod. "Is what I said."

"Yes, I suppose it is. I was just expressing it in a different way."

Mary picked up one of the baskets she had woven sometime ago and started for the door. "You come get me if Little Joe need to be fed."

"Yes, I certainly will."

When Mary stepped into the yard, she drew in several deep breaths. Having been cooped up in the cabin the last several days, she hadn't realized how much she'd missed being outdoors. The air felt clean and fresh as it always did after a good rain. She smiled, glancing at the trees and bushes bursting with green leaves. She felt one with nature, just like when she had been living among her people. Springtime brought new birth, new beginnings. Now it was the same for her and Jim in their small but sturdy cabin. She had given Jim a son, and because of it, she saw in her husband a new appreciation and even respect.

Mary studied her surroundings, taking in all the sights, smells, and sounds. The morning was certainly coming alive after nature's bath had rinsed everything off. She noticed droplets of water glistening in the morning light while slowly dripping from pinecones not yet opened by daytime warmth. Several chickadees splashed in a puddle, while nuthatches scurried up and down tree trunks looking for bugs. A thin layer of fog hung just above the surface of the nearby stream, and the ground smelled earthy, still damp from the rain. Mary knew it would vanish as the humidity disappeared, and a blue-skied day awaited them.

She stood several more minutes, breathing deeply and taking it all in, then finally moved toward the woodpile. A chipmunk dashed away as she approached. She set the basket on the ground and had just picked up the first piece of wood, when Jim stepped up to her. "Whatcha doin' out here?" he asked with a look of concern. "Shouldn't ya be inside resting?"

"I fine," she said. "Came to get wood for stove."

"Mary, that can wait. There's something I need to say," Jim said, moving closer.

She looked up, waiting for him to continue.

"This ain't easy for me, but it needs to be said. I owe you an apology for all the hurtful things I've said and done since ya came to live here with me." He cleared his throat loudly, while raking his fingers through the ends of his thick beard. "I'm especially sorry for the times I mistreated ya when I had too much to drink."

Is this truly happening? Mary wondered. Good things didn't come to her. She was afraid to believe something decent might happen. Was Jim having a change of heart?

Mary dropped her gaze, squeezing her eyes tightly shut as her mind pulled her back to the first time she'd been the victim of her husband's wrath.

Yawning, Jim pushed his chair away from the table, causing it to scrape noisily across the floor. "Think I'll take the chill from my bones," he said to no one in particular. His feet were clad in soft moccasins, and he plodded across the room to the cabinet full of his personal supplies.

Out came a full bottle of corn whiskey, and Mary watched with concern as he settled himself into one of the split-log chairs near the big stone fireplace. Jim's dog gave a noisy grunt and flopped onto the floor next to his master.

Mary drew in a deep breath. She wished Jim would take the bottle into the other room and be out of sight for the night. At one of the Rendezvous her tribe had attended, she had seen what the white man's firewater could do to the Indian. No doubt it would have the same miserable effect on any man, whether his skin was red or white.

Anxious to get to her loft, Mary hurried to finish her chores in the kitchen.

"Put another log on the fire!" Jim called, as she began her ascent up the ladder a short time later.

Mary hesitated. Hoping he would think she hadn't understood, she quickly scampered the rest of the way up.

Peeking down from above, she watched as Jim took a long drink from his bottle and wiped his mouth on his shirtsleeve. With a fierceness in his tone that Mary hadn't heard before, he screamed, "Get down here, now! If I have to come up there after ya. . ."

Trembling, Mary was already on her way back down the ladder and almost tripped when her foot got hung up on the bottom rung. She righted herself in time and went immediately to the wood box and placed two good-sized logs into the fireplace.

When she started back across the room, Jim reached out his hand and caught her by the wrist. "Just where do ya think you're goin'?"

"Me wish to sleep," she said, head down and eyes focused on the floor.

"You'll go when I say and not before!" he bellowed.

The pungent odor of whiskey wafted up to Mary's nostrils, and she fought the impulse to run away. It was all she could do to keep from gagging, as she swallowed the bitter taste of bile slowly creeping up her throat.

Jim shifted in his chair but didn't release his hold on her arm, causing her to wince in pain. She hated this man, just as she had hated Smoking Buffalo, the Blackfoot Indian who'd taken her captive and traded her to Jim.

He took another hefty drink, then finally released her arm. Believing she was free to go, Mary started toward the ladder.

Jim leaped to his feet, knocking over the wooden chair with a thud. "I didn't say ya could go!" With a few quick steps, he crossed the room and yanked the razor strap down from the wall peg.

Mary ducked, but it was too late. He struck her across the shoulders with a loud whack. She lifted her arms in order to protect herself, but the strap came down hard against her outstretched hand. She cringed as a large, red welt quickly appeared. I will not cry out, *she told herself.* I must not let him think I am weak.

A vein on Jim's neck bulged, and his breathing became heavy and labored as he cursed and threw her to the floor. There was no time to block the blows. His foot connected heavily with Mary's fragile ribs, and he pelted her several more times with the strap.

She groaned heavily but did not cry out. Her days of abuse among the Blackfoot had toughened her mind as well as her body.

The hair on Thunder's body stood straight up, and he growled. Jim cursed again and kicked the dog in the rump. "Shut up, cur! This ain't none of your business!"

The dog yipped and slowly retreated to the fireplace. Jim reached down and grabbed one of Mary's braids, yanking her roughly to her feet. He buried his face in her neck, and pulled roughly at her doe-skin dress with his large callused hands.

"I kill you!" she screamed. Her fists pounded against his muscular chest. She would not let him take her by force. Not without a fight.

"Oh, ya will, huh? We'll just see about that!" he roared.

Mary swallowed hard as a wave of nausea curdled her stomach. The mountain man was much stronger than she, and he'd been drinking the crazy firewater. If he really wanted to take her by force, there was little she could do about it.

She breathed a sigh of relief when he released her, but when she realized he'd lost his balance and was about to fall on top of her, she rolled quickly to one side.

Jim fell in a heap on the floor, passed out in a drunken stupor.

Mary stood quickly, staring down at him with disgust. He could lie there the whole night for all she cared. Looking over at Thunder, the dog returned her gaze and whimpered. It made her wonder how many times he'd been abused by his master.

She scampered quickly up the steps that led to her place of solitude. From childhood, she'd been taught to be strong in the face of adversity. Why did she feel so weak now? She had tried to be brave and hadn't let Jim see her fear, but the beating had been severe, making her wish she had never been born.

As Mary reached the last rung on the ladder leading to her loft, she paused and drew in a deep breath. Nothing mattered anymore. Life was empty and meaningless. She no longer had her Nez Percé pride.

Mary's thoughts were halted when Jim drew his finger gently across her cheek. "Can ya forgive me for bein' so hard on you, Mary?"

She swallowed hard, letting her gaze meet his. This was a side of Jim she hadn't seen before. In the year they'd been married he'd never apologized for anything. "I. . .I forgive," she murmured.

He pulled her into his arms and gently patted her back. "I threw out all my liquor last night when you were asleep, so there won't be none around to tempt me again."

Mary breathed a sigh of relief. As long as Jim kept true to his word, there would be no more beatings.

"From now on, I'm gonna try and be a better husband to ya," Jim added, continuing to pat her back.

"I be good wife to you as well," she said, leaning her head against his chest.

"You already are, Mary. You've been a good wife since the day you became Mrs. Jim Breck. Now, let me help ya gather that wood."

As Amanda sat in the wooden rocker near the fireplace, holding Little Joe, she found herself wishing she had a child of her own. If she'd married Nathan, as planned, she could be expecting by now.

She stroked the baby's soft cheek. His hair was dark, but it was too soon to tell if he would take after his father or mother.

Buck stirred from his mat nearby, and Amanda stopped rocking, fearful of waking him. She sat still several seconds, until she was sure he was still asleep, then resumed rocking the baby.

A few minutes later, Buck sat up and yawned.

"I'm sorry if I woke thee," Amanda said. "Was it the creaking of the rocking chair?"

He shrugged his broad shoulders. "I'm not sure what woke me, but it's okay. I've slept long enough."

"How art thou feeling?"

"I'm stiff, sore, and hungry," Buck said, stretching his arms overhead. He winced. "Ow! Guess I wasn't ready for that."

"Thou hast every reason to be sore."

"Yeah. I'm lucky to be alive."

"Would you like me to fix thee something to eat?" she asked.

"Naw, I can wait. Don't wanna interrupt what you're doin' there." He stared at her curiously, then eyed Little Joe. "Did Mary have her baby?"

Amanda nodded. "She gave birth to her son shortly before Jim found thee by the stream."

"Guess I've been too out of it to know what was goin' on. How long have I been here?" he questioned.

"Three days."

Buck whistled. "I don't remember much about anything."

"Thou hadst a fever, but it broke last night. It's the first time thou slept without throwing the blankets off." She sighed. "I was able to sleep better too."

"What do ya mean? Have you been keepin' an eye on me at night?"

"Jim and I have taken turns," Amanda answered. "With thy fever raging, we didn't think it would be good for thee to be alone."

"I appreciate that." Buck pulled his legs up to his chest and smiled. "You look kinda natural, holding that baby."

Amanda's cheeks warmed.

"So how come you're not married?"

She looked down at the infant in her arms and said quietly, "I had planned to marry a man once, but things did not work out."

"Oh, I see."

Amanda was glad Buck hadn't asked why. She didn't want to talk about it. Especially with someone she barely knew. "I'll put the baby down and fix thee some breakfast."

"Thanks. I am kinda hungry."

"If thine appetite is returning, that is a good sign."

"Yeah, I suppose."

Amanda went to the bedroom and placed Little Joe in the wooden cradle Jim had made. When she returned to the other room, she found Buck sitting at the table.

"You're not still thinkin' about goin' to the Spalding Mission, are ya?" he asked.

She nodded. "I will be on my way as soon as I find a guide."

He shook his head vigorously. "Now's not a good time to be travelin'."

"Why not?"

"We've had a lot of rain this spring, and the rivers are still swollen. If you're set on goin', you'll need to wait till the middle of summer."

"If I agree to wait until then, wilt thou take me?" she dared to ask.

Buck sat staring at the table. Slowly he raised his head and said, "I'll give it some thought."

Amanda smiled. "I appreciate that." She didn't know if Buck might reconsider because he really wanted to take her or if it was because he felt grateful for the care she'd given him. Either way, she hoped and prayed that he would eventually agree, because deep in her heart she felt that he was the man God had chosen to be her guide.

CHAPTER 19

Three days later, Buck was up and about, although moving slowly due to the pain he still felt from his wounds. The trauma left him feeling like he'd been stampeded by wild horses. Jim had cautioned Buck not to do too much, saying he was still in danger of ripping open the stitches on some of his larger wounds. But that was easier said than done. Sore as he was, Buck was getting antsy, and he didn't like feeling useless.

After breakfast, Jim had gone out to feed the livestock and chop some wood. Buck had wanted to help out, but Jim had said no, insisting that Buck take it easy because he looked like he hadn't slept well.

'Course I didn't sleep well, Buck thought as he sat in a chair on the porch, watching Jim do all the work. Buck wasn't cut out to sit around. He'd kept busy working since he was a boy. But then, living with Silas Lothard, he'd no choice. It was either work or be beat.

Thunder lay at Buck's feet, with his head between his paws, watching Jim as he moved around the yard. Buck grimaced and massaged his pulsating forehead. Just thinking about the injustices he'd suffered at the hand of that evil so-called stepfather made his blood boil. He hated Silas and was glad he was dead. A man like that didn't deserve to live. Buck needed to do something, anything, to keep busy and to prevent himself from remembering those days of living under Silas's rule.

Still in his bare feet, Buck rubbed his soles over the dog's back. "Life isn't fair, is it, ol' boy?"

Looking up at Buck as though he understood, Thunder wagged his tail, thumping the porch floor as he whimpered.

Whether Buck liked it or not, that unsettling time in his life had embedded something in him at a young age. It taught him to keep busy and never to be idle. Buck didn't have a lazy bone in his body, so now, because of his injuries, he felt lethargic and worthless. It seemed like any minute someone should be yelling at him for sitting around too much. But he knew he was among friends, and they were taking good care of him as he healed.

Buck yawned and breathed in deeply, letting the mountain air fill his lungs, listening to the shrill cry of his winged brother high overhead as if announcing to the world Buck's reappearance.

"Is the baby asleep?" Amanda asked when Mary came out of the bedroom where she'd fed Little Joe.

Mary nodded. "He good baby. Not cry much."

Amanda smiled. "You're right about that." She motioned to the kitchen table. "Should we sit and relax awhile? I'll fix a pot of coffee if you like."

Mary nodded and took a seat.

As the women drank their coffee, Amanda asked Mary to share some more things about her past.

"What you want to know?" Mary asked.

"I've been wondering how you were captured by the Blackfoot and how you survived the ordeal."

"My people make camp one evening on the plains," Mary began. "That night I could not sleep."

"Why not?" Amanda asked curiously.

Mary touched her chest. "Have great fear in my heart."

Amanda leaned forward, anxious to hear more about this. "How come?"

"Had a vision."

"What kind of vision?"

"See a yellow bird on a log. Then big buffalo come and step on bird." Mary touched her chest again. "Fear in my heart grew stronger, so I get up and walk to lake."

Amanda sat in rapt attention as Mary told how she'd left her parents' teepee and gone to the lake to bathe.

"When I dry and get dressed, I hear rumbling noise," Mary said. "Look up and see horse with Blackfoot rider coming toward me." She paused and took a drink of coffee. "I try to run but was not fast enough. He leap off horse and grab my arm."

Amanda's mouth went dry, thinking how frightened Mary must have felt. "What happened next?" she questioned, leaning slightly forward.

"I try to scream. He strike my face with rawhide quirt. Hurt much. Leave big welt." Mary touched her cheek and winced, as though reliving the horrible stinging pain.

Amanda gulped. "Then what?"

"He tie my hands and put piece of rawhide around my head so mouth is covered. Then he put me on horse, and we ride like the wind." Mary shook her head slowly. "I very foolish woman. Should not have gone to lake alone. It too late for regrets. Never see family or Gray Eagle again."

"Gray Eagle was the man you were supposed to marry, right?"

Mary nodded. "I never stop loving him though."

Amanda placed her hand on Mary's arm and gave it a gentle squeeze. While her situation was much different from Mary's, she could relate to it in a way, because she still felt something for Nathan. Whether it was love or simply a deep regret for what she'd lost didn't matter. Amanda's heart had been broken by Nathan's betrayal, and she didn't think she could ever open it to another man.

"Did the Blackfoot warrior take you to his camp?" Amanda asked.

Mary's head moved slowly up and down. "I ask myself every day if anyone will come for me. Wonder if I would see my people again."

"Have you asked Jim to try and find your people?"

"I ask once, but he say my life here now, with him." Mary's dark eyes revealed the depth of her pain.

Amanda didn't know what she would have done if she'd been in Mary's place. Would she have obediently stayed or tried to run away?

"At Blackfoot camp, I put in teepee with big buffalo painted on outside. Inside, sat two women. One very fat and mean. The other thin and ugly as dirt."

Amanda suppressed a smile. "Who were the women?" she asked.

"Not know at first. Later, found out they Smoking Buffalo's women."

"Was Smoking Buffalo the Indian who captured you?"

"Yes. His wives very mean. Make me their slave. Beat me all the time and make me do all the work." Mary scrunched up her face. "I hate them! Hate man who took me from my family and Gray Eagle!"

Amanda was shocked that anyone could treat another human being so cruelly. Seeing the look of bitterness on Mary's face, Amanda said, "Have you forgiven the Blackfoot who treated you so badly?"

Mary shook her head. "Smoking Buffalo never ask my forgiveness. Jim treated me bad when I came here too, but he say he sorry."

"It doesn't matter whether a person apologizes for the things they've done to us," Amanda said. "We still need to forgive them." She winced, thinking of the hurt she'd felt when Nathan broke their engagement. Though she might never fully recover from his betrayal, she'd asked the Lord to help her forgive Nathan, and Penelope too. It was the only way she could experience peace.

Mary sat several seconds, staring at the table. When she lifted her head, tears shone in her dark eyes. "There is more."

"What else would you like to tell me?" Amanda asked.

"Gray Eagle, he come to rescue me." Mary paused and swiped at the tears rolling down her cheeks. "Smoking Buffalo caught Gray Eagle and shoot him dead with arrow." She released a shuddering sigh. "Then Blackfoot tribe move on to different camp. Soon after, Smoking Buffalo give me to Jim."

"Do you have any idea why he did that?"

"He say his wives jealous. Not want me around." Mary slapped her hand on the table. "They evil people! I hate them all!"

"But you have a new life now, Mary, here with Jim and your son. You need to let go of the past, as well as the hate."

"That ain't always so easy," Buck said, stepping into the room with Thunder at his side.

Amanda looked up, startled. She hadn't realized he or the dog had come back inside.

He moved over to the table and took a seat across from Mary, while Thunder plopped down and leaned against the rung of her chair. Buck grunted. "Sometimes hate's what keeps a person going."

Shocked by his declaration, Amanda shook her head. "It's never right to harbor hateful thoughts against another person, no matter what has been done. Hate is like a wound that festers and never heals. Forgiveness is what brings healing."

Buck shrugged his shoulders. "There's no reason to forgive."

"Oh, but there is," Amanda was quick to say. She left her seat and moved across the room to get her Bible. When she returned, she placed it on the table and sat down. Opening the Bible, she read from Matthew 6:14 and 15: "Jesus said, 'If ye forgive men their trespasses, your heavenly Father will also forgive you. But if ye forgive not men their trespasses, neither will your Father forgive your trespasses.' "

"Tres-passes?" Mary tipped her head. "What that mean?"

"It means we must forgive those who have done us wrong," Amanda explained. "Smoking Buffalo trespassed when he treated thee badly."

Mary nodded slowly.

"Jesus is God's Son, Mary. When evil men crucified Him on the cross, He cried out to God, 'Forgive them, for they know not what they do.' If Jesus could forgive such a horrible crime against Him, then we should forgive those who have trespassed against us."

Buck glared at Amanda, but Mary sat staring at her hands.

"We are all sinners. None of us but God is perfect, for God cannot sin," Amanda went on to say.

Mary listened intently as Amanda read more from the Bible and explained the plan of salvation. "God's Word says in Romans 10:9: 'If thou shalt confess with thy mouth the Lord Jesus, and shalt believe in thine heart that God hath raised him from the dead, thou shalt be saved.' Wouldn't you like to do that, Mary? Wouldn't you like to ask

God to forgive your sins and live in your heart?"

"I. . .I not sure," Mary whispered.

"I've heard enough of this foolish talk!" Buck pushed back his chair, knocking it to the floor, and stormed out of the cabin, slamming the door.

Fighting for control, Buck hurried across the yard and stopped in front of the woodpile Jim had been cutting. Catching his breath and holding his hand against his chest, he looked Jim square in the eyes. "If ya don't do somethin' quick, that Quaker woman's gonna convert your wife to Christianity."

Jim stopped chopping wood long enough to wipe the sweat from his brow. "What are ya talkin' about, Buck?"

"She's in there right now, fillin' Mary's head with all kinds of stuff from the Bible—sayin' Mary needs to forgive and confess her sins to God." Buck spat on the ground. "When she got to that part I'd had enough, so I came out here to let ya know what was goin' on inside."

"Well, if Mary wants to do that, it's up to her," Jim said with a shrug.

Buck frowned. "You're kidding, right?"

"Nope."

"You've sure changed your tune in a hurry. It wasn't long ago that you didn't want that Bible thumper in your home."

"A man's got a right to change his mind." Jim lifted the ax and gave it a swing, splitting another log in two.

Buck stood with his arms folded, gritting his teeth. He couldn't believe that his friend was turning so soft. *Next thing I know, that Quaker woman will have Jim converted to her religion too,* he fumed. *Well, she'll never convince me that I should turn to God or admit that I'm a sinner. My mother always tried to do what was good and right, and look where that got her!* And as far as forgiving went. . . Buck knew that no matter how long he lived, he'd never forgive Silas Lothard for the things he had done.

CHAPTER 20

"I'm goin' back to my own place," Buck told Jim the following morning before the women got up.

Jim's bushy eyebrows raised into his hairline. "Ya can't. Ya ain't healed well enough yet."

Buck tapped his foot impatiently. "I need to see about my traps."

"I said before that I'd take care of your traps when I'm out checkin' mine." Jim lowered his voice. "I need ya here, Buck, to keep an eye on the women while I'm gone."

"Humph!" Buck scoffed. "Who'd be here watching 'em if I hadn't been hurt?"

Jim scratched the side of his head. "Well, I'd probably have asked ya to check my traps so I could stay with the women."

Buck motioned to the dog sleeping by the fireplace. "Thunder's here, and I'm sure the women will be fine while you're gone. I've wasted too much of your time with all this tending you've been givin' me."

"Thunder is a good protector, but I'd feel better if a man was here. You'd be helpin' me a good deal if ya stayed on, and I wouldn't have to worry about the women."

"You weren't worried about things before. What's got ya feelin' so antsy?"

Jim took a swig of coffee and wiped his mouth with the back of his hand. "Things are different now. I've got a wife and son to think about." Jim placed his hand on Buck's shoulder. "Will ya stick around the cabin for a while yet? It'd make me feel a lot better."

Buck hesitated, then finally gave a nod. He owed Jim a lot for the things he'd been taught, so he figured hanging around the cabin a few more days was the least he could do for his friend.

As Mary lay on the bed, nursing Little Joe, her thoughts wandered to the life she used to know when she lived among her people. Food gathering began in the spring, and she figured her tribe had already left their home along the Clearwater River to travel up to the high country, where roots and bulbs grew. Bitterroot and wild carrots were also collected, along with berries and nuts.

By July, the tribe would move farther on to the prairies to gather the sweet camas bulb. While the women did that, the men hunted, held horse races, and partook in various ceremonies.

By November, most of the tribes returned to their winter villages to wait until the next year, when they would do it all over again. Those were good days, and Mary missed them.

Thoughts of home and family always made her feel sad, and she usually shed a few tears. She missed her parents, and the thought that her son would never know his grandparents made her feel worse. Little Joe would not learn the Indian ways, at least not as Mary had known them when she was called Yellow Bird. Her son wouldn't follow behind his father, as Yellow Bird had done when she was a girl, learning about the different herbs and their purposes for healing. Instead, Little Joe would learn to set traps and prepare the catch for trading.

A vision of her father came to mind. Tall and strong, Laughing Wolf was highly respected among their people as an excellent horseman. Mary used to enjoy watching him break horses. Her heart swelled with a sense of bittersweet joy as she remembered the day he'd given her a pony when she was a young girl, full of joy and hope for the future. She reflected on the times they rode together or sat side by side on their mounts, looking out over the land. Laughing Wolf would explain to his daughter how life had been when he was a boy. She took in every word he'd said for, like many of the people in her tribe, she admired him greatly.

Then there was her mother, Small Rabbit. Mary could almost see her right now, bent over a weaving loom, her shiny black hair worn in long braids, her liquid dark eyes, warm and caring. Mother was a skillful weaver and had created many beautiful things—storage baskets, cooking vessels, and geometric-designed hats, often worn by some of the Nez Percé women. Yellow Bird's mother had patiently taught her how to weave, sew, cook, and do various other chores expected of the women in their tribe. Mary's heart ached to see her parents and share the news that they had a grandson.

Her thoughts drifted to her older brother, Little Bear. She wondered if he had ever married Smiling Squirrel, the Indian maiden he'd loved since childhood. Mary had been away from her family for more than two years. So much could have happened in that length of time. She wondered how many weddings, births, and burials she had missed.

This line of thinking conjured up thoughts of Gray Eagle, but she quickly pushed them aside. It hurt too much to think of things that would never be. She was no longer Yellow Bird, daughter of Laughing Wolf and Small Rabbit. Though not of her own choosing, she was now Mary Breck, wife of a mountain man, but she had finally come to accept that fact.

She glanced at the cradleboard leaning against the wall. She'd made it before Little Joe was born so she could strap him to her back whenever she went outside. She'd lined the board with rabbit fur and decorated the outside wooden pieces with colored beads she'd bought during their last visit to Fort McKenzie.

The sound of heavy footsteps coming into the room drew Mary's thoughts aside.

"Are ya done feeding the baby?" Jim asked, moving over to the bed. "Amanda has breakfast ready."

She gave a nod. "Our son sleeping now." Mary climbed off the bed and placed the baby in his wooden cradle, next to the bed.

"Ya did a good job makin' that," Jim said, pointing to the cradleboard. "But I'm wondering how come ya picked only yellow and blue beads. What's wrong with red or green?"

"Red and green good colors," Mary responded. "But blue and

yellow most important to me."

Jim scratched his head and snickered. "Don't see what's so important about them colored beads."

"Blue represent water, gift of life. Child is gift to us." Mary hesitated a moment, and when he made no response, she continued. "Yellow stand for sun. Sun rules over earth with greatness. It friend to water. Our child will be great like sun."

Jim eyed her curiously but remained silent.

"Must have water and sun to live," Mary explained. "Sun round like circle of life. We born. We die. We have children. They have children. Circle unbroken."

Jim pulled a hunk of dried rabbit from his pocket. "Injuns have some mighty strange ideas about things," he mumbled. "Everything's gotta have some kind of meanin', don't it?"

She nodded. "Everything has meaning. Birth of child bring meaning for us."

He grinned. "You're right about that. Never dreamed I'd feel such joy as when I first laid eyes on our son."

"Me wonder something," Mary said.

"What's that?"

"Do you believe in Great Spirit? Do you have guardian spirit to guide and protect?"

Jim shook his head. "Naw, that stuff's just for Injuns."

"I wonder if Great Spirit and God may be same. Amanda tell me about Jesus, God's Son. You know of this man?" she asked.

A muscle on the side of Jim's neck quivered. "I know all I wanna know, and that's enough!" His tone softened. "But if you wanna listen to all that stuff Amanda tells ya, that's up to you. I won't stop ya from hearin' her Bible stories."

Mary smiled. "It good that I listen. Maybe someday you listen too." She moved toward the bedroom door. "We eat breakfast now."

When they'd finished eating their meal, Jim announced that they were getting low on fresh meat so he was going hunting. Amanda looked at Mary to get her reaction, but she merely shrugged her shoulders.

"I'd like to go with ya," Buck announced.

Jim shook his head. "We talked about this earlier, remember? I need ya to stay here."

"If Buck feels up to hunting, maybe thou shouldst let him go," Amanda spoke up. "It will give Mary and me a chance to clean the cabin." Truth was, in addition to doing some cleaning today, Amanda wanted to read more scriptures to Mary. The last time she'd read to Mary from the Bible she'd seemed quite interested, and Amanda figured it was just a matter of time before she would have her first convert to Christianity. She was hoping to get through to Jim and Buck as well, but so far they'd both seemed closed off.

Jim finished drinking the last of his coffee. He turned to Amanda and said, "You're welcome to stay in this cabin for as long as ya want, but there's one thing we'd better get straight."

"What's that?" Amanda asked hesitantly. She had a feeling she knew what was coming.

"This is my place, which I built with my own hands, and I'll not have ya comin' in here tellin' me, Mary, or Buck what to do. Do I make myself clear?"

Amanda's face heated. "Yes, sir. I am sorry if I overstepped my bounds. I just wanted thee and Buck to know that Mary and I will be fine here by ourselves today. That is, if thou art agreeable," she quickly added.

Jim sat staring into his empty cup, then pushed back his chair and stood. "Buck stays. That's all there is to it! Oh, and we'd both appreciate if you'd quit sayin' *thee* and *thou* all the time."

Amanda flinched. If she said any more, Jim might ask her to leave. Without a guide, she had no place else to go. From now on, she would be more careful what she said and how she said it.

Jim rode out of a nearly barren stand of trees and down into the fertile valley below. He knew the wild game often came here in search of food. If he could bag a deer or an elk by noon, he would have it gutted and cleaned and be back at the cabin by suppertime. That would provide ample meat for a while.

Jim never would have thought it was possible, but he was much more content now that Mary had given him a child. He was glad for this newfound peace because the turbulence that had invaded his every thought, every action, since the loss of his first wife had exhausted him. He was also glad Mary had forgiven him when he'd recently apologized. Deep down he'd never wanted to treat Mary badly, but he hadn't been able to control his actions. His anger had been stronger than his restraint. If he cared for Mary, maybe even loved her, it would mean letting go of Lois, something he hadn't been ready to do. But since the birth of his son, Jim realized it was time to let go. Time to release the hurt and anger that had been eating away at his very soul. This baby boy had put a whole new perspective on life.

A quick movement of reddish brown caught his eye, and he saw two deer standing near the bordering trees. He brought his horse to a halt, unsheathed the gun, loaded, and fired. He dropped the five-point buck in its tracks, then watched as the doe, flagging her tail, ran quickly for cover.

The deer was soon dressed out and placed over the packs on the horse's back. Then Jim turned back in the direction of the cabin. It had been an easy hunt, and he'd be home earlier than planned.

A bloodcurdling war-whoop split through the air. Jim turned in his saddle. A painted Indian warrior was riding hard and fast across the open field, heading directly toward him.

Jim's throat went dry. If this Indian was part of a war party, more red men would follow. Would he be able to outrun them? If he were outnumbered, to stay and fight would surely mean death— or worse yet, capture. Stories among the mountain men often dealt with the extremes to which some Indian tribes would go in dealing out torture to their captives. Jim shuddered at the thought of what his fate might ultimately be.

He should probably say some kind of a prayer to prepare himself for the hereafter, but nothing came to mind, so he kicked Wind

Dancer hard in the sides and slapped the reins forcefully, urging the spotted stallion into a full run.

The Indian's cries became louder as he closed in on Jim. He turned, just in time to see the red man draw his bow. All Jim could think was that he might never see his wife and son again. Just when life had become more meaningful, was it about to be taken from him? Could God be so cruel to him once again?

CHAPTER 21

The arrow swished past Jim's head, coming so close it knocked his fur hat to the ground. White-hot anger bubbled in his chest, knowing how fast his life could have ended. He wasn't ready to die. He had too much to live for. He had a wife and a child. Mary needed a provider, and Little Joe needed his father. Jim had no choice. There wasn't time to run. He would have to fight to save himself. Fight for all he was worth.

Dust swirled from the ground as Jim halted his horse and quickly dismounted. He reached for his rifle still strapped to the side of his saddle. When he looked to the right, he saw the Indian dismount. The red man dropped his bow and pulled out a knife. In turn, Jim dropped his gun and grabbed his own knife. In an instant, Jim could have shot the Indian dead, but a fair fight was a fair fight. He stood his ground, crouched and ready to meet the charge of his opponent.

The Blackfoot warrior let out a war cry as he ran forward with the agility of a bobcat. Jim met the charge with the ferocity of a grizzly bear, and he grasped the other man's arm with unknown strength, forcing the Indian to drop his gleaming knife to the ground.

Jim felt some measure of surprise, and the Indian seemed to, as well, for Jim now had the upper hand. He knew he had only to thrust the point of his knife deep into the opponent's chest, and the encounter would be finished.

Jim lifted the knife in readiness, staring deep into the other man's dark eyes. What was it he saw there? Fear? Doubt? Questions? He wasn't sure, but for some unknown reason, Jim snorted and threw the knife aside. Then, using hand gestures, he indicated that the Blackfoot Indian was free to go. He hoped the red man understood, because if he didn't, Jim might be forced to kill him after all.

A look of surprise crossed the Indian's face. He muttered a few words in his native tongue, then following a brief pause, ran quickly to his waiting horse. He never looked back—just rode hard and fast into the stand of trees from which he had come.

Jim stood trembling for several moments, dazed and shaken. *Why'd I let that savage go?* he asked himself. *Why didn't I just kill him while I had the chance? He'll probably meet up with his Blackfoot party, turn around, and chase me, and I'll be dog meat for sure.*

He slapped the side of his head with the palm of his hand, wondering if he'd gone soft in the brain. "If I ain't careful, it could be my undoing," he muttered.

By early afternoon, Buck, tired of sitting inside the stuffy cabin, told Amanda he was going outside for some fresh air.

"That's fine," she said sweetly. "Mary's tending the baby right now, and I will be doing some cleaning, so it's the perfect time for thee to get some air."

He frowned at her. "Are ya ever gonna stop sayin' *thee* and *thou*? It really gets on my nerves."

Amanda blinked her blue eyes rapidly. "I. . .I'm sorry. I didn't realize it bothered thee so." She clasped her hand over her mouth and mumbled, "I mean, *you*, not *thee*. I will try to remember."

Buck grinned in spite of himself. She looked so innocent, looking up at him as though truly repentant. He guessed it shouldn't really matter whether she said *you* or *thee*, but Silas Lothard had used the words *thee* and *thou* whenever he forced Buck to sit and listen as he read the Bible every day, so when Amanda said them, Buck thought of Silas. Sometimes Silas forced Buck to memorize verses of scripture. Other times, he would use the verses against him, saying that if Buck didn't do everything he said, God would make something bad happen to him.

Buck blew out his breath. That was enough reminiscing for now. He needed to focus on something positive. "I'm goin' outside now," he said to Amanda. "Let me know when you're done cleaning."

She smiled and nodded. "Enjoy your time alone. I am sure it hasn't been easy for you being cooped up with two women."

Buck went outside, calling for Thunder to join him. When he stepped onto the porch, he stared across the clearing into the forest where Jim had gone. What he wouldn't give to be out there with his friend right now. The mountains he loved seemed to be beckoning him.

"What do ya say we take a little walk to the stream?" Buck said, reaching down to rub Thunder behind his ears. "We won't go far, and maybe by the time we get back the women will have the cabin cleaned."

Woof! Woof! The dog responded with a wag of his tail, circling Buck's legs.

Amanda got busy cleaning the cabin, but her mind kept wandering to Buck and his reasons for not wanting to talk about the Bible. *Does he think God's Word is only for women?* she wondered. *Does he believe he's not a sinner who needs to be forgiven? If so, then he really does need to be shown the way to God.*

Amanda's thoughts were interrupted by a knock on the cabin door. She was sure it wasn't Buck, because he would have just walked right in. But in all the time she'd been living here, they'd never had any visitors except for Buck. Standing to one side of the door, she opened it slowly, just far enough to see out.

A hefty, scraggly-looking mountain man wearing a squirrel-skin cap poked his head through the doorway. "Name's Seth Burrows, and I'm just passing through these parts. My mule drowned in the river and took my gun and supplies right with him. Thought maybe your man might have an extra one he could sell me."

Amanda wasn't sure how to respond. She glanced past the porch to see if Buck was in the yard but saw no sign of him. She hoped he hadn't followed Jim into the woods. To make matters worse, Buck had taken Jim's dog along, leaving Amanda and Mary with no protection.

"This is Jim Breck's cabin," Amanda told the man.

"Aw, and you must be Breck's woman." He cocked his head to one side, while looking Amanda up and down.

"Me Jim's wife," Mary said, joining Amanda at the door.

"I see. Well, where's your man?" Seth eyed Mary in a critical way.

"He hunting. Be back soon."

Seth grunted, pushed past the women, and ambled into the room, flopping into a chair at the table. Just his presence made Amanda feel uncomfortable, and she quickly uttered a prayer for their safety.

"So have ya got a mule I can have?" Seth asked, looking at Mary.

She cast a quick glance in Amanda's direction. Was she hoping Amanda would offer him one of the pack mules that had been with her when Harvey Hanson was her guide? That might be the Christian thing to do, but when Amanda headed west again, she'd have to travel lighter, with just one mule to carry her things.

"Besides the mule, I could really use a few supplies," Seth said, glaring at Mary as though she were his enemy. Amanda didn't know why, but it seemed as if this ill-mannered man felt contempt for Jim's Indian wife. Could he have had a run-in with Indians at sometime? Or perhaps he was prejudiced against them because of the color of their skin. Amanda had known people like that back in New York. Even a few people in their church thought they were better than others.

"How you know cabin is here?" Mary asked, giving no response to the man's request for a mule and supplies.

"I seen your smoke." Seth pointed to the fireplace. "Knew it weren't no Injun smoke signals, so I followed it, thinkin' I might find some help."

Something about the visitor didn't seem right, and Amanda had felt a keen sense of dislike toward him since he'd first entered the cabin. She brought herself up short, wondering if she too was being prejudiced. Or could the nervous feeling in the pit of her stomach be a warning that this man wasn't to be trusted? The sense of apprehension felt similar to when the Blackfoot had surrounded Amanda and her guide.

"I'm plumb tired," Seth said, yawning. "Have ya got a place where I can bed down for the night?"

Amanda drew back, wincing from the foul breath he'd just expelled. She looked at Mary and couldn't miss her look of surprise. At no point had either of them said the man was welcome to stay here for the night. *Where is Buck?* Amanda wondered again. *Did this horrible man do something to him?*

"Say now, I can sleep right there!" Seth motioned to the mat in front of the fireplace where Buck had been sleeping since he'd been injured. Amanda couldn't believe the nerve of this unpleasant man.

Seth sniffed the air. "Is that coffee I smell? If so, I'd sure like some." He turned to face Mary. "Pour me a cup." The man was so rude!

Mary nodded curtly, but before she started for the stove, Seth hollered, "On second thought, have ya got anything stronger'n coffee?"

Amanda looked at Mary again, hoping she could read her thoughts. If there was any whiskey in the cabin, she hoped Mary wouldn't offer it to Seth. She knew from seeing drunkards on the streets back home that it could do terrible things—turning a normally kindhearted man into a monster of sorts. And she was sure that Seth Burrows was no kindhearted man.

"Only coffee and water here to drink," Mary was quick to say.

Amanda breathed a sigh of relief.

Seth grunted. "Coffee it'll hafta be then."

Mary poured the man some coffee; then she stood with Amanda, watching the man gulp it down like he was desperate for something to drink. It was almost comical, because Amanda had never seen anyone drink hot coffee that fast before. She suspected at any moment that he'd let out a yell, but he acted no different than if he'd just swallowed some cold mountain water.

"Where's Buck?" Mary whispered to Amanda.

"I. . .I don't know," Amanda replied, keeping her voice low. "When I opened the door, I didn't see him anywhere in the yard."

"Say, ya wouldn't have anything for me to eat, would ya?" he asked, wiping his mouth with the back of his hand. "I ain't had nothin' in my belly since yesterday mornin'."

"There is some stew left over from our noon meal," Amanda said.

"I can warm that up for thee, Mr. Burrows." If the man really had gone that long without eating, they could hardly send him away with an empty stomach. Whether he was here to start trouble or just a poor fellow down on his luck, she hoped he'd be on his way after he ate. She was even considering letting him have one of the mules.

"Seth. Just call me Seth. And sure, I'll take some of that stew." He looked at Amanda, winked, and grinned.

Maybe if he eats, he'll leave quicker, Amanda told herself as she reheated the stew. If only Jim or Buck were here, or even Thunder. It was unsettling to think that she and Mary were alone in the cabin with this stranger. She wondered if Mary felt as uncomfortable as she did. The man was so big and his odor hard to tolerate. His presence seemed to fill the whole room. Amanda was tempted to walk outside and stand on the porch, hoping to see Buck approaching. But there was no way she would leave poor Mary and her baby alone with this brute of a man. Besides, to get to the door, she would have to walk past Seth, and she definitely didn't want to do that. *Where art thou, Buck? Please come back to the cabin, and soon.*

Chapter 22

W*a-a-a! Wa-a-a! Wa-a-a!*

"It's Little Joe," Mary said to Amanda. "I need tend to him."

"It's fine, Mary," Amanda replied. "Go do what you need to do."

Seth, apparently unmindful of the baby's cries, gulped down his plate of stew. Dribbles of the sauce clung to his beard as he picked up the dish to lick off what was left. This man ate like an animal, and the putrid smell of him had become overbearing.

The baby's cries grew louder, so Mary hurried to the bedroom to feed him.

Seth looked at Amanda. "So she's got a baby, huh?"

She gave a quick nod.

"Boy or girl?"

"Mary and Jim have a son."

"Ah, I see." Seth sneered at Amanda in such a way that it caused her to shudder. "What's a purty little thing like you doin' in a place like this?" he asked.

Trying not to let him see her anxiety, Amanda asked, "Didst thou get enough to eat?"

Seth rubbed his belly. "Oh yeah, but I could always use more."

Amanda took the bowl and started toward the stove. "I will get thee more stew." Before she could get there, Seth reached out his calloused hand and grabbed her arm. "Forget about the stew for now. I wanna talk to you, purty lady."

"About what?" she squeaked. "And please, let go of my arm." Amanda thought about saying she had a husband who was out for a walk, hoping that might cause Seth to think twice about touching her, but she'd never believed it was right to tell an untruth and doubted she'd be convincing if she did make up a story. If she lied to Seth, he'd probably catch on to the truth, and that might make matters worse.

"Well now, ain't ya jest the high and mighty one?" Seth tightened his grip and squinted his beady green eyes at her. "You ain't really in no position to be givin' orders."

Amanda's eyes burned, but knowing she needed to remain strong, she would not give in to her tears. She could smell the man's disgusting body odor even more clearly as he held her firmly in his grip. Her stomach churned.

"I'd be happy to serve thee more stew, or maybe some biscuits?" she said, trying to keep her voice steady so he wouldn't know how frightened she was.

"It ain't just food I'm hungry for," Seth said, jiggling his shaggy eyebrows.

Amanda twisted her body, trying to free herself from the evil man's grasp, but he held her tightly. She couldn't pry his fingers loose from around her arm. She gasped when he pulled her roughly against his side and then onto his lap.

"Let woman go!" Mary shouted, rushing into the room.

"Shut up, Injun!" Seth hollered. "This ain't none of your business!" He grabbed Amanda's chin, twisted her head toward him, and gave her a smothering kiss.

Amanda nearly gagged as she struggled to free herself from his grasp. She had never smelled anything so repulsive as this man's rancid breath. And she could only hold her own breath for just so long or she would surely pass out.

Mary leaped forward and clawed frantically at the man's neck and face. That only seemed to anger him further. "You're a real wildcat, ain't ya, you little heathen? Well, I can tame ya. I've taken on mountain lions that had more fire in 'em than any Injun, and I always won!"

Seth let go of Amanda, and jumped up, hurling the chair aside and knocking Amanda to the floor. He raised his arm, and *whack!* He backhanded Mary's face so hard that her head jerked to one side. Clasping his hands around Amanda's neck, he pulled her up and pressed her tightly to his chest.

She squirmed, coughing and gasping for air. *Oh dear Lord, help us, please!*

Mary bit the man's shoulder. He let out a yelp and released his hold on Amanda. The commotion woke Little Joe again, and he began to howl. Mary started for the bedroom, but Seth tripped her and she fell to the floor, hitting her head on the corner of a chair.

Amanda started crawling across the floor. If only she could get to the kettle of stew. It was still hot, and she might be able to use it as a weapon. She was almost there when Seth's bulky hand grabbed hold of her arm, and he commanded her to stand.

"Where do ya think you're goin', missy?" Seth buried his face in Amanda's hair, which now hung freely around her face. "Tryin' to sneak off, are ya?"

Amanda screamed when she looked over at Mary and saw blood running down her face. "Mary! Mary, art thou all right?"

"Aw, she's fine. Just a little whack on the head." Seth, breathing rapidly, kissed Amanda a second time. Turning her head away from his crushing lips, she tried to free herself from his grasp, but he was much stronger than she. He held her in a vise-like grip, and Amanda felt as if her spine was about to snap.

The cabin door flew open, and Buck burst into the room. "What's goin' on?" Looking at Seth, Buck rushed at the man and knocked him to the floor, but Seth didn't break his grip and took Amanda down with him.

Then, pulling Amanda up with him, the big man got up, grabbed his knife from its sheath on his leather belt, and held it against Amanda's throat. "Come at me again, and this woman is dead!" he bellowed.

Mary scooted across the floor to the bedroom, where Little Joe now whimpered. She hoped he would go back to sleep. Turning to watch the challenge between the two men, Mary wondered how she could help. Should she make a noise, hoping Seth would look her way? That might give Buck an advantage. Or should she find something to hit him with? If she could sneak up behind the crazed man and knock him out, they would be okay.

Too many times Mary had seen attacks like this one on women captives in the Blackfoot village. She was not about to let it happen here in her home. Not if she could help it.

Mary looked over and saw the kettle of hot stew. Steam rose readily from the top. Feeling more confident as she inched her way closer to the stove, she planned her attack.

———

Buck stood rigidly, trying to decide his next move. The crazed man meant business. If Buck didn't comply with his wishes, he would probably slit Amanda's throat. Buck had come across this type of man before, and his kind had no morals or conscience.

"Put down the knife," Buck demanded. "The woman's done nothin' to you."

"No way!" The man shook his head. "I aim to take what I want!"

Behind the attacker, Buck saw Mary edging closer to the kettle of stew. He knew what she was thinking, and he had to do something quick because she could end up getting hurt. Jim would never forgive him if he let anything happen to Mary or the baby.

Buck was about to pull his own knife out of the sheath, when the big man hollered, "Better not! You do like I told ya now, or the women will pay."

Amanda's face was paler than snow, her eyes wide with fear, as she hung limply over the intruder's arm.

Reluctantly, Buck placed his knife on the kitchen table, stepped back, and raised both hands, to show the other man his good intentions.

"That's better. Now open the door and stand aside," the man ordered gruffly.

"Just let the woman go." Buck's hands itched to lunge for his knife, but he couldn't risk Amanda getting hurt.

The man snorted loudly. "You ain't in no position to be tellin' me what to do. I'm takin' this woman as well as one of them pack mules I seen outside, and there ain't nothin you can do about it. Now open that door and stand aside!"

"Do what man says," Mary spoke up. "Don't let him hurt Amanda."

Buck held his breath, but the man didn't seem to notice that Mary had moved. Reluctantly, Buck edged his way toward the door and gave it a hard yank. It swung open, letting in a blast of warm air. If he was going to save Amanda, he'd have to do something quick.

The big brute maneuvered his way across the room, pulling Amanda helplessly along. Just as they stepped through the open doorway, Buck called, "Get him, dog!"

Thunder, who had been lying on the front porch, leaped to his feet and, with a piercing, wolf-like snarl, dove straight for the enemy's leg.

Caught off guard, the man let out a yelp and dropped the knife. Then he staggered and fell to the ground, taking Amanda with him.

Buck bent down and grabbed the knife. "Hold him there, Thunder!"

The dog bared his teeth, and his hair bristled as he hovered hungrily over his prey. Unless the man had no common sense, he wasn't going anywhere.

Buck bent down to check on Amanda, who was sobbing uncontrollably. Pulling her gently to her feet, he said, "Go back into the cabin." He then dropped to his knees and held the tip of the knife against the man's throat. "You hurt Amanda, and now you're gonna pay with your life."

Looking up at him with pleading eyes and trembling lips, the man begged for mercy. "Please don't kill me, mister. Your woman came on to me."

"You're lying—I know better than that!" It was all Buck could do to keep from taking the man's life right there on the spot. "I've seen your kind before. You take what ain't yours and don't care how ya get it. I oughta kill ya right this minute and be done with it!"

"Please, don't do it," Amanda pleaded from the porch. "God's Word says 'thou shalt not kill.' It wouldn't be right."

"If ya spare my life, I'll leave this place and be gone without another word," the big man said. "Honest, I will."

Reluctantly, Buck slowly lowered his knife. "Get up, ya filthy animal, and get outta here before I change my mind!"

The man rose slowly to his feet. "What about that mule I'm needin'? Ya know I can't make it outta here on foot."

"You'll be gettin' no mule. Now get going!" Buck shouted.

"But I need some form of weapon. My knife's all I got now that my gun and all the supplies I had are at the bottom of the river. Ya wouldn't send a man into the wilderness without some form of protection, would ya?"

Buck grunted through clenched teeth. "You ain't much of a man. You oughtta be grateful I spared your life."

The big fellow limped off, cursing under his breath, "I'll get even with ya someday; just see if I don't. You'll get your just reward."

As Buck watched the man disappear into the woods, he muttered, "It ain't me who's gonna get their just reward." Looking down at Thunder, he said, "Good boy! Now, stay out here and stand guard till Jim gets home."

Thunder looked up at him and whined. Then he took his place on the front porch. It wasn't likely that the intruder would return, but if he did, Buck wouldn't let him off so easy.

CHAPTER 23

M e fine," Mary said after Amanda had tended to the wound on her head. "Bleeding stopped now. No hurt."

Amanda smiled. "You're a woman of courage, Mary. You stood up to Seth Burrows and didn't back down."

"I think you were both pretty brave fightin' off a man of that size," Buck said, picking up the chair that had fallen over.

Mary's forehead creased. "Me not always a woman of courage. Once, when try to run away from Blackfoot, I scared of everything. But now, with baby son, I would fight like she-cat to protect him."

Amanda placed her hand gently on Mary's arm. "Would you mind telling us how you tried to escape the Blackfoot?"

"I tell you all about it," Mary said, glancing toward the room where her son now slept peacefully. "Many weeks I gather supplies for journey. When left alone in the teepee, I gather dried pemmican, buffalo jerky, and kouse cakes. Hid them under bedding. Put each in different place, so no lumps show through top of sleeping mat." She grimaced. "Winter come soon. I know if going to escape, it need to be then. Make choice to leave that night."

Amanda and Buck listened as Mary leaned back in her chair, closed her eyes, and relived the past.

———◆———

Yellow Bird lay motionless on her mat, listening to the sounds of the night. An owl hooted from somewhere outside, and one of the Indian ponies, corralled nearby, whinnied as if in response. Inside the teepee, she heard heavy breathing from the other two women, accompanied by the sound of Smoking Buffalo's deep snores.

Slowly, quietly, Yellow Bird crawled out from under her buffalo robe.

She waited until she was certain that everyone was asleep. Then, reaching under the mat for her food supplies, she tied them inside a piece of deer hide and slipped into her tunic and moccasins. She stuffed some larger deer hides under her sleeping robe, so it would appear as if she were still asleep. On hands and knees, she crept toward the door flap.

When Smoking Buffalo rolled over and grunted, Yellow Bird halted, holding her breath. She felt the blood race through her veins as she hunkered down close to the tent floor, waiting to see if he would awaken. His snoring continued, and she breathed a sigh of relief. She longed to reach out as she passed the sleeping man, snatch away the knife lying close to his side, and take her revenge. But it wasn't worth the risk. Freedom would be better than revenge.

The chill of the night air took Yellow Bird's breath away as she crawled outside the tent and stood. She shivered, looking down at her bare arms, realizing that she had carelessly forgotten to bring a buffalo robe from the lodge. She was tempted to go back and get one, but her fear of being discovered was greater than her reluctance to face the dreaded cold. She would have to find something else for warmth.

Yellow Bird knew the horses were well guarded, so her escape would have to be on foot. She walked carefully and quietly around the back of the teepee. It was pitch dark, as the silvery moon was hidden behind clouds, so she waited, giving her eyes time to adjust.

A stack of deer hides waiting to be cured were piled high. She pulled one off the top and wrapped it around her trembling shoulders. It helped dispel the cold, but the pungent odor was overpowering.

It will have to do, *she silently acknowledged. Hesitating a moment, she tried to decide which direction to take. Gathering what little courage she had, Yellow Bird made a dash for the woods.*

Her heart pounded so hard, she could hear the rhythm of it in her ears, and by the time she heard running water from the stream, she was nearly out of breath. The moon peeked out from behind the clouds, and she caught a glimpse of the stream just ahead. A few more steps and she was at the water's edge.

Yellow Bird looked for the shallowest part and waded quickly across, thanking Hanyawat that there had been no guards on the path she had chosen.

By the time she reached the other side of the stream, she was shivering badly. Her moccasins were soaked, and the hem of her tunic was also wet. She wrapped the smelly deer hide tightly around her shoulders, and ran for all she was worth. Yellow Bird didn't stop or even look back until the first light of day. She was hungry, thirsty, and utterly exhausted.

Dropping to a fallen log, she opened her satchel of provisions. She ate one of the kouse cakes but decided to save the rest, knowing she would need to make the few items of food last as long as possible. Since she would be following the river, heading upstream, she could get a cool drink of water whenever she needed one.

How Yellow Bird longed for just a few hours' sleep, but she was not yet far enough from the Blackfoot camp to stop. She had to keep going and hoped she was traveling in the right direction. If she had only paid closer attention to her surroundings when she'd traveled from her home to the Blackfoot camp with her captors. She prayed that her guardian spirit would guide her safely back to her people.

A chilling thought popped into her head. Even if she were successful in finding her way back to the camp from which she had been taken, the chance that her people would still be there was slim. Winter was coming, and they needed to go to their homeland along the Clearwater River.

As Yellow Bird trudged wearily on, a feeling of hopelessness flooded her soul. She was alone with no shelter, very little food, and no weapons. Now she wished she'd taken the chance and stolen Smoking Buffalo's knife. She might very well die out here in the forest. Yet she could not go back. She never wanted to see Smoking Buffalo or his cruel wives again. Any fate that might lie ahead could not compare to what she'd endured at the hands of her wicked captors. She had to go on, and somehow she must find the courage to survive.

The sun was high overhead when Yellow Bird stopped to rest again. Her tunic and moccasins had dried, and she had finally managed to warm up. She was about to collapse on the grass for a much-needed rest when she heard the sound of approaching horses. She turned and saw a group of

Indians riding toward her at a fast pace. As they drew nearer, she realized with agonizing fear that one of them was Smoking Buffalo.

Her heart thundered wildly, and she fled as fast as her legs would carry her. She could hear the yips and wild cries of the approaching Indians as they bore down on her, but she kept running.

In a short time they had gained on her, and one of the horses plowed straight into Yellow Bird's back. She dropped to the ground, the deer hide falling from her shoulders, and the satchel of provisions landing in the dirt.

She pulled herself to her feet, only to be knocked down again. The blow came from Smoking Buffalo. "You are my slave!" he cried. "You will pay for trying to escape!"

Yellow Bird knew the Blackfoot language well enough to understand how angry he was. She would surely be punished, if not killed, for her foolish attempt to escape.

She flinched when he grabbed one of her braids and yanked her roughly to her feet. "You come with me!" Smoking Buffalo jerked Yellow Bird toward his horse, and in one quick movement, threw her across the stallion's back, then mounted behind her.

The other five Blackfoot braves howled with laughter. No doubt they knew what her fate would be.

Yellow Bird's father had told her once that someday she would have strong power. Where is this promised power now? *she wondered bleakly.* Where is the strength of my guardian spirit? *She felt like a helpless fool as Smoking Buffalo held her firmly in place with one hand and guided his horse with the other. There was nothing left to do but wait and see what her punishment would be.*

Her body ached after hanging over the horse's back for so long, but Yellow Bird was more amazed at how quickly they'd returned to the Blackfoot camp. It had taken her all night and half a day to cover the ground they covered on horseback in just a few short hours.

As they rode into the village, many Blackfoot Indians looked up from their chores and smiled. Some laughed and cheered, pointing at the returning party bringing their runaway captive home. Even the children ran up to them, sneering at Yellow Bird.

When they reached Smoking Buffalo's lodge, the horses stopped. The master gave his slave a hefty push, and she fell helplessly to the ground. While the rest of the village went back to their business and the children continued to play, Smoking Buffalo dismounted, grabbed one of Yellow Bird's braids, and hauled her roughly into the teepee.

Yellow Bird expected to see Smoking Buffalo's wives there, but the lodge was empty. She swallowed hard, wondering what her fate would be.

Smoking Buffalo gave her little time to wonder. He jerked her toward the center of the lodge, directly in front of the fire pit. Yellow Bird cringed as he bent down, pulling her with him.

The heat from the burning coals reached out to her, and she was certain that her flesh was about to be burned.

Instead of thrusting her hand into the fire, Smoking Buffalo grabbed a slender piece of firewood and began to beat Yellow Bird with it.

She jerked back and forth, trying to dodge the blows, but it was no use. He held her firmly by the hair and continued to strike her legs, arms, and back. "You are mine, and you shall learn to obey! If you ever leave here, it will be because I say so! Do you understand?"

Before Yellow Bird could reply, he aimed one final blow to the middle of her back and threw her roughly onto a mat. "No food for four days! Hard labor as punishment!" he shouted.

Through tearfilled eyes, Yellow Bird watched as he stalked out of the teepee. Her bruised and battered body ached unmercifully, and she trembled violently. "I should not have tried to escape!" she sobbed. "I have no power and no courage. My guardian spirit has surely left me. Hanyawat no longer cares."

She dropped her head to her knees and let the tears flow unchecked. It was useless to think she could ever be free or happy again. Yellow Bird's fate had been sealed.

When Mary's story came to an end, she opened her eyes and blinked. "That day I vow never give in to my fears again." She clenched her fists until the veins on her hands protruded. "Seth Burrows, he evil man just like Smoking Buffalo." She looked at Buck, who sat at the kitchen table, eating a bowl of stew as he listened. "We glad you show up to help us, Buck."

Amanda nodded. "I shudder to think of what might have happened if thou—I mean you—hadn't come back when you did."

"I shoulda been here," Buck said with regret. "Shoulda stayed on the porch till you got the cleaning done."

"Where did you go?" Amanda asked, placing a cup of coffee on the table in front of Buck.

"When I went outside and saw what a nice day it was, I decided to take a walk." Buck pinched the bridge of his nose and frowned. "Guess I ended up goin' a little farther than I'd planned. I should have at least left Thunder with ya. Don't know what I was thinkin', and I'm sorry for letting you down."

"Thine apology is accepted," Amanda said, taking a seat in the chair across from him. "I. . .I mean, your apology is accepted," she corrected herself. "I am still trying to get used to the idea of saying *you* and *your* instead of *thee* and *thou*."

Buck shrugged. "Guess it's hard for people to change when they've been doin' or sayin' things a certain way for a long time."

She smiled. "That's true. As my father used to say, 'Once a Quaker, always a Quaker.' I think that includes the way we speak."

The whinny of a horse drew everyone's attention to the outside. "It be Jim," Mary said. "Me know the sound of his horse."

"Better let me take a look just in case it's not." Buck slid his chair away from the table. "Jim's been gone a long time. Someone coulda stolen his horse."

Amanda's eyes widened. "I hope it's not Seth Burrows. Maybe somehow he. . ."

Buck opened the door slowly and looked out. "It's Jim all right." He looked back at the women. "There's a deer draped over the back of his horse."

When Jim entered the cabin and saw everyone's serious expressions, he immediately grew concerned. "What's goin' on?" he asked. "Is everything okay?"

Mary and Amanda took turns telling him about Seth Burrows.

"He ask for mule," Mary explained, "but then he want more."

As Amanda related what had happened to her, Jim's anger mounted. "Where were you durin' all of this?" he asked, turning to Buck.

Buck's face reddened. "I. . .I needed some fresh air, so I took a walk."

Jim slammed his fist on the table. "You see why I asked you to stay? I was countin' on you to be here to take care of the women."

"I know, and I'm sorry," Buck apologized. "Guess I just wasn't thinkin'."

"No, I guess not." Jim sucked in a deep breath. "I've had a rough day, and then to come home and hear this. . . Well, if I still had some whiskey in the house, think I'd need to have some just to calm down."

"What happened?" Buck asked.

"I had a little run-in with an Injun today."

"What tribe?" Mary questioned, her eyes widening.

"I think it was one of them Blackfoot. He was probably after my horse, or maybe the deer I had, and I'm thinkin' he'd have probably killed me for it. Some Injuns would do just about anything for a good horse like mine."

"You hurt?" Mary asked with obvious concern.

He shook his head. "Naw, but I scared the daylights outta that man." He went on to tell about his encounter with the Indian and then said, "I didn't come straight home after that because I was worried the Injun might decide to follow me here." He grunted. "I sure didn't wanna lead him back to the cabin, so I took a longer way home."

"Till I'm recovered enough to return to my own place, I promise I'll stick close to the cabin," Buck said.

"Glad to hear it." Jim motioned to Thunder, lying under the table. "The dog has to stay here from now on too, 'cause I can't take the chance of anything like that happening again. Some Indians and even white men can be unpredictable, and it don't pay to let your defenses down."

Little Joe started crying just then, interrupting their conversation. "I feed baby now," Mary said. "When I come back, I fix you supper, Jim."

He reached out and clasped her hand. "I'm mighty glad no real harm came to you." He looked over at Amanda. "I'm glad you're okay too."

Amanda smiled. "We all faced some dangers today, but God had His protective hand on us."

Jim didn't admit it, but he wondered if she might not be right. He'd uttered a prayer out there in the woods, and everything had turned okay, so maybe God had been listening and protected him, as well as those at the cabin.

CHAPTER 24

For the next week Jim stuck close to home, watching over his family and making sure Buck didn't try to do too much. Buck was young and full of energy, and it was hard for him to sit around and do nothing but rest. Mary kept busy with the baby and helping Amanda with some of the meals, but Buck complained of being bored and needing something to do. So Jim suggested that Buck go fishing, which wouldn't overexert him. Jim had been tempted to go along, but after the scare they'd had, he wasn't ready to leave the women alone, even though Thunder would be with them. The women were back in a routine and seemed to have relaxed a bit since the episode. Jim knew his wife was a strong woman, but it truly surprised him to hear how courageous Amanda had been.

"Mary and I are going to study some passages from the Bible this morning," Amanda said when Jim entered the cabin after seeing Buck off. "Wouldst thou—I mean, would you care to join us?"

Jim was on the verge of saying no but changed his mind. If God had truly been watching out for him that day when he encountered the Blackfoot Indian, then he ought to at least listen to what the Bible had to say.

"Yeah, okay. I'll sit with ya for a while," he said, giving Amanda a nod.

She smiled. "As soon as Mary finishes feeding and changing the baby, we'll get started."

Sure hope I didn't make a mistake agreeing to this, Jim thought. *But I said I would, so guess I'd better follow through.*

As Buck sat on the grassy banks along the edge of the stream near Jim's cabin, he thought about Amanda and how pretty she was. She was also very complicated. She seemed meek and mild, but she didn't hold back—at least when it came to talking about religious things. He had to admit that she was gutsy. She'd proven that last week. Buck wished she wasn't one of those Bible thumpers, trying to cram religion down people's throats. Well, he guessed she wasn't exactly doing that, but she did take her Bible out regularly and read it to Mary. Whenever that happened, Buck made some excuse to go outside because he couldn't stand listening to what he felt was some story somebody had made up to make people think God loved them and would provide for their needs. *Well, He didn't provide for my mother's needs when she needed help,* Buck thought bitterly. *And where was God when Silas was whippin' the daylights outta me with his strap?*

Buck's fingers tightened around the branch he was using as a fishing pole. He pulled the bait up and left it dangling as his thoughts continued. He didn't need the white man's God or the Indian's Hanyawat. He could get by just fine, without any help from the spirit world. A man had to be tough enough to make it on his own in this world; that was just the way it was.

A bobcat kitten stood on the opposite bank, its stubby tail twitching ever so little. The small kitten didn't seem to notice Buck, but had its keen eyes on the bait dangling at the end of the fishing line. Back and forth the cat's head went, as the fish line blew gently in the breeze.

Buck smiled, watching as the kitten inched its way closer to the water. Buck couldn't help twitching his fishing pole, making the bait jerk at the end of the line. He held his breath, suspecting what the kitten was about to do next.

The little bobcat had reached the stream's edge. Slowly it crouched into position. Before Buck could blink again, the kitten leaped toward the teasing bait. Buck stifled a chuckle as the kitten plunged into the stream.

"Brr. . ." Buck shivered, realizing how cold that water must feel. And what a look of surprise on the kitten's face when it landed smack-dab in the middle of the stream. Its hazel-green eyes were as big as saucers. Buck couldn't help himself—he laughed out loud.

The bobcat leaped to the stream's bank, almost as fast as it had jumped in. Then it looked back at Buck, as though noticing him for the first time. The critter's grayish-brown fur was soaking wet, and droplets of water fell from its black-cuffed ears. The cat sat on the bank shaking each striped leg as if it had something stuck on the bottom of its paws.

Buck had been living in these mountains a long time and had seen plenty of bobcats over the years. He figured this kitten was over a month old, since that was when they usually started exploring.

Overhead, Buck heard a *kee-eeee-arr* sound, and when he looked up, his winged brother landed in a tall tree and sat, watching the baby kitten. Buck wasn't sure what to do, but he knew he wasn't about to remain there and watch the helpless kitten become a meal. Fortunately, Buck didn't have to worry for long. He heard what sounded like a screaming baby. Buck had heard that sound many times before. Anyone else hearing the sound might think it was an infant crying in pain, but the recognizable sound was that of an adult bobcat. Almost as fast as it had arrived, the kitten perked up and vanished, running toward its mother.

Even though Buck wanted to get back to work, especially helping Jim around the cabin, he was glad he'd taken his friend's advice and come down here to the stream. Otherwise, he'd have missed seeing the baby bobcat, and now it would be a memory he'd never forget.

Buck's thoughts went to Amanda again. She must have toughened up quite a bit since her departure from New York. If he agreed to take her to the Spalding Mission he'd probably think about her all the time. That, in itself, would be a good enough reason to say no to her request. Well, it would be several more weeks before the rivers became passable, so he didn't have to worry about taking Amanda anywhere right now. For the time being, all he needed to worry about was getting back to the business of trapping, and with or without Jim's permission, he was going back to his own cabin early next week.

———

Amanda took a seat at the table and opened her Bible to the Gospel of John. She was glad Jim had agreed to join her and Mary and hoped

God's Word would speak to his heart.

"In John 1:1–4, we read, 'In the beginning was the Word, and the Word was with God, and the Word was God. The same was in the beginning with God.'" She paused to look up at Jim and Mary, but their expressions were unreadable. Had they understand what she'd read? She would let them ask questions after she'd finished the passage. "'All things were made by him; and without him was not any thing made that was made. In him was life; and the life was the light of men,'" Amanda continued.

Jim and Mary stared at each other.

Amanda cleared her throat. "You see, God is the One true God, and the only way we can come to Him is through His Son, Jesus."

Mary nodded briefly, but Jim gave no reply.

Amanda turned to the Book of Romans and read chapter ten, verses nine and ten: "'If thou shalt confess with thy mouth the Lord Jesus, and shalt believe in thine heart that God hath raised him from the dead, thou shalt be saved. For with the heart man believeth unto righteousness; and with the mouth confession is made unto salvation.'"

"Saved from what?" Jim asked, leaning both elbows on the table.

Amanda smiled. At least she had his interest now. "By accepting Christ as our Savior, we are saved from our sins," she said.

"Me do this, last time we talked," Mary spoke up. "Me not want to die in sin."

Jim leaned back in his chair and gave his beard a quick pull. "Guess it's somethin' to think about all right."

"Would you like to pray and ask God to forgive your sins and acknowledge that you believe in His Son?" Amanda asked, looking hopefully at Jim.

He shrugged his broad shoulders. "I don't know. Maybe someday, but not now. I need to think on it awhile, I guess."

Amanda felt a keen sense of disappointment. She'd thought for sure that she was on the verge of leading Jim to the Lord. Maybe she'd said too much, too soon. Perhaps she should have eased into it gradually. But then, Papa had always taught that a Christian should be willing to boldly tell others about the Lord. *Boldly tell them,* she reminded herself, *but don't push. I wouldn't want Jim, or anyone else, to make a confession of faith until he felt ready.*

At least Jim had seemed to understand what Amanda had read, and she was pleased at the progress she'd made with Mary. Now if she could only get Buck to listen. Of course, she'd have to be careful not to push, because Buck had already made it clear that he wanted nothing to do with God. *But God can change a man's heart,* Amanda told herself. *The Bible says it's not His will that any should perish. I just need to pray that somehow Buck's heart will be softened and that one day he will hear God's voice and respond.*

CHAPTER 25

The following Monday, after breakfast, Buck announced that he felt well enough to return to his own place.

"Are ya sure about that?" Jim asked, after taking a swig of coffee. "I don't want ya goin' back too soon."

"I feel fine," Buck said. "And it'll be good to get back to my cabin and make sure nobody's messed with my things."

"The place was just like ya left it when I rode over there a few days ago," Jim said.

"Even so, I wanna see for myself. My little cabin's callin' to me, and I'm ready to go home."

Amanda had known this day was coming, but she still felt disappointment. She was accustomed to having Buck around and would miss him. It made no sense, really, but she found him intriguing. She wished she knew more about him. She'd asked him about it once, but he'd said his life was about his future, not the past. The only thing she knew about him was that he lived alone, wasn't married, and had learned his trapping skills from Jim.

She would miss the way Buck's square jaw stuck out in a stubborn way every time something was said that he didn't like. Even the scar on his neck from the bear's claws made his handsome face more rugged and striking. Under all that ruggedness, Buck had a tender way about him. She saw it every time he looked at Little Joe, and when he watched Mary and Jim interact around the cabin. As much as she tried not to think about it, Amanda found herself wondering if Buck had ever been in love or if he longed to have a family of his own.

What kind of future will Buck have? Amanda asked herself. *He lives alone, without even a pet.* Other than the hawk Mary had told her about, Buck was basically a loner. Having the hawk's presence nearby was at least something for Buck, but was that truly enough? *What will happen if he's not able to trap anymore?* she wondered. Both Jim and Buck had mentioned one time that it was getting harder to trap enough beaver and muskrats because their numbers were decreasing due to the demand for more pelts.

"When you go, we send meat, coffee, and pemmican with you," Mary said, smiling at Buck.

"Thanks, I appreciate that." He glanced over at Amanda but quickly looked away.

Amanda wondered if he'd been about to say something to her. Should she ask? No, that might appear too forward.

"I'm sure gonna miss Little Joe when I'm gone," Buck said. "I kinda like that little fella."

"You can come by to see him whenever ya like," Jim said, reaching over to stroke his son's shiny black hair.

Buck grinned. "I might just do that."

"You welcome here anytime," Mary put in.

"Would it be all right if I pray for thee now?" Amanda asked.

"You can pray for me all *thee* want when I'm gone," Buck said, his forehead creasing, "but I ain't in no mood to listen to no flowery prayer."

Amanda cringed. She had obviously offended him. "I. . .I am sorry. I meant no offense," she said, wishing she could take back what she had said. From the way Buck had responded to her Bible reading on several occasions, she should have known better than to suggest that she pray out loud for him, and to make matters worse, she'd used *thee* again.

"There's one more thing I'd better say before I go," Buck said, sliding his chair away from the table.

"Go right ahead," Jim spoke up. "You can say whatever's on your mind."

Buck looked at Amanda and blinked a couple of times. "I've. . . uh. . .thought things over and have decided not to act as your guide.

You'll have to find someone else to take ya to the Spalding Mission."

Amanda's shoulders slumped. She was sorely disappointed. "Is it because I asked if I could pray for you? Or have I said or done something else to offend?"

Buck traced his finger along the scar from the grizzly attack, running from his left eyebrow back to his ear. "Ya ain't done nothin',", he mumbled. "Just don't wanna go there, that's all."

"Don't worry about it," Jim said, tapping Amanda's arm. "I'll be takin' my furs and pelts to the Green River Rendezvous in a few weeks, and you can go with me, Mary, and Little Joe. Maybe somebody there will be willing to take ya to the mission."

Mary's eyebrows lifted as she looked at Jim. "We all goin' to Rendezvous?"

He gave a nod. "I'll be gone a spell and don't wanna leave ya here at the cabin by yourselves for that long."

"We enjoy goin' to Rendezvous," Mary said with an eager expression. "Much excitement and things to look at there."

Jim chuckled. "Well, just don't get too carried away with buyin' and tradin' things. I don't wanna have to buy another pack mule just to haul everything home."

"Other Indians be at Rendezvous?" Mary asked.

"That's right," Jim said. "Several tribes come to barter and sell."

Mary's eyes brightened. "Maybe some of my people be there. Might see Mother and Father again."

Jim frowned deeply. "It's not likely, but if they are at the Rendezvous, I hope you don't get any ideas about runnin' off with them." He motioned to their baby. "You and Little Joe belong with me."

Mary blinked. "I. . .I know, but—"

"If your family is there, which ain't likely," Jim said firmly, "you can spend some time with 'em, but when Rendezvous is over, you and Little Joe will be comin' back here with me."

Mary nodded.

Amanda felt sorry for her new friend. Leaving one's family by choice was one thing, but being ripped away from them through no desire of your own was unimaginable. Mary had told Amanda about her days as a captive of the Blackfoot, so she knew Mary had been treated cruelly. Even her time of being married to Jim hadn't been easy, although things seemed better between them since the birth of Little Joe. Still, if a husband cared for his wife, he should be willing to see that she was reunited with her family, even if it meant leaving the mountains and traveling to Nez Percé country. Amanda kept her thoughts to herself. She'd already overstepped her bounds with Buck this morning and didn't want to make the same mistake with Jim, especially since she was hoping he would soon be her second convert.

A short time after Buck left, Amanda mentioned to Jim that she thought Buck's refusal to take her to the Spalding Mission was because she'd done something to offend him.

Jim shook his head. "I don't know about that, but Buck can be hard to figure out sometimes. He had a rough life when he was a boy."

"Would you tell me a little about that?" Amanda asked.

Jim pulled thoughtfully on his beard. "Well, his pa was white and his ma was Nez Percé Indian. When his pa was killed by a Blackfoot Injun, his ma was taken captive and made to work as a slave."

"Same, like me," Mary put in, wrinkling her nose. "They probably beat her too."

"Could be," Jim said, "but Buck's ma was pregnant by her white husband when she was taken, and after the baby was born, she named him Red Hawk."

Amanda listened with interest as Jim went on to tell how when Red Hawk was five years old, the Blackfoot traded him and his ma to a man named Silas Lothard, who'd changed the boy's name to Buck. Jim grimaced. "The man claimed to be a Christian, but he sure didn't act like one. From what Buck said, Silas treated both him and his ma somethin' awful, callin' them heathens and beating them into submission." Jim took a drink of his coffee, then continued with the story. "One day Buck's mother tried to take her son and run away, but Silas caught 'em. As punishment, he traded Buck's ma to another man, but kept Buck, who was then ten years old. 'Course, Silas continued to mistreat Buck, and then one day when the enraged man was beatin' on Buck, he'd had enough and fought back. Silas ended up falling on his own knife, and once Buck realized the man was dead, he lit out on his own. Eventually, Buck and I met up, and I ended up teachin' him how to trap." Jim paused again for more coffee. "As you can probably guess, Buck has no regard for Christians and doesn't think he needs God."

"I see. I appreciate you telling me Buck's story. It helps me understand him a little better," Amanda said. "Now I understand why Buck seems so closed off to religion. He went through a lot at a very young age. No wonder he keeps up his guard."

Jim pulled out his pipe. "Yep," he said, before lighting it.

"Will Buck be going to Rendezvous too?" Amanda questioned.

"Probably so; he usually does."

"Will he travel with us?"

Jim shrugged his shoulders. "Don't know."

"Buck, he a loner," Mary said. "Like to be by himself."

I must remember to pray for Buck, Amanda told herself. *I shall pray that God will show him that not all who say they are Christians are bad.*

That evening as Jim stood beside the stream near his cabin, he noticed that the clouds he'd seen earlier had begun to break up, revealing a gloriously bright sunset that gave the trees a faint reddish-yellow color.

It wasn't often that Jim allowed himself the pleasure of indulging in the luxury of pure, simple relaxation, but this was one of those rare moments. He sniffed deeply of the clear, clean mountain air. It felt invigorating and reminded him that it was good to be alive and part of this great wilderness.

As the sun began to slip slowly behind the majestic Rocky Mountains, Jim felt the sudden need to share the experience with someone. He turned back toward the cabin to invite Mary to see the pretty sky.

When Jim entered the cabin, his son was lying on the bearskin rug on the floor with Amanda sitting on one side of him and Mary on the other. "Amanda, would ya mind watchin' the baby while Mary and I go outside to look at a sunset that's just too purty to miss?"

Amanda smiled. "I don't mind at all."

Jim grabbed Mary's hand and pulled her to her feet. "Let's go then, 'cause them colors will be gone if we don't hurry."

Mary hurried out the door behind Jim, giggling as she went. It was the first time Jim had seen her so carefree.

Once they were outdoors, Jim took Mary's hand and hurried across the yard. They stopped when they reached the stream and stood watching the sky until the sun slipped out of sight, taking with it all the beautiful colors. Standing with Mary made Jim feel as wonderful as the sunset. Now he knew what the words of scripture Lois had read to him once meant: "My cup runneth over." Lois had said the phrase meant that the person who wrote the verse had more than enough for his needs. That was surely how Jim felt these days.

"Whatcha thinkin' about?" Jim asked, as Mary stood quietly beside him.

"Just remembering some things from the past. Look forward to future with you and Little Joe," she said in a near whisper.

He turned and gazed deeply into Mary's dark eyes. "I'm lookin' forward to taking you and Little Joe to the Rendezvous. Maybe I'll see about buyin' a piece of glass for the kitchen window. How's that sound?"

"That be nice," Mary answered. "Much to be done before journey though. I make new clothes for us and Little Joe." She smiled at Jim. "Our son, he look like you, I think."

"Ah, but he's got your dark eyes and bronze-colored skin," Jim reminded her. "And ya know what else, Mary?"

"What?"

"I think our Little Joe is the most special child ever born."

She nodded. "That because he's yours and mine."

Jim grinned. He looked forward to the future—a future with his wife, Mary, and their wonderful little boy.

CHAPTER 26

The next few weeks were busy, as Mary tended to the baby and sewed them all new outfits to wear to Rendezvous. Little Joe's clothing was made from the softest skins, thinly scraped and tanned so pliable that they actually molded to his little body.

The clothing Mary sewed for herself and Jim was made from deer and bighorn sheep skin. She had tanned the leather until it was nearly white, then scraped it very thin, and finally rubbed it into soft leather, using white clay. She'd decorated the garments with porcupine quills dyed in the juice of huckleberries. She'd also used some tiny bones and animal teeth, bird quills, as well as colorful beads. These decorations were sewn in a variety of attractive patterns, using buffalo sinew to sew them in place. Mary made them new moccasins too, and for Jim, some extra fringed shirts and trousers from soft elk skin.

One afternoon, Mary sat at the table sewing some beads on one of the dresses she'd made. She smiled and watched as Thunder lay sleeping near the baby's cradle. She'd grown even fonder of the dog since Little Joe had been born, because Thunder was always close by the baby, watching over him as if he were his own. Mary wondered what would become of the dog when they left for the Rendezvous in a few weeks. They'd be gone for more than a moon, and even though Thunder, being part wolf, was an excellent hunter and could provide for his own meals, she wondered if he would think they had abandoned him and were never coming back.

Mary would have to speak to Jim about the dog. Perhaps she could convince him to allow Thunder to travel along to the Rendezvous. It would be added protection for them, as there were always dangers in the wilderness.

Mary was glad Amanda would be traveling with them, but she dreaded saying goodbye to her friend once she had found someone to act as her guide. She wished they could go with her to the mission, which she was certain was near her tribe's winter home. If she could just convince Jim to give up trapping and live among her people. But he was a stubborn man, and would probably never agree to such a thing.

———

The sun shone brightly, and the summer air felt warm and inviting as they set out one morning in early July. Jim led the procession, riding his spotted horse. Amanda and Mary followed on their horses, with Little Joe strapped safely to Mary's back in his cradleboard. Behind them were Amanda's two pack mules, Jake and Jasper, loaded down with some of their supplies and all of Jim's furs. Amanda's father's horse went too, carrying the rest of their things. Alongside Mary's spotted horse, Thunder ran friskily along, barking at every squirrel or small critter he managed to stir up.

Amanda smiled. She was glad Jim had agreed to Mary's request to take the dog with them. It seemed that Jim was much more pleasant these days. Their little boy had tamed his daddy quite a bit. Jim had begun to ask Amanda more questions about the Bible too. She hoped it was just a matter of time before he would open his heart fully to the Lord.

At midday they stopped beside a narrow creek where the water ran clear and swift. The warm sun had been beating down on their heads all morning, and the baby was starting to get fussy. Amanda was certainly ready for a break from riding and a refreshing drink of cold water. It had been several weeks since she'd been on horseback, and it would take a few days to get accustomed to being in the saddle again.

She watched as Mary unlashed the cradleboard and handed Little Joe down to his father. They both seemed in good spirits.

Jim knelt by the creek and sponged the baby's face with a piece of cloth he'd dipped in the cool, refreshing water. Mary and Amanda knelt at the creek beside him. Amanda splashed some cold water on her face and rubbed the back of her neck. Then she cupped her hands and took a long, invigorating drink. Her dry, parched throat felt the welcome relief that only clean water could provide.

"Guess we should've stopped sooner," Jim said. "I plumb forgot that women and babies need to stop more often. I've been used to bein' on my own for so long, reckon I don't always think straight about some things."

Mary smiled at him. "We be fine now. Cool water refreshing."

Amanda watched as Thunder, the horses, and the mules took their share of water from the creek. Then she sat on the grassy bank and drew in a deep breath. It felt good to stop and rest awhile. Thankfully, since she wore her father's trousers under her dress, she was able to ride like Jim and Mary rather than sidesaddle. She almost wished her clothing was made from animal skins, being so much softer than her own, but she'd have to make do.

Amanda turned her gaze from the water back to Jim. He was playing peekaboo with Little Joe and had the baby laughing at his funny antics. Mary sat nearby, watching with a smile. There was no doubt in Amanda's mind—the baby had changed this couple's lives. Jim had become gentler and much kinder since the birth of Little Joe, and Mary seemed more content and at peace with herself. Little Joe seemed to fill a special place in Jim's heart, just as he did in Mary's.

Amanda's thoughts were interrupted when Jim touched Mary's arm and announced, "We'd best be goin' now."

"Me feed Joseph first, then be ready to travel," Mary said, taking the child from his father.

They set up camp that night near another gently flowing stream. Jim busied himself building a fire and putting up a small lean-to, while Mary and Amanda got supper started. The clearing where they'd made camp was surrounded by tall trees. The pine and fir were a deep, verdant green, and they gave off a woodsy scent that brought a heady sense of peace and tranquility. It was so pleasant that Jim found himself wishing they could build a new cabin and stay right there. A slight breeze blew through the pines, giving it a whispering, soothing sound. Crickets soon chimed in, making their camp seem one with nature.

Jim usually had no trouble sleeping during the night in the wilderness, and he hoped the womenfolk would adjust quickly too. For him, all it took was a day of fresh clean air, and when he bedded down, he was asleep before he knew it. This time might be a little different, having the women and baby along. Although Jim needed the rest, he wouldn't allow himself to fall into a deep sleep in case something unwelcome ventured into their camp. What was more, it was a comfort to have Thunder along, because Jim knew the dog would alert him to any danger that might be out there, lurking, because in the wilderness most anything could happen.

By the time they'd eaten their evening meal and were getting ready to retire for the night, a light rain had begun falling.

"No wonder everything is so green around here," Jim said. "Hope it's just a short summer shower and doesn't last too long." A gentle rain could turn torrential in a matter of minutes and change an easy-flowing stream into a raging river.

Morning came slowly, with a dull gray sky hanging over the area. Little light filtered through the thick cloud cover. There was still a steady drizzle of cool rain, and Jim was anxious to get started. They'd been lucky so far that the rain hadn't turned heavy. He wished they didn't have to travel in the rain, but not knowing how long it would last, he didn't want to wait around the campsite any longer. So far, good fortune had been with them.

Jim was glad he'd brought his family along on this trip. He found himself enjoying Mary's company more all the time. He even had visions of them having more children, raising them in the serenity of the mountains, and teaching them the ways of wilderness survival.

He wasn't sure how, or even when it had happened, but Jim had allowed himself to fall in love with the Indian woman who had put up with his cantankerous ways and had given him a son. Not only did she cook and perform other household chores, she also did the tedious job of stretching and scraping the beaver and otter pelts he trapped. The young Indian woman was a hard worker, and Jim felt fortunate to have married her when he did. Though he didn't love Mary the same way he'd loved Lois, she was a friend and companion for life, and he hoped they would have many good days together in the years to come. Maybe one day she would love him too.

They traveled about fifteen miles that morning, and the rain continued. Very little was said as they rode along; their horses' hooves plodding through the mud. Little Joe slept soundly in his cradleboard, lulled by the gentle sway of the horse's gait and the sound of the rain.

Jim could tell his son would grow up to become a strong man. He thought about how Mary had chosen Little Joe's Indian name, Little Wolf. The wolf symbolized strength and endurance, along with intelligence as part of its instinct. Jim would teach his son all these principles, and if he taught them well, Little Joe would grow to be an honorable man, respected by all who would come to know him.

Jim's thinking shifted to the price he would get for his furs and pelts at the Rendezvous. The American Fur Company would be there, ready to pay good money for high quality furs and hides. He had a family to think of now and needed to provide for them in the best way possible.

Later that afternoon, Jim heaved a sigh of relief when the rain finally let up and the sun showed itself. The air was still humid, and a light fog drifted up the path, but it would make for easier traveling now that the rain had quit.

Jim thought about Mary again and hoped that she wouldn't decide to run off if her family was at the Rendezvous. He had a hankering to tell his wife a few things that had been on his mind today, but she looked awful tired, so what he had to say could wait till tomorrow.

Chapter 27

The sun streamed into the makeshift tent Jim had erected, where the flap had been folded back to let in some fresh air. Pushing her lightweight blanket aside, Mary rose from her mat, being careful not to disturb her sleeping son. She noticed that Amanda was already up and stirring around their campsite. Jim was not in the tent, and she wondered where he could be when the sun had barely risen.

He'd probably taken a walk or gone to the river to wash up. She would help Amanda with breakfast, and by the time it was ready, Jim would no doubt be back, hungry and ready to eat.

"Have you been to Rendezvous before?" Amanda asked as she placed the coffeepot over the hot coals.

Joining her friend at the campfire, Mary nodded. "Went with family sometimes."

"What's it like?"

"Many trappers. Also Indians. Men. Women. Children. Everyone go." Mary smiled, remembering the things she and her family had seen at the Rendezvous. "People sing, dance, tell lots of stories. Trappers trade and sell furs. Lots to look at. Lots to buy and sell. I like pretty beads."

"It sounds like an interesting event," Amanda said. "I'm looking forward to going." She touched Mary's arm. "But when I leave there, I shall miss you, my friend. It's like you are family, and I have known you for a long time. I will miss our long talks, and the time we've spent reading the Bible. Now that you have accepted Jesus as your Savior, our hearts are linked through the love of God." She glanced over at the baby, sleeping in his cradleboard. "And I'll miss Little Joe something awful."

"You wish to have a baby of your own?" Mary asked, rubbing her hands close to the fire. Since they were working their way down to the Rendezvous site in the valley, it was a little warmer than mornings up in the mountains. Even so, it was a bit chilly, and the warmth of the fire felt good.

"Someday I would like to be a mother," Amanda said, "but I'd have to find a good husband first, and I'm not really looking for one."

"You wish to marry strong mountain man?"

Amanda laughed. "Not necessarily, but he would have to be a Christian."

"Believe in God, like you?"

"Yes, he must be a believer, and someone I can trust."

"Buck no good husband then," Mary said, slowly shaking her head. "He not even want to hear about God."

"I know." Amanda's shoulders slumped. "I had hoped to reach him with the Gospel before I left Jim's cabin, but I guess it wasn't meant to be. I will pray that God will soften Buck's heart. Who knows? Maybe someone else will come into Buck's life, and they'll be able to reach him."

Jim had enjoyed a few minutes of solitude at the river as he washed up and spent some time alone with God. Last night Jim had seen Lois in a dream. She'd encouraged him to make peace with God, confess his sins, and acknowledge His Son, Jesus. Kneeling at the river, Jim had done just that this morning, and now he felt like a new man, ready to be the kind of father and husband God intended him to be.

Jim hadn't told Mary yet, but he'd decided that before winter set in, making it difficult to travel, he would take her and Little Joe to see her family at their winter home along the Clearwater River in Oregon Territory. As soon as he got back to the camp, he was going to surprise her with the news. *Maybe I'll even agree to act as Amanda's guide and take her to the Spalding Mission,* he decided. *From what I've been told, it's not far from where the Nez Percé camp.*

He dried his face on a piece of cloth, and was about to start back for camp, when a sudden chill went up his spine. He cocked his head to one side and listened. It was a dreaded noise that he'd hoped he'd never hear. The unmistakable vibration of a rattlesnake's tail caused him to look down. He held very still, watching the coiled snake a few inches from his foot and wondering why he hadn't seen it before. They weren't up in the higher elevations anymore, and Jim scolded himself for not watching for this type of danger more common in the valleys.

As though it could sense the danger, Jim's horse, hobbled several feet away, whinnied loudly. It was then Jim realized his gun was tied securely to one of the packs on the horse's back. If he'd been carrying it, he could have shot and killed the rattler with no hesitation. That left him with only two choices. He could back away slowly from the snake and hope it didn't strike before he reached his gun, or remain still and pray that the reptile would crawl away in the opposite direction.

His hands grew sweaty, and the muscles in his legs tightened as he contemplated what to do. After a moment's hesitation, Jim chose to back away slowly, but not before he sent up a quick prayer.

The snake lunged forward. The bite came hard and fast against Jim's ankle, and he winced in pain as the reptile's fangs sank in. It was too late for caution. Jim turned and started for his horse, but not before the snake caught him again, on the other ankle.

Jim was wet with perspiration by the time he reached Wind Dancer, and his ankles were growing more painful with every passing moment. He grabbed the gun and prepared to fire, but the snake had slithered away and was out of sight. He had to get to Mary, for she would know just what to do.

Jim threw himself into the saddle, urging his horse into a full gallop. There was no time to waste. The double dose of poison would travel fast.

I should've taken my knife and bled the wounds, he thought. *Well, Mary can tend to the bites with my knife and her healing herbs.*

Mary had just taken a pan of trout Jim had caught yesterday off the open fire, when Jim rode quickly into their camp. One look at her husband's ashen face told her immediately that something was wrong.

Jim dismounted and limped toward Mary. "What is it, Jim? Are ya hurt?" she asked, fear mounting in her chest.

"It was a rattler. He got me good!"

Amanda gasped.

"Did ya bleed wound?" Mary asked.

Jim shook his head. "Came right here. Ya need to tend it. The pain's really bad, and I feel weak and woozy."

"Lie down in tent," she instructed. "I do what I can."

Jim took off his moccasins and pulled up his right pant leg to expose the first snake bite, which was a little above the ankle. The area was severely swollen, and Jim was sweating profusely. Mary was afraid he might pass out, and she hoped she could keep him conscious.

"Mary," he murmured, lying on one of the mats. "I've gotta tell ya somethin'."

"No talk now," she told him sternly, moving toward her satchel of provisions. "Lie still."

"No! I need to say this now." Jim sounded desperate, as he reached his hand out to her.

Mary knelt next to him. "Speak if ya must, Husband." Maybe it would be better for him if he kept talking.

"I got right with God this morning, Mary. And I'm sorry for it now, but I've blamed God all these years for the death of my first wife." Jim's eyes glazed over as he looked at Amanda, who had knelt on the other side of him. "That's why I wouldn't let ya talk to me about the Bible at first."

"I understand, but if you have made things right with God and confessed your sins, then you have nothing to worry about now," Amanda said in a comforting tone.

Jim sucked in a ragged breath as he looked back at Mary. "I love ya, Mary, and if I live, then I'm gonna take you and Little Joe to see your family. I was anxious to tell ya that as soon as I got back, but wasn't figurin' on it goin' like this."

Mary swallowed around the lump in her throat. Jim's words had touched her soul. "I love you, Jim, but now I must tend wound."

With trembling hands and a heart full of mixed emotions, Mary heated Jim's knife over the flames of the fire. She could hardly believe he actually loved her, or that he planned to take her to see her family. Why did this accident have to happen now, when things were finally going so well?

When Mary returned to Jim's side, she noticed that the snake bite on his exposed leg was more red and swollen than when he'd first arrived back at their camp. She knew what must be done, and quickly made the incision. Then she proceeded to suck and spit out the poisonous venom. By the time she'd finished the unpleasant task, Jim's eyes had rolled back in his head, and his body began to convulse. He was soaked in sweat, and pale—so very pale.

Mary hurried to her parfletch and got out some willow bark to make a tea that would hopefully ease the pain and inflammation on his leg. Next, she made a poultice from plantain, which she placed on the bite. She tried to get Jim to drink the tea, but his body trembled so badly, he nearly choked on the liquid.

I have done all the things I know to do, she told herself. *Why isn't he responding?*

As Jim thrashed about, his other pant leg pulled up, and she discovered a second ugly wound. Quickly, she made another incision, sucked out the poison, and put a poultice on it. Once more she offered Jim some tea, while Amanda sat nearby, praying out loud.

Throughout the rest of the day and into the night, Mary tended to Jim, while Amanda continued to pray and take care of Little Joe. Thunder stayed close at hand, going to Jim and lying by his side.

Early the next morning, as the sun peeked over the horizon, Jim gasped his final breath.

"You cannot die!" Mary screamed. She placed her hand against his nose to feel for a breath. Nothing. She pressed her head against his chest and listened, but Jim's heart was silent.

"No! No!" she cried, throwing herself across his prostrate body.

Tears of despair coursed down Mary's cheeks. *Not now. This cannot be true!*

She lay sobbing for a long time, until Amanda's touch pulled her away. "You did everything you could for Jim. He's in God's hands now," Amanda soothed, gently patting Mary's back. "I'm so sorry for your loss."

Mary realized that Amanda was trying to comfort her, but she didn't want comfort. She wanted her husband—Little Joe's father. Jim was gone, and with him, their hopes and dreams for a future together.

CHAPTER 28

Amanda felt sick. What had started out as such a happy time had ended in disaster. It seemed she'd faced nothing but one mishap after the other ever since she'd left home. Was this what she could expect, living in the wilderness—things turning so quickly and changing her life forever?

Amanda glanced at Mary, solemnly swiping at the tears running down her cheeks. *What is to become of this young Indian woman and her son?* she wondered. *If only I could do something to ease her pain.*

Little Joe began to cry, and Mary rushed to her son, sweeping him possessively into her arms. She took a seat in the far corner of their tent, cradled the babe in her arms, and rocked back and forth as though in a trance.

Heavenly Father, Amanda prayed, *please give me the words to comfort Mary.*

Mary continued to sit and rock, singing a chant-like song. Amanda knew her friend needed to grieve in her own way, so she took one of the blankets, covered Jim's body, and moved away to sit near the fire.

After some time, Mary placed Little Joe, who had fallen asleep, back in the safety of his cradleboard. Then she turned to Amanda and said, "Need to bury Husband."

Amanda nodded. "I'll get a shovel from one of the packs."

After the women dug the grave, Amanda watched while Mary went to Jim's saddlebag and retrieved his favorite pipe. Then she walked over and tucked it in Jim's hand. Mary looked at Amanda, but no words were needed.

They pulled Jim's body to the site and placed it inside his permanent resting place, along with the pipe. When they'd scooped the last shovelful of dirt over the grave and topped it with several large stones, Amanda quoted a verse of scripture and said a prayer. Feeling that Mary needed a bit more time, she started singing:

"Amazing grace! How sweet the sound
That saved a wretch like me!
I once was lost, but now am found;
Was blind, but now I see.

"Thro' many dangers, toils, and snares
I have already come.
'Tis grace hath bro't me safe thus far,
And grace will lead me home."

When Amanda finished the last stanza and started to move away from the gravesite, Mary tore her tunic at the neck and fell to her knees. Dredging up handfuls of dirt, she rubbed it onto her hair, face, and arms. Mary ended the ritual by cutting a piece of her hair.

Amanda didn't understand the reason for this, but figured it must be an Indian custom for mourning the dead.

Mary grieved until Little Joe demanded to be fed again. Despite Amanda's coaxing, Mary had only eaten a little rabbit stew. She had no stomach for food, but she knew she needed to eat in order to have enough milk to nourish her son.

Mary wasn't sure if they should leave the campsite or stay another night. They couldn't stay here indefinitely. They were getting low on many of their supplies at the cabin, and she had all of Jim's fur pelts and hides to sell or trade. She really had only one choice if she hoped to provide for herself and Little Joe. They must go on to the Rendezvous.

It would be difficult to travel without Jim, but she was thankful for Amanda's company. They also had the protection of Jim's rifle, as well as Thunder, his faithful dog. When they reached the Rendezvous and had traded for the necessary supplies, she would take Amanda to the Spalding Mission. There was nothing for her and Little Joe at the cabin now. She needed to return to her people's winter home. She only hoped she could remember the way.

Mary had been taught as a child that moss grew on the north side of tree trunks. She also remembered her father saying, "If you ride with the rising sun on your left, keeping the mountains behind, you will be heading south."

She had done her calculations and felt sure they were traveling south, but how far they were from the Rendezvous site, she had no way of knowing. Making a decision to pack up and head out, Mary told Amanda they would stop often to water and rest the horses.

———

As they traveled the trail, the scorching sun soared high overhead, and the horizon stretched endlessly ahead. The heat of the day was almost unbearable, and beads of perspiration gathered quickly on Mary's forehead and trickled down her face. She wiped them away with the back of her hand, knowing if they didn't find water soon, they would be in big trouble.

Little Joe was her primary concern, but she could see from Amanda's weary expression that she needed rest and water too.

Mary leaned over her saddle and spoke to Thunder as he walked listlessly alongside her horse. From the way he was panting, it was obvious that he too was thirsty. "Find water!" Mary commanded. "Find water now!"

The dog seemed to understand, for he perked up his ears, wagged his tail, and quickly lit out on his own, disappearing among the dry sage brush.

They hadn't ridden far before the dog was back, barking loudly and urging them to follow.

Mary drove her mare forward, along with Jim's horse, which now carried some of the pelts. Amanda did the same, and the pack mules trailed slowly behind, in need of quenching their thirst.

Soon, they came to a stand of green trees near a small stream.

"Good dog!" Mary cried, relieved that at last they had finally come to water.

She and Amanda dismounted, and as Amanda led the animals to the stream, Mary removed Little Joe from his cradleboard and sponged him off with the cool water, allowing him to suck on a dampened piece of the clean cloth. Then she drank deeply of the cool, clear liquid, until her thirst was satisfied and she felt refreshed.

After Mary and Amanda hobbled the horses, they put up a lean-to and placed the baby underneath. Instructing Thunder to watch over Little Joe, Mary gathered an armload of firewood and started a campfire. For the first time all day she actually felt hungry. She even thought about taking Jim's gun and hunting for fresh game but felt uneasy about leaving Amanda and the baby alone, even with the reliable dog there to watch over them. She would have to make do with the dried rabbit left in her pack.

Mary placed a pot of water over the hot coals to boil, then tossed in several pieces of dried meat. She could still see Jim's ashen face as he lay dying on the mat under their tent. A tear slid down her cheek. She missed the rugged mountain man more than she'd ever thought possible.

If she'd been living among her people, Jim's face would have been painted red, his body washed, clothed in a new garment, and finally wrapped in a robe.

They needed Jim's horse for the Rendezvous journey, but if it had been a Nez Percé burial, his horse would have been killed and left close to the gravesite. The deceased's personal valuables were also placed in the grave, which was why Mary had put Jim's favorite pipe in his hand.

Had Mary been living among her people, she'd now be entering a yearlong mourning period. She'd cut her hair very short and wear old clothes until the year passed. Mary had decided not to cut her hair short, because they were heading to the Rendezvous. Remembering the type of men that showed up there, Mary didn't want to lead anyone to believe that she was without a husband.

She lifted her gaze toward the sky. *Hanyawat, why did you take*

Jim away from us now, when Little Joe and I need him so much? Despite her pain, she had to be strong and courageous. Little Joe needed her, and so did Amanda. She would do whatever it took to survive and to provide for their needs.

———

Amanda couldn't believe they had made it this far. Especially with what seemed like hours without water. Thank goodness Thunder was a smart dog and had led them to this lifesaving stream. Already she missed the cool air high in the Rockies. Sweat made her clothing stick to her all day. Oh, what she wouldn't give for a cool, refreshing bath. There was no way she was going to do that, however. She'd have to be content as she lay there looking up at the stars. The night air was cooling off some, so for that she was thankful.

Amanda couldn't help wondering about Buck. *If only he had agreed to travel with us, maybe Jim wouldn't have gotten bit by that rattlesnake.* Amanda figured Buck would have most likely been with Jim when it happened, and he might even have killed the snake before it struck. Hearing from Mary about Buck's skills, Amanda knew something like that would never have gotten by him unnoticed.

Was Buck back at his cabin thinking about her? If he was, they probably weren't good thoughts. She'd been a nuisance to him, and obviously he felt the more distance he could put between them, the better it would be for him.

Amanda fell asleep, wishing once more that there had been some way to guide Buck's path to the Lord. Somehow she'd failed. All she could do for Buck now was pray—pray that he would open his heart to the truth.

CHAPTER 29

As Mary and Amanda continued their travels over the next few days, a sense of foreboding and uneasiness come over Mary. She chided herself for fretting, yet the unsettling feelings remained. She neither saw nor heard anything unusual, but her concerns intensified with each step they took. Were they riding into some kind of danger? Could it be that some hostile Indians were nearby or maybe a wild animal, hidden by brush and waiting to attack? Was Hanyawat or her guardian spirit trying to warn her?

Mary thought about Buck and wished that he was with them. He would have offered them protection; she was sure of that.

They rode on, but when Mary didn't see or hear anything out of the ordinary, she decided that perhaps her irrational fears were just from missing Jim so much. She took a deep breath, in an attempt to clear her head. *I am a Nez Percé, and I will get through this. I have been through far worse, and we will make it.*

Dusk was settling over the land, and deep purple shadows engulfed the dense forest. A cool evening breeze blew softly against Mary's face, and she relaxed in her saddle for the first time all day. Perhaps there was no danger after all.

As they mounted the crest of a hill, they saw the site of the Rendezvous along the Green River basin in the valley below them. Mary sat taller in her saddle, feeling proud that they'd actually made it. She looked over at Amanda, who also sat higher in her saddle. *Her father must be proud if he is watching from above,* Mary thought.

With the Rockies behind them and the valley below them, they could see for miles—as far as their sight could reach. Their horses snorted, with nostrils flaring, no doubt getting wind of the fresh grasses below from the recent rains.

Smoke curled up from different areas of the site, and the smell of food reached Mary's senses, making her mouth water. She heard Amanda smack her lips and knew that she too must be hungry. Their horses grew restless, pawing at the dirt, no doubt anxious to feed on the valley grasses.

After a short rest, Mary and Amanda urged their mounts forward. As they drew closer to the compound, Mary thought it was strange that there were no clusters of teepees camped in the open area. Though she had only been to a few Rendezvous, she remembered that the white trappers who went there always camped in canvas tents or teepees, as did the Indians. Maybe she was mistaken. Perhaps this was not the Rendezvous site after all. They could have been heading in the wrong direction all this time, and this could be some other compound. Surely if this was the place of Rendezvous, there would be white men and Indians roaming everywhere.

Mary knew the only way to know for sure was to ride in, but a sudden wave of fear washed over her. She longed to have Jim by her side, but no amount of wishing would change the sobering fact that her husband was dead.

Little Joe started to cry, and Amanda looked at Mary expectantly. "Is everything all right?"

"I-I am not sure." Mary tried to reassure her baby with soft, comforting words, but it was obvious that he sensed her fear.

There were a few men milling around, and they gave Mary and Amanda a curious stare. She wasn't sure if it was because they seldom saw two women riding in alone, or if it was because of the squalling baby, strapped to her back. Nevertheless, neither of the women made eye contact. Just seeing some of those men and the way they'd looked at them, made Mary uneasy.

She halted her horse and asked one of the men for directions to the main post. He pointed to the largest of the log structures, and she nodded and stopped the horses at the hitching rail. She instructed Thunder to stay outside, then taking her crying son down from his cradleboard, she and Amanda entered the post.

Mary had to let her eyes adjust to the dimness as they entered the wooden building. The door closed behind them, making her and Amanda both jump. The only light streamed in from one window. As Mary's eyes took in the interior, she saw that there were just a few men inside, and one of them was sitting in front of a huge stone fireplace with his feet propped up on an empty supply crate. Figuring he must be the man in charge, Mary gathered up her courage and stepped up to him. "This be the place for Rendezvous?"

With barely a glance in her direction, he mumbled, "Rendezvous was supposed to be here, but it was moved farther south to a clearing called Horse Creek. It's along the Green River too, and you know what?" Without waiting for her reply, he said, "You're the second person in here today askin' about it."

"How far it be?" Mary asked.

The man spit his chewing tobacco into the fireplace, and flames sizzled as it made contact. "Reckon it's about half a day's ride from here. Too bad ya didn't get here a might sooner. The trapper that was here earlier was headin' there too. You and your party coulda rode with him."

Mary didn't feel inclined to tell him that except for her, Amanda, and Little Joe, she had no party. It would be safer if none of the men knew they were traveling alone. So she merely nodded and said, "Thank you." Then she and Amanda left the building and hurried toward their waiting horses.

That evening, as Amanda and Mary directed their horses to the wide green meadow covered with ample grass and surrounded by trees, Mary announced that this had to be Horse Creek clearing. Campsites with Indian and trapper's teepees and canvas tents stretched as far as the eye could see. How many different Indian tribes were represented here, Amanda could not be certain, but there were a lot of them.

Wagonloads of supplies, mule trains packed with all kinds of dry goods, and canoes piled high with bundles of animal pelts filled the center of the clearing to overflowing. All around, white men dressed in buckskins, with long, shaggy hair and faces bronzed and weathered, milled about with Indians. Many could be seen drinking together or bartering. Some were engaged in fist-fighting brawls. Whiskey wagons were scattered around, and Amanda cringed when she noticed several men so drunk they staggered about. Some men were too liquored up to even stand, and those in this condition found beds on the ground wherever they chose. Other groups of men sat huddled together, playing cards or throwing dice for high stakes.

Amanda guided her horse around a drunken trapper who had stumbled out of a tent. She shuddered, wondering if she, Mary, and the baby would be safe here.

Mary stopped her horse in front of one of the Rocky Mountain Fur Company's supply wagons, dismounted, and went to speak to the man in charge, while Amanda stood near the horses. "Me have otter and beaver pelts to trade," she announced.

"If you've got enough, you can trade for whatever you like. Some prices are steep, but them beaver skins will bring ya a fair price, that's fer sure," the man replied.

Mary nodded. "Have many beaver pelts."

The man squinted at her through halfclosed eyelids. "Where's your man? Usually it's the man who brings in the furs for trading."

"He not here. Me do trading," she answered.

"Your man ain't with you, huh? Well, I'd be more'n happy to fill in for him," another man spoke up.

As Mary whirled around, Amanda stiffened. She thought they had seen the last of Seth Burrows, but apparently she'd been wrong.

His thin lips pressed into a sly grin as he spotted Amanda. "Hello again, purty lady."

Amanda's heart pounded. She hoped he wouldn't cause them any trouble.

"Well, why don't ya say somethin', or has the cat got your tongue?" Seth sneered at her. "Or maybe you're just so surprised to see old Seth that you're plumb dumb speechless." He glanced back at Mary and grinned. "Bet you're wonderin' how I survived with my leg bleedin' and me with no supplies." Without waiting for her to reply, he hurried on. "Well, it weren't easy at first, but lucky for me that I found my way into the campsite of a band of friendly Flathead Injuns. After tendin' to my leg, they gave me food, clothes, and all the supplies I needed, including a horse. I holed up with 'em awhile, till I was able to be on my way again."

Amanda noticed that Seth was dressed in a new leather shirt, decorated with quills and beaded embroidery. It was probably one he'd been given by the Flatheads. His thick, pitted face was coarse with the growth of a new beard, and his hair was matted and uncombed.

Mary said something in her native tongue and started to walk away from the vulgar man, but he reached out a grimy hand and caught her by the shoulder. "Now jest where do ya think you're goin? I was talkin' to you and the purty white lady, and ya don't never turn your back on someone when they're conversin' with ya. Why, it just ain't polite!"

"Please, Mr. Burrows, leave us alone," Amanda pleaded. "We want no trouble from you."

Ignoring Amanda's request, he tightened his grip on Mary's arm. "Say, where is that mountain man of yours anyways? Did he get fed up and boot ya outta his cabin?" He eyed their pack mules. "Or maybe you just ran out on him and robbed the poor fellow blind."

Why doesn't someone come to our defense? Amanda wondered. *Don't they even care that this man is harassing us?*

Thunder had been waiting patiently by the horses, but he leaped forward and gave Seth a low, warning growl. The hair on the dog's back bristled, and Amanda wondered if he remembered the man's voice. Thunder's lips curled back, showing his sharp white teeth, never once taking his eyes off the vile man. All Mary had to do was give Thunder the signal, and his teeth would sink into Seth's skin, just like before.

"Call your dog off now, or I'll shoot him dead!" Still holding on to Mary, Seth gripped his rifle with his other hand.

Please, Lord. Please help us, Amanda fervently prayed.

CHAPTER 30

Be still, Thunder. Man will not hurt us," Mary said as calmly as possible. She did not wish to let Seth know how afraid she was, nor did she want to create any trouble that might interfere with her trading.

Seth laughed, an evil and sadistic sound. "Now, that all depends on whether ya cooperate with me or not. If your man ain't about, then I guess you'll be needin' some male company."

He gave her a quick wink and grinned wickedly. "I came from the original site for Rendezvous yesterday, and I know for a fact that supplies worth thousands of dollars were brought here by the St. Louis Fur Company. The old man at the fort said so." He motioned to the supply wagon nearby. "Now, with all them supplies available, you'll be needin' to trade off your beaver pelts to get some necessary things. Supplies is high priced, and a body's gotta know how to barter real good, or else you'll get took. I figure a dumb woman like you don't know much about tradin' or barterin'. For half of everything you've got, I'll act as your interpreter." He winked at Mary again.

She stiffened. Her determined gaze moved to his hardened face. "I speak white man talk. No need to talk for me."

"Is that right? Well, when you've had a taste of my sweet lips, I think you'll change your mind." He puckered his beefy lips and made a boisterous kissing sound.

The men who stood around hooted with laughter. It was the fuel Seth needed to continue, for he released Mary's arm and reached out his callused hand to stroke one of her long braids. "Ya can play hard to get all ya want; it makes no difference to me. If your man ain't here, then you're fair game for anyone who's man enough to take ya."

Seth grabbed Mary's arm and jerked her so roughly that Little Joe, who was strapped to the cradleboard on her back, began to cry. Mary recoiled, remembering the last time they'd seen Seth and the way he'd treated her and Amanda.

The men standing nearby laughed even harder.

"Now look what you've done," one of them called. "Ya made her papoose start to bawl!" He made a howling sound, mimicking the baby's cries.

"Stop!" Mary shouted, shaking her fist at him.

"Leave us alone!" Amanda cried from where she stood nearby.

Holding his rifle with one hand, Seth lifted her chin roughly with the other. He bent down and placed a smothering kiss forcefully against her mouth.

Mary pulled away angrily and spit in the evil man's face.

He responded by slapping her hard across the face. Then he turned to the crowd and hollered, "Hey, friends, have any of ya ever kissed a woman whose lips don't move? Well, maybe ya oughta try it sometime!"

The men laughed uproariously, but their mirth was quickly interrupted by the sudden appearance of a horse and rider.

A young mountain man sat straight and tall on the back of his horse, a compelling silhouette with the sun at his back. His dark eyes, barely visible under his hat, flashed angrily. "Let the woman go!" he shouted.

Mary looked up at the man and felt pure relief. Buck McFadden, tall and rigid, looked as if he was waiting for Seth to make a wrong move. He had come to their rescue yet again.

"This ain't none of your business, boy, but if ya really want to make it so, then get on down from that horse of yours, and we'll settle this matter man to man!" Seth bellowed.

"Leave the women alone, and there won't be any trouble," Buck said, squinting his brown eyes into slits as he dismounted his horse.

"No way! This one's comin' with me." Seth clutched Mary's arm even tighter. "Now, if ya don't wanna fight, get outta here right now!"

Some of the men who moments ago had encouraged Seth, cowered back and made a wide berth around the two opponents. Others lit pipes and stood smirking, as if hoping for a good fight to begin. Still others reached deep into their pockets, bringing out money to place bets.

Buck gave Seth a piercing look; then his gaze darted quickly to Amanda, whose face had turned ashen. Turning to face Seth and Mary again, he said sternly, "Let her go!"

Seth shook his head. "No way! She's mine for the takin', and ya ain't stoppin' me this time."

"Ah, let her be," one of the onlookers hollered. "There ain't no sense in gettin' into a fight that might lead to someone's death or could get ya kicked outta Rendezvous, all because of some purty woman."

"Women ain't nothin' but trouble anyways—especially an Injun," another man spoke up. "Besides, if ya take her, you'll be strapped with the brat kid."

Seth relaxed a bit and shrugged his broad shoulders. "Guess you're right about that. This woman ain't worth much anyhow." He eyed Amanda, who was visibly shaking. "I'll have a chance some other time with you, purty lady, just ya wait and see." He leaned close to Mary. "Why don't ya go on back to your man—wherever he may be?" He said it loudly, as though for the benefit of those who were listening. Then, in a hoarse whisper he mumbled, "This ain't the end of it though. Remember these words: You two women ain't seen nor heard the last of old Seth Burrows."

CHAPTER 31

Amanda trembled as she watched Seth turn and walk away with a group of other uncouth men. She could almost feel Buck's eyes upon her, and that made her quiver even more. She swallowed hard and forced herself to look at him.

Buck studied Amanda as though he was seeing her for the very first time. Then he reached out and placed a gentle hand on her arm.

She swallowed hard and fought against the burning tears that threatened to spill over. Whether it was from fright or anger over what had happened to Mary, a few of the tears escaped and trickled down. Just the mere fact that Buck was standing here was enough to make her cry. She felt ever so grateful he'd shown up when he did.

Buck went to Mary. "Did he hurt you?"

Mary rubbed her arm where Seth had held her in his grip. "I be fine now. I glad you are here."

Buck glanced around. "Where's Jim? Why wasn't he here to defend you and Amanda?"

Mary's shoulders slumped as she lowered her head. "Jim dead."

Buck's eyes widened as he jerked his head and drew in a sharp breath. "Wh–what happened?"

Mary explained about the rattlesnake bites. "I try to save him, but it be too late. Amanda and me bury Jim's body and come to Rendezvous with his furs."

Buck looked questioningly at Amanda, and she nodded. "It was a shock to both of us."

He rubbed the heel of his palm against his chest. "This is bad news. I feel a great sadness in my heart hearing this." His mouth twisted grimly. "Jim was like a big brother to me. I-I will miss him very much."

"Me also," Mary said, her voice trembling.

Amanda's heart went out to them, knowing firsthand how hard it was to lose a loved one. She too felt the loss of the intimidating man. In good time, Jim had softened up to her, and Amanda had felt safer with him around.

"What will ya do now?" Buck questioned.

"Sell Jim's furs," Mary replied. "Then head to winter home near Lapwai Creek." She reached over her shoulder and touched the cradle-board holding her son. "I need to see family. Little Joe need to meet grandparents."

Amanda blinked. This was the first time since Jim's death that Mary had mentioned going home to her people. "Does that mean you will accompany me to the Spalding Mission?" she asked.

Mary nodded. "Me, you, Little Joe, and Thunder. We all go west when done here at Rendezvous."

Buck shook his head vigorously. "That's not a good idea, Mary. It wouldn't be safe for you to travel without a man."

"We have no man," Mary said. "Have Jim's gun and dog for protection."

"Huh-uh. I won't allow it," Buck insisted. "If you're set on goin', then I'll be traveling with ya. The least I can do for my friend Jim is to make sure his family is kept safe." He glanced at Amanda. "But there's one thing I need to make clear."

"What's that?" she asked.

"You can read your Bible and pray all ya want, but there's to be no preachin' on this trip. At least not to me," he quickly added.

That will be hard, Amanda thought. But having Buck travel with them to show the way and offer protection was an answer to prayer. She met his gaze. "I shall not say one word about the Bible or God, unless you ask me first."

"That ain't never gonna happen," he shot back.

We'll have to wait and see about that. Amanda looked at Mary and said, "In the meantime, I think we should find a place to put up our tent for the night, because I am tired, and I'm sure you and the baby are as well."

Mary nodded. "We sleep good tonight. Trade furs in the morning."

Mary made sure that Joseph's cradleboard was tied securely to her back, then she mounted her mare. Amanda did the same. Leading the pack mules and the other two horses, they rode through the camps of white men and Indians alike. Mary was uncertain of where to set up their camp. She knew they must find a place where they'd feel safe from Seth Burrows, so she couldn't risk putting up their tent in a secluded area where they'd be by themselves.

They ended up stopping in front of a band of Flatheads, since Mary knew they had always been friendly with her people. She dismounted and spoke to one of the Indian men in sign language, asking if they might be welcome to camp among them. The man nodded and pointed to a small clearing where they could set up their tent. Buck pitched his tent close by and went to tend the horses. Mary would go to bed feeling safer than she had since the death of her husband. How thankful she was that Buck had shown up. Deep down, she knew it would not be safe for her and Amanda to travel alone, but she would have done it if necessary. She would do anything to be back with her family. She only hoped they would be happy to see her and would accept Little Joe.

While the women got some grub together, Buck took care of the horses and pack mules, watching as they munched hungrily on the grasses. It was good to be around Mary and Amanda again, and his stomach growled loudly, eager for food. But Buck needed some time alone with thoughts of his good friend Jim.

How could this have happened? Jim was the one who had taught Buck everything he knew about survival in the mountains. "Always be conscious of your surroundings," Jim would say. "That's the best way to make sure you're safe."

Once, when they'd traveled to one of the forts together, Jim had saved Buck from a rattlesnake he hadn't noticed that was coiled near his feet. "Not all rattlers warn ya," Jim had said. "Some strike without givin' any kind of notice." Buck had never forgotten Jim's words, and it had saved him several times after that.

Could this be what happened to Jim? Buck wondered. *The rattler gave no warning?* He groaned. *If only I'd been with him. If I just hadn't left to hurry home to my cabin. If I'd agreed to travel to Rendezvous with 'em, maybe Jim would still be alive.*

It did no good to dwell on these things. All the "if onlys" got a person nowhere, especially when it came to death. He had learned early on that once something, or someone, took a person's life, that was the way it was, and no amount of praying or wishing could change the situation. It was hard to think about Little Joe growing up without his father, and Mary now without her husband.

Trying to shake off his negative thoughts, Buck watched twilight fall upon them. The first stars appeared overhead as the day's light slowly faded. Here in the valley, he could see far into the horizon. He looked back toward the mountains standing tall against the blackening sky.

After he'd healed from the bear attack, he'd longed to return home. Usually opening the door to his little cabin had been inviting, but this time, it felt empty and lonely. What was the difference from before, when the silence and solitude had always been most welcome? Buck knew the answer was right on his lips, and try as he might to repel the thoughts, his mind kept wandering to what it would be like to share his life with someone. He couldn't stop thinking about a woman being there to welcome him home each time he went out trapping. What would it be like to have a son of his own? Someone to teach all the things Jim had taught him. Buck even wondered how it would be to marry someone like Amanda. She sure was pretty. But it could never work. He had known right from the start that he couldn't live with someone as religious as her. Their views about things were too different. Better to just be friends, and nothing more.

The smell of food cooking reached Buck's nostrils, and Thunder came to stand by his feet. "Is it time to eat, ol' boy?" Buck asked, reaching down to pet the dog's head.

As if understanding what Buck had said, Thunder turned in a circle, then headed back to the campsite where Amanda and Mary had a fire going. Thunder woofed a couple of times, as though to make sure that Buck was following.

"I'm comin'!" Buck called. He checked on the horses one more time and headed for the campsite. *All I need to do is get Amanda to the mission,* he decided. *Then there will be no more thoughts of her.*

Chapter 32

When morning dawned with a bright, full sun, many Indians and trappers had already begun to make their way back to the main camp, where traders had set out their goods and were anxiously awaiting the first buyers of the day.

Mary decided to try to make her trades so they could be on their way. She had no plans to stay until Rendezvous was over, as so many others in attendance would do. She wanted to leave as soon as possible. That way, hopefully no one would follow them. Buck had gone hunting for fresh game, and Amanda had agreed to watch Little Joe while Mary was at the main camp trading her furs. After the encounter they'd had with Seth Burrows the day before, she knew better than to put her son in a dangerous position again. If trading went well, they could leave and get as far away as possible from that man.

Mary made sure that Jim's gun was with her this time. She would be ready to take on anyone who might offer trouble, for she had too much to live for now.

In a flurry of frenzied activity, furs of all kinds were either being sold or traded for guns, ammunition, traps, blankets, tools, and various food supplies.

Just as Mary was finishing up with her business, she heard loud, obnoxious laughter. She turned and saw Seth Burrows heading her way.

Instinctively, her hand tightened over the rifle she held by her side. She was fully prepared to shoot the man, but only if it became necessary.

"I see you're still tryin' to peddle your furs. Need some help now, do ya?" Seth asked, grinning slyly as he stepped up to her.

185

"I need no help," Mary answered firmly.

"Now look here, I'm gettin' a little fed up with all your sass! I'm thinkin' that trapping beaver is a sight easier then figurin' out a woman, especially one like you. I thought maybe ya might be glad to see me, seein' as to how your man don't seem to be around. Maybe you don't have a man a'tall. Is that how it is?"

Before Mary could offer a reply, Seth pulled a knife from his sheath and held it next to her side. "I've been denied the pleasure of your company before, and I won't be deprived of it again. I aim to take ya as my woman, so there ain't no use in fightin' it." The ill-bred man smiled wickedly. "I'm glad to see ya ain't got that brat kid of yours with ya today, 'cause you're goin' with me!"

Seth held the tip of the knife against Mary's back, and she knew it would be impossible to raise her rifle and fire without being stabbed. She looked around helplessly, hoping someone might see what was happening and come to her aid. Everyone appeared to be engrossed in their trading business. No one seemed to care that she was about to either be killed or taken at knifepoint. No one except for her faithful dog.

Thunder, who had been standing on the other side of Mary, let out a low, throaty growl. Seth pulled his knife back momentarily, as he took a moment to glance at the dog.

In that brief instant, Thunder leaped at the man, toppling them both to the ground. It was impossible for anyone in the area to ignore the man and dog rolling around in the dirt. Thunder growled and snapped, while Seth cursed between gasps of ragged breath.

Mary raised her gun but held her fire. She could not run the risk of hitting Thunder instead of the evil man so she would wait until she could get a clearer shot.

"Do not shoot him, Mary! That would be murder!"

Mary turned. Amanda stood directly behind her, holding Little Joe. Next to her stood Buck, rifle in hand. Suddenly, Seth cried out. Mary looked back at her enemy on the ground. A deathly silence hung in the air, as the dog moved slowly away from Seth's unmoving body.

Mary gasped when she saw that Seth's own knife was stuck firmly into his chest. In trying to slay her dog, he'd fallen against his weapon.

"Is he dead?" one of the traders asked in a casual sort of way.

"Looks like it. He don't seem to be breathin'," another man said, as he bent down for a closer look. He placed his hand on Seth's bleeding chest. "Nope. There ain't no heartbeat a'tall."

Amanda could hardly believe that Seth Burrows lay dead on the ground, and no one seemed to care. Apparently these ill-bred men needed the Lord as much as—or even more than—the Indians she felt compelled to minister to.

Two men stepped forward and carried the body away. The others carried on with their business, as if nothing out of the ordinary had just happened. Apparently Seth Burrows had no friends among these crude mountain men.

"It is good that you did not take revenge on him, Mary," Amanda said. "Revenge is God's business, not ours."

Mary silently reached for Little Joe and held him tight.

Buck stood, shaking his head. "I'm sorry, Mary. I shoulda got here quicker. I came as soon as I got back from hunting and Amanda told me where you'd gone."

"I fine now, thanks to Thunder," Mary said.

As Amanda led Mary away from the crowd, Mary paused and said, "My dog. Must see to him. He could be wounded."

"I'll take a look," Buck offered. He bent to examine Thunder. "He ain't hurt, Mary," he said, smiling as he looked up at her.

Relieved, Mary called for Thunder to follow them.

"We no longer have anything to fear from that evil man, Mary. I am glad God kept you from taking revenge," Amanda said as they made their way back to their tent.

Buck snorted, but Mary gave no reply.

"God was watching over you, Mary. He cares for His children."

Still no response.

I hope Mary's faith isn't wavering, Amanda fretted. *Surely she must see that God's hand of protection was over her today. I am thankful Mary didn't shoot Seth.*

Even though Mary had confessed her sins and accepted Jesus as her Savior, she needed to learn more about God. In the days ahead as they traveled farther west, Amanda hoped to teach Mary many more things, and hopefully, Buck would learn them as well.

CHAPTER 33

Amanda slept better that night than she had in several weeks. The knowledge that Buck was sleeping outside their tent and had agreed to be their guide gave her a measure of hope and peace that she'd not had in many days. Instead of waking up every hour or so, thinking she'd heard something, Amanda slept until the sweet singing of birds awoke her.

She stepped from the tent, feeling renewed of body, mind, and spirit. Stretching, Amanda looked toward the sunrise and breathed in the dawn's cool air. It was a glorious morning, with a sky so bright and blue it nearly took her breath away. This place reminded her of the lake near her home in New York, where she had often gotten up early just to catch a glimpse of the sun rising, its soft colors reflecting in the water.

Amanda rubbed both arms. It was a bit chilly, but all too soon the day would warm up, and any shade they found would be most welcome.

She walked toward the campfire, fully expecting to see Buck stretched out by the log where he'd placed a sleeping mat the night before. To her surprise, he was not there. Neither was the buffalo hide he'd slept on. She scanned the area quickly, but there was no sign of Buck. The only evidence that he'd been there was the burning embers from the fire.

"I think Buck might be gone," Amanda said when Mary joined her. "Maybe he's decided not to take us to Oregon Territory after all."

Mary shook her head. "Buck not go back on his word. He straight-arrow."

Amanda's brows lifted. "Straight arrow? What does that mean?"

"He not lie. When Buck say he do something, he do it."

"Where is he then?"

"He say last night that he had furs yet to sell. He probably doing that now."

Amanda relaxed a bit. Maybe she just needed more patience. Taking a seat on a log near the fire and opening her Bible, she said, "Would you like to sit with me and listen to some Bible verses before we start breakfast?"

Mary shrugged. "It be okay I guess."

Amanda wished Mary would have shown more enthusiasm, but at least she hadn't said no. She opened her Bible to Proverbs and read from chapter 3: " 'Trust in the Lord with all thine heart; and lean not unto thine own understanding. In all thy ways acknowledge him, and he shall direct thy paths.' "

Mary tipped her head as though pondering things. "It be hard to trust when things go bad."

Amanda nodded. "You're right, but if we don't trust God, our faith begins to waver."

"Waver? What that mean?"

"It means we begin to doubt, and when we start doubting God, we become afraid," Amanda explained. "Sometimes when our faith wavers, we become sad and discouraged."

"Me sad when Jim die."

"I know. Life isn't always fair, and we need God to help us cope and get through the painful things that happen to us." Amanda clasped Mary's hand. "Let's pray." She bowed her head, and Mary did the same. "Heavenly Father," Amanda prayed, "comfort our hurting souls, offer us hope when there seems to be none, and give us the strength to live for You. Amen."

When Amanda opened her eyes, she noticed a slight movement in the trees bordering the campsite. Was it a deer or some other wild animal? She squinted, trying to get a better look, and then she saw Buck step into the clearing, wearing a buckskin shirt and leggings that reached mid-calf. His flowing red hair was tied behind his neck with a leather band.

She sat motionless as he approached, realizing that her heartbeat had quickened. When he reached her side, he handed her three small fish. "For our morning meal," he said, grinning.

Amanda took the fish, gratefully returning his smile. "Thank you. I'll begin cooking them at once." She turned toward the fire, but glanced back, seeing Buck still standing there watching her. Amanda whispered a prayer of thanks for Buck's kind gesture.

When breakfast was over, Buck reclined comfortably on a mat in front of the fire. He'd been up since dawn and hadn't slept well the night before. Thoughts of the two women who were in his charge had kept him from getting more than a few hours' sleep. That, coupled with the warmth of the fire and a full belly, made him feel drowsy and ready for a much-needed nap.

As noises and mutters from surrounding camps wafted over his mind, Buck drifted off. He hadn't been sleeping long, when the sound of Amanda's voice jolted him awake. He turned to look. She sat on a log a few feet to his right, her long, golden hair hanging freely down her back, cheeks pink and glowing. She looked at him expectantly, with blue eyes shimmering like pools of liquid sunshine scattered on a cloudless day.

Something indefinable passed between them, but Buck shrugged it away. *This will not be easy,* he thought. *The white woman has a way of looking at me, and seeing her every day until we get to the Spalding Mission could be my undoing.*

But what would become of Amanda and Mary if he didn't take them? They could die in the wilderness by themselves. Mary was tough and used to roughing it, but Amanda wasn't cut out for that kind of life. Buck was amazed that she had made it this far without giving up. Maybe she had as much courage as Mary did. He thought about the encounters the women had with Seth Burrows, and how he'd saved them the first time, and Thunder had interceded the second time. Buck wished he'd been there to see the whole thing. There could be other men like Seth out on the trail, not to mention the danger from wild animals and hostile Indians. The ordeal with Seth had reinforced in Buck the need to accompany the women to the Spalding Mission.

Mary, who'd been in the tent feeding the baby, joined them by the fire. "You trade furs yet, Buck?" she asked.

He shook his head. "I'll do it soon, and then we can be on our way."

"My people not go south until *Wa-Wa-Mai-Khal*," Mary said. "If we leave soon we be there when they arrive."

"Wa-Wa-Mai-Khal?" Amanda repeated.

"When summer is over and salmon spawn," Mary explained. "When they return to homeland, along Clearwater."

"I look forward to meeting your family," Amanda said, smiling at Mary. "I am sure they will be excited to see you."

Mary nodded. "It be good to see Gray Eagle's family too. They need know he died trying to help me."

"Will it be hard for you to tell 'em?" Buck asked.

Mary nodded.

"You loved Gray Eagle very much, didn't you?" Amanda questioned.

"No need talk about that now," Mary said, rising to her feet. "He dead, same as Jim." She slowly shook her head. "I will love no man again. They who love me end up dead." With a grunt, she disappeared into the tent.

Buck could see from the sorrowful look on Amanda's face that she felt Mary's pain. This woman of courage sitting close to him was also a woman who cared about people and was sensitive to their feelings. She was nothing like Silas Lothard. Was it possible that she really was a Christian, who lived by the Bible and not her own selfish ways? Well, even if she was, Buck had no desire to have religion crammed down his throat. Since he'd been on his own, Buck had done things his way. He saw no reason to change.

CHAPTER 34

Amanda and her companions had just ridden into a meadow dotted with delicate yellow and white wildflowers, when she glanced up at the sky and noticed how blue and beautiful it was. She was glad she had someone to share the glory of God's creation with. Since her father had died, she'd been lonely, but having Mary and now Buck to talk to had brightened her days. Then there was Mary's precious little boy. What a joy he was, and such a good baby too. He hardly cried or fussed, unless he needed to be fed. It was hard not to feel the desire to be married and have children of her own.

"You awfully quiet today. What you thinkin' about?" Mary asked, moving her horse beside Amanda's.

"Oh, just wondering how it would be if I had a husband and children of my own," Amanda answered honestly, swaying with the horse's smooth gait. She sighed. "But I've come to the conclusion that it's probably not meant to be."

"How come?"

"My call is to be a missionary, and I need to keep my focus on that."

"Can you be a miss-on-ary and wife at same time?" Mary questioned.

"I suppose, if I found a husband who shared my beliefs."

"Pretty woman like you find good husband. Husband give good bride price."

"I don't understand," Amanda said.

"Many horses given to bride's father."

Amanda smiled. "White people don't do it that way, Mary."

"How then?" Mary asked.

"The man first asks the woman to marry him; then he usually gets her parents' approval. When they marry, the bride sometimes has a dowry."

"What is dowry?"

"It can be money or personal property. A dowry is given to the man she marries."

Mary's forehead creased. "Whites have strange ways."

"Perhaps that is because you do not know us that well, and don't fully understand our ways."

"Many things about Husband I not understand. Jim hard to figure out, but he was good provider. He not like some white men. They act like they better than Indian." Mary frowned deeply. "Last night I have dream about white men taking our land."

"Oh Mary, I hope that dream never comes true," Amanda said with feeling. "It wouldn't be right for the white man to take what belongs to the Indians."

"May not be right, but I believe it happen." Mary slowly shook her head. "Sad day it will be though."

They continued their ride in silence for the better part of the day, and when they stopped for a much-needed rest and afternoon meal, the weather had turned unbearably hot, making Amanda feel irritable. She wished they could ride at a more leisurely pace, because keeping up with Buck's energetic horse all morning had been a challenge. Upon seeing the river only a few yards away, it was all she could do not to wade right in.

———

Buck watched as Amanda wiped the perspiration from her forehead, then fanned her face with the brim of her father's hat, which she'd worn today. Mary too looked overheated, as sweat beaded on her forehead as she sponged Little Joe with a wet cloth.

"Do ya wanna stay awhile longer, or start riding?" Buck asked, feeling concern for their welfare.

"It would be nice to stay awhile," Amanda admitted. "I know it's too early to stop for the night, but if I could just sit and dangle my feet in the river a few minutes, I'd feel better."

Buck nodded.

Amanda headed straight for the water and took a seat on a large, flat rock. After removing her boots and long stockings, she rolled the pant legs on her father's trousers up to her knees. Stretching out her bare legs, she let them dangle freely in the cool, refreshing water. Buck watched as Mary, with Little Joe strapped on her back, waded into the water.

"Water feel good," Mary said, smiling at Amanda.

"Yes, it sure does," Amanda replied.

Buck liked looking at the white woman, with eyes as blue as the sky, and he hated himself for it. He felt a physical attraction to her, but there was something more that went beyond fleshly appearance. Amanda seemed capable of looking into his soul, and that made Buck nervous, for he was afraid of what she might see. It was like she could tell what he was thinking. He continued to stare at Amanda as she closed her eyes. Buck knew that being out here in the hot sun could dull one's senses, unbalancing a person's thinking. *My senses must really be messed up,* he thought as he contemplated the idea of diving under the water, then sneaking up behind Amanda and pulling her in.

Buck had to turn away. The sooner he stopped thinking about her, the better it would be.

"Aren't you hot?" Amanda called to him.

He turned back to answer, hating to admit how refreshing the water looked and how much fun it would have been to frolic there beside her, but Buck's stubbornness outweighed his need to relax. "Not really, but there will be many hot days ahead, so cool down now while ya can," he said.

She smiled with a look of contentment. "I know it's not very ladylike, but this feels almost heavenly."

"Heavenly?" He moved closer, hunkering down next to her.

"You know about heaven, right?"

"I know about the Book of Heaven."

She shook her head, and gave the water a little kick with her toes.

"The Book of Heaven, as you call it, is the Bible. It's God's Holy Word. Heaven is where God the Father, and His Son, Jesus, live."

Buck's dark eyebrows shot up. "God lives in a book?"

Amanda laughed. "No, of course not. God lives in heaven."

Buck paused to watch Mary and Little Joe. Mary had unwrapped her son and was dipping him gently in and out of the water. They all laughed as the baby squealed with delight, sending up a spray as he kicked his little feet.

"My son soon swim like fish." Mary smiled as she swirled Little Joe in a circle. Soon his eyelids closed in slumber. "I wonder, where is heaven?" Mary questioned after she'd wrapped the boy up and put him back in the cradleboard.

"Actually," Amanda began, "no one really knows where heaven is. However, since men of old often climbed a high mountain to speak with God, and since Jesus returned to heaven in a cloud, it is believed that heaven is up there somewhere." She pointed toward the sky, squinting against the sun as she did so.

Buck scratched his head thoughtfully. "Do ya think God's in the clouds?"

"Well, no, not exactly. I mean, we believe that heaven is somewhere up there. Perhaps far above the clouds," she explained. "But even though heaven is God's home, His Spirit resides on earth, and we can have Him living in our hearts if we only ask—"

"God can't be in anyone's heart," Buck interrupted, with a wave of his hand.

"Yes, He can," Amanda said with assurance. "God's Son, Jesus, was sent to earth to die for man's sins, and if we want Him to live in our heart, then we must ask Him to forgive our sins and cleanse us from all unrighteousness."

"Enough talk about God and sin! You said ya wouldn't preach on this trip, remember?"

She gave a slow nod. "I wasn't really preaching. I was just—"

"I see the baby's sleeping," Buck interrupted. "So I think it's time we get riding again."

Amanda opened her mouth as if to say something more, but her words were drowned out by the low rumble of thunder in the distance.

Buck looked up and saw that the once cloudless sky was now filled with dark, ominous clouds. "We'll either need to ride the storm out or sit here and wait for it to pass," he muttered.

"A summer storm?" Amanda shivered. "I wonder what kind of destruction it will bring."

CHAPTER 35

If the cold water from the river hadn't cooled Amanda off, the downpour that followed had certainly finished the job. Within minutes of the shower, she was drenched from head to toe. They had tried their best to outride the oncoming deluge. It moved too fast, though, for the horses to keep ahead of it.

Amanda clung to her saddle, keeping Buck within sight, but she couldn't help looking back to see if the worst was still coming. Through blurry eyes she saw a whitish wall of water at the forefront of the storm. She could smell the earth as sheets of rain fell from the dark clouds above, and the wind kicked up dust as it reached the ground below.

All too soon, the heaviest part of the cloudburst was overhead, and the raindrops pummeled Amanda's body, feeling like tiny daggers hitting her skin. Thankfully, they were traveling in another open meadow, so there would be no danger from falling trees. The lightning and thunder had ebbed, which was fortunate, because out in the open they would have been a target for lightning.

Remembering once more how her first guide had died, Amanda was thankful there was no more lightning. However, the wind and chilling rain caused Amanda's teeth to chatter.

Buck seemed not to notice, and he rode along at a fast pace, as though trying to outrun the storm.

The weight of the water had completely saturated the brim of her father's hat, and she felt it sliding down onto her forehead. She'd been hot and tired only an hour ago, and now she was chilled to the bone and even more exhausted than she had been before the storm. If the rain didn't stop soon, she'd be completely waterlogged.

She glanced over at Mary. The young mother had pulled a piece of lightweight canvas over her and the baby's head but gave no complaint about the weather. No sound came from Little Joe either. He slept soundly.

The rain continued to pelt their bodies as they rode on for more weary miles. It was beginning to get dark by the time Buck halted the horses, and still the rain came down.

Amanda felt more like a drowned cat than a prim and proper missionary. She was quite sure that every square inch of her body was saturated. No matter how hard she tried, she seemed unable to get dried off or warmed up. Her teeth chattered hopelessly. Her hair hung in a limp mass down her back. Her arms and legs felt numb.

It wasn't until she dismounted and stood shivering under the branches of a fir tree, that Buck finally noticed the condition she was in. "I didn't realize you were so wet," he said. "I'm more used to getting rained on, but you need to get dried off."

"Yes, I do, and so does Mary and the baby," Amanda said through trembling lips. "I'm chilled to the bone and wet clear through. I'm sure Mary must feel the same way."

"I'll start a fire. You two stay under the tree," he instructed.

Amanda smiled gratefully. In her condition she doubted if she could move a muscle. She knew Mary needed to feed Little Joe too.

The rain was beginning to let up, and using some dry pieces of wood that they carried in one of their packs, Buck was able to get a fire going. As soon as it was ablaze, Amanda moved to stand in front of it. When she began to sneeze, Buck said, "You need to put on some dry clothes."

"Buck is right," Mary agreed. "Not good to stay in wet clothes."

"I will, just as soon as I warm up enough to set up my tent," Amanda answered. Her clothes clung to her like a second skin, and the collar around her neck seemed to have grown tighter. Amanda groped at the material, pulling it away from her throat.

"I'll put up the tent," he said. "You need to stay by the fire."

Amanda nodded numbly. She was too cold and exhausted to

argue. Besides, she wasn't sure she had enough strength to lift any of their belongings from the back of the mules, much less erect a tent by herself; although she was sure Mary would have helped. Gratefully, she flopped onto a log, as close to the fire as she could safely get. "I don't know what we would have done if you hadn't agreed to accompany us on this trip," she said to Buck. "I want you to know that I am grateful for all your help."

Buck nodded, then turned away to set up the tent.

When Buck returned to the campfire, he found Amanda draped across the log, fast asleep. Her breathing appeared to be shallow, and she was wheezing between ragged breaths. He knew he must get her into the tent as quickly as possible. He bent down and lifted her as though she weighed no more than a baby deer. As soon as he entered the tent and placed Amanda onto her sleeping mat, she woke up. "Where am I?" she asked groggily.

"You're in the tent. You still need to get outta those clothes."

Amanda's teeth began to chatter again, and she sneezed several times. "I will, as soon as you leave."

"I'll see about fixin' something for us to eat." He smiled and stepped outside.

When Buck came back several minutes later to let Amanda and Mary know that supper was ready, he found Amanda sleeping again, although Mary had helped her into dry clothes. Her breathing seemed labored, and beads of sweat glistened on her forehead. She'd obviously taken a chill from the drenching rain, and he was fairly certain she had come down with a fever.

"Do you have any willow bark?" Buck asked Mary. "I think she's sick, and being wet from the rain hasn't helped."

She nodded. "Always carry willow bark with me."

"Would ya mind fixin' some of it for Amanda?"

"I do it now." Mary handed the baby to Buck. "You hold Little Joe while I make tea." Before Buck could respond, she hurried from the tent.

Buck tweaked Little Joe's nose, and the baby gurgled, looking up at him innocently. Buck couldn't believe how good it felt to hold the infant, and once again, he wondered how it would be if he had a child of his own.

When Mary returned, she held a tin cup full of freshly brewed willow bark tea, known for its ability to reduce a fever and take away pain. Mary woke Amanda and coaxed her to drink some of the tea.

Amanda roused slightly, moaning. "I'm so tired. Please let me sleep."

Mary held the cup to Amanda's lips. "Drink tea now. Sleep after."

"Drink all of it," Buck said.

Amanda did as he said. "It's so bitter, and my throat hurts," she said, groaning as her head dropped back to the mat.

"You have fever. Must rest and stay warm," Mary insisted.

Amanda coughed and covered her mouth. "At this rate we'll never reach the Spalding Mission."

"We'll get there when we get there. Now rest." Buck was about to leave the tent when the sound of pounding horse's hooves and the cries of Indian voices filled the air.

"You women stay here," he commanded. "I'll go see who's come to our camp."

CHAPTER 36

When Buck stepped out of the tent, he was met by a group of Flathead Indians. He felt relief, knowing they were usually a friendly tribe.

Buck held up one hand and gestured in a motion similar to a wave, the sign of welcome. The leader of the Flatheads dismounted from his horse and with some hand gestures signaled that his tribe would like to set up their camp nearby.

Buck had no objections, knowing there was safety in numbers. He told the chief so, using the proper hand signals.

Ducking back into the tent, Buck nearly bumped into Amanda. She gave him an anxious look. "Who are they? Are they friendly? What do they want?" Her voice was shaky and edged with concern.

Buck eased Amanda back onto her mat. "It's not good for you to be up," he said sternly.

"I tell her that," said Mary, "but she not listen."

"I wanted to see who was here and find out if you were all right," Amanda said, as she laid her head against the soft hides.

Buck grinned. "You were afraid for me?"

She nodded. "I am afraid for all of us."

"It's a Salish tribe," he explained. "Flatheads, as the whites call 'em, and they're gonna make camp along the river. It'll bring good fishing. There are probably many roots to dig for eating here too."

"Are they hostile Indians?" she asked, eyes wide and expectant.

Buck shook his head and fought the urge to reach out to her. She looked so frightened, and he wished to bring her comfort.

"Why are they called *Flatheads*?" Amanda questioned. "Do they have flat heads?"

"Some Salish tribes make the heads of their babies go flat, usin' headboards," Buck explained.

Amanda gasped, causing another round of coughing. "Why would anyone do such a horrible thing to a baby?"

"What seems bad to you, not bad to others," Mary interjected. "You don't understand Indian ways."

"You're right, I don't, but I'm trying to."

"Would ya like to get to know the Flatheads?" Buck questioned.

"Well, I suppose, but. . ."

"That's good." He leaned back on his elbows. "They plan to stay here long enough so their men can hunt for fresh meat."

Amanda's eyes widened. "You're planning to leave us here with those Indians?"

He nodded. "I won't be gone long, and I'm sure you, Mary, and the baby will be fine."

"But I don't know the Flathead language, and I'm sure they don't speak English, so how are we supposed to communicate?"

"Mary can speak to these people. And if ya want to try, do this." He held his hands in front of her and made the sign of greeting.

"Buck right. I make Salish talk," Mary interjected.

"You want me to talk to them with my hands?" Amanda sputtered.

"Yes, if you wanna try."

Amanda swallowed hard. *What is wrong with me? I've come through horrible storms, buried three men, lost all my supplies, and traveled for miles, all alone. Surely I should be strong enough to let Buck go hunting. Truly I should have enough faith in God to know that He has brought me this far and won't abandon me now.*

"Don't be afraid. The Flatheads won't hurt ya." Buck lifted the tent flap and stepped outside.

————

Amanda awoke several hours later to the sound of children's laughter. She opened her eyes and was surprised to see two young Indian girls staring down at her. The older one, who looked to be about ten years old, poked the other girl's arm and giggled. The younger one pointed to Amanda and said something in her native tongue, then she knelt on the mat next to where Little Joe lay sleeping.

Amanda had no idea how long she'd been asleep. She held her pounding head a moment, thinking about how miserable she felt. She spotted Mary then, sitting in the center of the tent, stirring something in a black cooking pot over a small fire. The smell of rabbit stew wafted up to greet Amanda's nostrils. *I must be getting some better*, she noted. *At least my nose has unclogged enough so that I can smell that delicious aroma.*

"You feel better now?" Mary asked.

"I feel more rested," Amanda replied, "but my throat's still sore."

"You need drink more willow bark." Mary stopped stirring the kettle and poured Amanda a tin cup filled with the same bitter tea she'd given her before. It was hard to get down, but Amanda forced herself to swallow it as Mary looked on. "You had fever and bad dreams. You call out once for Buck, then fever broke."

"What are these two young girls doing in our tent?" Amanda asked, not wanting to hear that she'd called out for Buck.

"They hear baby cry and want to see him."

"I guess all young children like babies."

"Want to hear somethin' funny?" Mary asked.

Amanda nodded, eager to hear anything humorous. Life had been too serious of late. She'd begun to think the west was full of violence and uncouth men like Seth Burrows.

"Flathead chief think Buck is your man."

Amanda's mouth dropped open. "Why would he think that?"

"Buck say they should look out for you."

"I'm sure he asked them to look out for you and Little Joe too."

"Maybe so, but they think you Buck's woman."

"Did you tell them I am not?"

Mary shook her head. "It better they think that."

"How come?"

"No Flathead man will bother you if they believe you have husband." Mary motioned to the tin cup. "Drink rest of tea now. It good for you."

Amanda did as she was told, then lay back down and closed her eyes. As she reclined there, half-asleep, she allowed herself to think about what it would be like if she were Buck's wife. Would they live in the mountains, while he trapped and traded? Would they live at the Spalding Mission and work together, teaching the Nez Percé about Jesus and helping them make a better life for themselves? Would they have children to love and cherish?

Don't be ridiculous, she chided herself. *Buck is not a Christian, and there's no way he would ever ask me to be his wife. Even if he did, I would have to say no.*

CHAPTER 37

Amanda, deep into sleep, was awakened by the sound of voices. She opened her eyes, and noticed that Mary was gone. She peeked out of the tent, hoping Buck had come back but saw no sign of him either. A few minutes later, Mary entered the tent with a young Indian woman, obviously with child.

"What's going on?" Amanda asked, covering her mouth to smother a sudden coughing spell.

"This woman, she about ready to give birth," Mary explained.

"But why is she here? Shouldn't she be with her family right now?"

Mary shook her head. "They say, no family. They all dead. Only husband is alive, and he out hunting."

"Surely there must be someone in her tribe who can help deliver the baby."

Mary pointed to herself. "They ask me."

"Why? Did you tell them that you had delivered Little Joe by yourself?"

Mary nodded. "I also say my grandfather was medicine man. He taught me some, so they ask me to help Silver Squirrel deliver her baby."

As Silver Squirrel moved across the teepee, Amanda gasped. Beside the fact that the young woman's stomach was twice the size that Mary's had been when she'd carried Little Joe, the woman's right hand was missing. "What happened to the poor woman's hand?" Amanda questioned.

"She used to be part of Blackfoot tribe. She do something they not like, so they cut off hand and leave her in woods to die," Mary replied.

"Oh, that is terrible!" Amanda's mind reeled with what Mary had just said. She shuddered at the mere thought of losing her hand.

"What happened to her then?" she asked.

"Flathead warrior, Two Moons, found her in woods. She weak from hunger and loss of blood. He carry her to his mother's lodge. They took care of her there. Save woman's life."

"She's fortunate that Two Moons came along when he did," Amanda said. "She may have bled to death."

Mary nodded. "They marry soon after that."

Amanda knew that if Mary was going to deliver Silver Squirrel's baby, they would probably be here among the Flathead for a while. She wasn't quite ready to take on this latest challenge, but she had already formulated a plan for when she was feeling better. Using Mary as her interpreter, maybe she could teach these Flathead Indians about the one true God.

Buck felt bad about leaving the women and baby alone but was sure they'd be safe with the Flatheads. They were out of fresh meat, and he'd hoped to bag a deer. He hadn't been so lucky though, but he did get a few rabbits. Since Amanda wasn't feeling well, she needed nourishment, and of course Mary needed to eat well in order to feed Little Joe properly.

As Buck headed back to their camp, he thought about Amanda. Her ways were odd, and she couldn't seem to stop talking about God. But there was something about the way she looked at him—something in her tone of voice. It was almost as though she were calling to him. Calling him to something he didn't understand. Calling him somewhere he didn't want to go.

Guiding his horse to a stop, Buck dismounted and headed for a small lake nestled in the forest. He was in need of a cool drink, and a quick swim would help clear his mind.

He tied the horse to a nearby tree, removed his shirt and leggings, and flung himself headfirst into the water. A few long strokes and Buck was in the middle of the lake. He turned over on his back and gazed up at the clear blue sky, dotted with puffy white clouds. It was a peaceful day, a time when his mind should have been at rest. But a multitude of thoughts had been troubling him ever since the white woman entered his life.

Floating effortlessly on his back, he closed his eyes, but a shrill cry in the sky overhead brought Buck's eyes open in a flash. Circling directly above was his red-tailed hawk. The bird's wings were outstretched, and it glided effortlessly, down, down, down, until it came to rest on the branch of a pine tree growing on one side of the lake.

Buck turned over, and swam quickly toward the shore. By the time he reached the shoreline, his hawk had flown to another tree. The flutter of wings, so close Buck could feel the gentle breeze, caused him to inhale sharply. Was his winged friend trying to tell him something?

Buck reached out his hand, and the beautiful bird landed on his arm. "What say you?" Buck whispered. "Have you a message for me?"

As suddenly as the hawk had appeared, it was gone, flying upward toward the sky.

A feeling of disappointment flooded Buck's soul as he watched the bird disappear. But as he looked down, he spotted a perfectly shaped red feather lying at his feet. It felt like a reminder that Buck's place was with his winged friend.

He bent down to pick it up, stroking it gently against the side of his face. "There's only way I can get the white woman out of my mind. I must take her quickly to the Spalding Mission and hurry back to my home in the Rockies."

CHAPTER 38

Amanda felt concern when a low moan escaped Silver Squirrel's lips.

"Her time is getting closer," Mary said. "Soon she will deliver baby."

"Is everything all right?" Amanda asked, trying to imagine what it felt like to experience the contractions Silver Squirrel was having. "She seems to be in so much pain."

"Everything seem normal," Mary responded. "Take longer for some."

Just then, another Flathead woman entered the tent. She said something to Mary, and Mary nodded.

"Who is she, and what does she want?" Amanda questioned.

"Her name Basket Woman. She came to help." Mary poured some water from an animal skin into a small wooden cup, then she helped Silver Squirrel sit up, placing several buffalo hides behind her back. She held the cup to the expectant woman's lips and told her to drink.

"*Katsa-yah-yah*," Silver Squirrel murmured.

"What did she say? Amanda asked.

"She say *thank you*."

Basket Woman made a low, guttural sound, and motioned for Amanda to move aside. It was obvious that she didn't want her anywhere near Silver Squirrel, so she quickly did as she was asked.

It's just as well, Amanda thought. *It wouldn't be good for Silver Squirrel or her newborn baby to get my cold.* She seated herself on a mat on the other side of the tent and picked up her Bible to read. She couldn't do anything for the laboring woman in a physical way, but she could certainly pray for her to have an easy delivery.

Time seemed to drag by as Silver Squirrel fought each passing pain, and Amanda continued to pray. Listening to the agonizing moans coming from the laboring woman was beginning to cause her concern. It was hard not to wince, but Amanda hid her feelings and offered reassurance each time Silver Squirrel looked her way.

Basket Woman went out of the tent and came back to give Mary fresh water, a pouch of freshly crushed herbs, and several handfuls of tree moss, which Mary explained was to staunch the flow of blood that would soon be forthcoming.

Silver Squirrel was crouched in the birthing position now, and Mary had coated the young woman's loins with bear grease. When Silver Squirrel gave a mighty push, followed by another, Amanda caught sight of a tiny dark head, about to enter the world. She held her breath as the new mother pushed again, and Mary, with hands outstretched, caught the slippery babe.

With the agility of a mountain lion, Basket Woman quickly cut the umbilical cord, cleaned the infant, and draped it across the new mother's stomach. It was a girl—a healthy-looking, copper-skinned girl with a set of lungs that equaled any cat's shrill cry. The newborn's head of black hair, still wet from the birth, was thick, just like Mary's little boy.

Amanda swallowed against the lump in her throat, thinking about the miracle of birth. In an instant, another human being had made an entrance into the world. How could anyone deny God's hand in something so precious, so astounding?

She glanced at Silver Squirrel, wondering if she was happy she had a baby girl, and was surprised to see the young woman's face screwed up in what appeared to be more pain.

Suddenly, Basket Woman scooped the baby off the mother's stomach and handed the squalling child to Amanda. Not knowing what else to do, Amanda grabbed up a small piece of rabbit fur and wrapped it snugly around the infant. What was wrong with Silver Squirrel? Was she in pain from the afterbirth that hadn't been expelled yet?

Silver Squirrel let out a piercing scream, and Mary positioned herself in front of the young woman once more.

Amanda watched in shocked fascination as another dark-haired baby made its lusty entrance. "Twins," Amanda murmured, almost reverently. From the size of Silver Squirrel's pregnant belly, Amanda had figured she was having quite a large baby. Now, her size made sense, with the new mother giving birth to two precious babies.

"*Its-welx!*" Silver Squirrel cried. She turned her head and spat on the ground.

"What did she say?" Amanda questioned. *Why doesn't Silver Squirrel look happy? She has two babies, and they look perfect to me.*

"She say, 'Huge monster,' " Mary replied.

Amanda had no idea what was going on, but what she saw next, horrified her.

Basket Woman mumbled a few words, grabbed the baby from Amanda, and held it next to the other baby. Silver Squirrel squinted her dark eyes as though in deep thought, then, with an agonizing moan, she pointed to the first baby that had been born. Then Basket Woman placed the baby in the crook of her mother's arm, scooped the other infant up, and promptly left the tent.

Amanda sat there, mouth open and heart racing. Where was Basket Woman going with the other baby? Was this some sort of a ritual when an Indian woman had twins?

Silver Squirrel's eyes were closed, no doubt from exhaustion, and her tiny daughter had begun nursing at her breast.

"What is going on, Mary?" Amanda asked.

Mary slowly shook her head. "Its-welx, the huge monster, has come. Flatheads believe evil spirit left Silver Squirrel bad omen."

"What omen?" Amanda asked. "Certainly you can't mean having two babies is a bad omen."

Mary nodded, frowning deeply. "They believe when two babies born, one stays, the other dies."

Amanda covered her mouth as she gasped. "Dies? Are you saying they plan to kill the other twin?"

"No kill. They take baby to woods and leave her. Baby's spirit will be taken soon."

"Her spirit? Taken by whom?" Amanda asked incredulously.

"Child will die from hunger or be eaten by wild animal," Mary replied. "It is the way of their people."

Amanda leaped to her feet. "They can't do that, Mary! It would be murder, and murder is wrong in God's eyes!"

"What you gonna do?"

"I am going to save that baby!" Amanda said with determination. "I cannot allow something like that to happen to another human being—especially an innocent child who just came into the world."

Amanda had respect for the Indian ways, but she didn't understand all of their strange customs. It was hard to condone anything that hurt a human or an animal, but with this one omen affecting twins, she simply could not look the other way. The innocent baby had no one to defend her, and Amanda didn't care if it was the tradition of this tribe or not. She was determined not to let anything happen to that darling infant girl!

CHAPTER 39

Coughing and gasping for breath, Amanda ran through the camp-site, looking frantically for Basket Woman. It was incomprehensible to think they would actually leave a newborn baby in the woods to die. She stopped and held her head as a dizzy spell came and went. Amanda knew she wasn't over her sickness, but finding that baby was more important than her own health right now.

Blinded by her tears, Amanda stumbled along but saw no sign of Basket Woman. *What am I going to do, Lord? Please help me find that baby,* she prayed, nearly choking on the sob rising in her throat. *Why are You setting so many trials before my path?*

Someone touched Amanda's shoulder, and when she whirled around, she was surprised to see Buck. "Where are ya going, Amanda?" he asked, tipping his head.

Amanda threw herself into his arms and sobbed. "Oh Buck, I am so glad thou art here!"

"What's wrong, and why ain't ya resting in your tent?" he asked, taking a step back, while holding Amanda at arm's length.

Amanda swallowed hard, fighting against another tirade of tears. She was so upset by this that she'd used the word *thou* instead of *you.* "Silver Squirrel had twins, but she's only keeping one. They—they are going to take the other twin to the woods and. . ." Amanda hiccupped on a sob and starting coughing. "They think it's a sign that some huge monster has come," she added after she'd gotten her coughing under control.

"It's sad," Buck said, "but this is the way of their people."

"That is what Mary said too, but it's wrong. Leaving the baby in the woods for some wild animal to eat is murder!"

213

"There ain't nothin' we can do about it, and the Flathead people are leaving today, so you'll have to let it go."

"Let it go?" Amanda clasped Buck's arm, wondering if he was crazy. "I can't do that. I need to save the baby! Please help me find where they took her."

Buck shook his head. "That would anger the Flathead people. They're doin' what they think is best, and it wouldn't be appreciated if we interfered." His forehead wrinkled. "Besides, what would you do with a baby?"

"I-I don't know," she stammered, watching as Buck turned and scanned the area, putting a little distance between them. "Maybe Mary would take her."

"Think about what you're sayin'," Buck said. "Mary has Little Joe to care for, and she has no husband to help out."

"But she's going home to her family," Amanda argued. "Surely they would help her raise both babies."

Buck folded his arms in an unyielding pose. "Let it go, Amanda. There ain't nothin' you can do. Now go back to the tent and rest. Ya look like you're about to collapse."

Amanda couldn't deny his judgment, but she couldn't get rid of the image of Basket Woman taking that innocent baby out to the woods and leaving it for dead. With God's help, she would find the strength to go to the woods by herself and search for the baby, because it was obvious that she wasn't going to get any help from Buck. What kind of a person was he, to let something like this go as if it meant nothing? Maybe she had figured Buck all wrong. If he thought this practice was okay, and could just let it go, then showing him the way to Christianity was even more important. But Amanda was beginning to doubt she could ever reach Buck, and that thought made her feel empty.

Amanda waited in her tent until the group of Flatheads rode out of camp. It was hard to believe they would leave so soon after Silver Squirrel had given birth, but she supposed they wanted to leave this place as quickly as they could so the new mother wouldn't be reminded that her other daughter had been left behind.

Heavenly Father, Amanda prayed, *that innocent baby out there in the woods does not deserve to die. Please show me where the infant lies.*

When Amanda's prayer ended, she glanced over at Mary, quietly nursing her baby. Buck was outside packing things up, and Amanda knew this might be her only chance. "I'm going outside for some fresh air," she told Mary. Then she slipped out of the tent before Mary could reply.

Sneaking around to the other side of the tent so Buck wouldn't see her, Amanda hurried away from the campsite and darted into the woods.

As Amanda walked on, she listened, hoping to hear the baby cry. But the only sounds were the rustling of leaves and the wind whispering through the pines. It was an especially warm day, and the child had only been out in the woods a few hours, so she hoped it was still alive.

Amanda followed a worn path through the forest, which made searching a bit easier. She wasn't sure where the path led, but it looked like the same type Mary had pointed out during their travels to the Rendezvous. The trails, Mary had explained, had been made by animals.

Amanda moved on, deeper into the woods, praying as she went, keeping cautious and staying alert for any little noise. She would have normally been nervous being in the forest alone, but her quest to find the baby made her more courageous.

Suddenly, she caught sight of a fawn walking in circles around a large pine tree. *That's strange,* Amanda marveled. *I wonder where the little deer's mother could be.*

Amanda stood watching it for several moments, then slowly, she tiptoed around the tree, following in the young deer's footsteps. Amanda was halfway around, when she heard a soft whimper. She turned to the left. Tucked inside a hollowed opening in the tree lay a newborn baby wrapped in a piece of moss. Amanda scooped the infant into her arms, brushing bits of dirt and leaves from its tiny body. Immediately, the child began to howl. "Oh, I thank Thee, Lord," Amanda murmured. "Thou hast surely answered my prayers." She knew without question that the Lord must have used the young fawn to guide her to the baby. The small deer was no longer anywhere in sight, but Amanda was thankful that God worked miracles, even through nature.

"Where's Amanda?" Buck asked when he entered the tent and found Mary packing up her personal belongings but saw no sign of Amanda.

"She go outside. Said she need fresh air."

"She went looking for that baby, I'll bet." Buck grimaced. "And if she went into the woods alone, she's bound to get lost."

Mary's eyes widened. "What should we do?"

"You stay here with your son. I'm goin' to look for her."

When Buck entered the woods a few minutes later, he cupped his hands around his mouth and called, "Amanda! Where are you, Amanda?"

He heard only the sound of the wind whispering through the trees.

Buck moved on, going deeper into the woods, and continued to call Amanda's name. He didn't know what he would do if he couldn't find her. She would die out here with no protection.

Suddenly, Buck heard the sound of a baby's cry. At least he thought that was what it was. Maybe it was a mountain lion cub or some other animal with a high-pitched cry. It could even be a bobcat, since their cry mimicked that of a baby's.

He took a few steps forward and listened. Then he saw Amanda walking on the path toward him, a baby in her arms.

"Oh Buck, I'm so glad to see you," she cried. "I found the other twin, and she's alive!"

Buck's jaw clenched. "I told ya not to go lookin' for that baby," he muttered. "What were you thinking? Don't ya know how dangerous it is for you to be out here in the woods alone?"

"Yes, I do," she said, looking up at him with tears in her eyes. "And that is why I had to find this baby." Amanda patted the squalling infant's back. "She would have perished for sure if I hadn't come looking for her, and I'm thankful to God that He sent a little fawn to lead me to the right spot." She smiled widely. "The child is alive. God has performed a miracle on her behalf."

"Miracle?" Buck scoffed. "What miracle will feed and care for this child?"

"I am going to care for the baby, and I'll ask Mary to nurse Little Fawn."

"Little Fawn?" Buck repeated.

"Why, yes. Since it was a small fawn that led me to the baby, I think the name is appropriate for her." Amanda looked down at the squirming infant nestled in her arms. "I think it's a fine Indian name, don't you?"

Buck folded his arms and thrust out his chin. "Ya can't keep this baby, Amanda."

"Yes, I can. I am going to take Little Fawn to the Spalding Mission, and nothing you can say will change my mind." She squinted up at him. "And don't try to stop me either. I am determined to do this, whether you like it or not."

Amanda was not going to back down, but having another baby along would make traveling even slower. *What is this woman thinking?* Buck asked himself. *And why does she have to be so stubborn?*

CHAPTER 40

W e need to get going," Buck said, trying to accept the fact that he wasn't going to change Amanda's mind about taking the baby. "I'd just like to know one thing."

"What's that?" she asked, stroking the top of the infant's head.

"How are ya plannin' to ride your horse and hold on to the baby?"

"I'll ask Mary to help me make a cradleboard for Little Fawn." Amanda smiled, gently kissing the baby's nose.

He frowned. "That'll take some time, and I thought you were anxious to get to the mission."

"I am, but I want to make sure my adopted daughter is safe." Amanda clung possessively to the baby, her blue eyes sparkling with determination.

Buck's eyebrows shot up. "You are planning to keep her?"

"Well, of course. I told thee that before."

"I thought you meant you were gonna take the baby to the Spalding Mission and leave her there." Buck squinted with annoyance, running his fingers through the ends of his hair. "And you're using the word *thee* again."

"I'm sorry, Buck," Amanda said, "but I slip back into saying it whenever I'm upset." She kissed the baby's forehead this time. "Since I'm the one who found Little Fawn, she's my responsibility. Just look how adorable she is."

He groaned, feeling more frustrated by the minute as he watched Amanda look lovingly at the infant. Didn't this woman have any idea what she was getting herself into, taking on a baby? Even with the baby just a few hours old, Amanda was quickly bonding with her. He figured that any more talk about giving the baby up would fall on deaf ears.

Buck couldn't take his eyes off Amanda as she stood rocking the baby while singing a lullaby. Amanda made his head ache more often than not. She also amazed him, which he didn't want to admit. Here was a woman who had journeyed all the way from New York and had lost her father on the way. Yet she'd continued on with only a guide to protect her. Back at Jim's cabin, she had told Buck how she and the guide had been stopped by a band of Blackfoot Indians, who'd suddenly let them go. Soon after, Amanda's guide had been killed, and then Amanda had become very sick. If it hadn't been for Buck finding her, he was sure she would have died.

Thinking back on all of this, Buck couldn't deny that this woman had courage. And the more he thought about Amanda, several other thoughts occurred to him. Still weak from having been sick, she had helped Mary with the delivery of Little Joe and taken care of things around the cabin until Mary got her strength back. She'd also taken care of him after the bear attack. Then there were those encounters with Seth Burrows. Now, Amanda's will to continue onward to the mission after getting sick again, and with a baby, no less, made her seem even more courageous. One day, she would no doubt make some lucky man a fine wife.

"We'd better get back to the campsite now, before you start sneezing and coughing again," Buck said, pulling his thoughts aside.

"You're right, we do need to get back," she agreed, "but it's the baby I'm worried about. She needs to be fed and properly dressed, and Mary can help with that."

"All right, let's go." Buck didn't know what he'd done to deserve all of this, but right now he wished he'd never met this Quaker woman with such a determined spirit.

———

As soon as Amanda and Buck returned to their campsite, Amanda entered the tent to tell Mary what had happened. "I found the baby," she said, hoping Mary would share her excitement.

Mary stared at the infant, then nodded and said, "This not a surprise. I knew you not rest till you found baby."

"It's a girl, Mary, and I named her Little Fawn. She needs to be fed." Amanda held the baby out to Mary. "Will you feed her for me?"

Mary nodded again. "I have plenty of milk." She motioned to Little Joe, sleeping on the mat beside her. "He satisfied baby."

Amanda smiled as a feeling of relief rushed through her that Mary hadn't turned her down.

"What you do with baby?" Mary asked after she'd taken the infant from Amanda and begun nursing her.

"I'm going to keep Little Fawn and raise her as my own," Amanda said without reservation. "She deserves to live, just as all babies do. The Flathead Indians were wrong in leaving her to die in the woods because of some silly superstition."

"It be their way," Mary stated simply.

Amanda shook her head. "But it's not God's way, and I live by His principles, not theirs."

Mary didn't respond, but she didn't tell Amanda she'd been wrong for taking the baby either.

Sometime later, after both babies had been fed and seemed content, Buck stepped into the tent with a wooden contraption similar to the cradleboard Mary had for Little Joe. "I lined it with rabbit fur," he said, handing it to Amanda.

"Thank you, Buck." Amanda felt moisture on her cheeks. She knew he didn't approve of her bringing the baby along, yet he was caring enough to see that the child was properly cared for.

"The baby's gotta have some place to ride," Buck said with a shrug. "Are ya ready to travel now?" he asked, looking first at Mary, and then Amanda.

Both women nodded and Amanda put the child in place. Then Buck tied the cradleboard securely to Amanda's back and helped her climb into the saddle. It felt somewhat awkward and a bit top-heavy, but Amanda was determined to carry her newly adopted daughter without a word of complaint.

Little Fawn fussed for the first several miles of travel, but after a while, she dozed off. Amanda offered a prayer of thankfulness that the baby seemed to be content, at least for the time being. Her biggest concern was whether Mary would have enough milk for both babies. She couldn't let the child starve to death.

Try not to worry, she told herself. *Just trust God to take care of Little Fawn.*

———

That evening, Amanda reclined on a sleeping mat inside her tent, with Little Fawn snuggled contentedly in the crook of one arm. It had been a long, tiring day, but she was thankful the tiny Indian girl was still alive. Amanda was also pleased that Buck had allowed her to keep the baby. She didn't know what she would have done if he'd forced her to leave Little Fawn in the forest to be eaten by some wild animal or die of starvation. She'd have never been able to live with herself if she had agreed to that.

Amanda tried to put herself in Silver Squirrel's place, wondering what it must have been like for the woman to have been forced to choose which daughter to keep. After only one day of caring for Little Fawn, Amanda felt a special bond with the precious infant. She would make any necessary sacrifice to assure the welfare of her adopted daughter.

The baby whimpered slightly, and Amanda whispered a prayer: "Dear Lord, help us to get the Spalding Mission safely, and protect my precious little girl."

———

Buck shifted restlessly on his deer hide mat in front of the campfire. It had been a long day—a day full of unexpected surprises. *Not all of them were bad,* he noted. Seeing how happy Amanda appeared as she held the Flathead baby caused him to wonder if taking the child had been the right thing to do after all. Amanda did seem to care about the welfare of the little girl, caring for the baby as if it were her own.

Buck turned his head and stared at the tent Amanda shared with Mary and Little Joe. She was sleeping in there with Little Fawn at her side. He could almost visualize Amanda's golden hair spread across her sleeping mat as she lay peacefully, with the baby sleeping soundly.

How many times recently, especially after Mary and Jim had become parents, had Buck thought about one day becoming a family man? It was easy now to understand how Jim, who had previously been so reserved, had changed after the birth of his son. Buck found himself changing too, especially seeing Amanda with the baby.

He quickly looked away from the tent where she slept. *I find myself thinking about her too much. I'll be glad when we get to the mission and my job will be done.*

CHAPTER 41

It had been nearly two weeks since Amanda discovered Little Fawn in the woods. Travel had been steady but slow. Much slower than Buck would have liked. He was anxious to get the women to the mission so he could be on his way home. The trek had become frustrating because each stop to feed the babies took precious time, but he was trying to be patient. Buck wasn't one for lingering in one place too long, especially not knowing if they were being followed or watched by the local Indians.

As Buck led the way, he felt as if their very lives depended on his keen sense of alertness. Bringing up the rear were the pack mules and the two extra horses bearing all of their supplies. Surprisingly enough, they hadn't encountered any other humans so far, and Buck hoped it would stay that way for the rest of their journey. He didn't relish the thought of meeting up with enemy Indians or, worse yet, white men who might want to cause trouble. The safety of Amanda, Mary, and their children was uppermost in his mind.

Thunder had been their constant companion, and the dog was a big help to Buck. With his keen sense of smell and good hearing, he had alerted Buck to threats several times. Just yesterday Thunder had been running up ahead and come across a mountain lion guarding the prey it had just killed. Snarling and growling, the big cat had eventually grown weary and run off, posing no threat to Buck and the women. Buck was thankful for Thunder's vigilance. The trip hadn't been easy on the dog, because the pads of his feet were starting to crack. Each evening Mary put some milkweed sap on them to promote healing and ward off infection. Even when the dog rested, he was watchful, which allowed Buck to get some sleep at night. He needed the rest in order to be on the alert during the day.

The terrain was getting more difficult in their travels, with more mountains to climb, not to mention the relentless mosquitoes that attacked them during the evenings.

It was suppertime now, and since it was almost dark, they had stopped for the night. Once again, the mosquitoes were buzzing around the camp, but the smoke from the campfire helped to keep them at bay.

Amanda was tending to her baby girl, using a fresh piece of dried moss as a diaper, the way Mary had showed her. Mary had also given Amanda some of Little Joe's clothes for Little Fawn to wear.

Amanda glanced up when she became aware that Buck was standing over her. "Little Fawn is doing quite well, don't you think?" she asked, flashing him a wide smile.

He shrugged and tried to keep his face a mask of indifference.

Amanda turned her attention back to the squirming child, and Buck was about to tend the horses when he decided to ask her a question. "How come you're so determined to go to the mission?"

"I've told you before," she replied. "The Indians need to know about God and His Son, Jesus. They also need to learn how to read, write, and till the land."

"Humph!" Buck scoffed. "The Nez Percé know the land well. Mother Earth gives 'em all they need."

"I realize that you have no desire to believe in God," she said evenly. "But I'm sure some Indians do. Otherwise, they would not have sent a delegation all the way to St. Louis in search of the Bible and white missionaries, asking them to come and teach their people."

Buck frowned. "Some may want that, but most are happy with the old ways. The majority of Indians don't want white men on their land."

"Don't you think the Nez Percé people will be interested in the Bible?" she asked. "Are you afraid I will corrupt them with my religious ways?"

Buck dropped his gaze to the dusty ground. "I ain't afraid of nothing, but you should be."

"What is that supposed to mean?"

Buck held up two fingers and furrowed his brows. "Two babies born of the same mother ain't good. The Nez Percé people may think this is a bad sign. They might see it as warning from Hanyawat."

"What kind of warning would the Great Spirit have in regard to an innocent young child?" Amanda retorted.

Buck grimaced. "Bringing a child of Its-welx, born to a Flathead woman, into the Nez Percé camp is not good. They may think the trouble meant for the Flatheads could come upon them instead."

Amanda wrinkled her nose. "That's the most preposterous thing I've ever heard! Even if there were bad omens, which I certainly do not believe in, they couldn't be transferred from one tribe to another, merely by bringing a child into their camp."

Could this lady be more stubborn? Buck wondered. Amanda sure had spunk; he had to give her that. Maybe that was one of the things that attracted him to her.

"*Lap-lap,*" he said, changing the subject as he pointed to a nearby bush, where a beautiful butterfly had landed.

"Lap-lap?" Amanda repeated, as she rose to her feet. "What does that mean?"

"It means, 'little butterfly.' See, it's right over there."

"Oh yes, I see it." Amanda smiled. "It's beautiful, another one of God's creations."

Buck grunted and walked away. It seemed like everything Amanda said had something to do with God, and he was getting tired of hearing it.

As Amanda sat in her tent with Mary and their babies that evening, they discussed their futures—Amanda at the Spalding Mission, and Mary hoping to find her people.

"Do you think when we get to the mission that your family will be near and that you'll be able to find them right away?" Amanda asked, holding Little Fawn and admiring the little girl's perfect face. She was glad her child did not have a flat head.

"Should be at camp along Clearwater River," Mary replied. "Should not be hard to find."

"Many times I have been afraid to move forward with my plans, but you have been a big part in helping me continue. It would be nice if we could still see each other from time to time," Amanda said, watching Mary as she nursed Little Joe. "Your friendship means a lot to me."

"I like that." Mary smiled at Amanda. "It be good to be among my people and teach Little Joe the Nez Percé ways. It also mean much to have you and Little Fawn nearby when my people camp near mission during cold winter months. You have become special friend to me. I already feel the peace we shall find there."

Amanda knew that no matter which path their lives took, once they got to their destination, the welfare of their children would come first.

Mary had been teaching Amanda how to sign with her hands so she could communicate with the Nez Percé Indians she would be ministering to. She'd taught her a few Nez Percé words as well.

Amanda often read to Mary from the Bible, and helped her memorize some verses of scripture. Buck kept a safe distance during Bible reading. He did, however, tolerate her prayers whenever they ate a meal together. Amanda hoped that eventually he would see the truth of God's Word and open himself to Jesus. If he didn't do it before he left them at the mission and headed back to his home in the Rockies, she feared he might never find the Lord. *What will it take for Buck to see the truth?* she asked herself. *Is there something more I can say or do?*

CHAPTER 42

The sun cast a colorful pink hue across the valley where they were camped, splashing everything with a bright glow. They'd stopped a bit earlier than normal because Little Fawn, now a little more than two weeks old, had been extremely fussy. Amanda knew it was probably the heat that tormented the child, but she worried. They'd put in a lot of miles today, and Buck had obviously sensed the child's need and made the decision to stop and make camp for the night.

Amanda was glad today's travels were cut short, for the unrelenting August heat was getting to her too. She would be relieved when their journey ended. All the mountainous trails they had traveled so far; the streams and rivers they'd crossed; and the forest they'd quietly ridden through had kept her nerves on edge because of what they didn't know that might confront them at any moment. What she wouldn't give for a deep, restful sleep in a real bed, but she knew that wouldn't happen until she was settled in at the mission.

Even with these anxieties, Amanda had never felt more connected with her surroundings. She'd never seen so much beauty in what God created than she had during this journey. She had also met Mary, whom she hoped would be her friend for life. And the most precious thing of all was that she now had a daughter to raise and teach about God. It scared her a bit, realizing there would be many challenges ahead. But with God's help, she would deal with whatever came along.

Feeling ever so grateful, Amanda climbed down from her horse and quickly undid the cradleboard. She was exhausted from the endless hours in the saddle.

Amanda lifted the baby out and placed her on a deer hide, near the cool river. Then she dipped one end of a torn shirt into the water, wrung it out, and placed it across the infant's forehead. Next, she dipped another piece of cloth into the water, and designed it into a cone-shape. The baby began to suck as soon as Amanda put the moistened cloth between her tiny lips, and soon thereafter, Little Fawn drifted into a peaceful sleep.

"Thank you for stopping, Buck," Amanda said, smiling up at him as he approached her.

"I couldn't let the baby keep cryin'," Buck replied, looking at the forest before them.

Amanda's gaze followed his, knowing they still had many more miles to go until they reached their destination. A sense of excitement mixed with a bit of trepidation fluttered in her stomach as she contemplated the new life that would be awaiting her at the Spalding Mission. Would this be her future? Would she and Little Fawn be accepted? She prayed they would, or else her journey and all the sacrifices she had made would have been for nothing. And where would she go if they weren't accepted? Certainly not back home to Dansville. Papa was gone, and there was nothing in New York for her but a flood of painful memories. No, Amanda felt sure her place was in the West, where she could create new memories.

"This area is truly beautiful. It's as if God is right beside us," Amanda said to Mary when she walked over to join them.

Mary nodded. "I feel this too."

Amanda and Mary, holding their babies, and Buck squatting down to pet Thunder, gazed at the tall trees. Amanda breathed deeply of the forest's rich scents, mingling with the sweet smell of fresh water before them. She looked over at Mary and smiled. "Little Fawn is alive because of you, and I appreciate what you've done for her."

"You the one who saved her," Mary said, shaking her head. "I just provide milk she needs."

"That's right," Amanda acknowledged, glancing at Buck as he pet Thunder, "and I thank you for that, Mary." She motioned to Little Joe as they both took seats on a log. "He seems to have grown so much these past few weeks."

Mary nodded. "He grow tall like his father someday. He already strong baby."

"Yes," Amanda agreed. "And I'm sure if Jim were alive, he'd be proud of both you and his son."

Mary lowered her gaze. "I miss husband."

Amanda touched Mary's arm. "I'm sure you do, but at least you have his son, and that has to be a comfort. Through Little Joe, Jim will live on."

Mary nodded briefly, then placed Little Joe on the deer hide beside Little Fawn. "Someday our children be good friends."

Amanda smiled. "I hope so, Mary. And I hope you and I will be good friends for many years too. We have come a long way together."

As Amanda and Mary sat and visited near the water, Buck couldn't take his eyes off Amanda. He began tending the fire, which really didn't need tending at all, but it gave him something to do. Amanda had taken her hair out of the bun she normally wore, and it fell down her back in silky waves. She was plain, yet beautiful. Her eyes were as blue as the afternoon sky. Her voice, so soft and lilting, often left him feeling a hunger such as he'd never known. Amanda's skin looked like silk, and a tan gave her a healthy glow. *Are all white women like this one?* he wondered. She seemed to be enveloped with an aura of love. It made him feel peaceful yet strangely uncomfortable. From the first moment he'd set eyes on her, Buck hadn't been able to get Amanda out of his mind. She was in his every thought, no matter how hard he tried to ignore it.

As Buck willed himself not to, his feet took him once again to where Amanda and Mary were sitting. He sat on the log on the other side of her, and his throat grew suddenly dry.

Amanda turned in his direction, just as Mary got up to leave.

Mary took Little Joe to the water's edge and sat down, dipping her feet into the coolness. She held her son and dipped his feet too, smiling when he squealed with delight. The river was clear, and looking out toward the center, Mary could see the bottom and a few trout lazily swimming into the current. Round, smooth pebbles of all sizes and colors covered the river's floor, which made it easy to walk on, so Mary decided to do just that.

She got up, holding her son snugly, and waded in, knee-deep. There she saw a large, flat rock to sit on, immersing herself in the water, halfway up to her chest. Little Joe was still very young, but even at this age Mary wanted him to have no fear of the water. Just like the last time, he seemed to enjoy it. As she held on to her child, supporting him underneath, she moved him back and forth, skimming the water's surface, and his little feet kicked with delight.

"You swim like little fish," Mary crooned. Hearing him giggle made her happy, with thoughts leading toward her people. What would it be like when she reached her tribe? Would they accept her son, who was half white?

As Mary picked up Little Joe, a bird called from the other side of the river. It was a joyful sound, and she watched as it came closer, quickly flew over her head, and disappeared out of sight. Seeing the bird was something familiar to Mary, and she watched in amazement as a perfect yellow feather drifted to the ground.

Memories flooded back to when she was a girl and had gone seeking her guardian spirit. She remembered in her weakness that day that her eyesight had grown fuzzy, and she'd swayed, trying to stay upright from fatigue. Then the golden bird had come and dropped a bright yellow feather. Mary's father had told her later that a yellow bird meant to have trust in using power in voice. Looking back on it now, Mary felt that her guardian spirit had been with her when she'd encountered Seth Burrows and had shown no fear. She was certainly scared on the inside, but her voice had not revealed it.

Mary had also been blessed with a beautiful singing voice— another gift from her bird spirit, the canary. And now, seeing her guardian spirit once again gave Mary new hope in what was to come once she found her village and people.

———

Buck's mouth felt like it was full of cotton when he leaned slightly toward Amanda, and their gazes locked. In that brief span of time, something indefinable passed between them. Then she smiled and looked away.

He fought the urge to touch her face and trace the line of her jaw with his fingertips. It was a good thing she'd looked away from him, for it only took a split second to be lost in those liquid pools of blue. To run the backs of his fingers over her smooth, tan skin was a temptation he could hardly control. Instead, he focused on their mules and horses. Buck couldn't let his imagination run away with him.

He got up to check on the livestock one more time and then decided to take a dip in the river. He needed to wash the dust off himself, but he also needed to cool his body from the heat of the day.

Buck made his way on a small path leading downstream so he could enjoy a private swim and clear his jumbled thoughts. The river looked refreshing and calm, with only a small current going straight down the middle. Buck could hardly wait to plunge into the water, and he was lucky to find a small inlet blocked by some rocks, which created a small pool, separate from the river.

Sitting on one of the bigger rocks, Buck removed his shirt. He was just getting ready to take off his trousers when he heard the sound of running horses in the distance. He turned the other way and cringed when he saw a cloud of dust and several Indian ponies heading toward their camp. Buck's chest tightened as he reached for his gun and hurried back to protect the women. Who were these Indians, and what did they want?

CHAPTER 43

Three fierce-looking Blackfoot warriors dismounted and stood before Buck. Thunder's hair bristled, and he bared his teeth, while standing close to Buck's leg.

"Be quiet, dog," Buck commanded, nudging Thunder to sit down. Using the hand signal for friendship and the greeting of "hello," he motioned for the men to take a seat by the fire.

Buck wasn't sure what was about to happen, but remaining calm and trying to stay friendly, while keeping unnoticeably cautious, was the best thing to do. He stood, waiting quietly while taking in all the details of the three men. They each wore a loincloth with leggings made from deer hide that went up to their hips. A belt was also included, along with a brightly designed shirt from the same material. Colorful beads adorned their moccasins, and the tall one had a necklace of grizzly paws hanging around his neck. Buck knew this piece was a sign of bravery.

The tallest of the three men made a low, guttural sound, then held up a string of fish that looked like they'd recently been caught. He made no effort to sit on the log near the fire or even crouch down on his haunches, like Buck had just done. Instead, he stood firmly in place, his eyes scanning the campsite as though he might be looking for something.

Amanda and Mary remained motionless, holding their babies tightly to their chests. Buck knew from their tight shoulders and rapid blinking that they were both afraid. Things had been going along so well lately; this was not what they needed.

After several moments, the taller Indian, who appeared to be the leader of the group, spoke to his companions in their native tongue;

although Buck didn't recognize any of the words. At least so far their demeanor didn't seem threatening.

The leader turned from the other man and faced Buck again. He held the fish a bit higher and pointed at the two blankets draped over the log near the fire, opposite where the women sat.

Buck nodded, realizing that the man wanted to trade the fish for the blankets. He had no problem with that. They had other blankets in one of their packs, so he would gladly give away two blankets, just to see these men be on their way. He stood, grabbed up the blankets, and handed them to their leader.

The man grunted and pointed to one of the horses they'd been using to carry some of their supplies.

"No, he can't have that! It was my father's horse!" Amanda shouted, although she didn't make a move.

With his head lowered, Thunder stood and released a throaty growl. Buck had to hush the dog once more, and Thunder obeyed, never taking his eyes off the warrior.

The Indian's eyes narrowed at the dog, seemingly unafraid. Then he pointed to the horse again.

Buck shook his head, but changed his mind when the Indian made a sudden advance toward Amanda, holding his knife. Extending his hand in a sign of peace, Buck moved quickly to the horse, and led it over to the men. He then handed the reins to the leader, hoping this would satisfy the Indians, and they would leave. Since Blackfoot were known for their excellent horsemanship and raided other tribes to take their best horses, Buck was actually surprised that the tall one would settle for the chestnut brown horse that had belonged to Amanda's father, and not the beautifully marked spotted horse that Jim used to ride.

The Indian grunted and dropped the fish across the log. Mounting his painted horse in one fluid motion, he rode away, pulling Amanda's father's horse by a rawhide rope, while the other two Indians followed.

Buck heaved a sigh of relief. Either Amanda's God or Mary's guardian spirit must have been watching over them, because he never expected the Blackfoot men to leave so quickly. He figured they would want more.

"You gave that man my father's horse!" Amanda hollered, turning an angry face on Buck. "What were you thinking?"

"I was thinkin' about you, Mary, and the babies," he replied in an equally angry tone. "If I hadn't given 'em the horse they wanted, we coulda all been killed."

"But thee had no right to give my father's horse away without asking my permission." Amanda's voice quavered, and Buck figured she was on the verge of tears.

"Would ya have given it?" he asked, already knowing her answer.

She shook her head. "No, I would not."

"Would ya rather that I gave you or Little Fawn to those Indians?"

"No, of course not, but. . ."

"Knowin' the situation, I gave 'em what they wanted, and now they're gone, so you oughta be glad for that." Buck wiped the sweat from his brow. "I'm surprised that Indian settled for so little though. They could have taken all our horses and supplies if they'd wanted to, or even done worse."

"Buck is right," Mary interjected. "We be lucky they only took blankets and one horse. Could have took everything—even us or babies."

Amanda nodded, her shoulders trembling. "I am ever so thankful that no one was hurt, especially our children."

"Me too," Buck said. "We're all lucky to be alive."

When Amanda lay beside Little Fawn in their tent that night, all she could think about was Buck and how he'd given away her father's horse in order to keep the peace with those Blackfoot Indians. Her last encounter with Blackfoot had ended when she'd shown them her father's Bible, and this time his horse had saved them.

Amanda scolded herself as she continued to think about things. She felt terrible that she'd given Buck a hard time because he'd given away Papa's horse. While it was good to be brave and stand up for oneself, at times, like today, the less that was said, the better. They were fortunate that the outcome hadn't been worse.

After the encounter, Mary had also explained to Amanda that Indians valued horses, so there was no reason to worry about her father's horse, for she was sure it would be well cared for.

I thank Thee, Lord, for keeping us safe, Amanda prayed. *Please continue to guide and direct us as we complete our journey. And when we get to the Spalding Mission, I pray that Thou wilt give each of us what we are looking for.* She paused and stroked Little Fawn's silky head. *And may my daughter grow up to be a woman of courage, who will love You as much as I do and be willing to serve You with her whole heart.*

CHAPTER 44

Days turned into weeks, and weeks into months. Summer was just a memory. The warm days had been replaced with cool, crisp mornings, and the bugs were no longer a nuisance. The aspens had turned a bright golden yellow and stood in stark contrast to the pine trees. Birds flew overhead in large groups, making their southward journey. Fall was upon them, and Buck said they might see some snow soon.

Amanda had always loved fall in New York. It pleased her to see that, although they were different species, the trees out West also showed off distinctive colors before the cold and gray of winter set upon them.

Although they were getting closer to their destination, they still had a ways to go. Amanda was weary of traveling and figured Mary, Buck, and especially Thunder were too. She knew they would all be glad once they reached the mission.

They'd encountered a few trappers along the way, as well as some Flathead Indians, who'd been hunting. Amanda had kept Little Fawn's face turned away from the men so she wouldn't be asked any questions about why she had an Indian baby. Every day she prayed that God would grant them traveling mercies and reveal Himself to Buck.

One evening, after Mary and Little Joe had gone to bed, and Amanda had put Little Fawn down, as well, she decided to sit by the fire awhile, because she couldn't sleep. She took a seat on a log across from where Buck sat. Thunder slept nearby, awaiting his turn to keep watch.

Amanda looked up at the star-studded sky, while taking her hair out of the restraining bun she wore every day under her Quaker bonnet.

"It's a beautiful evening," she murmured as a few ringlets sprang free and fell loosely around her face.

Buck nodded. "Cold though. Winter will be here soon, and it'll bring snow."

She shivered. "I had hoped to be at the mission by now. The idea of traveling in the snow worries me."

"Nothin' to worry about. We still have plenty of blankets to keep warm, and the horses are used to the cold."

Amanda rubbed her arms briskly. "If it's this cold already, I can't imagine how it'll feel once the snow flies. Will it get very deep?"

"Some areas end up gettin' closed off once winter's truly here, but we oughta be at the mission before the snow socks in too bad." Buck left his seat, took a blanket from one of their packs, and wrapped it around Amanda's shoulders. Then he seated himself beside her. "Is that better?"

"Yes, thank you." She smiled. "I have to admit I don't miss the bugs now that the weather has turned colder."

Buck nodded.

As a coyote's lonely howl sounded in the distance, they sat quietly for several minutes; then Amanda turned to him and said, "I know I have said this before, but I really appreciate all that you've done for us, Buck. We could not have made it this far without you."

"I do what I know is best," he replied with a brief shrug.

"You are a good man, Buck McFadden. Don't ever let anyone tell you different."

"You are the good one," he said. "Much better than me."

Amanda opened her mouth to comment, but her words were cut off when he touched her lips with his finger. She read the longing in his eyes as he gazed at her. Then he cradled her face in his hands and gently caressed her cheeks with his fingertips. He leaned closer, put his arms around her waist, and kissed her.

Amanda's heart thumped so rapidly she could almost hear it. The touch of his lips brought pure joy to her soul, yet a deep-seated fear crept into her fast-beating heart. So many times she had wondered what Buck's kiss would be like, and it was even more wonderful than she could have imagined. She could hardly breathe from this unexpected feeling. She wanted him to kiss her again.

What is wrong with me? The words came uninvitingly into her head. She was a white woman raised in a proper, Christian home. She should not be kissing a man who wasn't a committed Christian. Had she done or said something to give Buck the idea that she saw him as anything more than her friend? Although she'd never spoken a word about her feelings, could Buck tell what she'd been wishing for?

Even the friendship they had come to know was risky. *"Friendship can lead to love."* Amanda had heard her father say that many times. That had been the case in his marriage to Amanda's mother. Ruth Collins, a farmer's daughter, had wed Clarence Pearson when she was a young woman of seventeen. She was the oldest in a family of ten children, and her parents were anxious to see her married off so they would have one less mouth to feed. She and Clarence had begun their marriage based only on friendship, but later it had turned to love. Amanda's father had told her this when she'd become a young woman.

Using all the willpower she could muster, Amanda pulled free from Buck's embrace, and shook her head slowly. "I am sorry. I should not have allowed that to happen. I don't know what came over me."

Buck's forehead creased. "There ain't nothin' to be sorry for. I kissed you, so it's my fault."

"But I let you kiss me, because I wanted it." Amanda flinched as she admitted those words. It was not right for a woman to flirt with a man or let him know how much she was attracted to him. She'd heard her aunt Dorothy say so many times. Not that her father's sister had much experience with men. She was forty years old and still not married. She'd probably never kissed a man either.

Buck reached his hand out to Amanda, but she quickly stood up. "No, please! We must not let our feelings get in the way of good judgment." She swallowed hard and blinked back sudden tears. "I do care about you, Buck, but it would never work for us to be together."

Rising to his feet and standing in front of her, Buck felt a muscle in his cheek twitch as he held her gaze. "Is it because I'm part Indian?"

"No, it's not that," she assured him. "But you are not a Christian."

"You're right; it couldn't work out for us." Before Amanda could respond, Buck turned and stalked off.

Amanda's voice caught on a sob. "Dear Lord," she prayed fervently, "please make him understand."

She began to pace, twirling the end of her hair between her fingers. Every few minutes her eyes went to the stand of trees where Buck had tied the horses and mules. She still couldn't believe she'd let him kiss her. Worse than that—she'd enjoyed the kiss and had done nothing to discourage it. Amanda wondered what her father would say if he had seen her being held in Buck's embrace. Would he be ashamed of her brazen behavior? Probably so. Would he approve of her rescuing an abandoned Indian child? Most likely.

Amanda's father had always been an upright, godly man, and he'd raised his only daughter to be the same way. If he could have witnessed her behavior with Buck, he would have been appalled. And why shouldn't he be? Amanda was aghast herself. Not because she believed white people were better than Indians or that it was beneath her to kiss a man who was half-Indian. No, it was because she knew it was wrong to be unequally yoked with an unbeliever.

Amanda wondered if she would have reacted to any man's kiss the way she had to Buck's. Nathan had never kissed her on the mouth, only her hand. That certainly hadn't left her breathless the way Buck's kiss had.

The memory of Buck's gentle touch caressing her face and the pleasant feel of his warm lips upon her own lingered in Amanda's mind. How wonderful it had felt to be held so closely by him—almost as if she belonged there. "Right or wrong," she murmured, "I have fallen in love with Buck. But he must never know."

Chapter 45

Buck rode in silence, trying to keep his mind on the trail ahead and a wary eye out for any kind of trouble. So far they had been fortunate. They'd met up with several more bands of Indians, but none of them were hostile. They'd never asked for anything other than a simple trade of cooking utensils, blankets, or food. Thanks to their loyal companion Thunder, any threats from wildlife had also been kept to a minimum. If the spirits smiled down on them, they might make Fort Walla Walla by noon tomorrow.

It had been a long five months since Buck had first met Amanda. And oh, how things had changed between them since then. So many events had occurred during that time—some good, some bad. And somehow he'd managed to lose his heart to the beautiful white woman. They would soon part, when he would leave her and Little Fawn at the mission and return to his home in the Rockies.

Though she'd be gone from his sight, Amanda would never be gone from his heart. Of that much, he was certain. After the kiss they had shared, he would never forget her. He could still picture Amanda unraveling her hair out of the bun she wore every day. Buck had tried to think of other things, but it was difficult.

If only things could be different, he thought. *If she were Indian and believed as I do, then maybe. . .*

Buck drew in a deep breath and tried to shake the image of Amanda from his head. He was thankful she had respected his need to be alone when they camped each evening. Being close to her was pure torture, and he knew that one look from her intense blue eyes would have banished his resolve to keep her at arm's length.

He shook his head slowly. *I should not have agreed to be her guide.*

Was he ready to be on his own again? Would he be satisfied to once again have brother hawk as his only companion? One thing was certain: being around Amanda was more difficult than dealing with a band of hostile Indians.

When they awoke the following morning, a blanket of pristine snow covered the ground, giving everything a peaceful, serene look. Tree limbs dipped low beneath the weight of the wintry blanket, and powdery flakes of snow danced against the gray sky. The snow must have started shortly after they'd retired for the night.

When Amanda peered out the opening of the tent and saw Buck adding wood to their campfire, a sense of longing welled in her soul. Crawling out of the canvas shelter, she stood and stretched her legs. In a childlike manner, she couldn't resist facing the sky and opening her mouth to catch a few snowflakes on the tip of her tongue. Her delight lasted only a minute or so, and just that quickly, the childhood memory faded.

She bit her bottom lip and frowned, wondering if the snow might prevent them from traveling. But then, there was no wind, and the horses were surefooted. Their travels might be slowed, but she was sure they would make several miles, just as they had been doing each day, and every passing mile would bring them closer to their final destination. Her conflicting thoughts left her confused, Amanda realized, for she wanted nothing more than to arrive at the Spalding Mission. At the same time, she knew it could be their final goodbyes and that Buck would leave them at the mission and be gone forever.

Fort Walla Walla lay just up ahead. Amanda could see it as they crested a hill. It looked like a typical wilderness trading post, with log walls built high and its gates closed tightly against unwanted intruders. The compound stood in a clearing, with tall, snow-covered fir trees surrounding the buildings. It was a welcome beacon for weary travelers and traders alike.

Buck would soon be going back to his home in the Rocky

Mountains, and she would probably never see him again. Would he miss her as much as she would him? Would he regret not having sought out the one true God? Perhaps it was best that she would never know the answer to her burning questions. It would only bring more pain to her already broken heart to know that he ached for her as much as she did for him, yet would not give himself to the Lord.

Amanda's thoughts were interrupted by the sound of Buck's deep voice. "We'll get some supplies here and rest a few days," he announced.

She smiled in response, knowing they wouldn't be leaving right away. His concern for their welfare was evident, not only by the tone of his voice, but from the sincere expression on his handsome face.

Someone inside the fort must have seen them coming, for the large wooden gates opened, bidding them entrance to this wilderness post, where spirals of smoke drifted up from chimneys, and horses whinnied a greeting from the large split-rail corral.

As they entered the compound, Amanda spotted a tall man dressed in buckskins and wearing a long coat and hat made from an animal skin. He had long brown hair and a scruffy beard, peppered with gray. He reminded Amanda a bit of Jim, and she wondered if Mary had noticed it too.

Buck dismounted from his horse and came around to help Amanda and the baby down, as well as Mary and Little Joe. Amanda had no sooner stepped to the ground when the burly looking man stepped up to Buck and said, "You can put your horses over there with the others."

"I'll take care of it," Buck said, looking back at the women. "Amanda and Mary, you should take the babies and go inside the main building where it's bound to be warmer."

"You can follow me in," the man said to the women. "I've got some some grub warmin' over the fire."

As Amanda and Mary, carrying their children in their cradleboards, followed the big man toward the main post, Buck tended the horses. Amanda looked forward to spending a few days at the fort to rest up and replenish their supplies. Her happiness was heightened by knowing she'd be around Buck a little longer.

A blast of warm air greeted Amanda as she and Mary entered the log structure used as the main post. Bundles and stacks of supplies littered the floor along one side of the building. A huge stone fireplace graced one wall, and a roaring fire emitted enough warmth to heat the entire room. A black kettle hung in the center, with a stew-like mixture bubbling inside. Three split-log chairs sat in front of the fireplace, and a bearskin rug lay on the floor a few feet from the hearth.

It was a cozy, welcoming sight, and Amanda was more than willing to take a seat in front of the fire. First, however, she removed the cradleboard from her back, and gently lifted Little Fawn from her sheltered cocoon. Dropping to her knees onto the bearskin rug, Amanda placed her baby girl on the rug, thinking she'd been confined in her cradleboard all morning and needed the freedom to kick her legs and move her hands. Mary did the same with Little Joe.

The big man, who'd followed them inside, let his coat fall from his shoulders onto the back of a chair and moved toward Amanda. "The name's Bret Walker, and I'm temporarily runnin' this here tradin' post, while the postmaster, Pierre Pambrun, is off gettin' more supplies at Fort Vancouver."

Amanda got up and extended one hand toward Bret. "It's nice to meet you, Mr. Walker. My name is Amanda Pearson, and this is Mary Breck."

Somewhat awkwardly, he shook her small hand. "So where ya headed?"

"We are going to the Spalding Mission," she replied.

"What for?" Bret asked, getting out some bowls for the stew.

"To help Reverend and Mrs. Spalding educate the Nez Percé Indians."

He looked away from Amanda and eyeballed Mary. "She goin' there too?"

Amanda nodded.

"Oregon Territory ain't fittin' for a fragile female," he mumbled, handing Mary and Amanda each a bowl of stew. "Take a seat and warm your insides."

"We thank you for the food, Mr. Walker, and I am not as fragile as I might look," Amanda said through tight lips. "I have been through more in the last nine months than most women see in a lifetime." Seeing this as an opportunity to witness, she added, "My strength comes from the Lord. He brought us safely across many miles of wilderness."

Bret raised his eyebrows. "Really now? I thought it was that half-breed guide of yours who got ya here safely."

"Buck did lead us, but I believe God guided him." Before Bret could respond, Amanda asked, "Where is everyone? Surely you aren't here at the fort alone."

Bret chuckled. "It is kinda strange to see this big room empty of men in the middle of the day. Usually there's three or four who just like to mill around, soakin' up the heat and chewin' the fat."

"Where are men today?" Mary spoke up.

"Some are out huntin' and checkin' their traps," he answered, reaching into his pocket for a wad of chewing tobacco. "Others are holed up in the cabins here, waitin' out the storm that's no doubt comin'."

"Aren't you going to eat with us?" Amanda asked, watching him chew the tobacco.

"Later." Brett chuckled. "Truth is, I've been tastin' that stew while it heated up."

Amanda wondered how anyone could chew that awful tobacco. Just the thought of putting something like that in her mouth made her nauseous, but she was so hungry, she tried not to think about it.

"So, how long are ya plannin' to stay?" Bret asked, abruptly changing the subject.

"Buck, our guide, said we would rest here a few days, and then. . ."

Bret rose from his chair and moved toward the window. "Well, I think your man may have changed his mind, 'cause the gates just swung open, and he's ridin' for all he's worth."

CHAPTER 46

Amanda's heart gave a lurch. If Buck had ridden out, did that mean he was leaving them here and going back to his home in the Rocky Mountains? Had he decided not to take her and Mary to the Spalding Mission after all?

She'd thought about saying so much to Buck before they parted. Now she would never get the chance. *Maybe this is the best way,* Amanda thought. For she really didn't think she'd be able to say the things she'd gone over in her head so many times when it came time to say goodbye. Amanda knew the parting would not be easy. In her mind, the situation played out much differently, however. But she kept pushing those hopes and dreams as far from her thoughts as possible.

She turned to Mary and clasped her arm. "Buck is gone, Mary. He's left us to find our way to the mission by ourselves."

Mary shook her head. "Buck, he not do something like that. He say he take us to mission, he will do it."

"But you heard what the man said, Mary. Buck just rode out, and he never even told us he was going or said goodbye."

"He be back. Just wait and see." Mary gave Amanda's arm a gentle squeeze. "Come, now. I will feed our babies. Then we rest."

After Mary fed Little Joe and put him down to sleep in the small cabin they'd been given, she decided to take a walk around the compound while Amanda and the babies rested. Mary was tired, but she felt restless and needed some fresh air. She'd just stepped outside when an Indian brave, sitting straight and tall on the back of a beautiful spotted pony, rode in. His long, shiny black hair hung loosely against his broad, well-muscled shoulders, and as he drew closer, his dark eyes met Mary's with a look of surprise. "Yellow Bird? Is—it really you?" he asked in their native tongue, dismounting from his horse.

Mary's heart pounded as she steadied herself against one of the supply wagons and stared at the young man's face. It wasn't possible, but as he walked toward her, she knew for certain that it was Gray Eagle. But how could that be? Gray Eagle was dead; she'd seen the Blackfoot Indian kill him. Perhaps this was someone who looked like Gray Eagle. But he had called her by name. Mary's mind whirled with this unexpected turn of events, and she trembled so badly, she feared she might faint.

His dark eyes met hers, and their gazes locked. "Don't you recognize me, Yellow Bird? It's me, Gray Eagle. I feared I would never see you again." He placed a gentle hand on her arm.

"Oh Gray Eagle, is it really you? I thought you were dead."

"I was left for dead, but the wound I sustained from that Blackfoot warrior did not kill me," he replied. "My determination to live would not let me die."

Tears welled in Mary's eyes and ran down her cheeks. "If I'd only known. . . I grieved for so many moons."

"As did I," he said, moving closer. "After my wound healed I searched for you, but to no avail. Where have you been?"

Mary swallowed hard, unsure of where to begin. Would Gray Eagle understand about her life with Jim? What would he say when she told him about Little Joe?

"Are you all right?" Gray Eagle asked, his face a mask of concern. "Your eyes are full of fear, like the day I tried to rescue you but failed."

Trying to calm herself, Mary drew in another deep breath. "Why are you here at the fort?" she asked, thinking a change of subject might help. Seeing Gray Eagle like this was almost too much to comprehend.

"I and a few others from our tribe came to trade for supplies. How is that you are here, Yellow Bird?"

"Before I explain that, there is something you must know," she said, shakily.

"What is it?"

"Smoking Buffalo, the Blackfoot Indian who captured me, took me to one of the trading posts and gave me to a white man in exchange for some things he wanted."

"You have been living with a white man all this time?" he questioned.

She nodded. "His name was Jim Breck, and he was my husband. He changed my name from Yellow Bird to Mary."

Gray Eagle's brows lifted, and he sucked in his breath. "You are married?"

"I was." Mary dropped her gaze. "Jim is dead. He died from rattlesnake bites."

"Did you love him, Yellow Bird?" Gray Eagle's question came quickly.

"Not at first, but I grew to love him," she answered honestly.

"Oh, I see. I'm sorry."

"What of my family?" Mary asked. "Are they alive and doing well?"

He nodded. "Your parents and brother are living near the Spalding Mission for the winter months."

Mary clasped her hands over her mouth. "I am so glad. That's where Amanda and I are heading, and I look forward to seeing my family there."

Gray Eagle quirked an eyebrow. "Amanda?"

"She is a white woman and plans to teach our people about God."

Gray Eagle smiled. "Reverend Henry Spalding has been teaching our people about God. He reads to us from the Bible, but many of the People call it 'the Book of Heaven.'"

Just then, Mary caught sight of Amanda standing in the doorway, motioning for her to come. Mary wanted to stay and talk more with Gray Eagle. All the years she'd mourned for this man, and now he was here. It was all Mary could do not to throw herself into his arms, but more needed to be said. There were so many things she wanted to tell him.

"I need to go," Mary said. "Will you be here awhile? Can we talk later?"

Gray Eagle nodded. "Yes, we have much catching up to do."

Amanda had just gotten Little Joe settled and laid back down when Mary stepped into the cabin they shared. The look on her friend's face sent a shiver of apprehension up Amanda's spine. "Is something wrong, Mary? You look upset. Little Joe was a bit fussy, but he's okay now."

Mary took a seat beside Amanda. "You have talked of miracles, right?"

Amanda nodded.

"A miracle has happened."

"Is it Buck? Has he returned?"

Mary shook her head. "It is Gray Eagle. He is not dead."

Amanda sat trying to process what Mary had just said. She remembered Mary telling her about the Nez Percé man she had planned to marry before she was captured by the Blackfoot. "I thought you had said Gray Eagle had been killed at the hands of a Blackfoot Indian."

"Yes. He not dead though. Got badly wounded, but he survived. He here at the fort. We just talk."

Amanda clasped Mary's hand. "Oh, that is wonderful news! It is a miracle, and I am so happy for you!"

Mary's forehead wrinkled. "Gray Eagle know about Jim, but. . ." Her voice trailed off as she glanced over at her son, sleeping peacefully on a mat beside Little Fawn. "I not tell him about Little Joe."

"How come?"

"He may not want me if he know I bore a white man's child."

"But you just said you told him about Jim. Was he understanding about that?"

Mary shrugged. "I not know. He just say he sorry. He also say my family is camped near Spalding Mission. I anxious to go there when Buck gets back."

"You mean 'if' Buck gets back," Amanda corrected. "He's been gone several hours, and that is not a good sign."

"Maybe Gray Eagle would guide us," Mary said. "He will go that way too."

"Yes, maybe so. Would you ask him about it?"

Mary looked like she was about to reply, when Little Joe woke up again. "Me tend baby first. Then I look for Gray Eagle," she said.

Amanda smiled. Even though she would miss Buck's companionship, she was thankful God had sent Gray Eagle to potentially act as their guide.

While Little Fawn still slept and Mary tended to her son, Amanda decided to take the opportunity to read the Bible.

Taking a seat on a small wooden bench, she opened her Bible to Deuteronomy 31:6 and read silently: *"Be strong and of a good courage, fear not, nor be afraid. . .for the Lord, thy God, he it is that doth go with thee; he will not fail thee, or forsake thee."*

Reading those words was an affirmation for Amanda. God had brought her this far, through numerous trials, and He would continue to provide for her and Little Fawn and take them safely to their journey's end.

She closed her eyes and prayed, *Heavenly Father, I thank Thee for Thy many blessings, and for giving me the privilege of raising Little Fawn. Please continue to guide and direct me, and prepare the hearts of the Nez Percé people I am going to teach.*

When Mary finished feeding her son, she decided to take him for a walk, since Little Fawn was still sleeping and wouldn't need to be fed right away. "I be back soon," she told Amanda.

"Take your time. From the way my daughter is sleeping, it could be awhile before she wakes up." Amanda yawned. "In fact, I'm feeling the need to rest some more too, so I think I'll lie down beside her and try to sleep."

"That be good." Mary wrapped Little Joe in a warm blanket, then picked him up and went out the door.

After she'd stepped outside into the fresh, crisp air, she spotted Gray Eagle heading her way. Her heart pounded with each step he took, bringing them closer. When he approached, Gray Eagle's gaze moved from her face to the child in her arms.

Mary took a deep breath to steady her voice. "This is my son, Little Joe."

Was it displeasure she saw on Gray Eagle's face or a look of sadness? She could not be certain. "I see," he murmured. "When we spoke earlier, you did not say you had a white man's child."

"Little Joe has brought much happiness into my life," Mary answered defensively.

"Were you happy living with your white husband?"

"Not at first, but I learned to be happy."

His dark eyes clouded over. "I see."

Mary swallowed against the lump lodged in her throat. It was obvious that Gray Eagle would never accept her, knowing she had a half-breed son. *Should I still ask if he will be our guide?* she wondered. *Or would it better if Amanda and I set out on our own? I am sure if we asked Bret Walker, he would tell us the way.*

She didn't have long to ponder the issue, because just then Buck, with a dead deer slung over the back of his horse, rode into the compound. Mary knew Amanda would be relieved, and right now, she was too.

After Buck dismounted and explained that he'd gone in search of some fresh meat, she introduced him to Gray Eagle. But before she had a chance to explain that Buck was her and Amanda's guide, Gray Eagle announced that he had to get back to his campsite outside the fort. "May the Great Spirit be with you, Mary Yellow Bird," he said.

Mary watched him walk away, his last words resounding in her head, like an echo in the highest mountains. She wished they could have talked longer. She wished she would have felt free to ask if he still cared for her. But what good would it have done? He'd left in such a hurry, it was obvious that he no longer had any feelings for her. His last words had sounded like a goodbye. It was just as well, she decided. She felt unworthy of him, and was certain they could never have a future together. She was glad she hadn't asked Gray Eagle to travel with them to the mission. Buck was here now, and it was better this way.

CHAPTER 47

When morning dawned the following day, Buck, Amanda, Mary, and the babies prepared to be on their way. They'd originally planned to stay at Fort Walla Walla for a few days, but Mary was anxious to see her family. They already had some snow, but Buck had said it was best to move out early, before the full force of winter was upon them.

As they loaded their supplies onto the pack mules and Jim's horse, Mary noticed some Indians standing on the other side of the compound. She paid little attention to them at first, thinking more about the cold of the late autumn air and how she would keep Little Joe warm until the journey was complete. After a second look, she realized one of them was Gray Eagle. With him, was a beautiful young Indian woman whom she did not recognize. The woman laughed and leaned in close to Gray Eagle. They seemed intent on what they were saying, totally unaware of Mary's presence.

Mary sighed deeply. No wonder Gray Eagle seemed so anxious to leave. He'd obviously replaced her with this lovely young woman. As much as it pained Mary to see this, it was completely understandable. After all, she had been gone a long time. She wondered if the young woman might be Gray Eagle's wife. So many moons had passed; it seemed like a lifetime ago.

In spite of the ache in her heart, she could not make this her concern. She must remember that the past was behind her and she needed to concentrate on her life with Little Joe.

Mary was surprised when Gray Eagle headed her way. Thunder had been sitting close to her while she checked on her horse, and his tail wagged as Gray Eagle approached. Normally, if a stranger came anywhere near Mary, Thunder stood guard, with hair raised and a warning growl. It was almost as if the dog knew this Indian would not harm Mary in any way.

When Gray Eagle reached the place where Mary stood, their gazes locked. Time seemed to stand still. She looked up at him and swallowed hard, her mouth suddenly dry. Mary Yellow Bird took in all six feet of his muscular build. Time had been good to Gray Eagle, and it took all of her willpower not to reach out and touch his shiny black, flowing hair. It was as if, in that minute, they were linked together, back to those years when they were young and their love for each other was all that mattered. Her heart pounded so fast that her chest ached, and it was difficult to draw a breath.

Gray Eagle reached down to pet Thunder's head, and the dog wagged his tail even more.

"Can we talk?" Gray Eagle asked, his dark eyes piercing Mary's and making her forget about Thunder's reaction.

Mary cast a quick glance in the direction of the young woman who stood nearby, as though waiting for him. When Gray Eagle turned and whispered something to the woman, she nodded and walked away.

Mary glanced in the other direction and saw Thunder amble over to the place where Buck was still checking the supplies for the final part of their journey.

"What do you wish to say, Gray Eagle?" Mary asked.

He touched her arm. "I want to ride to the mission with you so we can talk."

She pulled back, hoping to erase what she was sure could never be. "You act as though you care about me, but I know you do not."

"I do care," he said sincerely. "I love you, Yellow Bird. I have always loved you."

"Have you forgotten that I have been with a white man—that I have a son by him?"

"No, I did not forget. I know that you did not ask to be captured or marry a white man, but he is gone now." Gray Eagle leaned close to Mary. "Everything will be all right. You will go home with me, and we will be married. I will love your son as if he were my own and will love his mother for all of my days."

Mary wanted to believe his promises, but could she? Her son was not all that stood in their way. "What about the Indian woman you are with?" she asked, rubbing the place on her arm where Gray Eagle had touched. "Does she hold a special place in your heart? Can you simply abandon her to marry me?"

Gray Eagle smiled. "Did you not recognize my sister, Running Fox? She is no longer a child, as you would remember her. She is a beautiful young woman and is promised to White Foot. They will be married soon."

Yellow Bird's mouth fell open, not knowing how to respond. She remembered back to the day when White Foot had asked for her hand in marriage, but she'd turned him down in favor of Gray Eagle. She was glad White Foot had found someone to love and relieved to know that Gray Eagle did not have a wife.

"Come, we will travel to the mission now," Gray Eagle said, excitement in his voice. "On the way, we will get caught up with each other's lives."

As Gray Eagle pulled her into his arms, Mary Yellow Bird no longer felt the air's wintry grasp. Was this why her spirit guide, the yellow bird, had visited her not long ago?

To the Nez Percé, yellow was not only the sign for victory, but it was also a symbol of joy. Except for the birth of her son, Yellow Bird hadn't felt pure joy such as this in a long time. Now, the feelings for Gray Eagle that she'd tried so hard to bury all these years came rushing back, making her nerve endings quiver. Did she dare hope for those long-ago dreams to be a part of her life once again?

An awkward silence fell between Buck and Amanda as they followed Mary and Gray Eagle out of the fort and onto the trail. With Gray Eagle agreeing to travel with them, Amanda figured Buck might go his separate way, and while part of her wanted him to continue on as their guide, another part almost wished he had gone back to his home. Seeing him every day and wishing for what she couldn't have was hard for her—maybe for Buck too.

If only he would set his bitterness aside and surrender his life to the Lord, she thought yet again. *Can't he see that not all Christians are like the man who abused him when he was a child?*

With a need to focus on something else, Amanda turned her attention to the snow-covered trees. They were beautiful, dressed in pristine white with boughs of green showing through in some places. Seeing the splendor of the trees made Amanda think of Christmas, which was just a month away.

Last Christmas she'd been betrothed to Nathan Lane. Amanda and her father had spent the holiday with Nathan and his family. It had been a lovely celebration, and after dinner she and Nathan had walked hand-in-hand through the snow, discussing their future. Amanda had been looking forward to becoming Nathan's wife, but that wasn't meant to be, and maybe it never had been.

Now why am I thinking of him? she asked herself. *My relationship with Nathan is in the past. My future is here in the West, telling others about Jesus and raising my precious baby girl.*

She glanced over at Buck, riding beside her on Dusty, his buckskin horse. Sitting tall in the saddle and looking straight ahead, he looked more like an Indian than a white man. Perhaps it was because they were in Indian territory, since Buck was part Nez Percé. Amanda wondered if he was anxious to spend time among his mother's people. It was a shame he'd been separated from his mother at a young age. No child should ever have to grow up without a mother. Amanda knew that better than anyone.

What would happen to Little Fawn if I was taken from her? Amanda wondered. *Would Mary take my daughter and raise her as her own?*

Amanda shuddered. She hoped and prayed nothing would ever separate her and Little Fawn.

"Are ya cold?" Buck asked when his horse nudged close to hers. "Would ya like a buffalo robe to wrap up in?"

She smiled. "I am fine, but thank you anyway." It pleased Amanda that Buck seemed concerned for her welfare.

Just then, Little Fawn started to cry. She was probably cold, or needed to be fed. Amanda hated to do it, but she turned to Buck and said, "Could we stop for a bit, so I can see what my baby needs?"

"Sure, no problem." Buck cupped his hands around his mouth and hollered for the others to stop. Mary and Gray Eagle reined in their horses. Then Buck helped Amanda down and lifted Little Fawn's cradleboard from her shoulders. The baby was crying even harder.

"Thank you for your kindness," Amanda said.

Buck smiled and gave her a nod.

Heavenly Father, Amanda prayed, *help me not to wish for what I cannot have.*

CHAPTER 48

O n the last day of their journey they had ridden about fifteen miles northward when Mary spotted Lapwai Creek. They were getting closer to the People's winter camp. Her skin tingled from excitement and anticipation. "We are going home," she whispered to Little Joe, who was in his cradleboard tied securely to her back. "Home at last, where I will once again be known as Yellow Bird."

Despite her enthusiasm, Yellow Bird felt some anxiety about going home. She'd changed so much since she was taken from her tribe, and nagging doubts plagued her about whether her son would be accepted. She wondered too if her home would be the same as she remembered it, and would the people be the same as before? When she entered their winter village, her life would change once again. She had been through many changes since her abduction, so with the Great Spirit's help, perhaps she could manage this change as well.

Yellow Bird was thankful for the comfort of her five-month-old son, whom she loved more than life itself. She appreciated too her faithful dog and protector, who had been her constant companion since Jim's untimely death, and she was thankful for her good friend, Amanda, who had led her to the Lord. Most of all, she was grateful that she and Gray Eagle had been reunited.

It was late in the afternoon when they arrived at the village. Many lodges stood in their customary circular pattern, and Yellow Bird noted that the Clearwater River was as pure and beautiful as she remembered.

As they rode into camp, Yellow Bird saw children playing among the huts, women cooking over campfires, and men sitting in small groups, visiting with one another while smoking their long pipes. It was a peaceful, happy scene, one that she had resigned herself never to see again. She sat on her horse, studying the village and watching her people.

When they were noticed, all activity ceased, as adults and children alike hurried to greet them. A rush of emotion brought moisture to Yellow Bird's eyes, and her heart quickened as Gray Eagle guided their horses through the crowd of people. She recognized the familiar lodge up ahead, with a picture of a large, white wolf painted on the front flap. The sight of it brought another tide of tears and long-buried emotions. There was no one outside the lodge, but figuring her parents to be inside, she turned to Gray Eagle and asked, "Would you please go in and prepare them for my arrival? I know I have changed quite a bit, but should they still recognize me, I do not want it to be a great shock. If Mother and Father think I am dead, they might believe they are seeing a ghost spirit."

Gray Eagle nodded. "I will explain where you have been all this time." He touched her arm. "I will tell them about your child and the death of his white father, and say that you are waiting outside their lodge."

Gray Eagle dismounted, then helped Yellow Bird down from her horse. As he entered her parents' lodge, she removed Little Joe from his cradleboard and waited nervously.

"Aren't you going in?" Amanda asked, joining Yellow Bird by her horse.

Yellow Bird shook her head. "Not yet. Gray Eagle go first to prepare them. It will be a shock to know I am here."

"I'm sure they'll be happy," Amanda said, slipping her arm around Yellow Bird's waist.

A few minutes later, Gray Eagle stepped out of the lodge with Yellow Bird's parents. As they approached, Yellow Bird's heart seemed to stand still.

Her mother, Small Rabbit, sobbed, tears flowing freely down her leathery cheeks. She wrapped her arms around Yellow Bird and murmured, "Welcome home, Daughter."

Her father, Laughing Wolf, stared at Yellow Bird, as though seeing her for the very first time. "You have been gone so long, we thought you were dead." He too gave Yellow Bird a hug. "We searched many days, but there was no trail to follow. We are thankful to the Great Spirit for bringing you back to us."

Yellow Bird was surprised to see the drastic change in her parents. They had both aged considerably. Worry and grief over her disappearance was no doubt the cause. Their hair, once dark and shiny, was now gray and lifeless. They had wrinkles where smooth skin had once been. Their dark eyes looked tired and sunken, and Mother looked thin and frail.

A twinge of guilt ran through Yellow Bird. She knew she had been the cause of their sorrow. If only she had stayed inside their teepee that morning so long ago, instead of going off by herself to take a bath in the lake. But nothing could change what had already been.

"Nothing gives me greater joy than to be back where I belong." Yellow Bird nearly choked on her words. All that she wanted to say seemed to be stuck in her throat. There were so many emotions she hadn't allowed herself to feel because she truly believed this day would never come.

For a few moments, while Amanda, Buck, and Gray Eagle looked on, Yellow Bird and her parents stood in silence, holding each other as if making sure this was real.

When Yellow Bird gained control of her emotions, she smiled and said, "Mother. . . Father. . .I want you to meet my son, Joseph Little Wolf, but I call him 'Little Joe.' His white father named him Joseph, and he allowed me to choose an Indian name as well." She paused and lifted the baby. "Can you open your hearts and accept this child as your grandson?"

Laughing Wolf took the boy from her and held him high in the air. "I am honored you chose to call him Little Wolf, and I believe I speak for your mother as well when I say that if the child is part of you, then you are both welcome in our lodge. This day has not only brought our daughter back to us, but it has given us a grandson as well."

Small Rabbit nodded and reached for the chubby baby. "He is a fine boy. Our first grandson." She smiled at Yellow Bird. "Except for his curly brown hair, he looks much like his mother. Come inside now, Daughter, for we want to hear the details about where you have been."

"Yes, we have much to talk about," Yellow Bird agreed. Then, remembering that Amanda stood nearby, she introduced her and explained that Amanda had come to help the Spaldings at their mission.

Laughing Wolf bobbed his head. "Their place is two miles up Lapwai Creek."

Amanda looked at Buck, who stood nearby. "Can we go there now?"

"We can go whenever you want," Buck said, "but wouldn't you rather stay here and rest awhile?"

Amanda shook her head. "I am anxious to speak with the Spaldings. Besides, Mary Yellow Bird needs some time alone with her family."

"What about Little Fawn?" Yellow Bird asked. "She will need to be fed."

Amanda laughed. "In my excitement, I'd almost forgotten about that. Perhaps we can come back later in the day, when it's time for her next feeding."

"Why don't you leave the baby here with Yellow Bird?" Buck suggested. "Then after you've talked with the Spaldings, we can come back."

"I am sure Little Fawn would be in good hands, but I'd rather keep her with me," Amanda said, removing her daughter from the cradleboard.

"What if baby cries for food?" Yellow Bird asked.

Yellow Bird's parents looked at her strangely. "I will explain things later," she told them. Then she gave Amanda a hug and said, "I take good care of Little Fawn. Promise."

Amanda hesitated but finally agreed.

Yellow Bird's heart went out to Amanda, because she knew she would feel the same way if she were separated from Little Joe, even for a short time.

Amanda kissed Little Fawn's forehead. "I will be back soon," she murmured. Then she handed the baby to Yellow Bird and mounted her horse.

As Buck and Amanda rode out of the camp, Yellow Bird followed her parents inside their lodge.

———

Amanda and Buck rode along the snow-covered trail, following the bends and turns of the Clearwater River. She thought about Mary Yellow Bird and the joy she'd seen on her face when she was greeted by her parents. Amanda was happy her friend had been reunited with her family, but she felt a bit envious. Amanda had no one at the end of her journey to greet her, except the Spaldings, and they were strangers. *If only Papa had lived and could be with me now,* she thought. *Oh Papa, I miss you so much. Perhaps you are with me in spirit.*

In an effort to squelch her tears, Amanda changed the direction of her thoughts. *I wonder what type of job I'll be given at the mission. I hope I am asked to teach the children.*

Amanda had taught school for a few years before her betrothal to Nathan, and she'd always had a good rapport with the children in her class.

Or maybe I'll be asked to cook and clean. While not Amanda's favorite tasks, she would do whatever was expected of her in order to help out, although it would be much harder to witness to the Indians if she was relegated to household duties and not allowed to teach or mingle with any prospective converts.

"You're frowning," Buck said, breaking into Amanda's musings. "Are ya still worried about Little Fawn?"

She shook her head. "I am sure she is in good hands with Yellow Bird and her family, and we won't be parted for long."

"Then why do ya look so sad?"

"I was just thinking about my future and what will be expected of me at the mission."

"I thought you were goin' there to teach the Nez Percé about God."

"I am hoping for the opportunity to do that, but I may be asked to do other things."

Buck shrugged his shoulders. "Ya did other things at Jim and Mary's cabin but still managed to tell Mary plenty about God."

Amanda smiled. "You're right about that." Yet again, she found herself wishing Buck was willing to listen to the scriptures. What a joy it would be to lead him to the Lord. How different things might be between them if he became a Christian.

Why is it that so many things in life don't turn out the way we want? she wondered. *I know it's not right to expect everything to go my way, but it would be nice to see more of my prayers answered.*

"*God always answers our prayers,*" Amanda remembered her father saying on more than one occasion. "*Sometimes He says yes; sometimes no; and sometimes He asks us to wait.*"

Waiting had been one of the hardest things for Amanda when she was a child. Waiting to see what presents she would receive on Christmas Day; waiting for Papa to give her money to buy material to make a new dress; and waiting for Nathan to declare his love and ask for her hand in marriage.

Now there I go, thinking about Nathan again, Amanda scolded herself. *Why can't I forget about him and let the past go? After all, I certainly wasn't first on his mind. No, my best friend had the privilege of that. Is there a part of me that still loves Nathan? Or maybe I am thinking of him because he hurt me so badly and I haven't truly forgiven him.*

Amanda needed to make peace with this, or it would plague her forever. She would make it a priority to ask God to remove all negative thoughts or wishful thinking about Nathan from her mind. She must reach into the depths of her soul and completely forgive Nathan for what he had done.

"Look up ahead." Buck jolted Amanda's thoughts once more. "This must be the place," he said as they guided their horses up to a log structure, much larger than Jim Breck's cabin.

Amanda couldn't believe after more than nine months of travel that she had finally made it to her destination. There it was—the Spalding Mission. She hoped that the Spaldings had received her letter and would welcome her help.

CHAPTER 49

As Amanda and Buck headed back to the Nez Percé camp that evening, Amanda thought about her meeting with Rev. and Mrs. Spalding. Henry Spalding hadn't been quite as friendly as his wife, Eliza, but he'd been cordial enough when he'd learned who Amanda was and she'd shared her reason for coming. The Spaldings said they had received Amanda's letter but had no idea when to expect her.

Eliza Spalding was a petite woman who'd recently had a baby girl, although Amanda didn't get the chance to see the child, as she'd been sleeping during their visit. Eliza had mentioned that the baby was fussy and thought it might be because she didn't have enough breast milk, so they'd begun supplementing with goat's milk. Amanda knew that unless Yellow Bird came back to the mission to live with her, she would probably have to resort to goat's milk for Little Fawn as well. When Amanda told them about the Flathead Indian baby she'd found and claimed as her own, she'd been relieved that they had accepted the idea of her raising the child at the mission.

The log structure the Spaldings lived in had been built by several of the Nez Percé Indians in the area, and they'd made one section of it their home. The other part served as a schoolroom and a place of worship. Rev. Spalding had explained that sometime in the future they would be moving their mission from its present site to a better location. At first, Amanda didn't see anything wrong with the area where the mission was now. Then the Spaldings explained that when they'd first arrived in November 1836, after a long journey with several setbacks, they had lived in an Indian teepee, until a suitable home could be constructed. But the mosquitoes were a serious problem in the summer, as well as the heat, so they wanted to find a better location.

During the visit they'd discussed what Amanda's duties would be, and it was agreed that she could teach some of the younger children and help out wherever was necessary. That suited Amanda just fine. She looked forward to settling in at the mission when she returned there with Little Fawn in the morning.

"You're awfully quiet," Buck said, halting Amanda's musings. "Are ya havin' second thoughts about helpin' out at the mission?"

She shook her head. "I'm just reflecting on everything the Spaldings told me today."

"Think you're gonna be happy living there?" he questioned.

"I believe God sent me on this journey and He helped me make it here, so that makes me happy," Amanda replied, without really answering Buck's question. The truth was, she'd be much happier if Buck were staying too and would agree to help out at the mission. But that was just wishful thinking. He'd made it clear that he would be heading back to his home in the Rockies soon, and Amanda was sure that, short of a miracle, Buck would keep true to his word.

———

"How is Little Fawn?" Amanda asked when she and Buck returned to Laughing Wolf's lodge in the Nez Percé camp.

"She is fine," Mary replied, motioning to the mat where Little Fawn and Little Joe lay sleeping. "How it go at mission?"

"It went well." Amanda smiled. "They want me to teach the small children, and I'll begin as soon as I get settled in there."

"When you plan to go?"

"Tomorrow morning." Amanda paused. "Would you go with me, Mary—I mean, Yellow Bird?"

"To see mission?"

"I think she wants you to live there with her there," Buck interjected, before Amanda could respond to Yellow Bird's question.

Yellow Bird's dark eyebrows shot up. "I belong here with family. We have much catching up to do."

Amanda nodded. "I understand that, but I was hoping you would continue to feed Little Fawn until she is weaned. I know it's a lot to ask, but. . ."

"She will come," Gray Eagle spoke up. "We both speak English, and we will come to mission and help where we can." He looked at Laughing Wolf and Small Rabbit. "Wouldn't you like to go there too?" he asked in their native tongue.

There was a long pause, and then Laughing Wolf nodded and said, "We will go see what it is like, and maybe we can help."

"What did your father just say?" Amanda asked.

"He say they will come too." Yellow Bird looked over at Buck. "You come also?"

Buck shook his head. "I'll be leavin' for my place in the mountains tomorrow, and I probably won't come back this way."

Yellow Bird noticed the look of disappointment on Amanda's face before she cast her eyes downward after hearing Buck's plans. It was obvious that she was in love with Buck. Yellow Bird was pretty sure Buck cared for Amanda too, so it didn't make sense that he'd be leaving. She wished there was something she could do to keep him from going, but it was Buck's decision, and she would not interfere. Maybe when he woke up in the morning he would change his mind.

When Buck awoke the following day, he gathered up his gear. It had snowed during the night, but had stopped, and he wanted to get an early start, before it began snowing again. Travel could be grueling in the high country once winter set in. If things got too bad, he might have to hole up at one of the forts until spring.

Buck felt a sense of regret as he looked at Amanda sitting near the fire, holding her daughter. *If only things could be different,* he silently fumed. *How many times have I said that to myself? Amanda is a Christian, and I am not. She's a proper-speaking, beautiful woman, and I'm a half-breed, rugged mountain man. We don't belong together, and it's better that I return to what's familiar to me.*

Even though Buck hashed out the reasons with himself, he knew that if he stuck around even for another day or so, it would be that much harder for him to leave. No, he had to go now, before he gave in to his desire to stay near Amanda.

"I'm headin' out now," he said, moving to the center of Laughing Wolf's Lodge, where Gray Eagle, Yellow Bird, and her family had gathered.

"You will be missed," Yellow Bird said with a catch in her voice. "Don't you want stay and eat breakfast first?"

He shook his head. "I'll eat on the journey. Your mother gave me some pemmican, and I have dried berries and meat, so I'll be fine."

"I will pray for safe travels," Yellow Bird said.

"Thanks for that." Buck glanced at Amanda. "I hope things go well for you at the mission."

She smiled, although it seemed to be forced. "I hope things go well for thee—I mean you too."

"Thanks." Buck hesitated a minute, then turned and rushed out of the lodge. Thunder sat next to his horse, as if he knew Buck was soon to leave.

After securing the rest of his gear, Buck hunkered down to pet the dog's head. "You take care of everyone, ya hear?"

Thunder responded with a lick to Buck's hand. The dog was as faithful as any animal could be. Buck would miss his four-legged friend.

As if waiting for their travels to begin, a lone *kree-e-e-e-e*. . . sounded, as Buck's winged brother circled overhead. Buck looked up and saw the reddish tint of the hawk's tail as it soared in the morning's light, and he knew without a doubt that the hawk would accompany him home.

"Well, Thunder, ol' boy, time's a-wastin'." Buck had to leave now before he changed his mind.

———

Yellow Bird sang one of her favorite Nez Percé chants while rocking Little Joe to sleep. For the past week since her family had moved their lodge to the mission site, she had spent time getting reacquainted with both family and friends while preparing for her forthcoming marriage to Gray Eagle. She was thankful everyone had accepted her and Little Joe, as well as Amanda's Flathead daughter. Yellow Bird was also happy to learn that her brother, Little Bear, had married Smiling Squirrel during her absence, and that they were expecting their first child in the spring. It would be nice for Little Joe to have a cousin to grow up with.

The time spent waiting for the wedding day, which would also happen in early spring, was a good chance for Yellow Bird and Gray Eagle to become reacquainted. Yellow Bird prayed daily that she would be a good wife and not disappoint her new husband in any way. It seemed that she had waited all her life to become Gray Eagle's wife, and while her thoughts were a mixture of apprehension and anticipation, she thanked God for the joy in her heart. She would always miss Jim Breck and the love they had come to know, and she would be certain that Little Joe learned about his real father when he was old enough to understand. However, nothing ever had, or ever could, come close to what she felt for Gray Eagle. She was certain he would make a good father for Little Joe, as well as any other children they might be blessed with in the future.

When Yellow Bird wasn't taking care of Little Joe and Little Fawn, she helped Amanda at the Spalding mission, acting as an interpreter, since she could speak both the Nez Percé language, as well as English. Two Feathers, another Nez Percé woman, also spoke English and did some of the interpreting, but she was new to the tribe since Yellow Bird had left, and Yellow Bird hadn't had the chance to get to know the woman yet.

Much to Yellow's Bird surprise, Rev. and Mrs. Spalding recognized her, and also she recognized them, because it turned out that Rev. Spalding had been the preacher who had performed the ceremony when she and Jim had gotten married. Little did she realize back then, that this was the same couple who were heading west to start a mission to teach her people about God.

Yellow Bird's parents, as well as Gray Eagle and his family, helped out with chores at the mission and seemed to enjoy the pictures from the Bible stories Eliza Spalding drew, as well as the songs that were sung during the worship services. Amanda seemed pleased and had told Yellow Bird that she hoped her family would come to know the Lord personally, just as Yellow Bird had done.

Yellow Bird looked down at Little Joe, snuggled peacefully in her arms. As she sang the babe a song, she thanked the Great Spirit one more time for giving her this special son.

―――

Sitting on a mat inside Yellow Bird's teepee, Amanda smiled as she observed the tender moment between Yellow Bird and Little Joe. She enjoyed hearing Yellow Bird's song. It reminded her of a lullaby. Perhaps it was a Nez Percé lullaby. It had certainly put the baby to sleep.

Little Fawn, now a little over three months old, was also sleeping. She'd fallen asleep after her last feeding. She was a contented baby and seemed to be doing well physically. *Of course, that's because of Yellow Bird,* Amanda thought with gratitude. *Little Fawn would not have survived without the nourishment Yellow Bird provided from the day I first found my precious daughter.*

Amanda glanced around the teepee, feeling grateful she and Little Fawn had a place to stay. Since there wasn't room in the Spaldings' log home for extra people, Amanda and her daughter had been staying with Yellow Bird and her parents in the teepee they had erected on the mission grounds. It was a good opportunity for Amanda to learn more of the Nez Percé customs, and Yellow Bird continued to teach Amanda some Indian words.

During the day, while either Yellow Bird or her mother kept an eye on Little Fawn, Amanda helped out at the mission, teaching the younger children, and doing whatever she could to make Eliza's life easier. The poor woman had her hands full, taking care of her little one, as well as instructing the Indian girls who had come to the mission to learn how to sew and do several other things. About one hundred children came to the mission every day, and Amanda enjoyed teaching them Bible verses and songs. Having no books to teach with, Mrs. Spalding had printed some books by hand and often drew pictures to depict some of the Bible stories. This took a good deal of time, so Amanda knew her help was appreciated.

Amanda liked keeping busy. It felt good to be doing something worthwhile, and it helped to take her mind off Buck, for she often found herself thinking of him and wondering how he was doing. It had snowed off and on the last couple of days, adding several more inches to the ground. Amanda could only imagine what it must be like as Buck ventured higher into the mountains. She hoped he would make it safely to his cabin, for the things she had learned about winter in the Rockies let her know how challenging it could be. She shuddered, just thinking about it.

Buck had been on the trail for seven days, and it had been snowing most of that time. Between the heavy snowfall and the driving wind, it was hard to see up ahead.

"What am I doin'?" he mumbled under his breath. "I need my head examined, traveling in weather like this." What he needed was a place to hunker down until the weather improved. Buck knew that the higher up he went into the mountains, the more challenging his trek would become. It was difficult now to see his brother, the hawk, with the snow falling as hard as it was, but Buck knew the red tail was there, for he could hear his call overhead.

Guess I should have holed up at Fort Walla Walla, he told himself. *But if I'd done that I would have been tempted to ride over to the mission and check on Amanda.* He clenched the reins tighter. *Would that have been so bad? I would like to know how she's doing.*

In spite of the furs he would be collecting, the idea of spending the winter in his drafty little cabin didn't hold much appeal now that Jim was gone and wouldn't be stopping over at his place for regular visits.

I could even stay in Jim's cabin, since Yellow Bird won't be goin' back there, but I'd still be alone and thinking about Amanda. Buck knew that no matter where he was, his thoughts would be on her.

Buck reined in for a moment, looking ahead, then glancing back from where he'd just come. He watched as snow kept falling, laying so heavy on the pines they could no longer support it. Buck was cold and miserable, especially now when snow from the branches ended up down the back of his neck. Did he really want to go any higher, where it would be even colder?

"What do ya say, boy?" Buck murmured, leaning over to stroke Dusty's neck. "Should we turn around and head back to the fort where it's warmer?"

The lathered horse whinnied as if in response.

"All right then," Buck said, turning the horse around, "let's head down to the fort, and we'll stay for the winter."

CHAPTER 50

M rs. Spalding would like you and your family to join us at the mission for Christmas dinner," Amanda told Yellow Bird the morning before the holiday. "Gray Eagle and his family are welcome to join us too."

Yellow Bird blinked as she looked at Amanda with a curious expression. "What is Christ-mas?"

"It is the day we remember Christ's birthday," Amanda explained. "Remember, I told you the story of how Jesus was born in a lowly manger."

"I remember story, but know nothing about Christ-mas dinner."

"It's the way many of my people celebrate, to remember the day of His birth. We get together for a special meal, sing songs about Jesus' birth, and read the Christmas story from the Bible." Amanda placed a gentle hand on Yellow Bird's arm. "Will you come and help us celebrate?"

Yellow Bird nodded. "I will ask the others too, but not till Gray Eagle returns."

"Where is Gray Eagle?" Amanda asked.

"He go hunting with White Foot. They hope to get a few deer."

"That would be good," Amanda acknowledged. "Since winter is starting out, I hope they have good luck before the weather gets even worse."

Making his way back down the mountains, Buck halted his horse and sat looking down at the Clearwater River. When he'd reached the top of the slopes overlooking the river, he'd found himself on a treeless, rocky plateau. During this snowstorm, Buck was glad he'd made the decision to turn back, for he knew it would have been a mistake to risk his life or Dusty's to travel higher into the Rockies. He'd been dealing with heavy snowfall all day, and the rocky path was slippery. He would be glad to get down the frozen slope and onto the level ground that followed the river.

His horse's flanks quivered from the day-to-day exertion, and Buck knew they both needed a rest. Buck had actually been planning to stop at Fort Walla Walla but had changed his mind, deciding to go back to the Nez Percé campsite to see Amanda instead. He still hadn't decided what to say to her. Nothing had changed between the time he had left and now, so he couldn't declare his love for Amanda or offer her any kind of a future.

So what is my purpose in going back? Buck asked himself. He'd convinced himself that he was returning to the Nez Percé camp so he wouldn't have to spend the winter alone, but Buck knew the real reason he was going back was to see Amanda.

"What am I hopin' for?" he muttered. "Do I think if I stick around long enough she'll accept me the way I am, and won't expect me to convert to Christianity?"

With hooves pawing at the snow, Buck's horse snorted, obviously impatient to go. Despite his own energy waning, all Buck could think about was getting back to the Nez Percé camp.

"Okay, okay, let's be on our way," Buck said, giving the reins a snap.

Dusty moved forward, but his hooves slipped on a frozen rock, partially hidden beneath the snow. Before Buck could intervene, horse and rider were sliding down the hill. Buck tightened his legs, gripping Dusty's middle, and hoping to keep his balance. But the hill was too steep, as the horse whinnied and labored, slowly losing the battle to stay upright. Unable to hang on, Buck fell off the horse, and as he landed, Dusty lost his footing and rolled over on top of him, with most of his weight on Buck's leg.

Buck groaned as his leg started to throb, fearing the worst, not only for himself, but for Dusty. *What was I thinking, pushing my horse like that?* He was almost sure his leg was broken. The pain was so intense he feared he might pass out. Miraculously, the horse stood up, shaking his mane, and Buck was relieved to see that, except for some blood coming from a cut above Dusty's back leg, the horse seemed to be unharmed.

Buck, on the other hand, didn't fare so well. He became instantly nauseous, seeing the bone showing through the skin on his leg through a tear in his leggings. What was he going to do now? He couldn't put any weight on it. He needed something to pull himself up so he could get back on the horse. But short of a miracle, he didn't see how that was going to happen, because there wasn't even a twig within his reach. Buck was certain that if he stayed here on the cold, snow-covered ground too long, he would freeze to death.

The longer Buck lay there, the worse he felt. Shivering against the cold and feeling something warm and sticky on his forehead, he reached up to touch it. When Buck withdrew his hand and saw blood, he knew it wasn't just his leg that had been injured. For some reason, though, his head didn't hurt. Maybe the cold had numbed the pain.

Kree-e-e-e-e. . . Kree-e-e-e-e. . . Kree-e-e-e-e. . .

Through squinted eyes, Buck looked up and saw his winged friend circling overhead. He felt even more nauseous and woozy and knew he was losing consciousness. The last thing Buck remembered was the red hawk swooping down, landing on his chest, and then flying off again. As blackness overtook him, Buck was sure all hope was lost.

Kree-e-e-e-e. . . Kree-e-e-e-e. . . Kree-e-e-e-e. . .

Gray Eagle looked up and spotted a red-tailed hawk circling overhead. Then it swooped down, just missing his head.

"I wonder what is going on with that hawk," Gray Eagle's companion, White Foot, said.

"I am not sure." Gray Eagle watched as the hawk flew up toward the hill in front of them and circled some more. After two or three times of circling, it swooped down again, screeching as it passed by Gray Eagle's head, so close he could have reached out and touched it.

"Look up there!" White Foot pointed to the hill, where a buckskin horse stood on the edge of a cliff.

Gray Eagle shielded his eyes from the glare of the sun hitting the snow and looked in that direction. "I can't be sure from here, but that looks like Buck McFadden's horse. I think we should go check it out."

"I thought you said Buck had gone back to his home in the mountains," White Foot said.

"He did, but maybe something happened to him and his horse wandered off. You can stay here if you want to, but I'm going to take a look." Gray Eagle snapped his horse's reins and headed for the hill. He was glad when he looked over his shoulder and saw his friend following. If there was any kind of trouble ahead, it would be better if there were two of them.

As Gray Eagle and White Foot cautiously ascended the snow-covered hill, the red-tailed hawk seemed to be leading them on as it continued to soar and swoop.

When they reached the ledge where the horse stood, Gray Eagle spotted a man's body lying in the snow. As they drew closer, he realized it was Buck.

"I think he is dead," White Foot said, after the two men had dismounted and knelt next to Buck. "He does not seem to be breathing."

Gray Eagle grimaced, noticing the blood seeping from Buck's forehead, not to mention the bone sticking out of his twisted leg. He placed his hand in front of Buck's mouth. There was a breath, but it was faint and shallow.

"Buck, can you hear me?" Gray Eagle asked.

No response. Not even the flutter of eyelashes.

"We need to find some wood and make a travois, because we have to get him back to camp right away," Gray Eagle told White Foot. "Maybe Two Feathers, the medicine woman, can save him. Buck is a good friend to Yellow Bird and Amanda. They will not take it well if he dies."

CHAPTER 51

When Gray Eagle and White Foot entered Two Feather's teepee, carrying Buck on a travois, they found the middle-aged woman with a blanket draped closely around her, weaving a storage basket. Two Feathers was small, with smooth bronze skin and dark brown eyes. Her hair was thick, and a few strands of gray intertwined with her long coal-black braids.

"What is it?" she asked, looking up at them with surprise.

"Our friend has been injured, and we brought him to you for healing," Gray Eagle replied. With White Foot's help, he carefully placed the travois on the mat beside Two Feathers.

"His leg is broken, there's a gash on his head. He's also suffering from the cold."

"He is barely breathing," White Foot put in. "The bone in his leg is sticking out too."

"I will do my best." Two Feathers placed the partially finished basket off to one side. "But I make no promises. If it be the Great Spirit's will for this man to live, then he shall."

Gray Eagle looked down at Buck. He still had not opened his eyes, nor given any kind of response when they'd talked to him. He feared the worst and knew he'd better head to the mission to let Amanda and Mary know what happened. After learning how close Buck had been to Yellow Bird's husband, it wasn't going to be easy to convey bad news about her longtime friend. Gray Eagle himself had acquired a great deal of respect for Buck, knowing how he'd protected Yellow Bird and Amanda as he accompanied them on their journey. If it hadn't been for Buck, Gray Eagle might never have been reunited with Yellow Bird again, so he was grateful to this man.

"We must leave now," Gray Eagle told Two Feathers, "but we will be back later to check on him." Motioning for White Foot to follow, Gray Eagle hurried from the lodge.

—◆—

I didn't ask this poor man's name, Two Feathers thought as she examined his leg. It was a bad break, and if it didn't heal properly, he might be crippled for the rest of his life. She would need to set the bone back in place and prepare a wet poultice of boneset to put on his skin. Then she would wrap the area in clay and change it daily. She'd also need to splint the leg with a straight limb from a tree to reduce mobility and allow the break to mend. First, however, she would give the man some wild black cherry juice to sedate him. She also needed to tend the wound on his forehead and give him some willow bark tea to reduce his fever. Then there was the matter of getting him warmed up, which she would do by covering him with blankets and adding more wood to the fire.

From the way the man was dressed, she figured he was one of those mountain men who trapped and traded for a living. His skin was dark, giving indication that he must have spent a lot of time in the sun during the warmer months. His thick hair was red, like the tail of a hawk, and he wore it pulled back and tied with a strip of leather.

Opening one eyelid to check the young man's pupils, she discovered that his eyes were dark brown. He was a handsome man, even with the scars she'd seen on his neck, arms, and chest.

Two Feathers was certain her ability to heal others came from the Great Spirit, and as she began to work on the man, she prayed for wisdom from above. She knew, however, that not all who were brought to her were healed, because some were too far gone by the time they got to her or had been injured too seriously. She hoped this man wasn't one of those, for he had a pleasant face. Not only that, but from the look of concern she'd seen on Gray Eagle's face, she assumed the injured man must be his friend.

—◆—

"You are back early today," Yellow Bird said when Gray Eagle entered her parents' lodge. "Did you and White Foot have success with hunting?"

He slowly shook his head. "We did not shoot any game."

"Then why did you return so soon?"

"We found Buck. He's been injured."

Yellow Bird's dark eyes widened, as her mouth gaped open. "What happened?"

"We're not sure, but we think he fell off his horse," Gray Eagle explained. "The horse has only a flesh wound, and White Foot is tending to the gash. Looking at the tracks left in the snow, it appeared as if the horse lost its footing and slid down the bluff. Buck will have to explain the rest if he comes out of it."

"But I thought Buck was returning to his home in the mountains."

"I am guessing he changed his mind and started back here." Gray Eagle shifted his weight. "He's hurt bad, Yellow Bird. We took him to Two Feathers, but he was barely breathing, and I fear he may not live."

She gasped. "Oh no! Does Amanda know about this?"

"Not yet. I wanted to tell you first, because I think it might be better if you give her the news."

"Amanda is teaching at the mission today." Yellow Bird rose from her mat. "I will ask Mother to watch Little Joe, and then I shall go see Amanda right away. I know she will want to see Buck."

———

Thunder had developed a habit of staying with Amanda, snoozing in the corner while she taught her class. But for the past hour, for some reason he had been restless.

She had just finished teaching a Bible story to a group of young children and dismissed them when Yellow Bird entered the mission. Thunder wasted no time running out the door.

"I need speak with you right away," Yellow Bird said, stepping up to Amanda.

"What is it? You look upset?"

"It's Buck. Gray Eagle take him to Two Feather's lodge."

"Buck is here?" *No wonder Thunder was acting so fidgety,* Amanda thought.

Yellow Bird nodded. "Gray Eagle and White Foot find him when they out hunting. They think he fell from horse."

"Is he hurt?" Amanda's heart pounded as she awaited Yellow Bird's answer.

"Gray Eagle say Buck might not live." Yellow Bird clasped Amanda's arm. "You will go with me to see him?"

"Definitely! I just need to see if Mrs. Spalding will keep an eye on Little Fawn for me. The baby is sleeping right now, so she shouldn't be any trouble."

"If Mrs. Spalding be too busy, we can take baby to my lodge and leave her with Mother," Yellow Bird said.

"It will be quicker if I leave Little Fawn with Eliza, because Two Feather's lodge isn't far from here. I'll go ask her." Amanda hurried away.

When Amanda returned a few minutes later, she said, "Eliza will watch Little Fawn, and since the class I was teaching is over now, my duties are done for the day." She moved toward the door, feeling more anxious by the minute. "Let's go!"

Heavenly Father, she prayed, *be with Two Feathers as she takes care of Buck, and please don't let him die, because he does not know Thee in a personal way.*

Amanda was about to open the flap of Two Feather's teepee, when the middle-aged Indian woman stepped out. "Oh, I did not know anyone was here," she said, looking at Amanda with furrowed brows. "I am too busy for visitors right now."

Amanda was glad Two Feathers spoke English. It was easier to communicate than if she had tried to use the few Nez Percé words she knew. "We are not here to visit," Amanda explained. "We came to see—"

"I am caring for a man with serious injuries," Two Feathers interrupted. "You must come back later."

"You not understand," Yellow Bird spoke up. "Man you are treating is our friend. We want see how he is doing."

"He is not awake, and I do not want him to be disturbed." Two

Feathers grimaced. "His breathing is shallow, but I am doing all I can for him. If it be the Great Spirit's will, the man will survive."

Amanda nodded. "Awhile ago, when I found out, I started praying for him."

"That is good," Two Feathers said. "You come back another day."

"All right, but when he regains consciousness, would you tell him that Amanda and Yellow Bird were here?"

Two Feathers bobbed her head. "Take dog back with you." Then she grabbed a container full of water and ducked back into her lodge.

Now Amanda understood why Thunder had been so anxious. When she and Yellow Bird had approached the teepee, the dog sat diligently nearby. Thunder must have known Buck was close and sensed that something was wrong.

Amanda looked at Yellow Bird and sighed. "I don't see why she wouldn't let us see Buck. I just wanted to see for myself how he is doing."

"Two Feathers know what is best," Yellow Bird said. "Right now we can do nothing for Buck." She patted her knee. "Come, Thunder."

The dog looked back at the teepee and whined but obediently followed the women.

Amanda knew her friend was right, but that didn't make it any easier to accept. The best she could do for Buck at this time was to keep him in her prayers.

CHAPTER 52

Christmas came and went with a flurry of activities, but Amanda had a hard time enjoying the festivities. Rev. Spalding had cut down a tree, which Amanda and Eliza decorated with the help of some of the Indian children. They'd shown the children how to make paper chains, and they roasted popcorn and strung that on the tree as well. Cookies and candy were given to all the mission students, and there was a big dinner for everyone who helped at the mission. Amanda had tried to get into the spirit of things, but the concern she felt for Buck hung over her like a dark storm cloud.

It had been difficult to have fun knowing Buck was laid up in bed, but Amanda had managed to put a smile on her face and help the Spaldings introduce Christmas to the Indian children at the mission, who had never experienced it before. It was interesting to see how the children reacted to the fresh greens, pinecones, berries, and candles that decorated tables and windowsills. The children's faces glowed, radiating with happiness that only Christmas could bring.

Turning her thoughts toward Buck again, Amanda reflected on how she had gone to Two Feather's lodge a couple of times but was always told that she couldn't come in. Two Feathers said the man she was caring for was not well enough for visitors. Disappointed, Amanda had returned to the mission. Yellow Bird had also tried to see him, but she too was sent away. This concerned Amanda even more. She hoped Two Feathers wasn't hiding something from them. What if Buck was worse off than she thought?

"It makes no sense that Two Feathers won't let us see Buck," Amanda complained to Yellow Bird as they ate breakfast together on the last day of December. "It's been over a week since Buck was

279

brought to her tent, and yet she won't let anyone see him."

"My father say Two Feathers good medicine woman," Yellow Bird replied. "I think she know what best for Buck."

"She might know about healing, but I see no reason why we can't pay him a visit."

"Two Feathers keeps him sedated," Yellow Bird said. "He would not know you are there."

"Maybe not, but it would make me feel better if I could see how he is doing and sit by his side awhile."

Yellow Bird touched Amanda's arm. "You very much love him, right?"

Unwilling to admit her true feelings, Amanda shook her head. "We have become friends, but there is no future for us together, so I will not allow myself to have strong feelings for him."

Yellow Bird snickered. "I think it be too late for that. I have seen the way you look at him." She paused and took a drink of water. "Same with Buck when he look at you."

Amanda shrugged. "It does not matter. Unless Buck becomes a Christian, we cannot be together, and he's a very stubborn man, so it probably won't happen."

"It happen for me and Gray Eagle," Yellow Bird said, smiling widely. "The Great Spirit brought us together."

Amanda was tempted to correct Yellow Bird and tell her that it was God who had brought her and Gray Eagle together, but she knew Yellow Bird thought God and the Great Spirit were one and the same. *And perhaps they are,* she thought.

"It's different for you and Gray Eagle," Amanda said.

Yellow Bird tipped her head. "How so?"

"You both have an interest in spiritual things, and you and Gray Eagle have become Christians."

Yellow Bird nodded. "Gray Eagle is good man. I look forward to becoming his wife."

Amanda smiled. "Will I be allowed to attend your wedding?"

Yellow Bird's head bobbed as she clasped Amanda's hand.

"Everyone in tribe will come. White friends too."

"I'm looking forward to it," Amanda said. She was truly happy for her special Indian friend. Yellow Bird had been through a lot in her young life, and she deserved to be happy.

"I haven't seen Gray Eagle at the mission for a few days," Amanda commented, taking their conversation in a different direction. "Has he gone hunting again?"

Yellow Bird shook her head. "Some other men from tribe are hunting. Gray Eagle and White Foot go to Fort Walla Walla for supplies. Reverend Spalding ask them to go. They be back soon."

"Ta'c meeywi, manaa wees?"

Buck's eyelids fluttered, but they would not open. It sounded like someone was speaking to him from a faraway place—saying "Good morning, how are you" in the Nez Percé language. Then the words were replaced with a song. . .a song he remembered hearing a long time ago. What was this gentle, sweet song, and where had he heard it before?

I am dreaming, he told himself. *Or maybe I'm dead. If I were alive, I could surely open my eyes.*

As the singing continued, Buck felt like he was floating on a cloud. In his mind's eye he saw a red-tailed hawk circling the cloud. How nice that his winged brother had come to join him. Perhaps he was leading Buck to the valley of death.

Buck shuddered, and cried out in pain. He wasn't ready to die yet. He needed to see Amanda, if only one last time. Her name was on the tip of his tongue, but he could not open his mouth to speak it. *Come to me. . . Come to me, my beautiful woman. I will love you forever, even in death.*

As Gray Eagle urged his stallion toward the mission, he thought about Yellow Bird and how he couldn't wait to marry her. For many moons he had hoped to have this union become a reality, and he had never given up the thought that one day Yellow Bird would return to him.

What a joyous occasion it would be having all their family and friends there to witness their union. He thought about Buck, lying in Two Feather's lodge, fighting for his life. *I hope my new friend will be there for my wedding. It would be a sad thing if he dies.*

"How much longer until we get there?" the yellow-haired man who rode alongside Gray Eagle asked, pulling his thoughts aside.

"Soon," Gray Eagle mumbled. He glanced over at White Foot and said in their native tongue, "This man seems very anxious to get to the mission."

White Foot nodded. "He probably cannot handle the cold. Yellow Hair need to toughen up."

White Foot was right; it was cold today, but at least it wasn't snowing like it had been a week ago. The weather could be unpredictable though, and he was glad the trip to and from the fort had been uneventful.

Gray Eagle glanced back at the yellow-haired man. They'd met him at the fort, when he'd arrived with some fur traders who had led him there. When Gray Eagle heard that the man was looking for someone to show him the way to the Spalding Mission, he'd volunteered to take him. It made sense, since that was where Gray Eagle and White Foot were heading. He wondered now if it had been a mistake when he'd offered to bring this man back with them. Because of this white man, who rode much slower than they did, the journey to the mission was taking longer than it should.

The man, dressed in fancy clothes, talked funny too. He seemed nervous, like he didn't really belong here. Gray Eagle had seen a few other white men like him before and wondered why they had ventured this far west. This man, who hadn't bothered to give them his name, said earlier that he was headed to the mission on important business but didn't say what. Gray Eagle figured he was probably coming to help the Spaldings teach the Nez Percé about God and how to live like the white man. Or maybe he was their chief and had come to check up on them—see if they were doing things the way he wanted to have them done.

Gray Eagle didn't mind them teaching his people from the Bible, but it wasn't right that they expected the Nez Percé to give up many of their customs in favor of the white man's way of doing things. Some of the Indian women and children who went to the mission had even begun wearing dresses like Amanda and Eliza Spalding wore. It didn't seem right to see them dressed that way. It went against the heritage of his people. They were learning to read and write in the English language too. Gray Eagle supposed that wasn't a bad thing, because if white men were going to share their land, then they needed to be able to communicate with one another.

Gray Eagle's thoughts halted when the Spaldings' log structure came into view. "There it is," he announced to the yellow-haired man. "That is the Spalding Mission."

———

Amanda had just put Little Fawn down for a nap, when Mrs. Spalding came into the room and told her that Gray Eagle was outside and wished to speak with her.

"Tell him I'll be right out." Amanda leaned over and kissed her daughter's forehead; then she quietly left the room. She couldn't imagine why Gray Eagle would want to see her. If he was back from his trip to the fort, it would seem more likely that he'd be asking for Yellow Bird.

Slipping her dark bonnet on her head and wrapping a woolen shawl around her shoulders, Amanda opened the door and stepped out of the cabin. She spotted Gray Eagle standing near his horse, and her heart nearly stopped beating when she noticed the yellow-haired man beside him.

"Nathan Lane! What are you doing here?"

Chapter 53

Dost thou not mean *thee*?" Nathan asked, stepping up to Amanda. "Art thou not still a Quaker?"

"Nathan, why are you here?" Amanda asked without answering his question. "And where is Penelope?"

"She is in New York. We did not get married after all, Amanda."

"Oh really, and why is that?"

"Because I still love thee." Nathan opened his arms wide, as though expecting her to accept his embrace. When she took a step back, he dropped his arms to his side. "I am sorry, Amanda. I never meant to hurt thee," he said. "Canst thou forgive me for breaking our engagement?"

Amanda clasped her hands tightly together to keep them from shaking. She remembered her father saying once that it was important to forgive someone who had wronged you, but that forgiving didn't mean you had to be in a relationship with them. Sometimes it was best to keep a safe distance from the person who had done you wrong.

"I have already forgiven you," Amanda said, trying to keep her voice calm. "And you needn't have come all this way just to ask for forgiveness. You could have sent me a letter."

Nathan shook his head vigorously. "That would not have been good enough. I needed to see thee in person and try to win thee back."

"I am not going back," Amanda said with conviction. "My place is here at the mission, teaching the Nez Percé Indians about Jesus and how to read and write." She glanced over at Gray Eagle, hoping he might say something, but he was busy putting the horses away.

"I am not asking thee to leave," Nathan said. "At least not until thy work is done here. I am willing to stay and help thee teach the Indians."

Amanda hardly knew what to say. In her wildest dreams she'd never expected Nathan to show up at the mission, much less offer to stay and help out.

What does all this mean? Amanda wondered. She'd thought she had moved on with her life. Was Nathan's coming here a sign from God that they were supposed to be together? Could she trust Nathan not to break her heart again? And what about Buck? Nathan's sudden appearance had taken Amanda by surprise. How would he feel once he found out she had a daughter? All these questions whirled in Amanda's head, making her more confused than ever.

———

Two Feathers smiled when she touched the young man's forehead and it felt cool. He had faded in and out of consciousness ever since he'd been brought to her. In part, it had been from his raging fever. Plus, she had kept him sedated. It would not have been good for him to thrash about too much with his broken leg and ribs. Now that the fever had broken, she would ease up on the sedative.

Two Feathers hummed as she stirred a pot of rabbit stew. The tantalizing aroma caused her stomach to growl. She'd been so busy caring for the injured man these past few days that she hadn't taken time to cook a decent meal.

As Two Feathers took a seat in one corner of her teepee, she thought about Amanda, the young white woman who had come by several times, asking to see him. *Perhaps the next time she comes by I will let her in,* Two Feathers decided. *Maybe this woman means something to him.*

Two Feathers didn't know why she felt so protective of her patient. It wasn't like he was a relative or even a friend. Until the day Gray Eagle had brought the man to her tent, she'd never laid eyes on him before.

Two Feathers rose from her mat and returned to the pot of stew, stirring it again and breathing in the delicious aroma. It was almost ready. Perhaps when her patient woke up, he would eat some too.

As Two Feathers poked the wood on the fire, she began to sing.

Buck opened his eyes and turned his head to one side, curious as to who was singing that chant-like song. He'd heard it before but didn't know where. As his eyes began to focus, he noticed an Indian woman bent over a heavy dark pot hanging over the fire. Her black hair was streaked with gray, and she wore two white feathers at the ends of her braids.

"Ah, you are finally awake," the woman said in English, turning to look at him. "I figured the smell of rabbit stew might cause your eyes to open." She left the pot and moved across the lodge, then knelt beside his mat.

Buck groaned when he tried to move. "Where am I?" he asked, taking short, small breaths. He couldn't breathe normally because it hurt too much. *Did I get run over by a stampede of buffalo?* Buck wondered. *It sure feels like I did.*

"You are in the Nez Percé camp, just outside the Spalding Mission," she replied.

"Who are you?" he asked.

"I am a medicine woman. You were brought to me when you fell from your horse."

Buck winced as a jolt of pain shot through his right side. "I remember now. The trail was icy and covered with snow. My horse slipped on a rock that was hidden under the ice. We went down, and he rolled over on me. The last thing I remember is seeing him stand up, and wondering if I would freeze to death."

"Your friend Gray Eagle found you and your horse," the woman said. "It was good he came along when he did, or you would have surely died." She touched his arm gently. "Your leg and several ribs were broken, and there was a gash on your head. Your body was cold, but the fever was hot. I have been caring for you many days."

"Thank you. I appreciate that. How's my horse?"

"Horse had only a small gash, but it has healed," she answered, reaching out to feel his forehead again.

Buck sniffed the air as his stomach growled noisily. "Is that stew I smell?"

She nodded.

"It smells mighty good."

"Would you like some?"

"I sure would. Some hot coffee too."

"I have no coffee," she said. "Just herbs made into a tea. Would you like some of that, or should I go to the mission house and ask Mrs. Spalding for coffee?"

"Maybe later." Buck grimaced as he drew in another quick breath.

"What is your name?" she asked.

"Buck. Buck McFadden."

The Indian woman gasped, and Buck jolted upright, despite the pain that shot through his side. "Are you all right? Why do you look at me in such a strange way? Did I say somethin' wrong?" Buck watched as she searched his face, going from his eyes to his nose, his mouth, and back to his eyes again. It felt as if she were trying to reach his very soul.

"McFadden?" she repeated. "And your first name is Buck?"

"Yeah. But it's not my real name. The name my mother gave me when I was a boy was—"

"Red Hawk," she said, finishing his sentence.

"That's right. How'd you know?"

Tears welled in her eyes as she placed her hand gently against his chest. "I am Two Feathers, and you are my son, Red Hawk. My prayers have been answered, for you have come back to me."

Buck sat, too stunned to say a word. After all these years, could it really be true? The tune she'd been signing suddenly came back to him, for it was the same song his mother had sung when he was a boy.

"Oh, my son, my son," she sobbed. "My eyes see you, and yet I cannot believe you are really here. My heart sings with joy; there is so much I want to tell you. We have lots of catching up to do."

Buck could barely speak around the lump in his throat, as she began to sing that song again. He was in his mother's lodge, and she had prayed for him. Did Two Feathers know of the white man's God, or was it the Great Spirit who had answered her prayers? It didn't really matter, he supposed. The important thing was that they had found each other.

"It is so cold out here," Nathan said, rubbing his hands briskly together. "Can we go inside and talk?"

Amanda wasn't sure she wanted to talk to Nathan. Seeing him so unexpectedly was a shock. What she really wanted was some time alone, and she needed to check on Buck. But she didn't want to be rude, and since Nathan had come all this way to see her, Amanda felt that she ought to at least take the time to talk to him. "Follow me," she said, motioning to Nathan.

When they entered the mission, Little Fawn was crying, and Eliza, looking more than a bit flustered, was holding her baby while trying to calm Little Fawn at the same time.

Amanda hurried across the room and picked up her daughter. "There, there, little one. I know you are hungry."

"I need to find Yellow Bird," Amanda told Nathan. "You can visit with Mrs. Spalding while I am gone." Before Nathan could reply, Amanda wrapped Little Fawn in a blanket and hurried from the cabin.

When Amanda stepped outside, she was relieved to see Yellow Bird heading her way. "Oh good, I am glad you are here," she said. "Little Fawn needs to be fed, and Nathan is inside waiting for me." She drew in a shaky breath. "He wants me back, Yellow Bird, and I don't know what to say to him."

"Who is Nathan?" Yellow Bird asked.

"He's the man I was supposed to marry before I left my home in New York. I told you about him, remember? I explained how he broke our engagement the night before our wedding and said he was in love with my best friend." Amanda disliked having to relive the hurt and humiliation of this all over again.

"Gray Eagle say he bring yellow-haired man here to mission, but he not know who the man was." Yellow Bird took Little Fawn from Amanda, and patted her back. "Let's go inside. I will feed baby while you talk to white man."

"Yes, I need to do that. I just wish. . . ." Amanda's voice trailed off. "Oh, never mind. We'd better get in, out of the cold."

When they entered the mission, Amanda was surprised to see Nathan sitting by himself, his hands stretched toward the warmth of the fireplace. Mrs. Spalding had apparently taken her baby and gone into their living quarters, leaving Nathan alone.

"I am glad thou art back," Nathan said, rising from his seat. "We have much to talk about."

"Yes, we do." Amanda nodded. She motioned to Yellow Bird. "This is my friend, Mary Yellow Bird."

"It is a pleasure to meet thee," Nathan said in his most charming voice. "I would shake thy hand, but it appears as if both of your hands are full holding thy baby."

"Oh no," Amanda was quick to say. "The baby is not hers; Little Fawn belongs to me."

Nathan's face blanched. "Thou art married to an Indian?"

Amanda shook her head. "I am not married to anyone. Little Fawn is from a Flathead tribe. I found her in the woods where she'd been left to die."

"What? I am confused," he sputtered. "Why would anyone in their right mind leave a baby in the woods to die?"

While Yellow Bird hurried off to feed Little Fawn, Amanda took a seat and asked Nathan to do the same. Then she relayed the story of Little Fawn. "It was horrible, Nathan," Amanda said, nearly breaking into tears at the thought of it. "After I learned what was happening, I went to the woods and searched for the abandoned twin. When I found the baby, I decided to name her Little Fawn and raise her as my own."

"I can understand how sorry thou must have felt for the infant," Nathan said, "but surely thee could have found a home for her with some Indian family."

Amanda shook her head. "I doubt that anyone would have taken her, considering how superstitious some tribes seem to be. Besides, I fell in love with the precious little girl right from the start and couldn't bear the thought of giving her up."

Nathan frowned. "This is most unexpected. I-I hadn't planned on raising someone else's baby, much less an Indian child."

Amanda's spine went rigid. "I am not asking you to raise my daughter. Where did you get such an idea?"

Nathan's face turned crimson. "I came here to be with thee, and I had hoped we could be married. If thou agreed to be my wife, would I not be expected to raise thy child?"

Amanda sat staring at the fire, unable to form any words. Did she still have feelings for Nathan, or had she left them behind when she and Papa left New York? Could she agree to marry Nathan, after his betrayal? "I need some time," she said. "A lot has happened to me since I left home. I am not the same person I was back then."

Nathan eyed her speculatively. "Thou art thinner and not as prim and proper as thou used to be, but thou art the same woman I fell in love when we lived in New York."

Amanda folded her hands to keep them from shaking. "If you will recall, you fell in love with my best friend, so I don't think the love you felt for me was very strong." She sighed. "Maybe you loved me more like a sister instead of someone you wanted to marry."

"It wasn't like that," he insisted. "I was just confused about us, and Penelope wooed me with her charms. Once I realized she was not the woman I thought her to be, I broke things off."

"Whether that's true or not, I am in no way ready to marry you," Amanda said, holding her ground. She would not allow herself to be taken in by Nathan's charms. If he was sincere, then he would have to prove himself.

"I understand," he said, drawing his fingers through the ends of his thick blond hair. "I will stay here at the mission and help out wherever I can, and when thou art ready, we will talk of marriage."

What if I am never ready? Amanda thought. *Will you go back to New York and forget you ever knew me, or will you stay here and make me uncomfortable for the rest of my life?*

"I have not met Reverend Spalding yet," Nathan said. "Is he somewhere with thy father?"

Amanda slowly shook her head. "Reverend Spalding left early this morning to speak with some of the Indians who live nearby, and my father. . ." She swallowed hard, afraid she might break down. "I regret to inform you that Papa passed away a short while into our journey."

Nathan's mouth dropped open. "Preacher Pearson is dead?"

"That's right. He was fatigued, felt pain in his chest, and died."

"I am sorry to hear that. Dost that mean thou madest the trip here alone?" Nathan asked.

"I was alone for a short time after our guide was killed by a falling tree."

"First thy father, and then thy guide?" Nathan's forehead wrinkled. "How didst thou make it this far without them?"

"It's a long story," Amanda said. "I have someplace I need to go right now, but I'll tell you all about my journey as soon as I get back. In the meantime, why don't you rest here by the fire? When Reverend Spalding arrives, perhaps you can ask him what you might do to help out at the mission. That is, if you haven't changed your mind."

"I have not. I want to offer my services in any way they might be needed."

"Very well," she said with a nod, wishing he'd had second thoughts about staying. "We will talk more when I return to the mission."

"Where art thou going?" Nathan asked as Amanda slipped her dark bonnet on her head.

"A friend of mine was injured when he fell off his horse, and I need to check on him. Would you please tell Yellow Bird when she comes back to the room where I went?"

Nathan nodded slowly. "I hope thou wilt not be gone long, for I am anxious to continue our conversation."

Amanda wrapped the shawl tightly around her shoulders and rushed out the door.

For more than an hour, Buck and Two Feathers tried to catch up on each other's lives. Two Feathers kept saying it was a miracle, and that the Great Spirit had brought them together, but Buck thought it was just a twist of fate. How thankful he was to know his mother was alive, because he never thought he'd see her again.

"It nearly tore my heart out when Silas Lothard sent me away and wouldn't allow you to come with me," Two Feathers said, gently stroking Buck's forehead. "But I never gave up hope of seeing you again, and I prayed daily that God would take care of you."

Buck nearly choked on the bile rising in his throat. "Oh, He took care of me, alright. He allowed Silas to beat me for no reason at all, and then he kept preachin' to me from that Bible of his." He narrowed his eyes. "I was glad when he died. An evil man like him deserved to die. I hope his soul went right past the gates of heaven and straight to—"

Two Feathers held up her hand. "You must not talk like that, my son. You must forgive Silas for the terrible things he did."

"Forgive him?" Buck shook his head. "I could never forgive that man for what he did!"

"You must, Red Hawk. If you're ever going to be free to live a life of peace, then you must forgive."

Buck was about to refute what his mother had said when he heard Amanda's voice outside the lodge. "Two Feathers, it's Amanda Pearson! I came to see how Buck is doing."

Two Feathers rose from her mat and said, "The white woman has come by many times to inquire about you. If you feel up to company, I will show her in."

"No, do not let her in. I need time to think about things before I speak to Amanda."

"Are you sure?" his mother asked. "I sense that you have things you wish to say to this woman."

Buck shook his head determinedly. "Whatever I have to say can wait till I'm feelin' better. Right now, I need to rest and think things through."

CHAPTER 54

For the next four weeks, Nathan helped out at the mission, and Amanda visited him whenever they both had a free moment. He was always friendly and seemed interested in hearing about the things that had happened on her trip. Amanda was surprised to see Nathan chip in and help with even the most mundane things, in addition to teaching some of the children how to read and write. Maybe she had misjudged him. Perhaps he really did care about her, as well as the Indian children, and wanted to share in her work here at the mission. But did she still love Nathan, and could she open up her heart and trust him again? As it stood, she couldn't say how she felt about Nathan. It was obvious that things weren't going to work out between her and Buck. He didn't want to see her and had made that clear every time she stopped by Two Feather's lodge.

Why doesn't Buck want to see me? Amanda asked herself as she sat in front of Little Fawn's cradle and rocked her gently to sleep. *If he really doesn't want to be around me, then why didn't he go back to his home in the Rockies?*

Gray Eagle had been checking on Buck regularly and let Amanda know that Buck's injuries were healing, although it would take at least another week or so until he could walk on his broken leg. Gray Eagle had also given Amanda some surprising news—Two Feathers was Buck's mother.

How happy they both must feel about that, Amanda thought as she stared down at her daughter. Maybe the reason Buck didn't want to see her now was because he was catching up on all the time he'd missed with his mother. It still troubled her, not being able to look in on him. She wished Buck would let her see him, even for just a short visit. She

293

had so many questions she wanted to ask.

Hearing someone come into the room, Amanda looked up and saw Nathan watching her. Her face heated at the intensity of his gaze, especially since she had been thinking about Buck. "I didn't know who had come in. I thought perhaps it was Eliza coming to say it was time for me to teach a Bible lesson to the children."

"I think she may be planning to teach the class today," Nathan said. "I saw her in the next room, showing several children some pictures she had drawn depicting the story of Daniel in the lions' den."

Amanda pinched the bridge of her nose. "Oh, that's right. I remember Eliza telling me last night that she would take over the class today so I could spend some time with Little Fawn." She smiled as she watched her daughter sleeping peacefully.

"I enjoy watching you with the baby," he commented. "Seeing the look of joy on your face makes me wish for a child of my own."

Amanda smiled. "Children are a blessing from God."

He moved closer to where she sat and knelt beside her. "If thou married me, we could have a whole houseful of children."

Amanda felt a flush of heat start at the base of her neck and run to the top of her head. "I wish thou wouldst not say things like that, Nathan. It's not proper."

"It is proper, because I love thee, and I want to make thee my wife." He grinned widely. "And it's good to hear you using the word *thee* again."

"I revert back to my old way of speaking when I'm flustered," she admitted.

Nathan placed his hand on her shoulder. "There is no reason for thee to feel flustered. I have spoken with Reverend Spalding, and he is willing to perform the ceremony if thou wilt agree to marry me."

Amanda wasn't sure what to say. She didn't want to hurt Nathan's feelings, but she wasn't ready to make a commitment. Fortunately Yellow Bird chose that moment to come ask Amanda if she would like to go for a walk.

"Yes, I would." Amanda smiled at Nathan. "Would you mind

keeping an eye on Little Fawn? She should sleep until I get back."

Nathan's eyes widened. "Well, I. . ."

"I won't be gone long, and if you're planning to be a father someday, it will be good practice for you." She winked at Yellow Bird. "Don't you think all prospective fathers should learn to care for a baby?"

"Pro-spec-tive?" Yellow Bird tipped her head. "What does that word mean?"

"It means 'future father,' " Nathan put in. "I believe Amanda is saying that someday, after she and I get married, I might become a father."

"That is not quite what I meant," Amanda was quick to say. "I have made no promises to become your wife."

As if sensing Amanda's frustration, Yellow Bird said, "Are you ready to walk?"

Amanda looked at Nathan. "Are you willing to watch Little Fawn for me?"

He nodded.

"Will you marry Nathan?" Yellow Bird asked as she and Amanda walked near the river. While the water in the middle of the river continued to flow, ice had formed along its banks.

Amanda sighed as the frigid breeze coming up from the river stung her cheeks. "I don't know. Nathan is attractive, charming, and seems to enjoy helping out at the mission, but I'm not sure I love him anymore."

"You love him once though, right?"

Amanda nodded. "At least I thought I did. After he broke our engagement, I was hurt and wasn't sure I could ever love another man."

"And now?" Yellow Bird asked.

"Now I'm not sure about anything." Amanda stopped walking and folded her arms, rubbing them briskly. "I keep thinking that maybe God brought Nathan here so we could be together and share in His work, but. . ."

"You are in love with Buck?"

"No. Yes. I mean, I don't know." Amanda frowned. "For a while I thought I might love Buck, but I know it would never work because he's not a Christian. Besides, I'm not sure how he feels about me. I mean, he won't even let me see him."

Yellow Bird reached up to stroke the yellow feather attached to one of her braids. "You have been praying for Buck?"

"Yes, of course."

"If it be Great Spirit's will, everything work out like it should." Yellow Bird started walking again. "Gray Eagle and I will get married soon. You will come to the wedding ceremony?"

Amanda clasped Yellow Bird's arm. "Oh yes. I would not miss it for anything."

"I need some fresh air," Buck said to his mother. "It's stuffy in here, and I feel like I can't breathe." He had to admit living in the teepee was better than being cooped up in his cabin, but there was nothing better than being outside, breathing in the fresh cold air.

Two Feathers smiled. "Would you like me to go with you?"

"No, I can manage." Buck reached for the walking stick Rev. Spalding had given him when he'd dropped by last week. He couldn't go very far with it and had to walk carefully, barely touching the heel of his foot on the ground, but at least he was no longer confined to the teepee.

During Rev. Spalding's visit, Buck had overheard him talking with Two Feathers about her recent conversion to Christianity and how he hoped she would share the Good News with others in their tribe. She'd assured him that she was, and then when she told him how the Great Spirit had brought her son back, Rev. Spalding said Two Feathers should begin referring to Jesus' Father as God, and not the Great Spirit. Then the preacher man looked at Buck and said, "What about you, son? Do you know the Lord personally?"

Buck, feeling more than a little irritated by the man's bold question, had merely grunted and said, "I know of God, if that's what ya mean." To avoid further questions, he'd rolled over on his mat and pretended to be asleep. It was hard not to listen to the verses of scripture Rev. Spalding quoted to Two Feathers about going into all the world and preaching the Good News. Apparently, the man had taken that to heart, because he and his wife, Eliza, had traveled a long ways to come here and tell the Nez Percé Indians about God.

At times Buck wondered if the words written in the Bible were true. Silas Lothard could sure quote a lot of scripture, but he didn't live by what he'd read. He had somehow twisted and turned the words to fit his own sinister way of life and had used them against Buck at every opportunity. Buck was glad his mother hadn't tried to force her religious views on him, although she did talk about how God had answered her prayers and how grateful she was. One of these days, if he felt like talking about it, he might question Two Feathers about her conversion. Right now, though, he just wanted to get outside.

"I won't be gone long, Mother," Buck called over his shoulder before leaving the lodge.

It was difficult to maneuver with the walking stick, and Buck would be glad when he didn't need it anymore. Fortunately, only a light dusting of snow covered the ground, so that made it a little easier to get around.

With each step, Buck breathed in deeply and felt the cobwebs in his head clearing. It felt good to feel the sunshine on his face, and its warmth seeped in, as if touching his soul. He enjoyed smelling the clean waters from the Clearwater River not far from camp. As he limped along, Buck could hear the water gushing and picture in his mind how powerful it must look.

Buck had only gone a short distance, when he spotted Gray Eagle heading his way. He appreciated the new friendship he'd made with the Indian. He hadn't had a good man friend since he'd lost Jim Breck.

"It is good to see you out walking," Gray Eagle said, joining Buck.

"I wouldn't really call it walking." Buck grunted. "It feels more like hobblin'."

"How long do you think it will be before you can walk on your own?" Gray Eagle questioned.

"Two Feathers says my leg is healin' well, so maybe another week or so."

Gray Eagle smiled. "That is good. You will be able to attend Yellow Bird's and my marriage ceremony in two weeks. The weather has improved, and we have decided not to wait until spring."

"You want me to be there?"

Gray Eagle nodded. "All family and friends are invited."

"I guess Amanda will be there as well?"

"Yes, and her friend, Nathan too."

Buck winced. He'd heard about the yellow-haired man who had traveled all the way from New York to find Amanda. He wondered if they would be getting married too. If they did, he couldn't do anything about it. He wasn't going to pretend to be a Christian in hopes of getting Amanda to choose him.

"Will you come to the wedding?" Gray Eagle asked.

Buck nodded. "I'll be there—hopefully without my walking stick."

CHAPTER 55

On the afternoon of Yellow Bird and Gray Eagle's wedding, Small Rabbit entered the lodge, carrying Yellow Bird's wedding dress. Even though Yellow Bird knew her mother had given up hope of ever seeing her again, she'd kept the dress they had made before Yellow Bird's capture by the Blackfoot.

Tears filled Yellow Bird's eyes as she gazed at the lovely tunic. She had come to accept the fact that she would never see the dress again, let alone wear it, and now here she was, preparing to put on the very same tunic she'd been planning to wear so many moons ago. In just a short time she would finally become the wife of her one true love.

"Oh Mother, thank you for holding on to this dress," Yellow Bird said, hugging Small Rabbit tightly.

"Doing so gave me hope, Daughter. It gave me something to cling to," her mother whispered.

The white, long-skirted, doe-skin tunic had been well made. Intricate decorations of brightly colored beads and porcupine quills, along with the long white fringe, completed the bridal dress. On her legs Yellow Bird would wear beaded doe-skin leggings, and her feet would be graced with smooth white moccasins.

Yellow Bird wore her hair in a single thick braid that hung halfway down her back. It was held at the bottom with a strip of rawhide, and her yellow feather had been tied into it.

"You must hurry and dress," Small Rabbit said, wiping tears from her eyes. "The other women are waiting to escort you to the ceremonial lodge, and they will soon grow impatient."

Yellow Bird laughed nervously as she slipped into her wedding clothes. "No more impatient than I am, Mother. I have waited such a long time for this special day. I can hardly believe I am actually going to marry Gray Eagle and that he has so graciously accepted my son."

Small Rabbit nodded. "I am happy that your guardian spirit watched over you and brought you safely back to us. The past and all its sorrows are behind you now. Soon your life will be as it once was."

Yellow Bird shook her head. "No, Mother, my life will never again be the same. I have learned much since I was taken from my family, and I hope I have become a better person because of it."

"Sometimes the trials we face help mold us until we become soft and pliable, just like cured rabbit skin." Small Rabbit gave Yellow Bird a hug. "I am proud to call you my daughter, for you have proven that you are strong, courageous, and wise. You will make a fine medicine woman, I think."

"I may not be able to fulfill that role, Mother," Yellow Bird responded, stepping into her moccasins.

"Why not? You have knowledge of healing herbs."

"I know, but Amanda wants me to help her work with the missionaries, teaching our people about the Bible. Besides, we have Two Feathers now, and she is a fine medicine woman."

"Do not speak to me about the Book of Heaven," Small Rabbit said sharply. "The missionaries use words from the book to get us to change our ways."

Yellow Bird clasped her mother's hand. "The Book of Heaven, as some call it, has many good things to say about God, who I believe is the same as the Great Spirit we have worshiped for so many years. I believe it was God who kept me alive after I was taken from my people. He got me through times when I didn't think I would survive, and it was Him who brought me home again. It was the cruel Blackfoot who stole me from my family, not God."

Small Rabbit shrugged her slender shoulders. "We will speak of this another time. Right now we must go, for Little Joe has already been taken to your aunt Shy Deer's tent so she can care for him. You, my daughter, have a wedding to attend." She kissed Yellow Bird's cheek. Then hand in hand, they left the teepee.

"Will you be going to Gray Eagle and Yellow Bird's wedding with me?" Buck asked his mother.

She shook her head. "One of the women in my tribe is in the early stages of labor, and I'll need to be close by when she is ready to deliver."

"Oh, I see. Maybe I won't go either."

"You said Gray Eagle invited you, right?"

Buck nodded.

"Then I am sure he will expect you to be there."

"I suppose."

Two Feathers left the pot of herbs she'd been mixing and took a seat on the mat beside Buck. "Is there something troubling you, my son?"

He nodded. Truth was, a lot of things were troubling him these days.

"What is it?"

Buck pulled his fingers down the side of his face, not sure where to begin. "I've been wonderin' about something," he said. "After all the horrible things you went through when you belonged to Silas Lothard, how could you accept Christianity yourself?" He scrunched up his face. "Don't ya hate that man for what he did, and aren't ya mad at God for allowin' it to happen?"

Two Feathers sat quietly. Then she rose from the mat and moved across the lodge to the place where she kept her medicinal supplies. When she returned, she held a black book. Buck recognized it as the Bible, because Amanda had one too.

Two Feathers took a seat beside Buck and, placing her hand on the Bible, she said, "While I have not yet learned to read all the words in this book, I know in my heart that what it says here is true."

"How can you be so sure?" he asked.

"Because when the Spaldings told me that God sent His Son, Jesus, to earth to die for everyone's sins, I believed it."

Buck sat, staring at the black book. "So what are you saying—that Jesus died for men like Silas?"

Two Feathers nodded. "His blood was shed for all. We just have to believe in His name and ask Him to forgive our sins."

"I'll bet Silas never did that. If he had, he wouldn't have continued to abuse us, and he wouldn't have separated a mother from her son," Buck said bitterly.

Two Feathers placed her hand on Buck's shoulder. "I do not know what was in Silas's heart, or why he did what he did, but I know that you must forgive him, just as I have done. Forgiveness is the only way to feel peace and be free from the pain. Reverend Spalding says the Bible teaches that we must forgive others, or God will not forgive us."

"I don't know if I can," Buck said, averting his gaze from the Bible.

"Yes, you can," she said with assurance. "You can and you must, but not until you pray and ask God to forgive your sins and invite Him to live in your heart. Only then will you feel peace and be able to forgive Silas, or anyone else, who has hurt you."

Buck's insides twisted as he fought conflicting thoughts. His mother was right, but he'd held on to his hate for so long, he wasn't sure he could give it up. Would he really feel a sense of peace if he asked God to forgive his sins? Could he find it in his heart to forgive Silas, who might have died in his sins?

Bringing a shaky hand to his forehead, Buck said, "I have done many things I should not have done, and I do need to ask God for forgiveness. However, I'm not sure I can forgive Silas for what he did to us."

Two Feathers placed the Bible in Buck's lap. "Close your eyes and pray. God will give you the strength and desire to forgive."

Buck did as she suggested, and when he opened his eyes again, a sense of peace flooded his soul such as he had never felt before. If he had known asking for forgiveness would bring him such relief, he would have done it sooner.

Fresh pine needles were spread over the floor of the ceremonial lodge in readiness for the wedding. A great deal of food had been prepared for the feast, waiting to be eaten by the bride, groom, and their honored guests.

It seemed as though most of the village was in attendance, though not all could fit inside the teepee, despite the fact that it was larger than most other lodges. Some stood outside and cheered as Yellow Bird entered the place where she would be wed. She smiled shyly, for she suddenly felt like a young girl again. This was not only to be a wedding feast, but a celebration of her return home as well.

Everyone inside the lodge formed a circle; then the women took seats on the ground within their half of the circle, while the men sat on the other side. Yellow Bird kept her eyes looking down, as was the custom for a woman in her tribe who was about to become married. She knew Gray Eagle sat in the circle of men directly across from her. It was difficult not to look up and seek out his handsome face.

They were first served steaming bowls of buffalo stew by several of the young, unmarried maidens. Then more girls followed, bearing baskets filled with several kinds of dried fruits and berries.

Yellow Bird wasn't sure she would be able to eat anything, for she felt too nervous to think about food. Out of politeness to their chief and the other guests, however, she forced herself to take a few bites of everything.

When the meal was over, the chief rose and stood in the middle of the circle. Gray Eagle and Yellow Bird joined him there.

Yellow Bird stole a quick glance at her soon-to-be husband. He was so handsome, with high cheekbones and a straight nose. But nothing prepared her for the joy that filled her when she saw his warm smile that told of his undying love and devotion to her.

The chief spoke a few solemn words over them, giving instructions as to the duties and obligations of marriage. When he finished talking, he tied a leather cord around their wrists, symbolizing that Gray Eagle and Yellow Bird were now joined as one.

The drums began to play, the men chanted, and the women danced in time to the rhythmic, singsong beat. *If anyone deserves to be happy, it is*

303

Yellow Bird, Amanda thought.

Amanda's throat clogged when she saw Buck standing across from her, watching the festivities. He looked different today. He wore a broad smile, and even from a distance she could see a twinkle in his eyes that hadn't been there before.

It must be because of the time he's spent with his mother, Amanda thought. *I'm happy they found each other. Then again, he may be smiling so brightly seeing how happy Gray Eagle and Yellow Bird are today.*

Amanda's heart fluttered when Buck looked at her and smiled. *I wonder if he plans to stay here, rather than going back to the mountains. It would make sense if he did, so he could be close to his mother.*

"This is quite an interesting ceremony, isn't it?" Nathan asked, stepping up to Amanda and leaning close to her ear.

"Yes, it certainly is," she replied. Amanda had been so caught up in wondering why Buck looked different that she'd almost forgotten Nathan was here.

"I hope it's our wedding we'll be attending next," Nathan whispered.

Amanda shivered. She still had reservations about making a commitment to Nathan. It might make it easier if he would stop pressuring her. Then again, his persistence must mean he really cared for her.

She glanced at Buck again and was disappointed when she saw him walk away. He'd obviously decided to leave the celebrations, and she couldn't help wondering why.

CHAPTER 56

After Buck walked slowly away, Amanda decided to follow him. He'd been avoiding her long enough, and she needed to know what was going on.

She turned to Nathan and said, "I'll be right back."

"Where art thou going?" he asked, looking at her strangely.

"I need to speak with someone." Amanda hurried away before Nathan could question her further.

Buck walked slowly, so it was easy to catch up to him. "Buck, wait a minute; I need to talk to you," she said, stepping up to him.

He stopped walking and turned to face her. "What about?"

"Why have you been avoiding me, and how come you left the celebration early?"

A muscle on the side of Buck's neck quivered. "I didn't think we had anything to say, but then I. . ." He dropped his gaze to the ground. "Never mind."

"Never mind what, Buck? What's going on?"

"Nothing."

"Please don't do this. Tell me why."

He gave no reply.

"I thought we were friends, but you're talking to me as if I were a stranger." She clasped his arm. "When I heard you'd been injured, I was worried and came to see you several times. But Two Feathers, who I understand is your mother, would never let me in." Amanda paused for a breath. "At first she said you weren't up to company, but the last time I stopped by her lodge she said you didn't want to see me. Is that true?"

Buck shrugged.

305

"Please explain why you didn't want to see me," she said, determination welling in her soul. Even though she and Buck could never be together as a couple, Amanda didn't want to lose him as a friend.

"You don't need me as a friend," Buck said with a stoic expression. "You have Yellow Bird, Gray Eagle, the Spaldings, and the yellow-haired man who is heading this way."

Amanda turned and saw Nathan coming toward them. She wished he had waited. Despite her irritation, she introduced him to Buck.

"I have heard much about thee," Nathan said, as he shook Buck's hand. "And I want to thank thee for guiding Amanda safely on her journey west."

"I can't take all the credit," Buck mumbled. "She had another guide before me."

"That's true, but you brought me most of the way," Amanda interjected.

In the midst of an awkward silence, Amanda heard her name being called. "Oh, that's Eliza," Amanda said. "I'd better go see what she wants."

Amanda hurried off, leaving the two men alone. Eliza had volunteered to watch Little Fawn that morning so Amanda could attend the wedding, and she had a feeling the baby might have become fussy.

———

"I need to go," Buck said, turning away from Nathan.

Nathan placed his hand on Buck's shoulder. "What is thy hurry? I was hoping we could talk for a bit."

Buck turned back around. "What about?" He really had no desire to talk to this man, but he didn't want to be rude either.

Nathan lifted his dark hat and drew his fingers through the ends of his thick blond hair. "I was wondering if Amanda told thee that she and I will be getting married soon."

Buck pinched the bridge of his nose, hoping to release some of the tension he felt. "No, she hasn't mentioned it, but I'm not surprised, since ya came all this way to be with her."

"That's right, and I love Amanda very much." Nathan's piercing gaze made Buck wonder if the man suspected that he had feelings for Amanda too. Well, if he did, he could think whatever he wanted; Buck wasn't about to admit anything to Nathan.

"I wish you well," Buck said. "Now, if you'll excuse me, my leg's startin' to hurt, and I need to get off my feet for a while."

"Certainly." Nathan started to walk away but turned back around. "Oh, and we will let thee know when the wedding date is set, in case thou would like to be there."

Buck merely grunted in reply. If Amanda was going to marry this prim little man, he was definitely not going to be there!

"Would you take this basket up to the mission house?" Buck's mother asked, the following day. "It has some herbs in it that Mrs. Spalding asked for."

"Can't you take it to her?" Buck had no desire to go anywhere near the mission where he might run into Amanda or Nathan.

"I would, but I am needed at White Foot's lodge. His mother, Shining Star, is ill."

"Okay, I'll take the herbs over to Mrs. Spalding." Buck gathered up the basket and stepped out of the teepee, breathing in the crisp air and taking a minute to admire the beautiful blue sky.

When Buck arrived at the mission a short time later, he decided to enter on the side where the Indian children were taught. He knew Amanda was one of the teachers but hoped Eliza would be teaching the class this morning.

When Buck stepped inside, he heard the shrill cry of a child. It wasn't the sound a baby made, so he knew it couldn't be Little Fawn or the Spaldings' baby. No, the cry was distinctly that of a child, and when Buck entered the classroom, he was stunned by what he saw. Nathan had a young Nez Percé boy lying across a wooden chair, his pants pulled down, and he was beating him with a switch. Nathan's hand was pressed firmly on the back of the boy's head, holding him in place so he couldn't get up. The child's exposed skin was covered with red welts, and Buck could easily imagine what the boy's clothing hid.

Buck stiffened. What did this man think he was doing? The all-too-familiar scene reminded him of the numerous times Silas had whipped him, and it made his blood boil, just watching the injustice.

"Let the child go!" Buck hollered, unmindful of the basket he carried as it dropped to the floor.

Nathan glanced at Buck briefly and mumbled, "Mind thine own business," and he kept thrashing the boy.

Unable to stand and watch any longer, Buck marched up to Nathan and yanked the switch out of his hand. "I have half a notion to use this on you!" he shouted. Then, remembering the sniffling child who still lay across the chair, he lowered his voice, touched the boy's head, and helped him to his feet. "It's okay now. There will be no more whipping. Go find Mrs. Spalding and tell her what this man did."

With tears rolling down his red cheeks, the boy pulled up his britches and hurried from the room.

Buck turned to Nathan, still struggling with the urge to hit him with the switch. "I never want to see you treat anyone like that again! Especially the children!"

Nathan's nostrils flared, and his face contorted, turning bright red. Pointing his finger, he snapped back, "Thou art no teacher here, and thou hadst no right to interfere in my discipline of that boy!"

"I have every right to step in when I see someone being abused like that," Buck countered, stepping so close to Nathan's face that he could smell the man's hot breath. "If I was not a Christian, I would knock some sense into you."

"Christian?" Nathan mocked, his lips curling. "What does a half-breed, uneducated mountain man know about Christianity?"

"I know that the Bible says we are supposed to do to others as we would have done to us. Would you want someone to put welts on your body the way you did to that innocent young boy?"

Sweat beaded on Nathan's forehead. "That child is not as innocent as thou might believe. He refused to wear the new clothes he was given, and then he would not memorize the verse of scripture that I gave him."

Buck fought the urge to put this pompous, self-righteous man on the floor and beat the stuffing out of him. But as a new Christian, he knew such a response wouldn't be right.

"What is going on here?"

At the sound of Amanda's voice, Buck whirled around. "I think you'd better ask him!" He motioned to Nathan as he stepped away from him.

Amanda looked at Nathan and tipped her head. "One of the young boys I have been teaching came to me, crying. When I questioned him, he said a man in here had given him a whipping." Amanda glared at Buck and pointed to the switch he held. "Why would you do such a thing, Buck?"

Buck tossed the switch into the fire and hurried out the door. He couldn't believe Amanda would think him capable of whipping the boy. Was she really the sweet, understanding woman he'd thought her to be, or could she judge him so quickly?

———

Tears welled in Amanda's eyes as she tried to come to grips with what Buck had done. But why had he done it, and what had brought him to the mission this morning?

"That mountain man had no right to interfere when I was disciplining the boy," Nathan said, pacing in front of the fire. "Thou wouldst not believe the things he said to me."

Amanda's hand shook as she pointed at Nathan. "*You* are the one responsible for the welts on that poor child's body?"

Nathan nodded. "He was disobedient and needed to be taught a lesson. And he would have learned that lesson too, if that so-called friend of thine hadn't interfered."

Amanda's jaw dropped. "So Buck took the switch from you?"

"That's right, and that is not all," Nathan shouted. "That half-breed had the nerve to stand here and call himself a Christian."

"Buck said he was a Christian?" Amanda could hardly believe her ears.

"That is what he said, all right, but I am sure he made it up just to make himself look good. He certainly didn't fool me."

Amanda grabbed her shawl and bonnet and moved quickly across the room.

"Where art thou going?" Nathan called to her.

"To see Buck. I need to find out if what you said is true."

CHAPTER 57

Amanda stood outside the door of Two Feather's lodge and called, "Buck McFadden, are you in there?"

No response.

"Buck, I need to speak with you!"

Still no reply. Was he inside the teepee, refusing to speak to her, or had he gone somewhere else after leaving the mission?

Boldly, Amanda pulled the teepee flap aside and peeked in. She saw no sign of Buck or his mother.

Where else could he be? Amanda wondered, stepping outside. She lifted her gaze upward. *Dear Lord, please point me in the right direction.* Biting her lip until she tasted blood, she scanned the sky, hoping to get a glimpse of the hawk that always stayed close by Buck, but all she saw were some vultures soaring in circles as they caught the upward breezes.

Just then, Gray Eagle rode up on his horse. "I am looking for Buck," he said after he dismounted. "Is he in the lodge?"

Amanda shook her head. "I don't know where Buck is. He was at the mission awhile ago, but he left. I figured he'd come here, but apparently he went somewhere else."

Gray Eagle glanced around. "I don't see Buck's horse anywhere, so he must have gone for a ride."

Amanda's heart pounded. "I hope he hasn't gone back to the mountains. I'd feel terrible if he left again before we had the chance to talk."

"I do not think he would do that," Gray Eagle said with a shake of his head. "Buck would not leave his mother."

Amanda sighed. She hoped Gray Eagle was right. "Something

happened at the mission while Buck was there," she said. "I need to talk to him about it."

"What happened?" Gray Eagle asked.

Amanda explained what she had witnessed, what Nathan had told her about the whipping he'd given the boy, and about Buck claiming to be a Christian. "Do you know anything about that, Gray Eagle? Could Buck have accepted Jesus as his Savior?"

"Yes, he did," Two Feathers said, walking up to them.

"Really? When?" Amanda questioned Buck's mother.

"A few days ago," Two Feathers explained. "Buck asked Jesus to come into his heart. He is a Christian now, same as me."

Amanda gasped. All this time Buck had been so against anything that had to do with religion. She could hardly believe he'd had a conversion. But then she had been praying for him for months. She felt such joy that God had finally answered her prayers.

"I need to find him," Amanda said, feeling desperate. "We have much to talk about."

Following a trail along the river's edge, Buck rode his stallion hard and fast. He didn't know what had upset him the most—seeing Nathan whipping that boy, the things Nathan had said to him about not being a Christian, or Amanda believing he had whipped the child. The thought of Amanda marrying that tyrant of a man made Buck feel sick to his stomach. Nathan Lane, with his pompous attitude, was no better than Silas Lothard. Amanda deserved better than that. She needed a husband who would love her and provide for her needs—someone who would treat their children with love and respect. If Nathan was capable of whipping an innocent boy until he had angry-looking welts on his body, he could do most anything.

The image of that poor child, so vulnerable, being held in place by a person twice his size, not to mention the humiliation of being hit in front of the other children, was enough to make Buck want to beat Nathan to a pulp.

Pulling on the reins to slow the horse, Buck realized what had to be done. "Come on, Dusty, we're headin' back!" Buck turned the lathered horse around and rode at a hard gallop.

At Two Feather's suggestion, Amanda waited inside her lodge, hoping and praying that Buck would return. After some time went by, she decided that she needed to get back to the mission to check on Little Fawn. Although Eliza was there with her, Amanda didn't like the idea of her daughter waking up and crying for her.

Amanda was halfway back to the mission, when she spotted Buck's horse running at full speed. Buck halted Dusty and stepped down, then he secured the horse to a tree.

"Amanda, I need to talk to you."

"Buck, I have something I need to say."

They'd spoken at the same time, and Amanda, feeling breathless, smiled and said, "Go ahead."

"You can't marry Nathan!" Buck blurted. "He's not the right man for you."

"I know that, Buck, and I am not going to marry him. I never made him any promises about marriage."

"Really?" A look of relief washed over Buck. "He said you had."

"He wasn't telling the truth."

"He's an evil man," Buck said, his forehead wrinkling. "I felt this in my heart the day we met, but after seeing what he did to that boy, I knew I was right."

"I agree. I was fooled by Nathan once, but never again." Amanda moved closer to Buck, and when she looked up at his face, it was all she could do to keep from throwing herself into his arms. "I'm sorry I ever assumed you had whipped that boy. You're a better person than that, and I should never have jumped to such a conclusion."

"I know what it must have looked like, and I forgive you," Buck said. "I'm glad you realize I could never do such a thing."

"I do have a question for you."

"What do you want to know?"

"Nathan said you claimed to be a Christian, and when I asked

Two Feathers about it, she said you had asked Jesus into your heart. Is it true?"

He nodded, a smile tugging at the corners of his mouth. "A sense of peace came over me when I did that, and I was finally able to forgive the man who had separated me from my mother. I still don't like what Silas did, but it doesn't eat away at my heart anymore."

Tears welled in Amanda's eyes. "Oh Buck, I am so glad. Hearing that you have become a Christian is an answer to my prayers."

"You know what would answer my prayers?" Buck asked, his voice a near whisper. He took a step closer until they were almost touching, never taking his gaze from hers.

"What's that?"

"If you would someday be my wife."

"Are. . .are you asking me to marry you, Buck?" Amanda held her breath, while her heart raced like a beating drum.

"If you will have me."

Amanda nodded. "Oh yes, Buck. I will marry you!"

Buck pulled her into his arms. "How soon?"

"As far as I'm concerned, I would marry you tomorrow," Amanda said with so much feeling she thought her heart would burst. Oh, how wrong she had been when she'd thought she was in love with Nathan back in New York, for she'd never felt with him what she now had with Buck.

He grinned, holding her tight. "That sounds good to me."

"We'll need to speak to Reverend Spalding and see if he's willing to perform the ceremony. I also want to talk to Nathan and let him know that I will not marry him. I'll suggest that he go back home as soon as possible."

"Would you like me to go along when you tell him?" Buck asked.

"No, this is something I need to do alone, and I should do it right now." Amanda squeezed Buck's arm. "After I speak to Nathan, I'll get Little Fawn and meet you back at your mother's lodge."

"I'll be there waiting, but I wish you'd let me go along when you speak to Nathan. I don't trust that fella."

"I appreciate your concern, but I'm sure I'll be fine. I am not afraid."

Buck bent his head and kissed her tenderly. "I love you, Amanda Pearson, my brave, soon-to-be bride."

"And I love you." She turned, calling over her shoulder, "See you soon!"

When Amanda entered the mission, she found Eliza sitting in a rocking chair, with Little Fawn in her lap.

"Where is Nathan?" Amanda asked, taking the baby from Eliza. "I need to speak with him."

"He's not here," Eliza said. "He left."

"Where did he go?"

"He asked one of the Indians to ride with him to Fort Walla Walla. When he can find a guide, he plans to go home."

"Nathan is going back to New York?" Amanda could hardly believe he would leave like that.

"That's what he said. I guess he decided that he didn't like it here after all."

"He was right to leave. It's for the best." Amanda nuzzled her little girl's nose. It seemed that God was in the business of answering prayers today. She could hardly wait to see what the future would bring.

Epilogue

Six months later

I*t all seems like a dream,* Amanda thought as she sat in the rocking chair Buck had made when he'd learned she was expecting a baby. Amanda and Buck had gotten married a week after he'd proposed, and three months later, Amanda discovered she was pregnant.

She smiled at Little Fawn, who was over a year old now and walking well on her own. How nice it would be for her young daughter to have a brother or sister to play with.

"Are you happy, Mrs. McFadden?" Buck asked, rubbing Amanda's shoulders.

"Oh yes, my husband, I am very happy." Amanda rose from her chair and went willingly into his embrace.

As Buck held her close, it was as though all the months of sorrow and disillusionment she'd encountered on her journey west had never existed, for Amanda was happier than she ever thought possible. She believed with assurance that God had brought her here to this place for a special reason—to offer a new way of life and a hope in Jesus to the Nez Percé people. It would take time and patience, but Amanda felt certain that she and Buck could help make a difference.

Some days would be good, and others might be full of despair, but no matter what happened or where God might lead them, she would do whatever God asked, for with His help, she could be a woman of courage.

The Story of Little Fawn Continues

WOMAN
of HOPE

WANDA *&*
BRUNSTETTER

CHAPTER I

Lapwai Valley
1854

Little Fawn squeezed her eyes shut, allowing the morning sun to lift the chill from her body. It was springtime, the season of new life and renewed hope. The ground had nearly thawed as the spring air continued to warm each week. Birds sang an announcement that winter was over. In this quiet haven where Little Fawn came quite often to think, she noticed several clumps of frog eggs along the shallows. Soon the tadpoles would emerge and turn into the frogs she loved hearing later in spring and early summer.

She glanced toward the hills. A short time ago, the *Nimiipuu*, known as "Nez Percé" to the white man, had headed east toward the Bitterroot Mountains. It was time for digging *keh-kheet*, the first root food of the season. When the weather turned warmer and days moved into summer, the tribe would travel farther onto the plains. They would gather camas bulbs and hunt for the great buffalo. The Nimiipuu were likely to meet friendly Salish Indians, sometimes called Flatheads, who might also set up lodges on the ceremonial camas grounds.

Others had told Little Fawn that the annual foodgathering was a joyous time. She couldn't speak from personal experience, however, since her parents had never taken her or her brother, Running Fox, out onto the plains. They always stayed behind, near the mission station that had once been active in the Lapwai Valley. With the exception of a few elderly men and women, and sometimes White Wolf and his family, Little Fawn and her family were the only other people to remain at their winter camp throughout the spring and summer months. Every year

Little Fawn asked if she could accompany their tribe, and every year her parents said no. She envied those who'd just left and wished she could travel with them.

She reached down, picked up a small pebble, and tossed it in the water. *I am seventeen summers. It's not fair that I always have to stay behind with my parents. I don't understand why they won't let me go.*

Little Fawn's mother, Amanda, was a missionary and had worked at the mission station in Lapwai Valley for several years before it closed. She'd helped Eliza Spalding teach the native women and children about the Bible, which the Indians called "The Book of Heaven." Even though the mission station had closed after Rev. and Mrs. Spalding left in 1849, Little Fawn's parents stayed on, hoping more missionaries or a preacher would come so they could start a church or open another mission in the area.

It had been a shocking and sad day, three years ago, when they'd received word about Eliza Spalding's death. The influence Eliza and Mother Amanda had on Little Fawn's life fed her desire to follow in their footsteps and teach the Word of God.

Little Fawn had accepted her parents' explanation of staying behind without question during her childhood days. But she was older and wiser now.

With a sigh, she dropped to her knees, gazing at her reflection in the pool of water dammed off by large boulders. The image staring back gave proof that she was no longer a child. Her adolescent facial features had been replaced with a slender, high-cheek-boned beauty. Instead of her usual braids, today Little Fawn had chosen to wear her midnight color hair loose and flowing.

Cupping her hands into the water, she splashed some on her face. "Oh!" Little Fawn giggled when the cold droplets stung her cheeks. Snow-fed water from the long winter months took her breath away as it ran over her smooth bronze skin.

In days gone by during the hot summer months when most of the other children were with their parents out on the plains, Little Fawn and Running Fox had swum here. The water was not as frigid as it was right now though.

Little Fawn leaned against a large rock while looking down at her deerskin dress. It was the first one she'd made for herself, right down to the delicate beadwork carefully sewn into the top. Her moccasins featured the same artistic beaded design as her dress. Little Fawn ran her hands over the colorful pearl-like orbs, happy with the finishing touches of her attire. Mother Amanda had taught her well in the craft of sewing, and today Little Fawn wanted to look special.

She stood and looked around then strode over to a small grove of trees. Glancing in the direction of the lodge of her beloved's parents, she frowned. *Where is White Wolf? He should have been here by now. Could he have forgotten about our meeting this morning?*

White Wolf, who'd been known as Little Wolf when he was a boy, was the son of Yellow Bird, a good friend of Little Fawn's mother. His real father, a white mountain man, had been killed soon after White Wolf was born. Gray Eagle had later become his stepfather when he married Yellow Bird.

Lifting her gaze to the surrounding hills, Little Fawn moved away from the river's edge. She enjoyed fishing with her father and helping her mother dry the fish they would eat during the cold winter months known as *HaOoKhoy*. They also traded some of the fish to other tribes. In return, they might receive deer or buffalo hides, shells for decorating, colorful beads, or wool blankets from one of the white men's trading posts.

Sitting down again, Little Fawn closed her eyes and hummed along with the distant melody coming from one of the old people who had stayed behind. Halfway through the song, something tickled her nose. Startled, she opened her eyes, surprised to see White Wolf holding a feather as he crouched beside her.

"You snuck up on me." Little Fawn tapped White Wolf's arm. "You should have said something."

"I was going to, but only after I took some time to gaze upon your beauty." White Wolf tickled her nose again.

"Give me that." She snatched the feather and entwined it with a few locks of her hair. The older White Wolf became, the more his skills were perfected. He had the stealth and slyness of a *k'oy'am'á*—a mountain lion. His boyhood looks had changed as well. He stood taller, with a muscular physique.

"I am sorry for being late this morning. I had chores to do for my mother, and then I stopped to check on my horses." White Wolf stood and reached out his hand.

Her face growing warm, Little Fawn took it, and he helped her up. "It's all right. You are here now. That is all that matters."

When White Wolf moved closer, Little Fawn's heart thumped like a herd of stampeding horses. His bronzed skin and dark eyes came from his Nez Percé heritage, but his curly red hair had been inherited from his white father. It wasn't his appearance that appealed to Little Fawn. It was White Wolf's kind, gentle spirit that drew her to him. She had been in love with White Wolf since they were children. But now her feelings went deeper than anything a child felt.

Little Fawn placed her hand on his arm. "I have a favor to ask of you."

He stroked the side of her face with his thumb. "What is it you would like me to do?"

"As you know, my desire is to be a missionary like my mother. I wish to take the news of God's love and plan of salvation to other tribes."

Nodding, he stood silently beside her.

"I can't do that unless I am allowed to go with the tribe when they head east each spring. But they have already gone and are getting farther away every minute."

"Did you ask your parents if you could go?"

Little Fawn nodded.

"I take it they said no, like they've done all the other times."

"You are right, but they don't understand. I need to go and was hoping you would take me. If we ride fast, there is time to catch up with them."

White Wolf's brows lifted high on his forehead. "I cannot go against your parents' wishes, Little Fawn. If I did, your father would never give his permission for us to be married."

A shiver traveled up her spine. "You want to marry me?"

"Of course. Surely you must know how much I love you." He slipped his arms around Little Fawn's waist and pulled her against his chest. "If Red Hawk gives his permission, will you marry me?"

"Yes, I will." Hope welled in Little Fawn's soul. *If White Wolf wants to marry me, then surely he will agree to go with me onto the plains.*

"You are so beautiful." His voice was low and husky.

A shiver ran through Little Fawn when White Wolf looked into her eyes. His gaze traveled to her nose, and finally her mouth. When he cupped Little Fawn's chin then tilted her head back, all she could do was stare dreamily at him.

He lowered his head and caught her lips in a kiss so sweet it warmed her from head to toe. When they pulled apart, she said in a breathless voice, "Please consider my request, White Wolf. I feel an urgency to tell others about the one true God. If you go with me, maybe Mother and Father won't mind, because they will know I am safe."

White Wolf shook his head. "I will stay here with you, and we can enjoy our spring and summer together."

"But what about how I feel? I cannot be a missionary if I remain here while the others are gone."

"Once we are married we can go out on the plains."

"But that could be too late."

"Too late for what?"

"For some of the people who need to hear about God now. What if they should die before they are told?"

White Wolf grunted. "I will not take you away from this place until we are married. We will have to wait until next year to go with the tribe."

With pursed lips, Little Fawn folded her arms, frustration quickly replacing the gentle moment they'd just shared. "If you don't love me enough to accompany me on this trip, maybe it would be best if we don't get married."

His mouth opened slightly, but he closed it again.

"I mean it, White Wolf."

He clasped her hands. "I do love you, but I will not take you out on the plains unless your parents agree to it."

"Puh! That is never going to happen."

"Then it's settled. We will wait until after we are married to go with the tribe. Next year will be soon enough."

Little Fawn pulled her hands out of his grasp as a rush of heat crept up the back of her neck. *No, it is not settled, White Wolf. If you won't go with me, then I will go out on the plains by myself.*

CHAPTER 2

V enison stew again, Mother?" Little Fawn's brother, Running Fox, grunted as he took a seat at the wooden table inside their cabin. Despite being more white than Indian, he dressed and tried to act like a Nez Percé brave. Although Thomas was his given name, when he turned fifteen two moons ago, he'd changed his name to Running Fox. Everyone but Mother called him by his Indian name. She had made it clear that, to her, he was still Thomas McFadden.

Little Fawn looked at their mother, waiting for a response to her brother's question, but Mother only nodded and ladled some stew into their bowls.

"Wish I could have gone with Father and Gray Eagle to Fort Walla Walla." Running Fox puffed out his chest. "I am strong, and my horse is fast, yet I never get to do anything exciting."

Mother reached over and touched his arm. "They went for supplies, Thomas. There is nothing exciting about that."

"Humph! We are Nimiipuu. We should have no need of the white man's supplies."

Little Fawn could hold her tongue no longer. "Have you forgotten that our mother is white, and our father also has white blood flowing through his veins?"

Running Fox scowled at her from across the table. "I have nothing against our parents, but I don't think we should rely on white men's supplies to survive." He turned to look at Mother. "I wanted to go out on the prairie with the tribe when they left this morning, but you said no. I would like to hunt for meat with the men, while the women cure hides and make pemmican. I'd even be willing to search for nuts, honey, wild plants, camas, and other roots and berries." His fingers clenched into his palms. "I don't want to stay here again, Mother, while most of the others are gone."

"I wanted to go as well." Little Fawn hoped this time she would get permission. "It's not too late for us to catch up with them."

Mother shook her head. "That would be something I would need to discuss with your father, and since he is not here. . ."

"I will wait till he returns, and then if he says I can go, I'll ride like the wind and catch up to the tribe." Running Fox's brown eyes darkened further.

"He will not be back for several days, and my answer is no, so this discussion has concluded." Mother folded her hands and bowed her head. "Now, let's give thanks to the Lord for our meal and all He has provided."

Little Fawn lowered her head and closed her eyes. She didn't peek, but she hoped her brother was praying. Running Fox could be so obstinate.

"We thank You, heavenly Father," Mother prayed in a reverent tone of voice, "for all You have provided. We ask You to keep Gray Eagle and my beloved Red Hawk safe as they travel to and from the fort. Please watch over the Nimiipuu people as they are out on the plains. Bless and keep my children too, and watch over them every day. Amen."

Little Fawn opened her eyes, took a biscuit, and passed the basket to Running Fox. As they ate their meal, she decided to ask a question that had been on her mind for some time. "I have been wondering about something, Mother."

"What is it, Daughter?"

"You gave my brother a white man's name when he was born. Why do I not have a white woman's name? You have never called me anything but Little Fawn."

Shifting on her bench, Mother cleared her throat. "As your father and I have explained, your parents were not able to raise you. So I brought you to the mission with me, to raise as my own daughter. Then, later, I married Red Hawk, so he became your father."

"Was my name already Little Fawn when you brought me here?"

Mother shook her head. "That is the name I chose for you."

This puzzled Little Fawn, but she chose not to pursue the topic. She would be leaving tonight, as soon as her mother and brother were asleep, so any more questions concerning her heritage could wait until she returned with the Nimiipuu in the fall.

When they finished their meal, Mother got out her well-worn Bible. "Tonight I will read from the book of Romans, chapter five, verses one through four." She turned to a page she'd marked with a feather.

Seeing the plume, Little Fawn thought about White Wolf tickling her nose earlier and couldn't help smiling. Remembering how things had ended between them, she pulled her attention back to what Mother was saying.

"'Therefore, being justified by faith, we have peace with God through our Lord Jesus Christ: by whom also we have access by faith into this grace wherein we stand, and rejoice in hope of the glory of God. And not only so, but we glory in tribulation also: knowing that tribulation worketh patience, and patience, experience, and experience, hope.'" She glanced at Little Fawn and then Running Fox. "Do you understand what those verses mean?"

Running Fox shook his head, but Little Fawn spoke up. "We are supposed to have peace when we go through bad times, because it helps us learn to be patient and builds our hope in God."

"Yes, it is something like that." Mother let her fingers travel, almost reverently, over the fragile page before her. "My faith was tested and tried over and over when I decided to become a missionary and come out west. God used many tribulations to make me more patient and strengthen my faith."

"Were there ever times when you felt like giving up?" Little Fawn inquired.

"Oh yes. There were days when I didn't think I had the strength to go on. I even questioned God's purpose in allowing me to leave the comforts of my home and travel to an unknown land." Mother's eyes misted. "When my father died, and then our guide soon after, I almost gave up hope."

"How come you didn't?" Little Fawn asked. She glanced at Running Fox, who seemed disinterested in this conversation.

"Whenever I felt like giving up," Mother continued, "I turned to God's Word for comfort and assurance. I would send up a prayer for guidance, and God always sent an answer."

"Was my father one of those answers?"

"Yes. He saved my life and brought me here, where I could begin my mission work." Mother yawned as she got up from the table. "Today has been busy, and I am tired. We should retire now."

White Wolf glanced at his mother, lying on her mat across their lodge. It seemed odd not to see his father beside her. But he had gone to Fort Walla Walla with Red Hawk and wouldn't return for several days. In addition to getting supplies for those who would not be going onto the plains, Gray Eagle and Red Hawk would hunt on the return trip. He hoped they would get something more than a few rabbits, like they had on their last hunting expedition.

White Wolf had told his mother he would be gone before she awoke tomorrow morning. He wanted to get away for a few days and do a bit of hunting on his own—and some thinking.

White Wolf's attention went to where his fifteen-year-old half sister, Shy Deer, lay sleeping. It was an appropriate name for the young girl. She rarely initiated a conversation, unless it was with Mother, and for the most part, Shy Deer didn't mingle much with other girls her age. White Wolf wondered if his sister had been born timid, or if it was because their family stayed close to home and didn't usually join the others in their tribe who spent half a year out on the plains. When White Wolf's family stayed here along the Clearwater during the summer months, there weren't many people for Shy Deer to talk to, except for Little Fawn, whom his sister seemed fairly comfortable with.

He rolled over on his mat and tried to sleep, but a vision of the woman he loved came to mind. It nearly broke his heart when she pleaded with him to take her to the plains.

But I can't do it without her parents' permission, White Wolf told himself, yet again. *Little Fawn needs to learn patience. Once we are married, we will be able to go wherever we want without anyone's permission.*

As Little Fawn lay on her sleeping mat, a buffalo hide covering her body, she listened to the even breathing of Mother and Running Fox. Once she was certain both were in a deep sleep, she slipped into a clean doeskin dress, grabbed a parfletch, and filled it with pemmican, dried fish, and deer jerky. After taking a spare blanket folded into a tight roll,

Little Fawn gave one final look in her mother's direction, before slipping quietly out the cabin door.

After getting her horse, Snow, ready for the trip, Little Fawn walked the mare out of the village, stopping briefly at the river to fill a water bag made from an animal hide. She felt thankful for the bright full moon to give her much-needed light. Without it, she would have a difficult time seeing what she was doing or where she was going.

A sense of excitement mixed with a bit of trepidation filled her senses, and a nervous sigh escaped her lips. Little Fawn would miss her family, but she would soon be joining the Nimiipuu tribe, and then she'd finally know what it was like to journey out onto the plain. By the time Mother realized Little Fawn was missing, she would be far away.

CHAPTER 3

Somewhere in the Mountains

Little Fawn shivered as she pulled the blanket aside and rose from her sleeping mat. She'd been on the trail two full days, with no sign of the Nimiipuu people or any other native tribe. She paused to look at the sky. The stars, still visible, were slowly fading from the awakening light of day. The weather was cooler than she'd expected, especially at night. She'd hoped the woolen blanket covering her each evening would provide the same warmth as her buffalo hide back home, but she had been proven wrong.

Spending nights alone was frightening. Every little noise had awakened her, so she hadn't slept much since leaving home. She'd never gone this far into the hills before and wasn't prepared for what it was like to be alone.

Little Fawn hoped her food supplies wouldn't run out before she caught up to the tribe. She'd only eaten a little, hoping to make it last, but already her belly growled from hunger. So far she'd been able to find water, as she had after stopping to bed down last night. After two days of traveling, the skin bag she'd initially filled was almost empty. Both she and her horse needed water. Fortunately, there was plenty of bunchgrass in these hills for the mare to eat.

To dispel her fears, she sang a song her mother taught her when she was quite young. *"Amazing grace! how sweet the sound, that saved a wretch; like me! I once was lost, but now am found, was blind, but now I see.'"* The words offered comfort and hope as she gathered her things and prepared to ascend higher into the hills. Although unsure of the way to go, she figured her tribe could have only gone up and over the first set

330

of hills. Little Fawn hoped sometime today she'd be able to pick up the Nimiipuu people's tracks. Since many of them traveled on foot and had surely stopped last night to set up camp and rest, she shouldn't be too far behind. If she rode hard and fast today, perhaps by this evening she would find them.

It concerned her that she hadn't come upon any areas where they may have camped. Little Fawn wondered if it was because they were skilled at erasing all traces of where they had bedded down each evening. Or was it because she was going the wrong way?

Once Little Fawn had her belongings and food supplies secured to her horse, she climbed on the mare's bare back as another day's journey began.

––––––––

Little Fawn pressed a hand against her sore tailbone, as she tried to sit straight on Snow's back. The chestnut brown mare with a black mane and tail had plenty of stamina. The horse, a present from her parents a few years ago, had a white nose and four white socks on each foot.

This third day of her journey had been long, and as she traveled what seemed like many more miles, Little Fawn nodded off several times. She forced herself to rouse and go a little farther.

The mare nickered softly as the hoot of a screech owl perched in a tree somewhere echoed against the mountains. The sound was not fearful or threatening, but it reminded Little Fawn that it was time to stop for the day and sleep.

––––––––

Morning came with a light, fragrant rain. Little Fawn awoke feeling as if she had been caught in the middle of a buffalo stampede. Her neck felt stiff, and her head throbbed unmercifully. Sleeping on the cold ground with only a thin mat between her and the dirt was not nearly as comfortable as the coziness of her parents' cabin. Her nose tickled, and a sneeze was forthcoming. She grabbed her blanket and stifled the noise. The last thing Little Fawn wanted was to be heard by a dangerous animal—or worse, someone unfamiliar.

Grabbing a piece of pemmican from her satchel, she strained to observe the winding path, leading farther into the mountains. Fog hung heavy in the air, making it difficult to see very far. She'd hoped to at least see smoke in the distance from the Nimiipuu tribe, but the heavy air made it impossible. It concerned Little Fawn that she hadn't come across signs of a campsite, horse prints, or anything else to indicate they had come this way.

Beginning the fourth day of her trek, Little Fawn had no idea if she was heading in the right direction. It was a fearful revelation. She had no choice but to pack her things up and move on. First, however, she bowed her head and offered a prayer. "Dear God: It was wrong for me to leave home and head out on my own without telling Mother or asking permission. But since I want to serve as a missionary, I am asking You to keep me safe and show me the way to the Nimiipuu people."

Little Fawn had no more than finished her prayer when she was startled by a harsh rumbling sound. She opened her eyes and turned her head. A painted Indian on an Appaloosa stallion rode straight toward her. Although she had never seen a Blackfoot warrior, Little Fawn had heard they'd been so named because they used prairie fire ash to dye their moccasins a dark color. She felt sure this man was from a Blackfoot tribe, for his moccasins were black.

The Indian appeared to notice Little Fawn about the same time as she saw him. As the man's horse galloped faster in his approach, he shouted something Little Fawn did not understand. Her first thought was to climb on Snow and try to outrun the Indian, but by the time she'd started for her horse, the Indian was upon her. She screamed, but it was a futile gesture. No one else could hear her.

An expression of delight covered his face as he dismounted and secured his horse to a bush. Trying to flee, Little Fawn tripped on a rock. Without looking behind her, she jumped up to run, but he grabbed her arm.

"Let me go!" she screamed at his fearsome face, hoping he would believe she was unafraid. The Indian was not fooled, for he struck her cheek with his rawhide quirt, proving he was the one in charge. She reached up to touch the welt on her cheek and clamped her teeth together in an effort not to cry out.

With expertise, the warrior tied her hands together, using a leather thong. He put his hand over her mouth and shook his head. Grabbing Little Fawn, he slung her over his horse like a sack of potatoes.

Her throat constricted. Little Fawn had heard terrible stories of Blackfoot capturing women from other tribes to use as slaves. Was this to be her fate?

The Blackfoot mounted the Appaloosa stallion and sat directly behind her. Little Fawn's head turned when he nudged his horse over to where Snow was tethered. Leading Little Fawn's horse behind him, she felt the strength of her captor's hand as he pushed it against the small of her back and held her tightly against his horse. Then they disappeared into the woods.

The tears rolling down her cheeks burned like fire as they connected with the lacerations on her face. She lay helplessly over the horse, chiding herself for being foolish enough not to leave a note for Mother. It was doubtful anyone would know the direction she'd gone, even if they did come looking for her. How far was she going to be made to travel this way? She was already uncomfortable from this awkward position.

I have to remain brave and not show how frightened I am. Little Fawn's greatest fear was not what her captor would do to her, but whether she would ever see her family or White Wolf again.

Lapwai Valley

Amanda clung tearfully to her friend Yellow Bird. "Little Fawn has been missing too long. This is the fourth day now, and I. . .I fear we may never see her again." She sniffed deeply. "I wish Red Hawk was here so he could go out and search for her."

Yellow Bird patted Amanda's back. "He and Gray Eagle should be back soon. I am sure once they get here, Gray Eagle will volunteer to go with your husband to search for Little Fawn." Yellow Bird paused and shook her head. "I wish White Wolf had not left so early to go hunting the morning after Little Fawn left. He could be out looking for her now."

Amanda slowly nodded. "If I only knew where she'd gone, I'd go there myself, but I don't have my husband's tracking skills. Our daughter could have been snatched from here by some enemy Indian—the way you were when you were a young woman."

"If she is with the Nimiipuu, then she will be back when they return in the fall," Running Fox spoke up. "I wish she would have asked me to go with her." He stood proud and pounded his fist against his chest. "I would keep my sister safe."

Amanda shook her finger at him. "Then I would have both of my children to worry about, so don't get any ideas about going in search of your sister."

"I can take care of myself," Running Fox boasted.

"When White Wolf returns from his hunting trip, he will be upset to learn that the woman he loves is missing." Yellow Bird's brows wrinkled. "I hope his father returns first. Otherwise my son will go after her alone, and we will have two children to worry about."

In the Mountains

Little Fawn felt certain her fate had been sealed when she and her captor caught up with a small Blackfoot party leading nine Appaloosa ponies. One of the Indians said something in his native language, and the man who took hold of her horse's reins responded with a guttural sound. The others hooted and pointed at Little Fawn when her captor pushed her off his horse. The warrior nodded toward some bushes close by, and she struggled to get up on her tingly feet as the circulation tried to return. But she needed desperately to relieve herself. At least they turned their backs and did not watch.

Little Fawn cringed as she thought about the terrible things that could lie ahead. She'd heard alarming stories about the dreaded Blackfoot. They'd been known to inflict gruesome punishment on their prisoners. She sent up a quick prayer and tried to push her fears aside by focusing her attention on the passing scenery. When she escaped—if she could escape—she needed to have memorized the way home.

The light rain had stopped, and the sun peeked through the clouds. After they rested, her captor pulled her up in front of him, but this time in a sitting position. It revolted Little Fawn when his arm came around her waist, pulling her against his chest. She tried to lean forward so there was no contact with this savage, but he held her tight. She felt the muscles in his arms and the strength behind them. He dominated her, and she knew better than to challenge this Indian further.

The Blackfoot traveled all day and into the night, stopping only a few times to water the horses and stretch their legs. They only had some dried buffalo jerky to eat, and Little Fawn was not offered much. Several times, she nearly passed out as black spots swirled in her vision. The need for food and sleep overtook her weary, battered body. She hoped her captors would make camp for the night, but they rode relentlessly on through the darkness, ascending the mountains with only the light of the moon as their guide.

Just as the morning sun rose from its place of sleep, the group halted at the top of a ridge. They sat a few moments, gazing down at the lush, green valley below. Gray curls of smoke drifted up from several campfires, and hundreds of Blackfoot Indians milled about the village.

As they began their descent, Little Fawn noticed some women bent over their cooking fires. Small children ran about, laughing and playing, and more than a hundred horses grazed outside the camp. *Probably Nez Percé ponies*, she fumed. *These evil men steal helpless women as easily as they take our horses.* She prayed silently. *Please, Heavenly Father, release me from these people, or let me die quickly. I do not want to spend the rest of my life as their prisoner.*

Chapter 4

In the Hills

White Wolf stopped his horse, Spirit Dancer, at the crest of a knoll and sat gazing at the river below. The morning mist hovered over the water, and the call of an eagle echoed against the surrounding hills. It was a calming scene, yet he felt no peace, despite his successful deer hunt and the rabbits he had snagged.

Early this morning White Wolf had woken in a cold sweat after a disturbing dream about Little Fawn. Her face had been shrouded within dense fog. But he'd heard her calling out to him in an anguished tone.

White Wolf lifted his gaze to the sky. *Is Little Fawn in some kind of trouble? Might she have gotten hurt or taken ill? Does the woman I love need my help?*

He urged his horse on, eager to return to his home along the Clearwater. White Wolf hoped and prayed that when he got there, his fears would be unfounded.

⬥

Blackfoot Territory

Cries of excitement echoed as the Blackfoot warriors entered the village, leading ten horses they'd probably stolen as well as Little Fawn, their prisoner. Many of the women, and even some children, pointed and jeered at her, speaking rapidly to one another in their native language. She cringed under their scrutiny. *They are probably talking about the many ways they plan to torture me.*

A large crowd closed in around her. The man who held her captive pulled the horses to a stop and dismounted. With one swift movement, he jerked Little Fawn to the ground. Her wrists were still bound, and she landed on her knees. "Please untie me," Little Fawn begged, holding out her hands. "I will not run away."

Her captor backed away, while the women and a few older children moved closer. Younger children stood by and curiously watched when the mistreatment began.

Little Fawn had no choice but to take the punishment. She huddled into a ball and tried to shield her face, hoping to protect herself from sprays of dirt landing over her already dusty clothes and from the women's feet pummeling her. Some of the children joined in, while others pinched her exposed skin. The warriors laughed at the scene.

Little Fawn bit her lip and tasted blood. After what seemed like hours, the punishment ended, and the villagers dispersed. Little Fawn was startled when her abductor grabbed one of her braids and yanked her to a standing position. He then hauled her across the compound to a teepee covered with buffalo hides. When he pushed Little Fawn inside, she barely kept her balance.

Little Fawn blinked several times to help her eyes adjust to the dark interior. Two young boys and an Indian woman, obviously with child, sat watching her. The children looked simply curious, but the woman's scrunched-up face revealed intense malice.

The warrior said something to the woman; then he nudged Little Fawn toward an empty mat in one corner. "Please remove the bands. They are cutting my skin." She held her hands out to him again. Surely he must understand.

With a noisy grunt, he turned and sauntered out of the teepee. Had the hateful man ignored her request because he didn't understand her language, or was he merely being cruel? Little Fawn surmised it was the latter.

The woman went back to feeding her children some buffalo stew and cornmeal cakes. The aroma was tantalizing, and Little Fawn fought against the hunger pangs gnawing at her.

A while later, the Blackfoot brave returned. This time another Indian woman accompanied him. He said a few words to her then gestured to his wife, who took their boys by the hands and rushed out of the teepee.

The warrior squatted in front of the fire, and the woman he'd brought along hurried across the lodge. She knelt in front of Little Fawn and reached out to clasp her bound hands.

Little Fawn studied the woman intently. She appeared to be about thirty summers, and a small, faded scar marked her left cheek.

"My name is Flying Dove," the Indian said in the Nimiipuu dialect. "What are you called?"

Little Fawn was surprised to hear someone among the Blackfoot speak her own language. "I am Little Fawn. I was captured and brought here against my will. Please speak to my captor and ask him to let me go."

Flying Dove shook her head. "Wild Elk found you. He claims you as his own, so he is free to do with you as he will."

Little Fawn gasped. "But I am promised to another—one of my own people."

"That does not matter. You are the property of Wild Elk now. He has the right to sell you, make you a slave, keep you as second wife, or have you killed. He tells me that for now at least, he wishes you to be his wife's slave." Flying Dove squeezed Little Fawn's hands. "You will live among the Blackfoot. After a time, you will come to accept this, and your old life will seem like nothing more than a distant dream."

"I do not wish to stay here. I could never forget my old life, and I do not want to be his wife's slave."

The woman's dark eyes held a note of sympathy, but she shook her head vehemently. "Do not fight what you cannot change. To fight will only mean pain. I know, for I was captured many moons ago. I was also part of a Nimiipuu tribe, and I fought my captors until there was no fight left. I was nearly beaten to death on several occasions." Flying Dove touched the scar on her cheek. "I finally came to accept my life. It was either accept or be killed." She smiled faintly. "I am content to live as Black Turkey's second wife. We have three sons and two daughters. The Blackfoot are my people now, just as they shall be yours."

Hot tears streamed down Little Fawn's cheeks as she thought once again of Yellow Bird's story about her capture by the Blackfoot when she was a young woman. Gray Eagle had found Yellow Bird and made an attempt to rescue her, but one of the Blackfoot Indians shot him with an arrow. Yellow Bird believed the man she loved had been killed. She'd tried to escape, but her captors caught up and brought her back to their camp. She was severely punished and after a time, traded to a white man who later became White Wolf's father.

Will White Wolf search for me? Little Fawn shuddered. *If he does, will he be killed or left for dead, the way Gray Eagle was?*

Flying Dove stood up. "Forget about freedom, Little Fawn. You would do well to cooperate with your captor. You are a beautiful young woman, and Wild Elk's beatings will make you ugly and old before your time. Heed my advice, and you will be happier."

"Happier?" Little Fawn screamed. "How can I be happy living here among my enemies?" She leaned forward, until her head rested on her knees, giving in to the tears she'd tried to hold back until now.

Sometime later, Little Fawn sat up and dried her eyes with the back of her hands. She glanced around the teepee. Wild Elk and Flying Dove were gone, and his wife and children had not returned. Seeing an opportunity to escape, although her wrists were still bound, Little Fawn peeked out of the teepee's opening. One of the Indians who had ridden with her captor sat in front of the lodge. No doubt he'd been told to guard the captive.

With mounting despair, Little Fawn moved back to her mat, noting that the Blackfoot lodge was similar to the Nimiipuu's summer lodges. She saw several leather bags hanging from the teepee's support poles as well as clusters of drying herbs and pemmican. A chairlike device, made of branches woven together was stored in the teepee. In the center of the teepee a large, black pot hung over the cooking fire. Piles of deer and buffalo skins were stacked in one corner for sleeping mats. Little Fawn wondered which one belonged to her captor, and where she would be expected to sleep.

A sense of terror moved through her body like a slithering snake, as she thought about Wild Elk. Flying Dove was right, for his capture had already caused her much pain. She looked down at her legs, where black-and-blue marks from the pinching spotted her delicate limbs. Little Fawn hoped the beatings would not become worse.

I should have listened to White Wolf. Little Fawn tried not to cry. He was only one year older than her, but in those eighteen years, White Wolf had gained much wisdom.

She whispered a prayer to God, pleading for strength to endure. Then she stretched out on the mat and let much-needed sleep overtake her dispirited body.

Little Fawn felt herself being jerked to her feet. In her sleepy state she thought she was dreaming, but Wild Elk's menacing, dark eyes drew her consciousness back to the stark reality that this nightmare was real.

The Indian no longer wore his war paint, so she was able to see his face clearly. He had deeply set eyes and a strong jaw accentuated by a long, jagged scar. His dark, flowing hair was held away from his face by a leather band.

When Wild Elk grabbed her bound hands and pulled her close to his muscular body, she stiffened against his unwanted touch.

He glared at her then jerked a knife from the sheath tied around his waist. Little Fawn closed her eyes, waiting for what she felt sure would be the sting of death.

In one quick movement, the Blackfoot warrior sliced the leather thong free from Little Fawn's wrists, and her arms dropped to her sides. With a renewed sense of courage, she darted toward the deerhide flap.

Wild Elk whirled around and grabbed her arm. With his other hand, he slapped her face hard, causing her head to snap back. A deep moan escaped Little Fawn's lips, and black spots swirled in her vision. Never had she felt so much anger toward anyone as she did this cruel man. Never had she been so abused.

The Blackfoot warrior pushed her toward the fire and pointed to the cooking pot. She looked up at him, waiting to see what he would do next. He ducked out of the teepee and returned a few moments later with three large rabbits, which he promptly threw at Little Fawn's feet. His meaning was clear. He wanted her to cook the freshly dressed game.

Little Fawn drew a deep breath. For the time being, she must accept her plight. She could not do as Flying Dove asked, however. No matter how long she was held captive, Little Fawn would never accept the Blackfoot as her people. Had God abandoned her, or could she have been put in this position to tell the Blackfoot tribe about Jesus and the plan of salvation? Perhaps in a strange way, Little Fawn had been given the chance to be a missionary. The question remained: Would these people listen?

CHAPTER 5

Little Fawn made her way to the stream. Women and children laughed and played as they bathed and then cleaned their clothes by beating them against the rocks. The first time Little Fawn had tried to bathe here, the other women pushed her away, so today she'd chosen a spot farther downstream.

Little Fawn dropped to the ground and removed her moccasins, wishing she could share in the merriment going on upstream. But her heart held no laughter. Her life was meaningless now that she was the captive of a Blackfoot warrior. If only she could speak their language so she could tell them about God. At least there would be some purpose for her being here.

Little Fawn stared at her hands, callused and sore from long hours of hard work. Wild Elk's wife made certain of that. Slow Turtle was an appropriate name for the woman. She was lazy and used the fact that she was with child to her advantage. Slow Turtle made Little Fawn do countless chores and beat her if she didn't do them quickly enough or the way she wanted them done. The discouraged young woman was kept busy from sunup to sundown, carrying water, hauling wood, cooking, sewing, curing hides, and caring for her captor's children.

She could hardly remember what it felt like to have a full belly. Her stomach, even now, growled in protest with the little substance she'd been allowed to eat that morning. After cooking meals for her captor, his wife, and their children, Little Fawn had to wait until they finished eating. She then got the leftover morsels.

Her only respite was after dark, when all was quiet in the camp. Last night before falling asleep, Little Fawn lay watching the stars through the hole at the top of the teepee. Gazing at them made her feel closer to God. She remembered her mother saying more than once that a person's greatest hope on earth was help from God.

Pulling her thoughts to the need at hand, Little Fawn removed her tunic and stepped into the chilly water to bathe. Her youthful body was covered with ugly black bruises, and the water stung her painful welts. While most of the wounds came from Wild Elk's wife, he too would often beat her. She felt grateful he hadn't taken her as a second wife and prayed that Slow Turtle's jealousy would prevent him from ever doing so.

Little Fawn thought about trying to escape during the night, but it was too risky, since guards were posted around the camp. All she could do was hope and pray that someone would rescue her. In the meantime, she needed to speak with Flying Dove again, to ask if she would act as her interpreter.

After Little Fawn finished her bath, she filled two water skins from a part of the stream where the water flowed over rocks. She'd just stepped away when she noticed Flying Dove and two of her children getting dressed after their morning baths.

Flying Dove sent the children off to play then moved closer to Little Fawn. "I see you have not heeded my words."

"What do you mean?"

"I can tell by your bruises that you have suffered much. When will you accept this life as your own?"

Little Fawn's voice trembled. "I will never accept it. I do not want to be part of Wild Elk's lodge."

Flying Dove flicked a hand in front of her nose. "I believe much of your abuse comes from a jealous wife."

Little Fawn nodded. "It is as you say. Slow Turtle hates me. She beats me no matter how hard I work. I believe the woman wishes I were dead." She gulped back a sob. "I wonder if that might not be for the best."

Flying Dove gave Little Fawn's arm a light tap. "I felt that way once, but it will pass. If you do not allow yourself to think about your past, you will adjust to life among the Blackfoot."

Little Fawn pressed her palms against her chest. "I could never forget my past. I will die with my family in my thoughts."

"For your sake, I hope you can learn to forget."

Little Fawn slowly shook her head "Even if I could, it would not change the way Wild Elk or his wife feel about me."

"Perhaps in time she will learn to accept you. Slow Turtle must respect her husband's wishes." Flying Dove spoke in a hushed tone. "A conversation I overheard indicated he still wishes to have you only as his wife's slave. And remember, my husband's first wife hated me once, but she is now my friend."

Little Fawn studied the top of her moccasins. "When you were captured, did you ever think about trying to escape?"

Flying Dove gave Little Fawn a firm shake. "Do not think such thoughts! You would be caught and punished severely."

Little Fawn swallowed hard. She believed Flying Dove spoke the truth. "I have a favor to ask of you."

"What is it?"

"Would you act as my interpreter, so I may tell Wild Elk, Slow Turtle, and the others about God?"

Flying Dove's forehead wrinkled. "You mean the white man's God?"

"Yes. He is the one true God—our heavenly Father. He sent His Son to earth to die so that—"

Flying Dove put her hand over Little Fawn's mouth. "Do not speak such words to me. There is no white man's God. Only *Han-ya-wet*—the Great Spirit." She pointed to the sky. "To speak of any other God could mean more punishment, or even death. At the Green River Rendezvous, Black Robe men tried to teach us from the white man's book. But our chief said we are to have no part of it. So you must keep quiet about your religious beliefs in this camp, and I will not act as your interpreter."

Tears sprang to Little Fawn's eyes. Their chief was wrong, but if she had no one to speak on her behalf, how could she possibly share God's Word and the plan of salvation? Had she been a fool to think she could be a missionary like Mother Amanda and tell others about God?

Little Fawn clutched the water skin tightly to her chest. "I must get this back to the lodge. Slow Turtle will no doubt be waiting for me with angry sticks for being gone so long."

———

High in the Hills

After his hunting excursion, White Wolf was glad to be heading home. He had done a lot of thinking while away from the village. He had made a mistake. Because of Little Fawn's focus on her desire to teach, rather than on him, he had let jealously get in the way of his better judgment. White

Wolf regretted not taking her to join the Nimiipuu so she could begin fulfilling her dreams. When he got home, he would apologize to her.

A few more hours of travel and he would be back at his village. But for now, he needed a rest, not only for himself, but also for Spirit Dancer. The sound of a gurgling stream drew him in that direction.

After guiding his horse to the water's edge, White Wolf rested up against a tree. He glanced to his left and noticed a feather caught in a vine. Examining the plume closely, he determined it had come from a hawk. White Wolf stared into the sparkling stream, with his thoughts going back a week—the last time he and Little Fawn had talked. He closed his eyes, and a smile touched his lips. Seeing the feather brought a warm feeling to his heart, remembering how he'd tickled the tip of Little Fawn's nose.

I should have supported her determination to teach the Word of God and gone with her to the plains so she'd be safe. White Wolf's left fist hit his other hand. *We could have talked it over with our mothers and tried to persuade them to allow us to go.*

White Wolf couldn't get home soon enough. He wouldn't be content until he saw Little Fawn and apologized to her.

A timid doe walked cautiously on the other side of the stream and gazed toward his horse. Seeing the doe's widened belly was a reminder that the birthing season was soon approaching. When the doe dipped her head to take a drink from the stream, she didn't seem to notice White Wolf sitting directly across from her. He blended in well with the surroundings, as he had been taught many moons ago. White Wolf could have had the perfect shot, but instead of adding more meat to his cache, he chose to enjoy the moment. When his horse whinnied, the doe stood straight and alert with her nose in the air; then she bounded off, disappearing over the nearest ridge.

His horse looked over at him as if to say, "You let her get away?" White Wolf grinned and shook his head. He walked over to Spirit Dancer and patted the black stallion's neck. "I did you a favor, boy. Now you will have less to carry home."

After rubbing the horse with cool water over his legs and back, White Wolf left the peaceful resting place to journey toward home. "Tomorrow I will know Little Fawn is safe."

Lapwai Valley

"What do you mean, Little Fawn is gone?" Red Hawk tipped his head as he stared at Amanda. "Where did she go?"

Amanda's voice trembled as she clutched her husband's arm. "We think she may have followed the Nimiipuu onto the plain. She's been gone seven days."

"Did you give her permission to go?"

"No, of course not."

"What about White Wolf? Did he go with her?"

Amanda shook her head. "But he's not here to ask. The same day she disappeared, he told his mother he was going hunting and would be away several days. He is not even aware she is gone."

Red Hawk dropped into a chair at the table. "I'm betting he used hunting as an excuse. My guess is, White Wolf and our daughter are traveling together. They've probably caught up to the tribe by now."

"Are you going after her?" Amanda took a seat beside him.

He shook his head. "What is the point? If she was determined to go and White Wolf is with her, then I'm sure she'll be safe."

Amanda's chin quivered. "It's not only her safety that worries me, Husband. What if by some chance Little Fawn comes across the same band of Flathead Indians we ran into seventeen years ago? What if she sees her twin sister?" Her voice rose. "Everything I've tried to protect her from could be exposed, and Little Fawn might never forgive me for keeping the truth from her." She swiped at the tears on her cheek. "Besides, if the Flatheads discover who she is, her life could be in danger."

"I don't believe they would harm Little Fawn." Red Hawk shook his head.

"How do you know?"

"If they did recognize her as the twin baby they'd left in the woods to die, they would likely see it as an omen or sign from the Great Spirit. Their superstitions might cause them to believe that our daughter has some kind of mystical powers." He reached over and touched Amanda's arm. "Think about it. How many babies left to die could have possibly survived? The Flathead tribe would have no way of knowing you found

345

the infant and took her to raise as your child." Red Hawk stroked her forearm. "I realize you are worried, but Little Fawn is no longer a baby, and we can't always be there to shield her. If she were alone, I would be concerned, but with White Wolf there, she will be protected. And once they are with the Nimiipuu people, they will both be fine."

Amanda hoped her husband was right, but the fear in her heart would not go away until she saw Little Fawn again. She would keep praying for their daughter until the day she returned.

CHAPTER 6

As White Wolf rode his horse into camp early the next day, he spotted his mother talking with Amanda outside of their lodge. He quickly dismounted and secured Spirit Dancer.

"My son, you have returned!" Yellow Bird hurried toward him.

"Yes, Mother. It is good to be home." White Wolf joined the women and gave his mother a hug.

"Is Little Fawn nearby? I wish to speak with her."

Amanda's chin trembled, and his mother shook her head.

"Where is she?" That strange, foreboding feeling he'd felt in the hills returned. "Has something happened to Little Fawn?"

"We don't know. My daughter has been missing for several days." Amanda drew a shaky breath. "We thought—even hoped—she was with you and that you were both heading for the plains."

"I have not seen Little Fawn since the day before I left." A muscle in White Wolf's cheek twitched. "I cannot believe she would leave without telling anyone where she was going." He pulled down on his chin. "I wonder. . ."

"What are you thinking?" his mother asked.

"I believe, like you, that Little Fawn went to join the Nimiipuu. She mentioned it to me the last time we spoke—even asked if I would take her."

Amanda clasped her chest with both hands. "If we had known she wasn't with you, Red Hawk would have gone looking for her. Now he and Gray Eagle are out fishing and may not be back for a few days."

"It does not matter. I will go in search of Little Fawn myself. Hopefully, I will be able to follow her horse's tracks."

White Wolf's mother clasped his arm. "No, my son. You must not go by yourself. Please wait until your father and Red Hawk return. Then all three of you can go looking for her."

With a determined set of his jaw, White Wolf shook his head. "I cannot wait that long. Little Fawn's life may be in danger. I will gather up some supplies and be on my way."

Blackfoot Territory

As Slow Turtle's time of delivery approached, she became harder to live with. She ate all the time, made Little Fawn cook and serve the food, and spent hours on her sleeping mat.

Little Fawn couldn't remember any other pregnant woman she'd been around being so lethargic. It was customary for Indian women to continue working right up to the time of their delivery. If a woman was sick or having an unusually difficult pregnancy, she might take to her bed for a time, but such was not the case with Slow Turtle. Her pregnancy appeared to be normal. She was simply a lazy woman who wanted to be waited on.

Since Little Fawn's grandmother was a medicine woman, Little Fawn was acquainted with the birthing procedure. She was aware that in order to have an easy delivery, a pregnant woman must not only get sufficient rest, but also the proper exercise. Slow Turtle rested plenty but got very little exercise.

One afternoon, Little Fawn tended Slow Turtle's two young sons, while the slothful woman took her second nap of the day. As Slow Turtle's slave, Little Fawn was expected to keep the boys quiet and entertained. She decided to take them for a walk to the lake.

Small Elk, five summers old, had been named after his father. His younger brother, Calling Bird, was nearly three summers. The little boy hung on to the hem of Little Fawn's tunic and whined. She had a feeling he didn't want to walk with her.

Small Elk said something that made his younger brother cry. Little Fawn practically had to pull him along the path, but eventually he cooperated. Small Elk ran ahead and was already at the water's edge when Little Fawn and Calling Bird reached the lake.

The older child ran circles around his brother, tormenting him with a stick.

"Stop that!" Little Fawn's patience was waning, and when she tripped on a boulder, trying to sidestep the rambunctious children, she fell face-first into the cold water.

The boys stood on the bank, laughing and pointing at her. As she trudged wearily out of the lake, shaking the water off the best she could, the children darted into the woods.

Little Fawn stepped onto the path and nearly ran straight into Flying Dove.

"I am glad I found you," the other woman said breathlessly.

"What is it? You look upset?"

A smile tugged at the corners of Flying Dove's lips. "And you look very wet. What happened?"

"I took a bath with my clothes on." Little Fawn's teeth chattered. "What did you need to see me about?"

"Slow Turtle's labor has begun."

"Am I expected to watch her children for the rest of the day?"

Flying Dove shook her head. "Someone else will care for them. You are needed to help with the birth."

"Why would she need me? Isn't Standing Tall a medicine woman?"

"Yes, but she is with another woman who is about to deliver." Flying Dove reached for Little Fawn's hand. "Slow Turtle is having a difficult time. You told me that your grandmother is also a medicine woman. Surely you know what needs to be done."

"I have had some experience, but—"

"There is no time for talk. You must go quickly. I will take the boys with me."

Little Fawn wasn't sure how much help she would be, but she had learned to do as she was told. So she headed toward Wild Elk's teepee, calling over her shoulder, "The boys ran into the woods. I hope you can find them."

Slow Turtle moaned and rolled restlessly on her mat while Little Fawn quickly changed into a dry tunic and dropped to her knees in front of the distraught woman.

Slow Turtle tried to resist when Little Fawn began to examine her.

"I am here to help." Little Fawn spoke in a calm voice, hoping that a soft tone would soothe Wild Elk's wife, even though the woman did not understand her words.

Slow Turtle finally settled down. She closed her eyes and relaxed against the mat.

It took Little Fawn only moments to see that the baby was quite large. An incision would have to be made, or else the laboring mother would tear. While she had never done the procedure herself, she had seen her grandmother do it. She wished she spoke the Blackfoot language, so she could explain to Slow Turtle what she needed to do.

Little Fawn scanned the drying herbs overhead. When she located some valerian root, she made a sedative tea and offered a cup to Slow Turtle.

Flying Dove entered the lodge as Little Fawn was gathering blankets and strips of deer hide to aide in the delivery.

"What can I do to help?" she asked.

Little Fawn nodded toward Slow Turtle. "She is fairly sedated, but will need to be held down while I make the cut."

The other woman's dark eyes became pools of concern. "Cut? What will you cut?"

"The baby is large, and I must make an incision outside the birth canal. If I do not, she will tear and could possibly bleed to death," Little Fawn explained, as she moved back to her patient.

Flying Dove nodded. "Do what you think is best."

"I cannot do it without a knife."

"I will look through some of the parfletches." A few moments later, Flying Dove handed Little Fawn a small knife.

With only a moment's hesitation, Little Fawn poured some of the herbal tea over the knife and instructed Flying Dove to hold the patient down. Quickly, she made the incision, and then smeared bear grease on Slow Turtle's loins.

The laboring woman groaned as Flying Dove helped her sit in a crouched position.

After several hard pushes, Little Fawn saw the baby's dark head pass through the birth canal. She caught the slippery child as it made its lusty entrance into the Blackfoot world.

It was a large boy with a pair of healthy lungs.

Little Fawn placed the infant across his mother's stomach then cut and tied the umbilical cord. She went to a sewing parfletch and withdrew a bone needle and some buffalo sinew. While Little Fawn stitched Slow Turtle's incision, Flying Dove cleaned the baby and wrapped him with strips of soft deer hide.

By the time Wild Elk returned to their lodge, both mother and child rested peacefully.

Flying Dove said something to him then motioned to Little Fawn. "I explained that his wife's delivery was difficult, but you knew what to do, and because of it, he has a new son."

Wild Elk barely glanced at Little Fawn before moving toward Slow Turtle to get a better look at the son nestled in the crook of his wife's arm. For a brief moment, Little Fawn saw tenderness when Wild Elk gazed upon the newborn's face. He conversed briefly with his wife then stood and turned to Little Fawn.

She froze in place, not knowing what to expect. *Is he angry with me? Did I disappoint him?* Little Fawn could not read his emotion. *Is he not happy that I helped his wife deliver a healthy baby boy?*

Wild Elk mumbled something, turned, and walked out.

While Little Fawn hadn't expected thanks from her captor, at least she wasn't being punished. But as hard as she tried to find joy and meaning in life, Little Fawn's heart held no hope.

CHAPTER 7

All around the village, fires burned and fresh meat hung to dry from a recent buffalo hunt, while children and dogs ran about playing. The smell of smoke hung thick in the air as a small party of men mounted their horses and rode out of camp. Little Fawn wondered if they were going out to hunt game again or perhaps steal more horses.

Many of the older Blackfoot men sat around campfires, smoking their long pipes and visiting. Some of the women had gone to the lake to bathe and then wash their clothes. Others were at camp, sewing, cooking, or taking care of their young children.

When Little Fawn entered Big Elk's teepee, she found it empty. She preferred to be alone and was glad when the others were not around to taunt or torture her. She was exhausted after helping the women prepare hides from the buffalo recently killed—a long and tedious process.

She placed the water skins next to the cooking pot and began to prepare a venison stew. Once it was bubbling, she picked up a piece of deer hide and threaded a bone needle with a thin piece of buffalo sinew. As Little Fawn sewed a new tunic for Slow Turtle, she let her thoughts wander toward home. Did her family and White Wolf think about her? Had they assumed by her disappearance that she'd joined their people to dig roots and hunt on the plains?

Loud voices pulled Little Fawn's thoughts back to the present. She set her sewing aside and went outside to see what the commotion was about.

Several Indian men had gathered in a circle, and a young woman, not much older than Little Fawn, stood in the center. They prodded her body with long sticks, while shouting unfamiliar words in their native tongue. The poor woman, Shining Waters, looked terrified, as if she knew what was coming.

Little Fawn spotted Flying Dove in the crowd. "What is going on? Why are those men tormenting Shining Waters?"

"She has done a terrible thing," Flying Dove whispered. "She refused to accept her husband's new wife and tried to run away. Now she must be punished in whatever manner Black Bear chooses."

Little Fawn's hand went to her mouth. "Being hit with sticks in front of everyone? Is that the punishment her husband ordered?"

Flying Dove shook her head. "That is only the beginning of her sufferings. Black Bear has decided to mark her for life so everyone will know she is an unfit wife."

"How will he mark her?"

"By cutting off the tip of her nose. Then she will be cast from his lodge to fend for herself."

Little Fawn gasped. "How could he do something so terrible to his own wife?"

"It is the way of our people."

"These Blackfoot are not *our* people. They are cruel, and I claim no part of this tribe."

Flying Dove touched Little Fawn's trembling shoulder. "Not all are cruel. Red Turkey is good to me in most ways. If I am punished, it is because I have done something to displease him, and I deserve it."

"Deserve it? If you displease your husband, you deserve whatever punishment he gives? Is that what you believe, Flying Dove?"

"It is what I know. My husband has the right to do as he chooses."

"If I were married to White Wolf, he would never deal so harshly with me, no matter what I may have done." Sadly, Little Fawn turned away as two young braves threw Shining Waters across Black Bear's horse. They mounted and rode out of camp, laughing and cheering.

Shining Waters was about to meet her fate. She would be disfigured for life—however long that might be.

As Little Fawn started back to the teepee, hot tears rolled down her cheeks. She too was a marked woman, only her mark did not show on the end of her nose. She was scarred by the anger she felt toward Wild Elk. Little Fawn cried for Shining Waters—and for herself.

In the Mountains

White Wolf had been tracking Little Fawn's horse several days and hoped he was getting close. He needed to rehearse his speech for when he did find her. After that, he might kiss her soundly and promise to marry her.

"I love Little Fawn, even when she is stubborn," he said to Spirit Dancer as the stallion drank from the stream where White Wolf had stopped to refresh himself. "I should have suspected she would strike out on her own, especially after I had that bad dream."

White Wolf closed his eyes, and an image of Little Fawn appeared. "I've loved her as long as I can remember. Her smile is so warm it could melt the coldest winter snow."

While the horse continued to drink, White Wolf took a piece of dried fish from his pack. As he ate, his mind drifted back to the days when he and Little Fawn were young and carefree. It was a time when life was uncomplicated and full of promise.

It will be that way again, he told himself. *After I find Little Fawn and am holding her in my arms.*

Lapwai Valley

Amanda paced the length of the cabin, stopping long enough to stir the cooking pot a few times. She was in no mood for supper this evening. In fact, until she knew her daughter was safely home, Amanda didn't think she would ever care about food. If Red Hawk were here right now, he would have gone with White Wolf in search of Little Fawn.

"You should have let me go with White Wolf," Running Fox said, as though he could read her mind. "I am a good tracker, and I'm sure I could find my sister."

Amanda paused to rub her forehead. "The last thing I need is for both of my children to be out there on their own."

Running Fox lifted his chin. "I wouldn't have been alone. Yellow Bird's son would have been with me."

Amanda went to the cooking pot and dished her son some stew. She wouldn't admit it, but he was right. If she trusted anyone to keep him safe, as her husband would have done, it would be White Wolf. He had the necessary skills for survival and would put them to good use.

Amanda prayed for the day White Wolf would bring her daughter back, unharmed.

"Enough talk about this, Thomas." She handed the wooden bowl to him. "As soon as your father returns from his fishing trip, he will go in search of Little Fawn too."

The cabin door opened, and Yellow Bird stepped in, along with her daughter, Shy Deer. "I came to see how you are doing." She moved to stand beside Amanda.

"Not well. I'm worried sick about Little Fawn," Amanda admitted. "What if White Wolf doesn't find her? What if something bad happens to both of them?"

Yellow Bird slipped her arm around Amanda's waist. "Where is your faith?"

Amanda sighed. "Even I, a woman of faith, can experience doubts and be filled with worry. I am human after all." She touched her chest. "This feeling of dread haunts me, but I'm trying to live my faith."

Yellow Bird nodded. "I too am concerned for our children's welfare." She glanced at Shy Deer, sitting at the table beside Running Fox. "I wish White Wolf and Little Fawn were still young, like these two. It was easier back then. Even so, I do have confidence in my son's ability to bring your daughter home."

Amanda managed a smile. "You are right on both accounts." She clasped her friend's hand. "Let us pray now—for White Wolf to find Little Fawn and for their safe return."

In the Mountains

White Wolf checked on Spirit Dancer one more time then spread out his bedroll nearby. He wasn't ready to end the day's search, but dark had come quickly, and he had no choice. After traveling all day, rest was what he and his horse needed.

With his head resting on his folded arms, White Wolf looked up at the ebony sky. Like the wilderness surrounding him, the heavens with millions of twinkling stars filled him with a sense of vastness.

I wonder what Little Fawn is doing right now? Is she watching the stars too? He shifted his position. *When Little Fawn becomes my wife, we will watch the stars together. Becoming her husband cannot happen soon enough.*

White Wolf groaned. He felt restless and agitated. *This would not be happening if I'd done what Little Fawn asked.*

A coyote howled in the distance, cutting through the night's peacefulness. Spirit Dancer nickered then settled down. The dried fish White Wolf ate earlier would have to do. In the morning he would eat before continuing his search. But for now, he ignored his protesting stomach and willed himself to sleep.

As White Wolf rolled onto his side, he prayed the morning would come fast. *Maybe tomorrow I will find Little Fawn.*

CHAPTER 8

The next night when White Wolf stopped to rest, he found it hard to sleep, despite his fatigue. Had Little Fawn found the Nimiipuu people and headed out with the tribe to the plains? If so, why hadn't he seen their tracks, along with those from Little Fawn's horse? His eyesight was blurred from an all-day search looking for the smallest of signs.

Rubbing his eyes and then pounding his fists, White Wolf grew angry. "I will not let my hope be defeated." But the gnawing fear he'd had since his dream about her increased with each passing day. White Wolf's greatest worry was that Little Fawn's life might be in danger. Until he looked at her lovely face and saw for himself that she was all right, he would not have any peace.

As White Wolf pulled his bedroll from the pack on his horse's back, he lifted his face toward the star-studded sky and sent up a prayer. "Heavenly Father, please protect Little Fawn and lead me to her."

The following day, as the sun rose to its highest position, White Wolf came across a band of Salish Indians, known to some neighboring tribes as Flatheads. He'd heard they were called that name because they did not follow the tradition of putting cedar cone-shaped headdresses on their babies, which forced the infant's head to become pointed. To those who followed the traditional custom of reshaping the skull, the top of Salish people's heads appeared flat.

The Salish territory extended from the crest of the Bitterroot Range to the Rocky Mountains and centered on the upper reaches of the Clark Fork of the Columbia River. They hunted elk, deer, bison, and small game, and also gathered edible plants such as bitterroot, various types of moss, camas, and wild onions. Fishing was also important to the Salish, as it was to the Nez Percé and other Plateau tribes.

As White Wolf approached their camp, one of the tribe's men looked in his direction and gave an acknowledgment, using sign language with his hands.

White Wolf greeted him in return. Through sign language, he asked if a young woman had passed this way, riding an Appaloosa. When the man shook his head, White Wolf moved on.

Blackfoot Territory

Little Fawn lay motionless on her sleeping mat, listening to the sounds around her. An owl hooted from somewhere outside, and one of the horses whinnied, as if in response. Inside the teepee, she heard the heavy breathing of Slow Turtle, accompanied by the rumble of Wild Elk's deep snores. The boys slept soundly, while the baby cooed softly beside his mother.

Flying Dove was wrong. Little Fawn had not accepted the Blackfoot people as her own, nor had she given up hope of being rescued someday. But maybe it was wishful thinking. Even if someone was looking for her, they might never come across this Blackfoot camp.

Little Fawn gulped back a sob. *If they were to find this encampment, how would they get past the guards to set me free?*

Closing her eyes, Little Fawn reflected on the scripture from Romans her mother had read before they'd gone to bed the night she'd snuck out of their cabin. According to one of the verses, she was supposed to have peace while going through bad times because it would build hope in God.

Dear Lord, Little Fawn prayed, *please give me a sense of peace and the strength to endure. I want my hope to be in You.*

The following afternoon while Slow Turtle napped, Wild Elk stepped into the teepee and handed Little Fawn two plump rabbits. Then he mumbled something while gesturing to the cooking pot.

Even though she didn't understand his words, Little Fawn got the message. He wanted her to cook the rabbits for their evening meal. She gave a brief nod and said, "*Latawah*—friend. I wish to be your friend." Little Fawn didn't know what had possessed her to say such a thing. It was doubtful he understood her language, and even more unlikely that he would want her as his friend. But if she could gain his trust, perhaps by using Flying Dove as her interpreter, it might be possible to tell him about God.

Wild Elk grunted in response. Then he turned and stalked out of the lodge.

She sighed. *If only God would provide a miracle that would help me get through to these people.*

High in the Mountains

After five days of trying to locate Little Fawn's trail, White Wolf came upon tracks that only her mare could have made. Snow's prints were easily identifiable, since her left rear hoof had a small crack. A brief moment of hope was replaced with alarm when he saw another set of tracks. Little Fawn was not alone. Another rider and horse were with her.

Following the trail, White Wolf came to a small stream. Crossing the shallow water, his hopes diminished when he got to the other side and saw no sign of any hoofprints. Looking up ahead, and then to his left and right, he summoned up the skills he'd learned through trial and error as he grew up.

"Let's try this again, Spirit Dancer." White Wolf guided his stallion back across the water to where he'd first crossed. After searching awhile, he noticed some overturned rocks under the shallow water's surface. These were the signs he'd been hoping to find, which led White Wolf farther downstream.

A sigh of relief escaped his lips when he discovered evidence of where they had exited the water. While tracking two sets of hoof prints, White Wolf discovered two sets of footprints. He got off of his horse and hunkered down for a closer look. More disturbing than seeing these impressions in the dirt was noticing signs of a struggle.

White Wolf wiped at the beads of sweat running down his forehead. Little Fawn must have been taken hostage and had no doubt been escorted somewhere against her will.

He jumped back on his horse. The trail they'd made was easy to follow, and he quickly headed in that direction.

After traveling awhile, he saw smoke rising in the far distance. White

Wolf would have to operate with caution and use methods he'd perfected.

Making his way toward the smoke, he chose his path carefully. He tethered Spirit Dancer in a dark shaded area of trees. Then he went the rest of the distance on foot.

Soon White Wolf found a point from where he could observe the village without being seen. He spotted Little Fawn's mare, but a guard stood too close to the horses, so White Wolf didn't dare make a move. If he could find a way to slip in and free Little Fawn, they'd both have to ride on his stallion and leave her mare behind.

White Wolf had a few ideas for rescuing her, but he would do nothing reckless. *I must be patient and choose the right time.* White Wolf would wait and observe the goings-on in the Blackfoot camp. How long it would take, he did not know, but getting Little Fawn out safely was his only concern.

For several hours, White Wolf remained in his hidden position, watching the Blackfoot camp. He'd glimpsed Little Fawn when she went to get water at the far end of the village. It was difficult to see her struggle then stop to rest from carrying a heavy container of water. For a brief moment, she looked up at the sky as if saying a prayer to the Father above. White Wolf had to keep himself from running to her. More unnerving, as she stood there before going into a tent, was seeing black-and-blue marks on her much-too-thin legs. White Wolf wanted to punish the person who had inflicted such abuse on her. He wanted Little Fawn to be safe and away from this savage tribe and would like nothing more than to give her abductors what they deserved.

I'm as much to blame as the person who did this. White Wolf closed his eyes and willed himself to bring his anger under control. If only he had agreed to take Little Fawn to the plains, this would not have happened. He would have been there to protect her. Perhaps this was his punishment for not wanting to be a missionary and tell others about the Word of God.

White Wolf offered another heartfelt prayer. *Please give me the opportunity to free Little Fawn, and protect us both as we make our escape.*

CHAPTER 9

Exhausted from another day of hard work, Little Fawn crawled onto her sleeping mat. Closing her eyes, she let thoughts of home fill her mind. It was the only thing that brought even a small measure of comfort to her aching soul. As each day passed, she became more despondent, convinced that she would never see White Wolf or her family again. Yet she tried not to give up hope.

Little Fawn wished she could sneak out, hop on her horse, and flee. But she was smart enough to know it wasn't as simple as that.

A few times, she'd caught glimpses of Snow out in the meadow among the other horses. When Little Fawn was close by, the mare seemed to sense her presence as well. Little Fawn recognized her horse's whinny among the snorts and neighing of the rest of the herd. With Snow's ears perked and her soft nickering, Little Fawn was content that the Blackfoot treated all horses well, and her mare was safe. Even though the thought of escaping with her horse was on Little Fawn's mind, the last thing she wanted to do was put Snow in danger. The warriors might kill her horse if she tried to escape and failed.

Her thoughts turned in another direction. Earlier today, she'd dealt with Slow Turtle's temper and abuse again. Somehow, during those punishments, Little Fawn kept her reflexes under control. She wanted to fight back, lash out, and prove she was not a coward. But her Christian beliefs proved to be more powerful, so she chose to follow the Golden Rule and the things she wanted to teach by example. *"Do unto others as you would have them do unto you."* Many times, Little Fawn had to repeat to herself, *"Love thy neighbor as thyself."* It was the only way she could get through this ordeal.

Tears stung her eyes. *So here I will stay, waiting and hoping for a miracle.*

Little Fawn recited Psalm 39:7. Her mother had taught it to her when she was a young girl. *"And now, Lord, what wait I for? My hope is in thee."*

She closed her eyes. *That is my prayer, Lord. For I know You are my only hope. Please give me the faith to believe.*

White Wolf waited until nightfall, when all was quiet in the Blackfoot camp. Even the guard who stood by the horses sat against a tree with his head lowered in slumber. Like a cat slinking up on its prey, he snuck into the village and went behind the teepee he'd seen Little Fawn go into earlier today.

Slowly, White Wolf sliced a hole in the back of the dwelling. He stood, quietly listening, making sure he hadn't been detected. The only sounds he heard now were heavy breathing and someone's deep snores. White Wolf had to be careful. Here in the enemy camp, not only was Little Fawn's life in danger, but his as well. So far, his ingenuity and competence worked to his favor. Because of his cunningness, not even a dog barked, or was disturbed, when he'd crept into this village.

"Little Fawn," he whispered, but she did not respond.

Without making a noise, White Wolf pulled the buffalo hide apart and crept inside. "Little Fawn." He kept his voice down.

When someone stirred, he crouched on his haunches and held his breath. It was difficult to see inside the dimly lit lodge, with only the coals from the fire giving light. The last thing he wanted to do was wake the wrong person.

White Wolf moved closer to the smoldering logs in the center of the teepee. Squinting his eyes as he glanced around, he spotted Little Fawn lying on a mat not too far from him. He crawled over to her and placed his hand across her mouth, in case she didn't realize it was him and should cry out.

Little Fawn's eyes snapped open. Someone had their hand clamped over her mouth. *Please don't let it be Wild Elk.* Had he come to take her as his wife? If so, she would fight until she had no fight left.

"Little Fawn, it's me," a voice whispered in her ear. "I've come to get you."

Her heart hammered fiercely. Could she be dreaming, or was he really here? Perhaps God had answered her prayers. Little Fawn reached up to touch his face. White Wolf was real. It was no dream.

Slowly, he took his hand away from her mouth. "Get up, Little Fawn. I'm taking you home."

She did as he said, taking time only to look around to be sure no one else was awake. Little Fawn felt relief when Wild Elk rolled over with his back to them and kept snoring, while Slow Turtle, along with her children, slept on.

Grasping her hand, White Wolf led the way out through the cut he'd made in the teepee. Then cautiously and quietly he guided her out of camp until they reached the spot where Spirit Dancer was tethered. Without a word between them, White Wolf assisted Little Fawn onto his horse. Climbing up behind her, he grasped her waist and the two escaped into the night. Little Fawn was certain the prayers she had offered were the reason no one in the Blackfoot camp saw them and they were able to escape without getting caught.

As they rode out of the area, her mare's distant whinny reached Little Fawn's ears. Leaving her horse behind was difficult, but knowing all the horses were well guarded in the Blackfoot camp, she felt sure they would not be able to get Snow.

Little Fawn hung on to Spirit Dancer's mane, filled with happiness that she and White Wolf had been able to escape, but sad that they were leaving her horse behind. *I'm sorry my precious Snow. Stay safe.*

In the Mountains

For the first time in many days, Little Fawn felt free, riding in front of White Wolf on his mighty steed as they put miles between them and the Blackfoot camp. She was exhausted, and as they rode double on his horse, her greatest comfort was feeling White Wolf's arm protectively around her as she leaned against his muscular body. He was strong like her captor, but White Wolf's touch was gentle, not possessive and controlling like Wild Elk's. Little Fawn relaxed fully against White Wolf's chest and let the motion of his horse lull her to sleep.

When they stopped to rest, White Wolf helped Little Fawn down, took her into his arms, and held her close. In a voice thick with emotion, he said, "When I found out you were gone, I was scared of losing you." He gently patted her back. "I'm sorry for refusing to take you to the plains, Little Fawn. I should have realized how important it was to you. Together, we could have gone to your parents and sought their permission."

Tears pooled in her eyes. "I am sorry too. I was foolish to go out on my own. I should have been satisfied to wait, like you said, until after we are married." Little Fawn boldly grasped the sides of his face.

White Wolf needed no persuading, as their lips met, full of emotion. Little Fawn didn't want the kiss to end. She clung to him, afraid to let go while he hugged her even tighter.

White Wolf slowly pulled back, and their gazes met once more as he ran his fingers across her delicate cheek. "We will never be parted again, my Little Fawn."

Never had she felt so loved. "Oh White Wolf," she murmured, "can you ever forgive me? How could I have jeopardized what we have between us? What if you had never found me?"

White Wolf put a finger to her lips. "It is behind us now. We must rest a short while, and then keep moving. I don't want to take the chance of the Blackfoot following us when they wake up and find you are missing."

The journey that lay in front of them was long, but Little Fawn could not imagine God would have brought her and White Wolf together without getting them home safely.

Lapwai Valley

The following morning, Amanda heard the sound of horses' hooves. Running Fox rushed in. "Mother, come quick! Father and Gray Eagle have returned."

Hurrying from the cabin, her heart stirred with relief as Red Hawk dismounted his horse. Gray Eagle did the same. Yellow Bird rushed out of her dwelling and into Gray Eagle's open arms.

"I am so glad you are back." Amanda clutched her husband's arm, before he drew her into his embrace. "White Wolf returned while you two were gone hunting, and when he heard Little Fawn was missing, he went looking for her."

Grasping her shoulders, Red Hawk's posture stiffened. "So I was wrong? He didn't go with her?"

Amanda shook her head. "We can only hope that Little Fawn caught up to the tribe and nothing bad has happened to her." Her voice caught. "I am afraid for her, Buck. My mother's instinct tells me that our daughter is not with the Nimiipuu." In Amanda's emotional state, the fact that she'd called her husband by his white name barely registered with her.

Red Hawk's fists tightened as he planted his feet in a wide stance and glanced over at Gray Eagle. "As soon as I gather some supplies I will go looking for her and White Wolf."

Gray Eagle stepped forward. "And I will accompany you, my good friend. We must find our children."

CHAPTER 10

In the Mountains

It was morning again, and the winds that had come up the night before had finally quieted. As White Wolf and Little Fawn headed toward home, their bodies were in perfect rhythm with the galloping black stallion they rode. A hurried feeling had overcome them, striving to get closer to their destination. Even Spirit Dancer seemed to sense the urgency, his glossy black mane streaming behind him while his feet pounded the dusty ground.

Sweat lathered on the steed's back as they paused on the crest of a hill to catch their breath. The shade from the trees provided welcome relief from the warming sun.

White Wolf sat erect when he saw two riders in the distance, heading toward them. Concerned that they could be enemy Indians, he nudged Spirit Dancer behind a thicker grove of trees and waited, holding tightly to Little Fawn.

"What if they are Blackfoot?" Her voice trembled.

"Do not worry," he said, hoping to reassure her. "I am here to protect you."

As the riders approached, kicking up a swirl of dust, Little Fawn turned and looked at White Wolf with a gaping mouth. "It's all right. It is my father and Gray Eagle. I recognize their horses."

White Wolf nodded. "They must be back from their fishing trip. I bet they're out looking for us." Cautiously, he directed his horse out from behind the trees. Sure enough, as the riders drew closer, he could see that it was their fathers.

Galloping toward them, White Wolf lifted one hand and waved it about. He'd never been so happy to see two people in all his life.

As soon as Red Hawk and Gray Eagle stopped their horses, Little Fawn leaped off the snorting Spirit Dancer. As she approached her father's horse, he dismounted and swept her into his arms. "I am relieved to see that you are alive. How are you, my daughter?"

"*Ta'c wees*—I am good." Tears pooled in her eyes. "I'm sorry, Father Red Hawk, for leaving Lapwai Valley without telling anyone."

Red Hawk nodded. "You are right—it was wrong. But we will not talk of it now."

"Did you find the Nimiipuu people on the plain?" Gray Eagle questioned, grasping White Wolf's arms.

"No," Little Fawn answered for Gray Eagle's stepson. "I was captured by a Blackfoot warrior before I could catch up to our tribe." Her voice caught on a sob. "I was beaten and used as a slave until White Wolf risked his life to rescue me." She paused for a breath. "It grieves me to say that I was not able to convert anyone to Christianity while I was with the Blackfoot, even though there was a Nez Percé woman who could have acted as my interpreter. And since White Wolf and I had to make a quick escape during the night, I had to leave my horse behind."

"That's right," White Wolf put in. "We couldn't risk trying to get Snow from the area where the horses were being guarded, even though the sentry was asleep."

Red Hawk lifted Little Fawn's chin so she was looking directly at him. "Horses can be replaced; people can't. And I have no doubt your mare will be well cared for. I am just glad you are safe. Your mother will be too." His forehead wrinkled. "She has been beside herself ever since you disappeared."

Little Fawn's chin quivered. "I am sorry for the worry I caused. It was foolish of me to run off. I hope Mother will not be too upset with me."

"No more than she was upset with me for not going after you sooner." Red Hawk placed his hand on her head. "You see, at first, I believed White Wolf had gone with you. So I thought you'd be protected and didn't see the need to go after you. But then when Gray Eagle and I returned from our fishing trip and learned that White Wolf had been hunting when you disappeared from our home,

I realized what a mistake I had made."

"We were thankful to hear that my son had gone in search of you as soon as he found out you were missing." Gray Eagle gestured to White Wolf. "I have confidence in his skills. Plus, this young man cares deeply about you, Little Fawn, and would take every precaution necessary to carry out his plan."

"I know, and I care about him too." As she looked at White Wolf, who stood proud and tall, Little Fawn was once again reminded of how much she loved him. Even so, she felt bad about going home without completing her mission. Not only had she not led one person to the Lord since she left home, but she hadn't even been able to share the Gospel. That was the whole reason she'd wanted to go out on the plains. Would she ever get her chance to be a missionary, or was Little Fawn destined to spend the rest of her life in Lapwai Valley?

After a brief time of refreshing themselves with water and some jerky and letting their horses cool off, the four began their journey home. They had only gone a short ways when they encountered the same group of Flatheads White Wolf had seen several days ago. He was surprised to see they were still camped in the same area and felt glad they'd happened upon these friendly Salish people.

White Wolf looked over at Red Hawk. "Would it be all right if we stopped here awhile? We have been traveling at a fast pace, and Little Fawn is tired. I think it would be good for her to rest a day or so."

Red Hawk nodded slowly. "We will stay the night and leave for home in the morning."

Little Fawn looked at her father with gratitude. Lifting her hands and opening her palms, she murmured, "*Katsa-yah-yah*—thank you."

When Little Fawn got down from White Wolf's horse, she noticed several of the Salish women looking at her with strange expressions. Had they never seen a Nez Percé woman before? Or perhaps they were merely curious about her, wondering who she was and why she and the men had stopped in their camp.

Red Hawk explained that he knew the Flathead language and would speak to the chief to see if it was okay for them to spend the night. While he sought out the leader, and White Wolf and Gray Eagle tended the horses, Little Fawn meandered around. Following a group of children to a nearby stream, she observed a young woman with flowing black hair standing near the water's edge.

Feeling drawn to this woman, and thinking she might be able to communicate with her through sign language, Little Fawn approached from behind. "*Ta-c halaxp*—good afternoon." While she assumed the Indian maiden wouldn't understand what she'd said, Little Fawn figured her greeting would at least get the young woman's attention.

The Salish woman turned around. Little Fawn's head jerked back, and the other woman's eyes widened. Little Fawn didn't know how it was possible, but this Indian looked almost identical to her.

Little Fawn stared at her lookalike, and the other woman looked intently at her. It was as though she were holding her mother's looking glass and seeing her own reflection. But how could this be? In all her seventeen years, Little Fawn had never met anyone who resembled her in such an uncanny manner. She felt compelled to communicate with this young woman.

With a hand signal for the young maiden to wait, Little Fawn ran to the area where Gray Eagle and White Wolf had gone to take care of the horses. "Where is my father?" she asked, barely able to catch her breath. "I need to speak to him right away."

"He's talking to the chief—asking if it's alright for us to stay here until tomorrow," Gray Eagle responded.

White Wolf put his hand on Little Fawn's arm. "What is wrong?"

Little Fawn pointed toward the stream. "There's a young woman over there, and. . ." She blinked rapidly, unable to finish her sentence.

His brows lifted in question.

Little Fawn gestured again to the stream, thankful the maiden was still waiting. "I need my father to speak to this woman on my behalf."

"For what reason? I don't understand."

"Because it's strange that we would look so much alike."

"Here comes Red Hawk now." Gray Eagle pointed in the opposite direction.

When Red Hawk joined them, Little Fawn quickly told how she'd seen the young woman at the stream who looked almost identical to her.

"I can't speak the Salish language, Father, but would you speak to her for me? I wonder if she too noticed that we look alike." Little Fawn touched her chest. "It is odd, but in the few moments we stood together, I felt as though we had a connection."

Red Hawk shifted his weight as he looked in the direction of the stream. Then, taking Little Fawn by the shoulders, he looked directly into her eyes. "Your mother was hoping to keep this truth from you, but now that you have seen this woman who looks like you, I feel you have the right to know."

Her eyebrows lifted. "Know what?"

"You have always known that Amanda is not your birth mother, nor am I your father by blood."

Little Fawn nodded. "The only thing Mother has ever told me is that my parents couldn't keep their baby, so she decided to raise me as her own."

Red Hawk glanced at Gray Eagle, standing stoically beside him. Releasing his grip on her, he looked back at Little Fawn. "Yes, that is correct, but there is more you don't know."

She clasped his arm. "Please, tell me."

"Your birth mother's name is Silver Squirrel, and your father is Two Moons. They belong to the Salish tribe."

Little Fawn's mouth went dry. "So I am not part of the Nimiipuu?"

He shook his head. "You are Salish. When I was acting as Amanda's guide to Lapwai Valley, we stopped along the way for a spell and made camp with this Salish tribe. It was during that time when Silver Squirrel gave birth to twin girls. Amanda witnessed the birth and was quite upset to learn these Salish people believed that if a woman had a multiple birth, it was a bad omen." Red Hawk paused, swiping his tongue across his lower lip. "Your mother, Amanda, has lived in fear that you would find out about this someday. That is why she did not want you to go out on the plains with the rest of our people. She was afraid if you ever ran into your twin, it could be dangerous for you."

Little Fawn tipped her head. "Why would it be dangerous? Did my birth mother give me to Amanda?"

"No. You see. . ."

"Does Amanda believe that if Silver Squirrel were to see me again, and realize I am the twin she gave away, she would want me back? Is that what you are saying, Father Red Hawk?"

He shook his head. "The truth is, Little Fawn, your birth mother was only allowed to keep one of the babies she bore." Red Hawk swallowed so hard, she saw a lump in his throat move up and down. "So according to the Salish tradition, the other baby was taken out to the woods and left."

"Left?" White Wolf shouted. "Was Little Fawn left to die in the woods from starvation or to be eaten by some wild animal?"

Little Fawn covered her mouth with the palm of her hand.

Red Hawk glanced around, as though someone might hear their conversation, and his voice lowered when he spoke again. "When Amanda heard this, she became even more upset and went to the woods to search for you. I followed her there. Seeing a fawn circling a tree is where she found you, unharmed. Amanda believed the baby deer was sent by God in order to lead her to you. That is why she gave you the name Little Fawn." He stopped talking and drew in a breath. "Amanda loved you from the moment she found you, and she's been a good mother to you ever since."

Little Fawn's chin quivered as tears filled her eyes. "I am grateful she saved me, but I don't understand how anyone could leave a newborn baby alone in the woods to die."

"That's murder," White Wolf spoke again. "We should leave this place and these superstitious people right now."

Little Fawn, barely able to speak around her swollen throat, murmured, "We cannot leave yet. Surely this tribe needs to know God. It is a shame Mother Amanda couldn't have reached them with the Gospel." She clutched Red Hawk's arm. "Since you speak the Salish language, won't you please say we can stay longer so I can get to know my sister and tell her and the people here about the one true God?"

"We will stay long enough to tell them, but then we need to be on our way home."

CHAPTER 11

For the next two days, Red Hawk acted as Little Fawn's interpreter so she could communicate with her sister. He'd also spoken to the young women's mother about the twins. When the truth came out that Little Fawn was the baby who had been taken from her and left in the woods to die, something unexpected happened. Silver Squirrel, Two Moons, and even their tribe's chief, saw Little Fawn's survival as a good omen. Being superstitious, they believed her appearance to them now was a type of miracle—that she'd been sent by the Great Spirit. Therefore, they treated Little Fawn with respect, although no one seemed to understand the concept that there could be only one God, who sent His Son, Jesus, to earth as a baby.

With this turn of events, Little Fawn wished to remain in the Flathead camp longer, to get to know her twin sister better, and with the hope of making her true-blood people understand about God. However, Red Hawk insisted they needed to go home.

"And I cannot allow you to remain here by yourself," he told Little Fawn as she stood near her twin sister. "Amanda would be very upset if I returned to Lapwai Valley without you, and since you cannot speak the Salish language, it would be difficult for you to communicate with them."

White Wolf stepped forward. "I agree with Red Hawk." He slipped his arm around Little Fawn's waist. "Even though the people here seem to be in awe of you now, they might change their mind, and then your life could be in danger. I want you to go home with me."

Little Fawn's muscles tightened as she lifted her chin. "But I need to make these people understand about God. I believe that is why He led us here."

"All right then," Red Hawk agreed. "We will stay a few more days—long enough for you to tell them more about the Good News. Since they believe your being here is a good omen, perhaps they will listen to you through me."

Little Fawn smiled. This was finally her chance to be a missionary, and the first people she wanted to tell about Jesus were her birth mother, father, and twin sister. She only hoped they would listen.

A bird sang nearby, as if it were announcing another day's end. Today had not gone well, but Little Fawn would try again tomorrow. She could only hope another day of teaching them about the Gospel might make someone from the Salish tribe become open to the possibility of what they were being taught.

Little Fawn expelled a frustrated breath as she watched the sun slowly descend in the western sky. *How did Mother Amanda get through to the people and make them understand the Word of God?* She felt determined to make this work. It was only the first day for the Salish to hear what she wanted to teach them, and Little Fawn had to admit she'd been a bit nervous as well. She was eager for everyone to accept Jesus as their Savior, the way she had done. In her haste, she had to be careful not to rush out the words and confuse them with everything she'd come to know about God. But even explaining things slowly, she wasn't sure her father's words would be understood. Perhaps when all was quiet and those they taught climbed into their sleeping mats for the night, it would be easier for everyone to process what they'd heard from her earlier today.

Little Fawn lifted her face to the glowing sky. The puffy clouds had turned a golden yellow, and near the horizon, a deeper orange began to set in.

Little Fawn became alert when she felt someone behind her, but as soon as his hands touched her shoulders, there was no mistaking who it was.

"I was wondering where you got to." White Wolf wrapped his arms around her and pulled her against his chest.

"I needed to take a walk and find a quiet place to think." Little Fawn sighed as she relaxed. Together, they stood peacefully, watching the clouds turn into more fiery colors.

"Maybe I'm not good enough to teach." Little Fawn rested her head against White Wolf's shoulder. "Do you think I'm wrong in trying to do so?"

He turned his head and tenderly kissed her temple. "It's only been a short time since they heard the Good News, and it's a lot to process for people who have lived by the same customs all their lives." White Wolf looked directly into her eyes. "Just give it some time."

"You are right, but I'm not sure a few days will be enough to get through to them."

"If it does not seem that you're getting through to the Salish when you and Red Hawk teach them again tomorrow, maybe after we are man and wife, we can seek out this tribe another time, and you can try ministering to them once more. But right now, I only want to talk about one thing— you and me."

"You would return here with me?" Little Fawn could hardly believe what he'd said.

White Wolf nodded. "Yes, and perhaps Red Hawk will teach us the Salish language. After hearing the story of how you and Singing Sparrow were separated so cruelly at birth, I have come to realize how important it is to tell others about God and the way He wants us to live. No parents—Indian or white—should ever agree to sacrifice their child. Two Moons and Silver Squirrel should have taken their twin daughters and left the Salish camp." He stroked her arm gently. "I am thankful Amanda went to the woods in search of you. If she had not taken you away, you would not be with me today."

Little Fawn's heart throbbed, seeing the loving way White Wolf looked at her. His touch was tender as he stroked her cheek. If ever there was a time she could melt like the snow on a warm spring day, it was now. Little Fawn had begun to understand things more clearly and was happy they would soon be going home. She felt bad for putting her loved ones in danger and would give up on the idea of being a missionary if necessary.

"If you still want to marry me, I will stay close to home and be content to be surrounded by family and friends," she murmured. "I love you so much, and will never intentionally put you in harm's way again."

"I would marry you right now, if I could." White Wolf spoke softly.

Little Fawn giggled. "If we married before getting home, I do not think our mothers would be happy with us, and our fathers would get scolded too."

"Then I want to marry you as soon as we get back." White Wolf nudged her chin with the knuckle of his finger. "And the first spring after we are married, we will go with the Nimiipuu people onto the plains, so we can tell other tribes we may see along the way about God.

"Thank you. I will look forward to that." Little Fawn tilted her face up to meet the kiss she felt sure he was going to place on her willing lips. No more words were spoken as she clung to her future husband.

As the stars above twinkled in the darkening sky, Little Fawn felt a sense of emptiness when White Wolf stepped back. "We need to get our rest. In a few days we will be traveling again."

"Yes, we should get back to camp, or our fathers will wonder what happened to us."

———

For the past two days Little Fawn had preached to the Salish people, using Red Hawk as her interpreter. No one except her twin, Singing Sparrow, seemed interested in hearing about God or the Bible. Little Fawn felt discouraged. She'd hoped for a better response from her blood people and didn't want to return to Lapwai Valley, knowing she hadn't reached anyone for the Lord. Apparently, this Salish tribe preferred to hold on to their superstitious traditions and beliefs, rather than put their faith and trust in God.

In addition to her disappointment over their rejection of the Gospel, Little Fawn and Singing Sparrow had spent so little time together. There was a lot that hadn't been said, and Little Fawn feared if she left now, she might never see her twin sister again.

When Little Fawn tried to communicate with her birth parents about Jesus, she was met with indifference. Rather than being overjoyed with the Good News, there was a wariness about them—like they didn't want to accept her God. This seemed strange to Little Fawn, since the heavenly Father was everyone's God.

Even though my blood parents see my coming here as a good omen, they have not asked me to stay and be part of the Salish tribe. Nor have they shown any interest in the holy Word of God. Little Fawn grimaced, as she gathered some food supplies in readiness to return to Lapwai Valley. Truthfully, she would never feel as though Two Moons and Silver Squirrel were her parents. How could she, when she had not met them until a few days ago? Amanda and Red Hawk had raised her and poured out their love in so many ways. While she might be a Salish Indian by blood, in her heart, Little Fawn was a Nez Percé maiden, pledged to marry White Wolf, and for that she felt thankful. As much as it would hurt to leave her twin and blood parents behind, Little Fawn would pray for them and look forward to the day she and White Wolf would seek out this Salish tribe after they were married.

When it came time to leave the camp, Little Fawn sought out her sister to say goodbye, as she had done with her parents the night before. She found Singing Sparrow outside Two Moon's tent, talking with Silver Squirrel. It appeared as if they were arguing. Silver Squirrel shook her finger in Singing Sparrow's face, and the young maiden kept shaking her head. *I wonder what they are quarreling about.*

Little Fawn took a step toward them, but, with a shake of her head, Silver Squirrel held up her hand. Then she turned back to Singing Sparrow and said something in their native tongue. Little Fawn was on the verge of finding Red Hawk to interpret what was being said, but before she could make a move, Singing Sparrow grabbed a deer hide pack, slung it over her shoulder, and motioned for Little Fawn to follow her.

Little Fawn turned to look at Silver Squirrel, but the older woman was gone, leaving Singing Sparrow and Little Fawn by themselves. At her sister's urging, Little Fawn followed her over to a gray-and-white horse, pawing at the ground, as if in readiness to go somewhere. Then Singing Sparrow motioned for Little Fawn to get on the horse's back.

Without question, Little Fawn did as her sister requested. As soon as she was on the mare's back, Singing Sparrow climbed up behind her. *What is going on? Where does she want us to go?*

Little Fawn's twin directed her horse to the place where Red Hawk, Gray Eagle, and White Wolf waited with their horses. Then touching Little Fawn's back, she spoke to Red Hawk.

"What did she say?" Little Fawn asked. "What is my twin sister telling you, Father?"

Tilting his head to one side, Red Hawk rubbed his chin. "Singing Sparrow said she wants to go with us. She wishes to know more about

God and spend time getting to know you better. She is eager to go to the Nez Percé camp in Lapwai Valley, while her tribe goes out on the plains. Her parents have given their permission, so she will join up with them again in the fall."

Little Fawn's lips turned upward. "That is good news." She looked over at White Wolf, who stood by his mighty steed. "Would you mind very much if I rode with my sister—at least part of the way?"

Smiling, he shook his head. "We have many days in the future to be together. It is good for you to spend time with your twin."

"Thank you." A sense of joy came over Little Fawn, as the party of five rode out of the camp. Perhaps if Singing Sparrow became a Christian, when she was reunited with her parents in the fall, they might be willing to listen to the truth of God's Word.

CHAPTER 12

Lapwai Valley

Our husbands have been gone nearly a week, and I can't help but worry." Amanda looked at Yellow Bird and frowned.

Nodding, her friend took a seat at Amanda's table. "I worry too, but it will not bring the men home any sooner."

"What if they don't find Little Fawn and White Wolf?"

Yellow Bird placed her hand on Amanda's arm. "They will not come home without them."

Amanda's throat felt so clogged she could barely swallow. "This is my fault. If Red Hawk and I had agreed to take Little Fawn out on the prairie, we would all be there now, and my daughter would not be missing."

"Blaming yourself will not change what has happened. We must not give up hope." Yellow Bird rose from her chair. "Let's go outside and see what our other children are up to."

Little Fawn's heart swelled with joy as they neared the Lapwai Valley. Home had never looked so good. And for her, this truly was home. For now, she had no desire to be anywhere else.

Sitting on White Wolf's stallion, Little Fawn glanced over at Singing Sparrow, riding tall on her horse. No apprehension showed on her face. Little Fawn thought her sister might be nervous about visiting a strange place with people she'd only met a few days ago, but Singing Sparrow showed no fear.

Little Fawn was eager to get to know her twin better, and teach her the Nez Percé language. She wanted to learn the Salish language as well. It wasn't fair that she and her sister had been separated at birth. She shivered at the thought of having been left to die. The superstitious belief that a mother giving birth to twins was a bad omen was one more reason the Salish Indians needed Christ.

As they entered the compound, Mother Amanda and Yellow Bird stepped out of the cabin and ran toward them. But when Mother caught sight of Singing Sparrow, the smile left her face.

Everyone dismounted, and while Yellow Bird greeted her husband and son, Red Hawk gave his wife a hug. Then he explained where they'd been and everything that happened. When he told how they'd discovered Little Fawn's twin sister, and that he'd told Little Fawn the truth about the way Amanda had found her as a baby, tears filled Mother's eyes. "I am sorry you had to find out this way. I've wanted to tell you but didn't know how. I was afraid the truth would be too painful for you."

"It was distressing to learn that my blood people wanted me to die, but something good has come from me learning that I have a twin sister." She slipped her arm around Singing Sparrow's waist. "Mother, I'd like you to meet Singing Sparrow—my lookalike sister."

Tearfully, Mother Amanda gave the young woman a hug. "It is good to meet you. I was there when you were born."

"She does not understand white man talk," Little Fawn explained. "But Red Hawk speaks her language, so he can tell her what you said."

Red Hawk stepped forward and told Singing Sparrow what Amanda said.

With a slight dip of her head, Singing Sparrow nodded, before saying something to Red Hawk.

"What did my sister say?" Little Fawn asked.

"She said she is glad to meet the woman who saved her twin's life."

Amanda smiled. "I am happy she is my daughter." She looked at Red Hawk and then Gray Eagle. "Thank you for bringing Little Fawn home."

Red Hawk motioned to White Wolf. "He deserves the praise more than we do. White Wolf is the one who rescued Little Fawn from the Blackfoot."

"That is right," Gray Eagle added. "They were on their way back here when we came upon them."

Amanda gasped, and Yellow Bird took hold of Little Fawn's hands. "Were you treated badly?"

Little Fawn nodded. "But I am all right now." She realized that Yellow Bird understood, since she had been through something similar when she was a young woman.

White Wolf slipped his arm around Little Fawn's waist. "I love Little Fawn and would have sacrificed my life to bring her home." He turned to face Red Hawk. "May I speak with you tomorrow about a suitable bride price?"

Little Fawn held her breath as she waited for her father's reply. She didn't know what she would do if his response was negative.

"Yes, we will talk tomorrow. But right now we need to get Singing Sparrow settled in and spend time with our families."

As they walked toward their separate dwellings, Little Fawn glanced back at White Wolf. He looked at her too before entering his family's lodge. It seemed his smile reached hers, and a sense of contentment filled Little Fawn's soul.

After sharing the evening meal with her parents, twin sister, and Running Fox, Little Fawn stepped out of their cabin. The western horizon drew her to the edge of their village, like it did not long ago at the Salish camp. She'd never seen anything more beautiful as the sunset glowed with brilliance, but perhaps it was because, once again, she was seeing it from home. The sky blazed with color from the deepest red, to orange, and then yellow, where the sun dipped below the skyline. A few gray clouds lingered, and as she watched their colors deepen to a rich purple hue, it seemed like an invisible artist had added pink highlights to the image.

Little Fawn's spirit felt as glorious as the sunset, and she sent up a prayer of thanks. She was home where she belonged, safe and sound with family, and the man she loved was home too. A feeling of serenity flowed through her like never before. Perhaps it took being away from those she loved to make her realize what should come first.

When Little Fawn thought about what could have happened, her body shuddered. But her prayers had been answered, leading the person of her destiny to find her and save her from being a captive the rest of her life. White Wolf had freed her from the bonds of slavery, where if never found, she would have grown old before her time. She prayed that the Blackfoot would take good care of her horse, but Little Fawn doubted she would ever see her mare again.

As she watched the horizon turn translucent, Little Fawn sent up another prayer of thanks for uniting her with Singing Sparrow. The one good thing about her abduction was meeting her twin sister on the way home. Otherwise, she would have never known she had an identical twin. *This chapter in my life taught me a valuable lesson.* Little Fawn gazed at the horizon. *I will never again risk being parted from the people I love.*

Goosebumps rose on Little Fawn's arms as she sensed someone behind her. She turned around and locked eyes with her handsome White Wolf. It seemed ages ago when he'd snuck up on her and tickled her nose with a feather unlike now, when she'd sensed his presence. He had the strength of a wolf and the stealth of a mountain lion, and soon this wonderful man would be her husband. White Wolf's broad shoulders, and muscular arms made her feel safe and protected when she was enveloped in his embrace. Except for a section of hair braided with a piece of rawhide on the one side, this night, he'd kept the rest loose and flowing. White Wolf was not only handsome, but he truly was a good man—kind and gentle with the children and elderly folks of the village. Even as a boyhood friend, this quality had drawn her to him. White Wolf would be a great leader someday. Little Fawn made a vow that she would never, of her own free will, put miles between them again.

No words were spoken as she gazed up at this handsome warrior, cherishing everything about him. In an instant, they clung to each other, locked in a strong embrace, and their lips met in a lingering kiss. When the tender moment ended, Little Fawn turned around. Leaning against his chest, she watched the glow of the fast-fading sunset.

"It seems the sky is our friend again tonight." White Wolf's arms held her close while they watched the last of the fiery sky fade below the skyline.

A sigh escaped Little Fawn's lips when White Wolf kissed the back of her neck. "Yes, but now we are home where we should be. Are you ready for tomorrow, when you speak to my father? I hope he doesn't give you a hard time."

As they watched the first of the twinkling stars appear in the darkening twilight, White Wolf whispered, "I am not worried. It will be fine."

The next morning White Wolf wasted no time coming to speak to her father. Little Fawn reached for her mother's hand as they stood outside together and waited for Red Hawk's response.

Several seconds went by, as if he were teasing White Wolf, for it was quite clear her intended was a little bit nervous. Then Red Hawk placed both hands on White Wolf's shoulders. "I am willing to speak with you about a bride price. But know this—my daughter is worth more than five, or even ten ponies. So you had better promise to treat her well."

"I will treat her with the best care any husband could offer," White Wolf replied.

Red Hawk looked like he was about to say something more, when a distant neighing echoed in the morning's stillness. All eyes turned to the white-socked horse running into their camp. The mare pawed the ground and whinnied again as if searching for someone.

Little Fawn could not believe her eyes as she ran toward her horse. At the same time, the mare's ears perked up. "Oh Snow, you came home!" Little Fawn hugged her mare as Snow greeted her with more nickers. "How did you get away?"

White Wolf joined her, as did everyone else, each greeting the lather-soaked mare. "It does not matter how she has returned to us. What matters is that she is here." And then he added, "Little Fawn, your journey home is complete."

She smiled at the look of love she saw on her beloved's handsome face. Little Fawn looked forward to their wedding day as well as the opportunity to spend many days with Singing Sparrow. But most of all, she was eager to share more about the Good News with her sister and anyone else who would listen. For she had become a woman of hope, who'd learned to put her trust fully in God.

A NOTE FROM THE AUTHOR

The area known as Lapwai Valley became part of the Oregon Territory in 1848 and a part of the Nez Percé Indian Reservation in 1855. It then became part of the Idaho Territory in 1863. This was also the time when troops were assigned to the Lapwai Valley, and Fort Lapwai was established as a response to the 1860 gold rush on Nez Percé lands.

Fort Lapwai became part of the State of Idaho when Idaho was admitted to the Union as the forty-third state in 1890. The town of Lapwai, where several churches are now located, remains the seat of government for the Nez Percé Indian Nation. Since 1948 the Nez Percé Indians have been self-governing with an approved constitution and by-laws. Due to the influence of missionaries and preachers many Nez Percé Indians were converted to Christianity.

ABOUT THE AUTHOR

New York Times bestselling and award-winning author Wanda E. Brunstetter is one of the founders of the Amish fiction genre. Wanda also enjoys writing historical fiction. She has written close to 90 books translated in four languages. With over 10 million copies sold, Wanda's stories consistently earn spots on the nation's most prestigious bestseller lists and have received numerous awards.

Wanda's ancestors were part of the Anabaptist faith, and her novels are based on personal research intended to accurately portray the Amish way of life. Her books are well read and trusted by many Amish, who credit her for giving readers a deeper understanding of the people and their customs.

When Wanda visits her Amish friends, she finds herself drawn to their peaceful lifestyle, sincerity, and close family ties. Wanda enjoys photography, ventriloquism, gardening, bird-watching, beachcombing, and spending time with her family. She and her husband, Richard, have been blessed with two grown children, six grandchildren, and two great-grandchildren.

To learn more about Wanda and her books, visit her website at www.wandabrunstetter.com.